THIS
BOOK
KILLS

To Mum, for everything

First published in the UK in 2023 by Usborne Publishing Ltd., Usborne House,
83-85 Saffron Hill, London EC1N 8RT, England, usborne.com.

Usborne Verlag, Usborne Publishing Ltd., Prüfeninger Str. 20, 93049 Regensburg,
Deutschland, VK Nr. 17560

Text copyright © Ravena Guron, 2023

Cover illustration by Leo Nickolls © Usborne Publishing, 2023

Map by Lucy Morris / Imageremedy.com © Usborne Publishing, 2023

A CIP catalogue record for this book is available from the British Library.

FMAMJJASOND/23   ISBN 9781803705415   7999/03

Printed and bound using 100% renewable energy at CPI Group (UK) Ltd, Croydon, CR0 4YY.

RAVENA GURON

THIS BOOK KILLS

USBORNE

HEYBUCKLE SCHOOL

NOBILITAS ET PROSPERITAS

REGIA CLUB RULES!

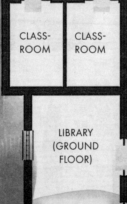

6TH FORM COMMON ROOM

5TH FORM COMMON ROOM

ADMIN OFFICE

STAIRS

3RD FORM COMMON ROOM

SCHOOL HALL

MAIN CORRIDOR TO CLASSROOMS

CLASS-ROOM

CLASS-ROOM

4TH FORM COMMON ROOM

STAIRS

LIBRARY (GROUND FLOOR)

TOILETS

TRO RO

ENTRANCE HALL

WOODS

FIELDS

MRS GREYTHORNE'S OFFICE

WAITING AREA

STAIRS

CORRIDOR TO STAFF ACCOMODATION AND OFFICES

DISUSED CLASSROOM (MR WILLET)

DISUSED CLASSROOM

STAFF ROOM

TOILETS

CORRIDOR TO CLASSROOMS

TOILETS

KITCHEN

BACK CORRIDOR

STORAGE

DINING ROOM

ROOM WITH ENTRANCE TO CELLARS

DRIVEWAY

1

I'll make it clear from the start: I did not kill Hugh Henry Van Boren.

I didn't even help. Well, not intentionally.

Mum thinks I've got some latent trauma hanging around. She's not a psychologist or anything – she just watches loads of documentaries, and believes that makes her an expert on everything. Apparently, writing down what happened will help me *process*. I think that's a load of crap, but when I politely said that out loud, Mum got that steely look in her eye which said, *Better do what I say, Jess Choudhary, or I will beat you with this slipper.*

Mum's never actually beaten me. She just threatens The Slipper.

Anyway, I'm going to pour the truth into this notebook, even though I'd rather forget the entire thing.

Let's get cracking with my tale of misery and woe.

* * *

The week before Hugh was killed, I witnessed the first sign of trouble brewing.

I was sitting alone at the end of one of the long, polished wooden tables in the dining room. My best, and only, friend, Clementine-Tangerine Briggs, had decided to skip dinner so she could spend more time focusing on her new venture – a podcast detailing the sad plight of the Titicaca water frog. It was nicknamed the "scrotum frog" and was apparently very close to extinction (Clem was adamant that ugly creatures deserved to be saved too). And yes, Clementine-Tangerine is her real name – her parents said fruit was the biggest seller in their chain of organic superstores, and big sellers made them money, and Clem's parents love money.

I had a book propped up on the crystal jug of orange juice in front of me. I wasn't actually reading, but I'd brought it along so people would think I'd intentionally sat by myself, to be alone with my thoughts. Mysterious, too cool to have friends. I'm sure everyone was fooled.

There was a big, empty space around me at the table, as if I repelled people. Further down the bench, my roommate was gossiping loudly with her friends. Their shrill laughter grated on my ears, but I still wished I could slide down and join them.

I never would, though. I didn't fit in at Heybuckle School. No matter what I did, or how nice I was, everyone else would always see me as the poor kid, the charity case.

Every so often, I turned a page of my book, to make the whole act of *mysterious loner* look more believable.

When I was about halfway through my fish and chips, Millicent Cordelia Calthrope-Newton-Rose (also, unbelievably,

8

a real name) made her grand entrance, slamming open the wooden doors of the dining hall.

Millie sashayed down the empty space in the middle of the hall, her hips swaying like she was on a catwalk. Her blonde curls hung loose around her shoulders, and her deep blue eyes narrowed as she scanned the crowds. Her regulation grey skirt was hitched up around her waist to show off her long legs, and her tie dangled around her neck like a fashion accessory. She always wore her uniform like that – not even the teachers dared to tell her off.

"Where's Hugh?" she demanded.

Her voice carried across the room, but no one spoke up. I was at the other end, as far from her as I could possibly be. Still, I made myself smaller. Hugh rose from where he had been sitting, nestled comfortably amongst his squad of friends just metres away from Millie. Like her, he was incredibly good-looking, with curly blond hair and rosy cheeks. He rarely smiled, his face carved like a stone sculpture, and was over six foot, with broad shoulders from all the time he spent exercising. They could have ended up being a famous modelling couple, they were both so pretty. You know, if he hadn't cheated on her and then got killed.

"Here I am, babe," Hugh said, sticking his hands in his pockets. His tone was bored. "What's wrong?"

"What's – wrong?" Millie's voice was strangled. "You lying, two-faced piece of—"

"Oh. You found out." Hugh took his hands out of his pockets and smoothed down his red-and-gold Heybuckle tie. His expression was indifferent, almost resigned, like he'd been

9

expecting this day to come. "Maybe we shouldn't talk about this here—"

"You CHEATED on me," roared Millie. "You lying scum, you absolute piece of filth. FILTH." She got right up in his face, screaming the word again and again like a wind-up toy that had got stuck.

Hugh shrugged, looking unconcerned as the words slid off him. "I feel like we've become two different people," he said.

He was acting so reasonably, half the dining hall seemed to be nodding along with him, even though he was the cheater and Millie was in the right. Millie seemed to sense the mood shift in Hugh's favour, because she screamed, grabbed a pitcher of orange juice, and tossed the drink in his face. Some of the juice sploshed down onto his shirt.

"What the hell!" said Hugh, frantically rubbing his eyes. "Someone get me some water – she's got it in my eyes – they're burning—"

Hugh's friend, Eddy, reached for the jug of water in front of him, but Millie was quicker. She flung the water at Hugh.

"Do you all want to know who this *scum* cheated on me with?" She waved the empty jug above her head.

Hugh ineffectively dabbed at the yellow blotches on his formerly starch-white shirt with a wet tissue, his cheeks flushing red. "This is going to *stain*," he said. "Urgh, it's disgusting, I'm going to have to throw it away." He looked more upset about his shirt getting dirty than his girlfriend of three years ending their relationship.

The teachers at the head table were frozen, a few with their forks halfway to their mouths. The kitchen staff hung out of the hatches, watching in astonishment. None of the adults would stop Millie before she spilled the truth. I knew what was coming, and I couldn't do anything about it.

Millie was looking around again, and I wished even more that I had friends to sit with. On my own I was vulnerable, like a weak gazelle about to be picked off by a cheetah. I tried to hunch over further, but Millie's gaze had fixed on me.

"You," she breathed, stomping towards me.

Everyone turned to look. My cheeks burned red. People started whispering, the dining hall filled with the noise of leaves swishing in a gentle breeze.

Crap.

I had never been more aware of my tongue. Was it always pressed to my teeth like that?

"Where is she?" Millie towered over me, her rose-scented perfume – definitely designer, most certainly eye-wateringly expensive – almost overwhelming. "Where's that boyfriend-stealing little trollop?"

My mind went blank, and my throat closed up. I couldn't speak, even if I wanted to.

Hugh looked up from his ruined shirt. "Leave Jade alone," he said with a sigh, as he dropped the mulch of wet tissue onto the table. "I'm the one you're angry at."

It would have been heroic if he wasn't still dripping in diluted orange juice. And, I wasn't about to correct him in front of everyone, but the boy had been in most of my classes since we were thirteen, and three years later still didn't know my name. It's not like *Jess* was that hard to remember.

Millie threw her head back and let out a guttural scream.

Her hair flew wildly about her face, while her eyes darted everywhere. "Scum!" she shrieked. "Scum!"

I wondered why she loved the word *scum* so much, and why she hadn't used a normal swear word yet, but it turned out she'd been building up to it, like a singer warming their vocals for the grand finale of a song. She started throwing every bad word in the book at Hugh, her voice getting plummier and plummier as he didn't react to any of the insults.

"You *humiliated* me—"

"You've humiliated yourself, babe," said Hugh in a gentle voice.

"Don't you dare call me *babe*. I will kill you," she screamed, her smeared mascara making her look like she had two black eyes. "I – will – kill – you."

And then she did.

No, I'm kidding, that's not what happened. Though this story would be a whole lot shorter and way less stressful for me if that's how it had all gone down.

Instead, the door to the dining room opened and my best friend Clem walked in.

Everyone looked at her, including Millie.

Who let out a yell so high I bet some dogs ten miles away pricked up their ears and barked.

Clem stopped, confused.

And Millie charged.

2

It was at that point the teachers remembered what they were being paid to do.

"Millicent Cordelia," boomed Mrs Henridge, my English teacher. "I think you need to go to the headmistress's office."

Headmistress Greythorne was a stern, no-nonsense woman, who looked like she thought spending a Saturday night polishing her certificates commending her for service to the school was the epitome of a good time. She also commanded instant respect, and even Millie would dread a visit to her office.

Millie had paused halfway to Clem. I don't know what she was planning to do, maybe rugby tackle her? But even she wouldn't disobey a direct order from a teacher. She scoffed, flicking her hair over her shoulders.

"This isn't over," she said to Clem, loud enough for her voice to carry.

Clem looked from Millie to Hugh. She scrunched up her nose, like she always did when she was thinking. Then a light seemed to come on in her eyes, and her lips stretched into a wicked smile. *Oh, no.* I knew that smile. She had come up with An Idea.

She picked up a pitcher of orange juice, just like Millie had done. Everyone started whispering, and even Millie looked confused. Was Clem going to chuck the juice at Hugh too? Or Millie?

But Clem, without breaking eye contact with Millie, turned the contents of the pitcher on herself, letting every single drop splash over her uniform.

"There," she said to Millie. "I saved you the effort."

Millie snarled. I thought Clem had made her point, but she picked up yet another pitcher of orange juice.

"I was named after this drink!" she said as everyone started clapping.

"Pour it, pour it!"

Clem poured the pitcher, properly smiling like she was having the time of her life. Then she picked up a third.

"Clementine!" said Mrs Henridge, finally getting to her feet. "Stop that at once – orange juice is for drinking, for goodness' sake. Go get yourself cleaned up. And, Millicent, get to the headmistress's office *now*."

Millie's eyes slid past Clem, to me, and she gave the tiniest of smiles. The message was clear: I'd known about Clem and Hugh. I was going to be a target as well. A shudder passed through me as she turned on her heel and left the dining room with her chin jutting out, her head held high.

Now all eyes were on Clem. She was short, with cropped copper hair that stuck up in weird tufts, and she had an impish look about her which made teachers peg her as trouble. The

14

sleeves of her blazer were rolled back, and she wore brightly-coloured badges saying stuff like RECYCLE and NOBODY CARES. One of her socks had fallen down.

She shook her head like a dog, spraying droplets of orange juice everywhere.

"I'll be right back!" she announced to the room with a grin, and sauntered out.

Everyone's eyes swivelled to Hugh, who was looking after her with a silly, lovesick expression on his face. He might as well have had hearts for eyes.

Gingerly, he left his table and walked carefully from the room, his arms hanging stiff by his sides. Millie had aimed well, so most of the juice had landed on his face. Yet he was acting like his shirt was a priceless work of art ruined by the small blemishes of yellow. He'd probably spend the next three hours having a shower and burning every last trace of the shirt.

I went back to pretending to read my book, on edge as I waited for Clem's return. She didn't take long, coming back fifteen minutes later with damp hair and fresh clothes that she had pinned her badges to. She walked over to me as if she didn't have a care in the world. It hit me that, despite all their obvious differences, there was a certain similarity between Millie and Clem. The money they came from gave them a certain sort of confidence, like the world was theirs and they were giving other people the right to live in it.

Clem sat down opposite me, and immediately snaffled some of the now-cold chips on my plate.

"How's it going?" she said, as if nothing had happened.

I stared at her (much like everyone else in the room). Clem

15

continued to chew, like she hadn't noticed.

"My podcast is a bust, just so you know. I'm starving – why didn't you get more chips?" Clem pulled my plate over to herself, scoffing down the remains. "No one cares about the sperm frogs."

"Scrotum frogs," I automatically corrected. Then I blinked, because she still hadn't acknowledged what had happened. "Millie knows about you and Hugh, in case that wasn't obvious." I glanced over my shoulder at Hugh's empty spot. Everyone else had gone back to talking at their normal levels of volume.

Clem avoided meeting my eyes, choosing instead to stare at my chips. "That orange juice scene…was not my finest moment," she said. "I mean, er, Millie had every right to get angry."

"Yes," I said.

"It's just…I saw what she'd done to Hugh with the juice and I got mad. He hates mess." She lowered her voice and leaned forwards. "It's because when he was younger, these robbers broke into his house and stole loads of stuff – only, they couldn't tell what was valuable because his parents own all this weird art stuff that looks like everyday objects. So they stole his crayons and his wooden train set and his favourite toy elephant, Roger, and trashed the place afterwards and now any sort of mess reminds him of that…"

"*Really?*" I said, my mouth hanging open.

Clem grinned at me as she turned to the chocolate cake and custard I'd been saving. She was eating like she'd been on a hunger strike – which she had once tried.

"No, you wally. You believe anything! Hugh's just weirdly

neat and I wanted to stick up for him." She took a deep breath. "Millie was going to find out about us eventually. Hugh has been thinking of ending it for a while."

"And you're certain he loves you?" I asked. "There's that old saying – if he'll cheat with you, he'll cheat on you."

"He does love me," she said, her voice sure, like she was announcing that tomorrow the sun would come up. "And I love him. He's sweet – and, yeah, he's a bit serious but that's only because he's a deep thinker."

I raised my eyebrows. Hugh wasn't unintelligent, but I bet if he had the choice, he would have happily paid someone else to do his thinking for him.

"But what if he decides to get back together with Millie? They've always been inseparable – remember that year he decked out the entire common room in roses for her birthday and paid a bunch of the choir kids to follow her around the whole day and serenade her?"

It was my final attempt to show Clem that Hugh and Millie would end up together no matter what. Our school was for kids aged thirteen to eighteen, and they'd started dating in our first year, within a week of knowing each other. They were like magnets or something – at least their mouths were. I was certain they would grow up and get married and have tall blond babies together.

"Well, if he loved Millie so much, why'd he start things with me?" asked Clem.

I could tell she was just humouring me, but I pressed on anyway. "For attention; to prove he can get any girl he wants – I can list a whole bunch of reasons." It was no use – I'd tried so

17

many times to tell Clem the whole thing wasn't a good idea. Ever since she told me about it, nine months ago – just before the summer holidays.

"Well, you can sit here and worry about all those reasons," said Clem, getting to her feet. "Or, you can come with me and we can see if Hattie has any chocolate we can steal – and if you're too slow making up your mind, I *will* eat it all without you!"

She was gone before I had a chance to respond. I smiled as I slid my now-empty plates onto the metal trolley where all the dirty dishes went.

Our friendship was, in many ways, an odd one. Clem probably could have been as popular as Millie. But when I'd been eating alone on the third day of school, feeling miserable and wishing I could *just go home*, Clem had slammed her dinner tray down opposite me.

"I heard Miss Bilson and Coach Tyler used to date. How gross is that?" She leaned over and swiped a few of my chips.

I stared at her, with no clue what was going on.

"You know how I found out? Apparently last year someone actually saw them *kissing*. In the staffroom, where anyone could see in through that massive glass door. I mean, I'm all for public displays of affection, but the teachers have entire flats to themselves to kiss in – with little kitchens and everything…"

She'd gone on, seemingly not caring that I was too awkward to respond. When we were done with dinner, she told me we would be hanging out in her room and painting our nails. And after a while, I began to feel grateful to her. I couldn't believe she picked *me* to hang out with, when she might have been friends with anyone. I couldn't believe she was including me.

When I was comfortable with her, I started to talk back properly. And she'd smiled, and we'd been best friends ever since.

I hurried out of the dining room, to where Clem was waiting in the corridor. We made our way through the dark-panelled hallways until we reached the trophy room.

Most of the corridors in the school led to the trophy room, which wasn't actually a room but a large, circular space that connected the entrance hall to the east and west wings of the school. It was here that Headmistress Greythorne normally hovered after dinner, making sure all students were *quietly* making their way to evening activities. But now she was miles away in her office, probably laying into Millie and telling her that nice, respectable students *didn't* threaten to kill their cheating boyfriends.

On the other side of the trophy room were the enormous front doors. At 10 p.m. every night these doors were locked, not that break-ins were much of a worry. Heybuckle School was nestled in acres of land in the middle of the English countryside.

High, thick stone walls marked the school's boundaries, much to the chagrin of people like Clem who thought it'd be fun to break out (though of course there was nowhere really to sneak *to*. We needed to take coaches or taxis just to get to the local village, which was at least ten miles away from us).

So, after 10 p.m. the whole school basically became a prison, with no way out until morning – apart from the alarmed fire exits.

"It's a bit weird, Mrs Greythorne not being here," said Clem, jerking her thumb at the trophy room as she came to a stop.

"Yeah – she's with Millie…"

Clem's face had a weird, tight expression on it. Clearly, she was finally thinking properly about the consequences of her reckless decision to fall in love with Hugh. Maybe she would come to her senses, and that would be the end of it.

"Hopefully Millie doesn't get into *that* much trouble with Mrs Greythorne," Clem said, nibbling her bottom lip and ruffling her hands through her hair, making it stick up even more. "This wasn't her fault." But Clem had never managed to be serious for long. It only took a few seconds for her to perk up as she whipped her phone out of her blazer pocket. "I bet she's already posted about this online – I can't wait to see what the legendary Millicent Cordelia Calthrope-Newton-Rose has *deigned* to say about me." She pressed her lips together as she scrolled. "I can't believe it – she hasn't said anything…"

"Why do you sound so disappointed?" I said, unable to stop myself smiling. It was one of the things I loved about Clem. Insults slid right off her and she never cared what anyone thought.

"No, wait!" said Clem, holding up her hand. "Here we go. Oooh… She's posted a *terrible* photo of me and added little devil horns. Oooh, there's a whole bunch of them. I personally think, though, she should have made more comments about my hair – it's awful at the moment, all stick-y up-y. It was a really stupid decision to cut it myself – never let me do that again." Clem paused her commentary as she looked at me. "What if I accidentally like something on her page? Let me use your phone to stalk."

"My phone's dead."

It had run out of battery a while ago, but I hadn't got around to charging it. I didn't feel the need to message people in school, not when I saw them every day. And Mum had taken to using emails like texts, sending me all sorts of random news articles, like how people who drank apple cider vinegar straight from the bottle lived to be a hundred.

A few years ago, the school tried to introduce a rule where we had to hand in our phones during the day. I hadn't really cared too much, but other students made a huge fuss – which the school paid no attention to, until the Regia Club got involved. The Regia Club's real name was *Sodalitas Regia*, meaning "Royal Secret Society" in Latin, but over time the Latin had got mixed in with English. It was one of Heybuckle's many odd traditions: a "secret society" made up of a select few students – the poshest ones at school who came from hundreds of years of generational wealth. People often joked that the Regia Club were the ones really running Heybuckle, because when they told you to do something, you listened – and that included the teachers. Members supposedly went on to work in super influential jobs in banking, journalism, top law firms, high-up roles in government – using their network of ex-members already in those positions, who were happy to boost the career prospects of the current crop.

The Regia Club had put posters up around school that said stuff like THE REGIA CLUB DOESN'T SUPPORT FASCISM and HAVING OUR PHONES IS A HUMAN RIGHT. Then, lo and behold, everyone could keep their phones, as long as they didn't go off during class. Heybuckle tried to keep control of internet usage by putting a bunch of blocks on the Wi-Fi, taking comfort from the fact that the signal was poor. But someone savvy had figured out a workaround on the blocks, and now everyone could post crap on social media to their heart's content, a freedom Millie had apparently taken advantage of.

"Fine, I'll just be extra careful," said Clem, turning back to her phone.

"Jess," said someone behind me.

I whirled around. Summer Johnson (straightforward name – she was a scholarship student like me) was striding from the direction of the library, her blonde hair pulled into a tight, high ponytail, her intense brown eyes fixed on me. Of course she had skipped dinner to work. The girl never stopped.

It was too late to pretend I hadn't heard her, and I knew at once what she wanted to talk to me about: our assignment. Summer and I were supposed to be writing a short story together for Gifted and Talented, a waste-of-time class we had to attend. Heybuckle offered loads of "extras" that my old school didn't, like beekeeping society and automobile society – stuff we could put on university or job applications to make us *stand out*. A few years ago, the school board got worried that too many students weren't participating in any additional activities. They decided to take away a precious free period slot from everyone in the upper two years, and replace it with a forced extra-curricular – either Gifted and Talented or volunteering.

I didn't pick volunteering because there was no choice about the activity you were assigned. I wouldn't have minded gardening or something, but other potential options included things like volunteering in care homes, and I couldn't risk

22

having to make small talk with people. So, I picked Gifted and Talented (or, as everyone called it, G&T). To get in, we had to explain what "gifts" we could share (I said writing), and then also include a few academic weaknesses someone else in the class could teach us (I suck at maths). We could then put "peer tutoring" down on our CVs and hey presto, not one single person would leave Heybuckle without appearing to be *well-rounded*.

Summer had suggested writing a murder mystery story for our G&T assignment, but we'd spent ages squabbling over what direction to take it in and what sorts of things to include (I wanted lots of random, wacky details, and Summer basically wanted to kill our readers through sheer boredom).

With any other project, I would have just gone along with what Summer wanted – but not writing. It was one of the few things I was actually confident in.

"*Help me?*" Summer said through gritted teeth. Her skirt was just below knee length, perfectly in accordance with the school rules on uniform.

I shrugged. "I thought it was a fun addition."

"This is supposed to be a serious short story—"

"Literally no one cares about G&T," interrupted Clem, looking up from her phone.

Summer full-on growled, like a bear.

"I think the stuff I came up with was quite inventive," I said.

"The twigs aren't inventive," snapped Summer. "They're *ridiculous*. What kind of murderer kills someone and sticks around long enough to gather a bunch of twigs and spell out the words *HELP ME*?"

"The creative kind," I said, trying not to get frustrated. I'd been really proud of that idea – the body in our story was found in a forest with twigs spelling *HELP ME* just out of reach of their grasping fingers. I liked the idea of creating something so out there and wild that no one else at Heybuckle would even think of it.

Summer's eyes rolled so far back I wondered if they could get stuck staring at her giant brain.

"I refuse to include those absurd details – the murder weapon being a *trophy* of all things was bad enough."

"Hey, I thought that was great," I said. It had come to me on a whim, as I walked through the trophy room on my way to one of Clem's lacrosse matches.

"Oooh, Millie's posted that story about me and the hot peppers," said Clem. Her stomach gurgled, loud in the silence of the corridor. "Come *on*, Jess, if I don't eat some chocolate now, I shall *starve*. I'm so hungry I could eat ten of those hot peppers, even if I would have to drown myself in milk afterwards."

"Could have just stabbed the guy." Summer folded her arms, ignoring Clem's comments. "But *no*. Trophy to the skull."

"Are you going to write it up or not?" I said, losing patience.

Summer and I had been taking it in turns to scribble down our additions. It would have been easier to work with an online document, but Mrs Henridge had a weird rule about creative writing. She said it didn't count if it wasn't handwritten, because that's how the best authors in history wrote their stories. Summer had volunteered to write the final version in her red spiral notebook, so it looked extra neat, and would carefully extract the paper to hand it in.

Summer's nostrils flared and she sucked in her cheeks. After a moment of silence, she huffed. "Fine. We'll have one last meeting in the library tomorrow morning to smooth out my section and then I'll write it up before class." She grimaced, like the words physically caused her pain, and stalked off up the stairs.

"That girl has a *lot* of issues," said Clem, staring after her.

3

I never liked Hugh. Even before he started seeing Clem, I
thought he was a weasel. I think my dislike stemmed from the
moment I met him, when we were forced to do awkward icebreaker sessions in our first class.

I remember that moment well, because I was already
regretting accepting my scholarship at Heybuckle School. The
building was too grand, the uniform too formal. There were
only six hundred students in total across the five year groups so
it was hard to blend in. And there were all these weird traditions,
like waking up at the crack of dawn on the first day of every
term and hiking up a nearby hill, trying to keep a candle alight.
If you got caught with your flame burned out, then you had to
go all the way back down to the bottom of the hill and try again.
On my first go, it was a really windy day and I had to go up the
hill five times, spattered in mud, exhausted and close to tears.

But the worst part of being at Heybuckle was how, when I
told everyone my name was Jesminder, I got loads of confused
looks, like they didn't believe it was a real name or something.
I missed my old school in London, where I didn't stick out,

where I'd grown up with everyone and we all laughed about our overbearing parents with fondness.

During the icebreaker session, Hugh's eyes kept flicking over to Millie and I could tell he didn't want to be paired up with me. We were supposed to be asking each other questions, and then I would introduce him to the rest of the class, and he would introduce me. So far, I'd been the one to do all the asking.

"Where are you from?" he said at last, flicking a small, scrunched up bit of paper at Millie's curls with a ruler. She turned to glare at him, and he grinned.

"Er – London," I said, shifting in my seat.

He looked at me properly, his eyebrows drawn together. "No, where are you *from*?"

"London," I repeated through gritted teeth. I could tell what he was really asking, but I didn't have the answer he wanted: I was from London. I was born there, I was raised there. I had never been to India.

He tried a different tack. "Where are your *parents* from?"

"London," I said again. They'd both been born in London, though my dad had passed away when I was two.

"No, I mean where are you *really* from? Where's your family from?"

At that point I decided it would be less exhausting to let him get away with his determined stereotyping. "India. Punjab."

"Why didn't you just say that?" He rolled his eyes.

And when it came to introduce each other to the class, I could tell everyone he was Hugh Henry Van Boren, and one day he would be a duke, and he'd grown up in a ten-bedroom country house, and he had two dogs and three cats.

27

And he could tell everyone I was Jasminther Something, and I was from India.

I had one G&T class a week, run by Mrs Henridge, who had only started working at Heybuckle in September but already felt like part of the fabric of the school, developing a reputation as an exacting teacher who dished out detentions like sweets. She wore pinstripe suits and had a voice like a foghorn, which she'd used to drown out Summer's arguments about how being paired up with me to write a short story was a waste of time.

Summer was already in class when I arrived, sitting in the front row. She gave me a single, curt nod.

"Jess," she said.

"Summer," I replied.

This was how most of our interactions went – just because we were the only scholarship students in our year, it didn't mean we had anything in common. And it certainly didn't mean we had to be friends.

I sat in the middle row, on my own. My forced extra-curricular slot was on a Tuesday afternoon, when Clem had lacrosse practice. I hated classes without her because it meant I had no one to talk to. But the classroom looked out over the school playing fields, so I could at least watch her charging around the field, dodging everyone with super speed.

Arthur Applewell arrived next. He was short with mouse-brown hair and hardly spoke. He never went out into the sun if he could help it, which meant his skin was the colour of sour milk.

His twin sister, Annabelle Applewell (always Annabelle,

never Annie, which she had once snapped at a teacher) followed him in, sitting at the other end of my row and getting out her nail file. The twins rarely acknowledged each other.

Annabelle had been part of the four-person dormitory I was in for my first three years at Heybuckle. When we reached fifth form and got to share with just one other person, Annabelle had been assigned as my roommate. But even though I'd lived in close quarters with her for so long, I barely knew anything about her beyond the basics (she snored and liked painting and gossiping and showing off how much money she had). She was always civil with me, but she'd never bothered to try and be friendlier. Her friends were all loud and confident and splashily rich like her.

She used to have mouse-brown hair, like her brother, but she arrived at the beginning of this school year having dyed it peroxide blonde. During the weekends, when we were allowed to wear our own clothes, she decked herself head-to-toe in designer outfits, making sure she always wore items with the Gucci or Prada or Chanel label splashed across the front. Unlike Arthur, she put on a fake posh accent. When she was angry it slipped, and she dropped her Ts and her Hs – the Annabelle who had grown up in an ordinary semi-detached house in east London peeking through. That was when I liked her most.

I'd always found the Applewells an interesting family. Mr and Mrs Applewell had once earned a normal amount of money as lawyers for Z-list celebrities, but a few years ago they won a high-profile case and their net worth had quadrupled. Something of the tabloid culture of their clients seemed to have rubbed off on them. They had five children – four girls and one boy – and all their names started with A, giving them the initials AA. Like Alcoholics Anonymous. Or maybe the batteries.

Finally, Hugh arrived – and behind him was Tommy Poppleton, his best friend. I'd always thought Tommy was better-looking than Hugh – he had dark, messy hair, and green eyes which twinkled, like he knew a joke he wasn't willing to share. He wore his shirt sleeves pushed up, and had this sort of musky smell about him – it sounds gross, but something about it always made my knees go just a little bit weak.

They had to pass my desk to get to their seats at the back of class. Hugh fiddled with his phone, not even noticing me. But Tommy smiled at me and my lips twitched in return. We shared a few classes, but I'd never had a real excuse to talk to him.

I spotted Clem out of the window, leading the lacrosse team in a warm-up as they windmilled their arms in small circles. I hoped she would keep her wits about her. Millie was wearing the same neon-coloured bib as her, which meant they would be on the same side – but I wasn't convinced that meant Clem would be safe.

Millie's announcement in the dining room a week ago had spurred Clem and Hugh to officially start going out. They were constantly getting told off for kissing in corridors. I had barely seen Clem, but I tried my best to be happy for her…despite the fact they always looked super lovey-dovey and it made me want to hurl. Hugh hadn't even started a fight with Clem when she accidentally dropped his bag in the mud.

Millie, meanwhile, walked around like a ticking time bomb waiting for the opportune moment to explode. I ducked down corridors when I saw her coming, hoping she'd forget I'd known about Clem and Hugh. But I couldn't avoid her friends as well, and they all smirked when they saw me, like they knew Millie was planning her revenge.

A shrill whistle blew from outside. A game of lacrosse had begun.

Summer shoved back her chair and turned around.

"Here's the final short story," she said, thrusting a wad of papers at me.

I scanned the pages quickly, just to make sure she hadn't snaked me and *forgotten* to include the twigs and the trophy and the body position.

"I see it's all in order," I said, pushing it back to her.

She gave a satisfied smile and put it on Mrs Henridge's desk.

From outside, there came a scream, followed by another. Millie had tackled Clem, and they were rolling around on the ground. The coach was blowing his whistle, but neither girl seemed to care.

We all gathered by the windows to get a better view – except for Arthur, who remained seated. He had glanced at the commotion and then promptly went back to thinking about whatever it was he was thinking about.

I winced as Millie got on top of Clem and raked her manicured nails across Clem's face. Clem howled and shoved Millie backwards, their lacrosse nets lying forgotten by their sides.

"Really, they don't need to fight over me like this," said Hugh with a massive grin on his face, his breath fogging the window.

"You're an absolute arsehole," snapped Summer.

31

"At least I don't have a stick up mine," replied Hugh, without looking at her.

"Well, I can remove that stick, but you, Hugh Henry Van Boring, will *always* be an arsehole."

I looked around, trying to catch Summer's eye and give her an approving smile – and caught Tommy's instead. He was biting the inside of his cheeks, like he was trying not to laugh as well. I looked away at once, staring at the ceiling until I had the desire to giggle firmly under control.

Clem and Millie were still fighting, and I was so engrossed in hoping my best friend would be okay that I didn't even notice Mrs Henridge come into the room.

"Good afternoon, all – what are you looking at?" Mrs Henridge's high heels clacked as she marched over to the window. "Oh dear heavens, why isn't anyone stopping them? What is that teacher doing?"

The coach clearly didn't want to pull them apart. I guess it was similar to how you wouldn't want to get into the middle of two fighting dogs, in case you got bitten. And, just like you would with dogs, the coach had managed to procure a large bucket of water, which he proceeded to pour over both the girls.

Their screams probably reached the nearby village.

"Okay, class, that's enough excitement," said Mrs Henridge, squinting at the coach with disapproval. "Let's get started."

I turned around. Hugh was already in his seat, still smirking to himself as he straightened up his textbooks and laid out his pen and pencil and ruler in exact, straight lines.

He caught me staring, and there was something in his eyes that at the time I couldn't quite place.

That class was one of the last times I saw him alive, which is why I guess his expression lodged in my brain. I only worked out what was off about the way he looked much, much later.

I'd looked at him expecting to see concern in his eyes, because Clem had almost been beaten up.

Instead, there was burning triumph.

4

Clem and Millie were put into isolation for the rest of the afternoon, and then Coach Tyler gave them his standard detention: clean all the school's sports balls. The detention took hours and all efforts were pointless because the balls immediately got dirty again the next day, which made it an extra cruel punishment.

Dinner started at 6 p.m., and Clem was allowed to eat with me in the dining room as long as she was at her detention for 6.50 p.m. sharp.

"She's such a cow," Clem grumbled. She stabbed her fork into her spaghetti and gave it a swirl, oblivious to Millie sitting at the table behind her and staring daggers at her back. "Honestly, she walks around with a face like a slapped arse. You'd think she'd be over it by now, not attacking me in lacrosse. And I didn't even get the chance to decide I was going to become a pacifist and not lift a single finger to fight back – that would have been hilarious though. She would have been *so* confused."

I was about to point out that it had only been a week since Millie's heart had been very publicly shattered, but was interrupted

34

by three first year boys standing up on the benches and mooning the teachers' table. At once the dining hall erupted into cheers as everyone started banging their cutlery on the tables.

"Regia Club! Regia Club!" people chanted.

I tried not to roll my eyes. The Regia Club didn't just settle for pulling strings at Heybuckle to make their own lives better (which the rest of the student body sometimes benefited from, as an unexpected bonus, like with the whole phone thing, or the fact they were rumoured to be responsible for the fifth form common room getting a refurbishment ahead of the poky staffroom). No, the chosen elite *also* occasionally sent anonymous texts or letters to the rest of the students at Heybuckle, setting out a dare for them to do. I lived in fear of getting a text: dares often involved stuff like skinny-dipping in the lake or streaking through the common room. Clearly, whoever was in charge thought the funniest thing in the world was people getting their kit off for a laugh.

The dares were all generally harmless, more embarrassing than anything else. But if you didn't do a dare, you had to forfeit. A nasty rumour might get spread about you, or everyone in your class might be told to stop talking to you for a week. Forfeits were super rare, because even if the punishments *sounded* tame, they weren't in practice; because we were at boarding school, you could never get away from it.

I think Headmistress Greythorne had tried to get the Regia Club shut down, saying it led to insubordination and bullying, but it was a tradition as old as the rest of the school, and would probably survive long after she'd left.

The mooning boys were sent to Mrs Greythorne's office

but their spirits weren't dampened in the slightest, because everyone was still cheering and clapping for them.

"Bet you anything they'll just have to write lines or something," muttered Clem as they walked past. "Not do manual labour like me."

At 6.30 p.m., Clem and I left the dining hall. She went to her bedroom to get changed out of her school uniform and into one of her baggy tracksuits.

"At least they're not going to make me wear an orange jumpsuit," she said. "It would clash horribly with my toilet-brush hair."

I headed to my own room, eager to return to the climax of the thriller I was currently reading. But, when I approached my bedroom door, I heard angry voices that even the thick oak door couldn't muffle.

I entered to find Annabelle had her friend Lucy Huang over. I knew Lucy fairly well because we were *somehow* always chosen to be in the school's prospectus, fake laughing and pretending we were having loads of fun. If I had a penny for every time I'd actually sat on the sweeping lawns of Heybuckle School chatting with my group of diverse friends, I'd be about as rich as I am now – which is to say, I'd still be incredibly poor.

But like I didn't want to be friends with Summer just because we were both scholarship students, I didn't want to be friends with Lucy just because we happened to be two of the few *diverse* students at school. Lucy was even worse than Annabelle for gossiping, and probably equally as rich.

Annabelle and Lucy had fallen silent when I entered the room. They obviously didn't want me to overhear whatever they had been arguing about – probably something like whether *this* celebrity was hotter than *that* celebrity. Annabelle had loads of posters of famous people tacked next to her bed, even though we weren't supposed to put anything on the walls. Her side of the room was half hidden by plastic bags filled with clothes; she liked to order hundreds and hundreds of pounds' worth of items and try them on, sending back anything she didn't like.

Knowing I wasn't wanted, I decided to mooch over to the library. It took me a while to gather my books, and then I spent ages trying to find my calculator, before remembering Clem had borrowed it and not given it back. Annabelle tossed me hers, clearly to get me to leave.

When I started making my way to the library, I found the corridors to be eerily quiet, my footsteps echoing on the highly polished hardwood floors. Most people were probably still at dinner, hanging out in their rooms, or in the common room. A cool draught blew at my neck; Heybuckle was an old building, too large for the number of pupils. There was a lot of empty space, lots of unused classrooms. It felt like I was miles away from another student, until I turned into a stone stairwell that led down to the main corridor and ghostly voices floated up to me. I froze as I recognized Millie's plummy tones.

"You need to stop, okay?" she hissed, her voice echoing from the bottom of the stairwell.

I hovered, not wanting Millie and whoever she was with to know they were no longer alone, but stuck to the floor by the irresistible urge to eavesdrop. I checked my watch; it was 6.46 p.m, so she was cutting it fine if she wanted to get to detention on time.

37

"But you've *always* let me help you with stuff," said a boy, whose voice I couldn't place – the stairwell was so echoey and all the boys at Heybuckle sounded the same, enunciating every word like they had taken elocution lessons from the queen. "I'd do anything for you—"

"You need to get over this *stupid* little crush," snapped Millie. "And you're going to make me late for detention. Get out the way—"

"What changed?" said the boy, his voice more urgent now. "Just tell me and I'll fix it—"

"*Get out the way!*"

There was a grunt, and the sound of a door slamming shut.

"That hurt!" said the boy, but if he was speaking to Millie, it was clear she was already gone. I waited a few seconds before continuing down the stairwell, but when I reached the bottom it was empty.

I quickly put the conversation out of my head, happy Millie's mind seemed to be on something other than plotting revenge on Clem for a change. Anyone else would have been dying to find out who Millie's secret admirer was, but I had no interest. Clem's little romance with Hugh was all the drama I needed.

I spent the rest of the evening trying not to rip my hair out as I attempted to do my maths homework. You'd have thought that, since we were at boarding school and therefore never at home, we'd have no homework.

Not true. They called it "prep", but an apple is an apple, even if you call it a pear.

The maths homework I'd been set was awful, and I felt like I was wading through treacle trying to get to the solution. I know

I'm not the brightest bulb, but I'm not awful either. I have a great memory. It's not, like, photographic or anything, but I definitely have a knack for remembering things. It was how I got my scholarship – I just did loads of old Heybuckle School entrance exams, and the same questions came up in the version I did.

Clem didn't understand why I cared about maths so much. "You like English – why does it matter if you're terrible at maths?" she always said.

But it mattered to me. Everyone else at Heybuckle acted like they were so brilliant, even if a lot of them weren't – *fake it until you make it* seemed to be the unofficial school motto; a skill I didn't have. No one ever acknowledged how *making it* for most Heybuckle students involved simply waiting for the day their parents could get them into a top-level job with one of their friends. I continued to muddle along, always feeling like I had to prove I deserved my place at Heybuckle, even when I scored higher than half the class in tests. People like Clem went through life knowing it owed them something, so that's how life treated them. People like me owed life something instead.

Mum said Heybuckle would give me all the opportunities she never got. She left school at sixteen to get a job – back then, going to university was unheard of in our family, and her parents only understood that having a job, any job, made you money, which they so desperately needed. My grandparents couldn't speak English, conversing only in Punjabi. When they were alive, I used to struggle through conversations in broken Punjabi with them, neither of us fully understanding the other. Then they died, so I had no real reason to speak Punjabi any more. I gradually forgot it, my last real link to India dying with them. I straddled an odd line – people would never look at me and straight away consider me English. But I couldn't slip into a life in India – I was too British for that.

And the more I learned at Heybuckle, the more I realized I still didn't have the opportunities the other students had. They could go travelling and see the world with their parents' blessing. They could plan to take jobs that they loved but which paid a pittance, knowing their real income would be from their mums and dads. I had to think smart, practically, about what I wanted to do next. I had no safety net.

So, yes, maths was important.

I stayed in the library all evening, struggling through my homework. People kept filtering in and out, but I kept my head down, doing my best to focus. At closing time, I gathered my stuff and set off to my room, the way taking me past the fifth form common room. Gaggles of people were streaming out, heading for bed. This included Hattie Fritter, Clem's roommate, who awkwardly fell into step with me because we were going the same way.

Hattie was one of those salt of the earth people, who loved going on hikes and anything to do with nature. She was quiet and so was I, which meant we hardly had anything to talk about. I said goodbye at my bedroom door and slipped inside. Annabelle was already asleep, which was odd because she usually stayed up well into the night texting people. I got ready for bed in the dark.

* * *

I met up with Clem at breakfast the next day. There was something weird about the atmosphere in the dining room. Most people were chatting and laughing like normal, but a few had serious, scared looks on their faces.

We sat down at one of the long tables and it was almost like watching a fire slowly spread, as one by one people's faces became solemn. Kate Dulfity, whose family owned a chain of high-end jewellery stores established in the early 1800s, walked past us with a big group. She had flame red hair and freckles, and always looked slightly concerned, like she had lost something – which she probably had. She was super disorganized, famous for leaving items all around school – her water bottle, her book bag, her laptop. I didn't know her well, but she was in my maths class, and was also one of Clem's friends from lacrosse. Clem told me the lacrosse girls often told Kate to meet them an hour before they needed her, because she had no concept of time – probably because she'd left her phone and watch lying around somewhere.

"Hey, Kate," called Clem. "What's going on?"

Kate stopped, and so did all her friends, bunching together as if for safety.

"Not sure," she said, a little nervously. "The Regia Club graffitied this…violent version of the school logo in one of the corridors no one really goes down. It's an odd prank for them – they normally like an audience, don't they? Plus their pranks don't involve destroying school property."

"I heard they voted in a new leader a few weeks ago," said one of her friends, "who wants a *change in direction*." She said the words ominously.

41

"It's a secret society, how'd you hear that?" said Kate.

"Nothing's ever *really* a secret, is it?" said her friend.

The weird atmosphere continued into first period. When I first started at Heybuckle I'd found it odd how each period was only forty minutes long, with a five-minute gap between to get to the next class. The day felt lengthy, with five periods of lessons on Mondays and Tuesdays and eight on Wednesdays, Thursdays and Fridays.

Miss Bilson, my biology teacher, set us a worksheet to do, which was strange because she normally put a lot more effort into lessons. We all cracked on, until someone figured out she had printed the worksheet from a random website. People got their phones out and started copying the answers from online, but Miss Bilson didn't comment. About halfway through, Mrs Greythorne's assistant came in and told Clem to go to the office.

"Probably to do with the whole Millie thing," said Clem, rolling her eyes. She tried to sound carefree but was given away by how pale she had gone. Even she couldn't want round two of detention.

I went to double maths alone. Two of the twelve seats stood empty – Tommy wasn't there, and neither was Eddy, Hugh's other closest friend. Summer sat in front of me, her entire body rigid with tension.

Instead of my usual maths teacher, Coach Tyler shuffled in. His bushy moustache twitched as he looked around the room, clutching a clipboard to his chest. He looked out of place indoors, his yellow polo shirt and crimson shorts suited to jogging along with students doing laps around the fields.

Normally he appeared the epitome of health, but today his face was grey and drawn.

"Where's Mr Rhubarb?" Kate asked.

Coach Tyler had started to wipe the whiteboard clear, revealing patches of damp under his arms.

"Not up for class today," he said with a grunt.

"Is it because of...of what Hattie found this morning?" asked Kate.

Coach Tyler paused, turning around with a frown. "How did you hear about that?"

"*Everyone's* heard by now," said Summer, in her usual disparaging tone.

I hadn't heard anything about Hattie, but I didn't want to ask. The back of my neck prickled as I started to imagine wild explanations, like Hattie had found a pile of bones in the woods because Heybuckle had been built on an ancient graveyard. Or she'd found—

I clenched my fists, forcing myself to stop. I had a habit of imagining doomsday scenarios, probably because of all the thrillers I read – great for writing stories, but not helpful when I just needed to listen to the conversation to find out what was happening.

"Do you know *why* Hattie was walking through the woods this morning?" said Coach Tyler, dropping his voice a little bit. He didn't need to. The entire class was listening intently.

At least I knew *that* reason. Clem moaned constantly about Hattie waking her up every day as she got ready for an early morning walk. Hattie always went the same way, through the school woods, because the path led to a hilltop and some

43

stunning countryside views.

"We shouldn't be speculating," said Summer. "It's not right. What cover work has Mr Rhubarb set for us?"

I tried not to groan. I wanted to hear the gossip, not do maths. Trust Summer to ruin things. The class went on in silence until the bell rang for break. I headed to the common room, not sure what I would do when I got there – I wouldn't have anyone to sit with. I got out my phone, to check if Clem had messaged me to say where to meet her. But the cracked screen remained blank, even when I pressed the power button as hard as I could; I still hadn't got around to charging it.

When I got to the fifth form common room, I found people crammed in together, huddled in small groups and whispering. There were way more people than normal, especially since the sunlight flooding through the enormous bay windows hinted at a lovely spring day.

Annabelle was with Lucy. I tried to squeeze past, but Annabelle stopped me, her jaw chomping up and down on some chewing gum.

"Jess, I was hoping I would see you," she said, each word carefully pronounced.

Like always, I wondered why she didn't just speak in her real accent.

I frowned. Annabelle normally ignored me.

"What's up?"

"Have you heard from Clem? What has she said?" Lucy leaned forwards, her eyes wide.

"Er…no, I haven't seen Clem since this morning," I said. "Why?"

44

Annabelle gaped at me, her mouth hanging open to reveal her chewing gum stuck to her back teeth. "You mean you haven't heard?"

Obviously not. "No – there's been loads of weird rumours going around today."

Annabelle had always loved gossiping, but she paused, exchanging a look with Lucy. "Well, Hattie came running into school this morning, basically hysterical. She'd gone through the woods on her walk and...and..." Her voice shook. "Apparently he was just *lying* there... Blood everywhere..."

"Who?" I asked.

"Hugh. He's dead."

5

By fifth period everyone knew Millie had killed Hugh.

She'd lured him out to the woods and then attacked him (strangled him, stabbed him, dug an enormous hole that he fell into, dropped a giant rock on his head). The details were different depending on who you talked to.

She had the motive – he'd cheated on her – and she'd threatened to kill him a week before he was murdered. It was like every cliché in every murder mystery I had ever read: the jealous ex-girlfriend killing her former lover. Like everyone else, I was convinced she was the murderer.

And no one had seen her, or Clem, all day. I tried to go past Mrs Greythorne's office, hoping to get a glimpse of her, but two bulky policemen told me to keep walking. I imagined arguing with them, forcing them to let me in. Bursting triumphantly into the room and racing to Clem's side, where I knew she needed me to be.

Instead, I walked away, my stomach burning with self-loathing. I couldn't risk getting in trouble. One of the many conditions of my scholarship involved maintaining a clean record, and while I didn't know exactly what the limits of that were, interrupting a murder investigation was definitely a no-no.

I looked out for Tommy or Eddy at lunch, but they were still absent. The next two periods passed quickly, and the question on everyone's lips was the same: how did Millie think she would get away with it?

The teachers went around with harried looks on their faces, and I wondered how the school would break the news to our parents. Mum would probably have a fit and then be hugely torn between ordering me home where she could keep an eye on me in the safe streets of London, aka the murder capital of the country, or telling me to never go out of sight of the teachers.

In my final class of the day, English, we were told there would be a special assembly after dinner. In a move that highlighted the seriousness of the situation, Mrs Henridge gave up trying to teach us, and instead put on a film that no one watched. People whispered in small groups, and she didn't tell them to stop.

I kept looking over at Clem's empty seat beside me and wondering where she was, if she was okay.

Arthur was on my other side, doodling what I think were supposed to be robots in a notebook. He looked up suddenly and caught me staring.

"So how do you think she did it?" he said.

"What?" I blinked. He was acting like we were already in the middle of a conversation.

"Got him out to the woods. You think she told him she wanted to get back together?"

I couldn't believe he wanted to jump from never talking to me at all, to discussing theories about how exactly Millie had killed Hugh. I shrugged, turning back to the film and pretending like I was really interested in the argument going on between the two characters.

Arthur either didn't pick up on how uncomfortable I was, or did and carried on anyway.

"I'm willing to bet he knew the whole cheating thing hadn't put him in her good books, right? So, how'd she manage to convince him to sneak out of school in the middle of the night so she could murder him? You know what else I don't get, though?"

I couldn't ignore his direct question, not when he had turned his entire body to face me.

"What?" This was the longest conversation I'd ever had with Arthur, and I was starting to get the impression he was a bit of a weird one.

"Why'd she let everyone in school hear her threatening to kill him?" Arthur tutted, shaking his head. "She must not have cared about the consequences. Must have been a real heat of the moment thing – she always struck me as the *too emotional* type. You know how girls can be." His lip curled, like he considered having emotions to be the peak of weakness. "Maybe even when she was luring him out there, she didn't know what she was going to do. But then she saw him, all on his own, and he told her how much he loved Clem – and it's not like the two of them were subtle about being together this week. Couldn't turn a corner in this school without the fear of running into them sucking face. So, I guess she saw red, and something snapped. And she just kept hitting and hitting…"

Arthur's eyes became unfocused, like he was imagining the scene – and enjoying it. And then, in perhaps the most bizarre part of the whole interaction, he turned back to his doodling, and didn't speak to me again for the rest of the lesson.

We all lined up to file into the school hall, an enormous, circular room, with large windows allowing light to flood across the polished floorboards.

Mrs Greythorne stood by the entrance, nodding up at shell-shocked students as they passed. Despite being tiny, she only ever wore flat shoes. Her grey hair was normally pulled tightly into a bun, but there were strands coming loose, hanging limply around her haggard face. There were heavy circles under her eyes; she looked like she hadn't slept in weeks.

"Miss Choudhary," she said, her face grim. She knew the names of every student in school. "Would you follow Inspector Foster, please?"

Inspector Foster was nearly six foot, with a fringe of brown hair that fell into her eyes, the sort of hairstyle I had when I was five. Her thin lips seemed to fall naturally down into a frown, like gravity was working extra hard on them.

My stomach swooped as I tried to come up with a way of avoiding going with her. Clem would've said *no thanks,* and stalked into the hall, and that would have been the end of it. Instead, after an awkward few seconds where I stared at Mrs Greythorne like my brain had been switched off, I gave a small squeak and meekly followed the inspector down the hallway. My ears burned as everyone stared.

"Am I in trouble?" I managed to ask as we went up a flight of stairs.

"No," she replied.

I could sense she wasn't in the mood for a conversation, and in any case I had watched enough documentaries with Mum to know I shouldn't say anything to a police officer without a lawyer present. Or something.

The inspector led me to the corridor outside the gallery at the top of the school hall. I stopped, and gasped. At the end of the corridor someone had painted an enormous version of the school logo, a red-and-gold shield with a crown-wearing dragon inside. Except the painter had added extra details; the dragon's wings were clipped, with chains around its ankles – and blood dripped from a knife protruding from its throat. The blood blurred into the red background of the shield. In the corner, in black paint, were the initials *S.R.* The Regia Club.

Someone had placed little orange cones blocking off the area round the graffiti, and there was a discarded bucket and sponge lying pushed to one side. I guess the cleaners hadn't had much luck scrubbing it off.

Graffiti wasn't common at Heybuckle, and I could see how Kate had thought this Regia Club prank was an odd one. The whole point of the club was to put on a show that said, *See, we're the exclusive overlords in charge of everyone's puppet strings and we can make you do stupid stuff in public for our entertainment.* Even amongst the rich kids, there was a hierarchy. But this didn't feel stupid, it felt calculated. The new leader, whoever they were, clearly wanted to do things differently.

And now, after what had happened with Hugh…the graffiti

took on a more sinister meaning. Had Hugh been *part* of the Regia Club? Was this a twisted memorial for him?

The inspector's frown deepened as her eyes flicked to the graffiti, before she pushed open a door leading off the corridor.

"In you go," she said shortly.

I entered the gallery, which was a sort of theatre-box type structure that looked out onto the hall. Below, the entire school buzzed as they took their seats.

A few chairs had been placed in a row in the gallery, and sitting on them were Tommy, Eddy and Clem.

"Jess," she said, almost tripping as she got to her feet and lunged at me, hugging me so tightly it hurt. Her whole body trembled. When she pulled away, I was startled by her tear-stained face. I had never seen her cry before. "I just don't believe – it's not true. It's a nightmare, Jess."

Until then I'd been treating Hugh's death in an abstract sort of way. Like something you would hear on the news, and then change the channel and forget about. But looking at Clem's pale face, her red hair startling against her blood-leeched skin, it suddenly hit me.

I would never see Hugh again.

I would never speak to him, or look at him. I would never see him walking down the corridors with his friends, or sitting in the dining hall. He would never smile, never laugh, never pay someone to do his homework for him. His textbooks would always remain pristine.

He would forever be seventeen.

I found myself blinking back tears. His poor *parents*. He'd had two dogs and three cats and they were probably waiting for the school holidays, for him to come home.

But he was never coming home.

Clem clutched my hand, pulling me to the seat next to her. Her palms were clammy, and I couldn't even begin to imagine how she was feeling. Our entire friendship, I'd always been the one who felt things too deeply, who cried when I didn't do well in a test or when the other kids were mean to me, and Clem had always been there to tell me to buck up, and then would distract me with one of her wild ideas. Now it was my turn to be her rock, but this was beyond any of my experiences. Dad had died when I was too young to know what was going on, and when my grandparents passed away, I was comforted by the fact they had managed to live long lives and had been healthy right up until the end.

But Hugh was seventeen and death was supposed to be one of those things that happened to other people. All I could do was squeeze Clem's hand, and know it wasn't enough.

I looked over at the other people in the gallery. Tommy and Eddy were obviously being kept away from the rest of the school to stop people questioning them. As Hugh's inner circle, they would now be like celebrities.

Tommy clenched the arms of his chair, his knuckles white. A muscle in his jaw jumped, and his unblinking eyes bore down on the currently empty stage.

Eddy looked equally shell-shocked, hunched in the middle of the row, running his hands through his mess of sandy hair that stuck up in all directions. His brown eyes were framed by thick lashes that looked wet, and he was even paler than normal, his freckles stark against his skin.

I'd never really spoken to him before – he talked to Clem

a lot, but I didn't register on his radar. From what I could tell, he liked to latch onto people who were richer than him, or more popular, or more talented, and then bragged about their achievements like they were his own. When Heybuckle finally won a football tournament, he'd stood up in the common room and invited everyone to a party, even though he'd only been a substitute and didn't play a single match.

Hattie wasn't in the gallery. She was probably still in counselling or something. Finding a body would be something to haunt you for the rest of your life – even worse if it was someone you knew.

Clem clasped my hand, her eyes fixed on a point on the ground. I was glad she didn't want to speak. I didn't know what I would say if she did.

The door to the gallery squeaked open, and I looked behind me, expecting to see another police officer.

Instead Millie walked in, dressed head to toe in black.

"What's *she* doing here?" I said without thinking, a little bit too loudly.

Eddy whipped his head around. Even Tommy and Clem looked up.

Millie ignored me, dragging a chair backwards. She sat down behind us, her back straight, her hands folded neatly in her lap as she gazed ahead. Her face was expressionless, and apart from a slight quiver to her cherry-red lips, she looked remarkably well put together.

I couldn't believe it. Why hadn't Millie been arrested? How could she be sitting there so calmly, waiting for Mrs Greythorne to make a speech?

53

"Jess," muttered Clem.

I dragged my eyes away from Millie.

"Why's she here?" I whispered. "Do you want me to ask them to make her leave?" And even though the very thought made me nauseous, I gladly would have got up and said something if it meant Millicent Cordelia Calthrope-Newton-Rose was never allowed within ten metres of Clem again.

Clem whispered, "She's in pain too."

She hadn't heard. She didn't know what Millie had done. She'd been with the police all day – she was in shock.

She hadn't put two and two together.

"Clem, she… She killed Hugh." I said it as gently as I could.

But Clem was shaking her head. "I was with her all evening, sorting out the stupid balls…" Clem broke off, tears flowing thick and fast down her face now. "The police say they think he was killed after he left dinner at seven, and before bedtime at 10 p.m. I was with her that *entire time* at detention. She didn't do it, Jess."

I didn't fully understand what that meant at first. It took me a few seconds to process that if Millie hadn't killed Hugh, someone else had.

And they were on the loose in Heybuckle.

6

Headmistress Greythorne stepped up to the podium. She tapped the microphone, and at once all noise ceased. She cleared her throat.

"By now I'm sure thousands of rumours have spread about what happened last night. A student, Hugh Henry Van Boren, sadly passed away."

Not "was killed". *Passed away*. Like he'd drifted off in his sleep. Like he hadn't been found in the middle of the woods by one of his now forever traumatized classmates. Mrs Greythorne clearly wasn't going to go into what had happened. She was trying her hardest to gloss over the fact that a student had been murdered in her school.

"I'm sure you'll all appreciate that this is a very difficult time for those who knew Hugh best. I urge you to respect the privacy of those who were closest to him." She took a deep breath. The microphone picked it up, the static crackling around the room. "For now, the school woods are off limits to students. There are police tapes cordoning them off."

Tommy had stood up, and was leaning against the balcony,

his gaze so intense he probably could have burned a hole into Mrs Greythorne's brain.

"Hugh was…was found this morning by a student, who is currently with their parents. I know this is a difficult time, and you must all have so many questions, but please do not attempt to contact this student."

Clem sniffed loudly. Snot ran down her face and I wished I was one of those people who carried tissues with them.

"Hugh was a popular, well-liked boy. Many of you in this room will be affected by his passing." Mrs Greythorne's voice shook. "Counselling will be available for all students. Please do speak to a trusted member of the faculty if you feel you need it. Anything you say will be confidential…" She hesitated and looked at the front row. There were a few adults in plain clothes I had never seen before. Police.

She didn't know for sure whether anything we said in counselling would be confidential, I realized. If someone used the session to announce they'd been the one to knock off Hugh, surely that would have to be shared with the police?

The school hall had never been so quiet. It was like people were afraid to move.

"And…and there will be a continued police presence in our school," Mrs Greythorne went on. "Over the course of the next few days, the police may want to speak to some of you, to ask if you have any knowledge of yesterday's events. We will be contacting parents to let them know of the current circumstances. Of course, any student has the right to refuse to speak to the police, but I urge you – if you have any information, please, *please* come forwards."

There were murmurings now. People were as confused as I had been. They all thought Millie had killed Hugh. They didn't understand why the police needed to ask any more questions.

"This school has always been a family, and together we shall help each other through this most terrible of tragedies. For now, let's have a minute of silence for Hugh – to remember one of the stars of our school, taken much, much too soon."

After the assembly was finished, Clem got shakily to her feet. She swayed, and I grabbed her arm.

Inspector Foster blocked the exit.

"Just a moment, ladies. I think it's better if we let the rest of your classmates clear the corridors before you go back to your rooms."

I nodded. Clem didn't need the whispers and the stares of the other students right now.

Tommy and Eddy hovered behind us in silence. Millie stood a little way off, staring blankly across the emptying assembly hall with her arms folded. While we were waiting, Mrs Greythorne arrived.

"I just wanted to say goodnight to you all, and that you should try to get some rest."

Mrs Greythorne smiled at us, and I could see why she'd been in charge of the school for so many years. She was strict, but she had a motherly sort of quality to her which she could switch on at a moment's notice.

"I think the corridors are sufficiently clear now, Inspector. The students should be okay getting to bed. It's been a long day."

Tommy and Eddy filed out. Millie waited a moment before following.

"Jess," said Mrs Greythorne, turning to me. "As Hattie has gone home to be with her parents, Clem has requested you stay in her room tonight."

Clem tugged on my sleeve. "I hope that's okay, Jess? I just don't want to be alone."

"Of course," I said, shocked she even had to ask.

Mrs Greythorne nodded at me. "I'll arrange for some overnight things to be brought to Clem's room. Sleep well, ladies."

We walked back slowly, arms looped. I felt like a crutch, holding Clem upright.

"I can't believe this is happening," said Clem as we walked through the now silent corridors. "The police had all these questions for me. When's the last time I saw him, what's the last thing we talked about? Did anything seem off? Did he seem worried about anything – scared of anyone? Did he ever mention any enemies? They kept pressing and pressing…"

For a brief moment I considered the possibility that someone random had killed Hugh, a murderer who had got past the school's high walls, and the security guards who patrolled the borders, and all the cameras over the entrances. Who snuck into the school without anyone becoming suspicious, and found Hugh in his bedroom after dinner and lured him out into the woods to kill him – then left his body behind.

Or maybe it had been a professional hitman. Hugh's family were rich – maybe they had crossed the wrong person, and Hugh's murder was revenge.

But then I settled on the most likely answer. Someone in school – perhaps someone I saw every day – a teacher, even, or a student, had killed Hugh. And the idea they were walking around school, blending in like nothing had happened, was terrifying.

We reached Clem's room, and I switched on the light. Her bedroom was the same size as mine, but hers had a wide window which normally provided views over the school fields. Now, however, it just looked out upon darkness.

Hattie's side of the room was relatively tidy, but Clem's half always looked like someone had come along determined to chuck everything in the most random location they could. Her desk chair had clothes stacked on it and her lacrosse sticks lay in a pile by her bed, along with her muddy kit. Most of the desk space was taken by two teddies that Hugh had given her for their one-month anniversary. One teddy wore a clementine-orange dress, and mismatching socks, the other a three-piece suit. The teddies sat propped up against her history textbook, their little arms crossed. They were the only neat things on Clem's side; Hugh had carefully brushed down their fur and rearranged them regularly, before they could start to gather dust.

Clem collapsed on her bed, lying face down, and I perched on the edge of Hattie's mattress. Clem's breathing was steady, and for a while we sat in silence. Then there was a gentle knock on the door, and I pulled it open.

Mrs Henridge was holding my old flannel pyjamas and my toothbrush. Annabelle must have given them to her.

"Here you go, Jess," she said. She hesitated for a second, like she was about to say something else. But then she seemed to change her mind, because she just said, "Goodnight."

"Night, miss," I said.

Clem still hadn't moved, so I decided to get out of my uniform and into my pyjamas. I hurriedly took my blazer off, and my phone clattered out of the pocket and onto the floor.

"What's that?" Clem looked up.

"Just my phone," I said, picking it up and numbly clutching it.

School was normally like a bubble, with all the problems we dealt with contained inside. What grades we were all getting, what extracurriculars we were doing, who was going out with who. But the bubble had burst. The news about Hugh would have leaked into the outside world. Mum had probably messaged me about it.

"Can I borrow your charger?"

There *were* lots of unread messages from Mum, asking if they were still feeding me okay, and did I want any new socks, and never mind she'd already bought me a jumbo pack of thirty because they were on sale. But there was nothing about Hugh; maybe it hadn't yet leaked online.

It would only be a matter of time, though. Alumni of Heybuckle School were powerful, influential. I bet a lot of favours had been called in to stop enormous BREAKING NEWS headlines flashing up in all the rags, but even with all the will in the world, the school wouldn't be able to suppress this.

I hated having notifications on my phone, so I flicked through each one, to make them go away.

Mum, Mum, Mum – Blocked Number.

"No way," I muttered, dread creeping up my spine.

Everyone knew what getting a message from a private number meant. Unless I happened to be getting a random spam message, the Regia Club had chosen me for a dare.

But surely not. Hugh had literally just died. They absolutely *couldn't* be worrying about whether they could get me to run around school during prep banging pots and pans together. Not unless they had the message on some sort of auto-timer, so it had been scheduled to send out before everything happened.

I tapped on the message and for a moment I couldn't register what I was reading.

I read it once.

Twice.

But the words didn't change.

Thanks for the inspiration. I couldn't have killed Hugh without you.

7

I didn't tell Clem about the message.

She had her back to me as she grabbed a pair of silk pyjamas from her drawers. I climbed into Hattie's bed, and every so often would reread the text, hoping it would disappear, or a second one would appear being, like, *gotcha*.

"You okay?" said Clem, as she flicked the bedroom light off. "You've gone all quiet."

"Fine, yeah," I replied, my voice coming out oddly strangled. "Night."

Clem's breathing got slower, and she started doing these little snort things. Even after everything that had happened, she still had the unnerving ability to fall asleep almost instantly.

I, on the other hand, knew I'd be getting no sleep. I burrowed under the sheets so the light wouldn't wake up Clem and opened the message yet again.

Sent Wednesday, 9.16 p.m.

Around half an hour ago.

I didn't understand. If Hugh had been killed yesterday, why would someone wait a full day to send me this?

Maybe this *was* a Regia Club prank. A sick one. It was under new leadership, and from the graffiti on the wall it seemed like the new leader wanted to take it in a darker direction. The Regia Club had always been about wielding power, either by making people carry out pranks, or pulling strings to make life at Heybuckle more pleasant for its members. Heybuckle management listened to them because any time they did as the Regia Club asked, the school got a big donation from an anonymous source – probably a parent of someone in the club.

That was how the club kept on the good side of the majority of the school – to protect their anonymity, the things they demanded for themselves often trickled down to everyone else as well. They'd once put a poster up in the dining room demanding lobster for Friday dinner instead of fish and chips, and the entire school had feasted on the most expensive meal ever. But now it seemed like the club was more about breaking rules and getting under people's skins.

Well, this message had certainly got under my skin.

But then I considered the other possibility. This could be an actual text from Hugh's actual murderer.

The police had told Clem that Hugh was killed between 7 p.m. and 10 p.m., when the school was locked up for the night and all the alarms switched on. The school was only unlocked at 6 a.m., and he couldn't have been killed in the morning, because there would have been a big difference between a fresh body and one which had been outside all night.

I looked at the message again. It made it sound like I was an accomplice or something, like I'd had a hand in Hugh's death. I'd be a good suspect – the Indian kid from the poor background, jealous of everything Hugh had. His influential family was probably baying for blood. The school might try to make an example out of me, try to claw back their good reputation by taking my scholarship away.

It took me hours to fall asleep, but by then I had worked out what I needed to do: talk to the one student who actually knew something about the crime. I had to speak to Hattie Fritter.

While I waited for Hattie to return to school, I, like everyone else, read all the news reports about Hugh, trying to glean any information about the case. But Heybuckle and Hugh's family must have really called in all their favours, because there weren't any actual facts to be found. Most of the articles had a few short sentences describing what we already knew: that Hugh's body had been found in the woods and the police were investigating.

The rest of the news stories were bulked out with focus on Hugh's background as the golden boy with a blessed life, a distant relative of the royals, the brilliant athlete with everything to live for, set to inherit millions of pounds and hundreds of acres of land as part of a huge country estate.

It was surreal, seeing Hugh described that way. To me, he was a classmate who existed on a different plane – we went to the same school but lived in different worlds.

Mum repeatedly attempted to ring me. When I eventually returned her call, she launched straight into the lecture I'd been expecting: *stay out of trouble, keep away from any press, keep your head down, don't go out of school after dark, don't walk in the grounds or corridors on your own, keep in sight of a teacher at all times.*

I said *Yes, Mum* and reassured her as best as I could. I almost pointed out that I was probably miles off the murderer's radar – but then I remembered the *thanks for the inspiration* text and I stopped talking.

It took Hattie three days to come back to Heybuckle, and when she did, she looked exhausted. People respected Mrs Greythorne's request to leave her alone. They kept a safe distance and talked about other things to take her mind off it. Everyone really stepped up, and it was nice to see the school banding together and being mature about the whole thing.

Obviously, I'm kidding. The moment Hattie came back to school it was like sharks smelling fresh blood. They all circled around her, waiting to take a bite.

Clem was relieved because it meant some of the heat was taken off her. She was the tragic girlfriend left behind and she was drowning in the sympathy of the entire school. Even Arthur got in on the act, drifting out of his world of obliviousness long enough to say he was sorry for her loss, though there was something off about the way he said it. The words sounded rehearsed, rolling unnaturally off his tongue.

Millie seemed to be basking in the glow of the whole thing. She strutted around school out of her uniform, dressed in all black like a designer-clad Hollywood widow, with big sunglasses, a veiled hat and blood-red lipstick. She knew the teachers couldn't stop her without coming across as heartless.

"Don't you think it's a bit…odd of Millie, though?" I said at breakfast to Clem, as I watched Millie laughing with her friends

65

as she adjusted the veil attached to her black fascinator. "She doesn't seem to be affected at all."

"People handle grief differently," said Clem, rather wisely for someone who had spent last night gulping alcohol she'd bought from an eighteen-year-old student who had smuggled it in from a day out at the village. I was worried she'd go back to being old Party Clem, which is who she'd been before...well, before she got with Hugh.

Last year she'd been very much out of control. Not so much in school, but on holidays she would do all sorts of wild stuff. Like setting fire to her mother's wedding dress or getting caught skinny-dipping in her neighbour's pool. I never told those details to Mum, who probably would have tried to ban me from being friends with her.

Then after last summer, Clem had come back to school a different person, still with the same confidence, but also deeply ashamed of her past actions.

"It's textbook, isn't it?" she'd said. "Rich girl whose parents don't give me enough attention, so I screw around to make them notice me." She shrugged. "I can't act however I want just because *they* let me." She'd started counselling and since then I hadn't seen her touch a drop of alcohol.

But now I was worried the shock of Hugh's death would send her spiralling. I hoped speaking to Hattie would kill two birds with one stone – I would find out a bit more about what had happened to Hugh, maybe something that would help Clem deal with everything... And I'd also be able to figure out who had sent me the creepy thank-you text – and why.

Clem had lacrosse practice on Saturday mornings. She sped

off, while I went to find Hattie. My hunch was that she would be in her room, hiding from everyone. That's what I would have done if I was her.

I knocked gently on Clem and Hattie's door.

"Come in," said a soft voice.

I went inside. Hattie was sitting at her desk, flicking through a textbook.

"Oh, hey, Jess." Hattie shut the book. "I was expecting you to come see me."

"You were?" I asked, surprised.

"Yeah – I mean, I know Clem must want to ask about… about…" She cleared her throat. "But I don't think she's got it in her to. So I guess she wants you to find out?"

"Yes," I said, glad to have confirmation I was doing the right thing for Clem.

"Mrs Greythorne didn't want me telling people – they're trying to keep the whole thing hushed up, but I've heard reporters keep trying to get secret interviews with students. Plus, loads of people's parents want an investigation into how this could have happened." Hattie shrugged, tucking a piece of her frizzy hair behind her ear. The tip of her nose was red – I guess with cold. She had the window wide open, and the late April air was nippy. "Can I count on you not to tell anyone but Clem?"

I nodded, and my heart started beating faster as I wondered what she was going to say.

"I'd got up slightly earlier than usual for my morning walk and snuck out quietly, because Clem was still asleep. I followed my normal route – and then I got to the clearing in the woods…"

Hattie's voice wavered. Her skin had a tinge of green to it. "He was just lying there – and there was so much blood..."

She squeezed her fists into balls.

"I – I won't go into what he looked like. There was this enormous gold trophy lying on top of his hands—"

"A trophy?" I interrupted. I couldn't stop myself. My stomach had started churning.

She nodded. "I went up to him and there were these twigs—"

"—spelling *HELP ME*," I finished, as my knees gave way and I sat heavily on Clem's bed.

Hattie stopped, confused. "Yeah... How did you know?"

She was looking at me oddly. I needed to think of a lie, fast.

"I spoke to a police officer – he let it slip... I didn't think it was true."

I couldn't tell if she believed me. I don't think I'd have believed me, if I was her.

"I've got to go," I blurted, before fleeing Hattie's shrewd stare.

I ran to the nearest bathroom, where I locked myself in a stall, and whipped my phone out.

Thanks for the inspiration. I couldn't have killed Hugh without you.

Someone had used my short story as the basis for Hugh's murder.

68

8

I felt like I was walking around with a giant sign on my head that said *I know something about the murder.* I wanted to go to the police. This was information that could help them. They could work out how someone had read my short story in the first place – although it wouldn't have been hard. Mrs Henridge didn't even lock her office door. Anyone could have snuck inside and taken photos.

Maybe they could trace the text message I had received, figure out who had sent it through GPS stalking, like people did in spy films.

But something stopped me from walking into Mrs Greythorne's office.

I was supposed to be keeping my head down, getting good grades, and leaving Heybuckle with the opportunities Mum dreamed of for me. Confessing I had something to do with the murder of one of the school's most celebrated students would make me the centre of attention for all the wrong reasons.

So, I kept quiet.

* * *

The rest of the weekend passed in a blur, and I wished everything would go back to normal. But that was impossible with the police still hanging around, asking questions.

I knew Hattie would eventually talk to Clem about what she had found in the woods. She would mention she'd told me first, and I would look terrible if I didn't speak up about how my short story had inspired the murderer.

Clem and I were sitting in the fifth form common room, alone in a corner. We'd just finished lessons for the day, and most of the squidgy couches were empty, because people were outside in the acres of Heybuckle's green grounds enjoying the sunshine – although the woods were still roped off.

Clem fiddled around on her phone, while I had a book resting on my lap. I had been trying to find the right moment to bring up the whole twigs-spelling-help-me thing (*why* hadn't I just listened to Summer and gone with a straightforward stabbing? No one could say I'd inspired a straightforward stabbing).

Tommy was sitting nearby with a few friends. They weren't close enough for me to listen in on, but they were getting quite rowdy – well, everyone but Tommy. Since Hugh's death, his eyes had lost a bit of their twinkle, and he didn't smile as much as he used to. I had an urge to get up and just…wrap my arms around him and tell him everything would be okay. And then he would sort of relax into me and tell me he'd always had a thing for me, and he was glad something was finally happening—

"Earth to Jess." Clem waved her hand in my face, and I snapped out of my daydream.

I'd been staring at Tommy. I probably even had a bit of drool at the corner of my mouth.

"Do you think I should dye my hair pink?"

"It's against the dress code," I said, turning my attention back to Clem. "No unnatural hair colours."

"They won't say anything to me," said Clem, her tone light. "I'm grieving, remember?"

I hesitated, and she must have caught something in my expression because her face went serious.

"What's wrong?"

It was time. I decided to say it fast, and then it would all be over.

"I have to tell you something. And this is going to sound ridiculous, but I have proof, okay?" I got out my phone. My hands were shaking as I clicked over to the text message. "But believe me, I didn't have anything to do with it."

"What're you talking about?" said Clem with a laugh. She took my phone from me, and the grin slipped off her face. For a moment she was silent, and I worried she would storm out. "What's this?"

"Remember the short story I wrote for G&T?"

Clem nodded, still looking at the phone, her eyes fixed on the screen like she could will the words to rearrange themselves into something that made sense.

"When Hugh's body was found…" My tongue had swollen up. I couldn't get the rest of the words out. I tried again. "Remember I had all that stuff in my story about the twigs, and…and the trophy and everything?"

Clem nodded again, her head bobbing up and down like a toy. She finally looked up, staring at me. Her lips were pursed, and she clutched my phone so tightly the veins on the back of her hands popped.

71

"That's how Hugh was found," I said. "Exactly like in my short story."

"I don't understand," said Clem. "Who sent you this?" She waved the phone at me.

"It's a blocked number… I thought maybe it was the Regia Club. As some sort of sick prank. But now I'm thinking it's someone piggybacking off their anonymous text style…and it's from whoever killed Hugh."

"Why the *hell*…?" She raised her voice, and Tommy and his friends looked around.

I smiled at them, to say *nothing going on here. We're not discussing how I potentially inspired a murderer to kill Hugh Henry Van Boren. Everything is fine.*

"Sorry… I just don't understand," she repeated. "If it was the…the killer who sent you this – why would they send you this…thank you? Killers aren't typically known to be a polite bunch." She blinked a few times, fiddling with her helix ear piercing, which she normally kept covered by her hair because it was against school uniform policy. "Have you told the police?"

She'd asked the one question I didn't want her to. "This whole thing is just some sick joke or something—"

"You haven't told them?"

"No, because…" But all my reasons suddenly sounded incredibly stupid. How could I tell her I didn't want anything to do with this, not when she was so wrapped up in it against her will? "I wanted to tell you first." I hated myself, but I wanted to salvage *something*, so Clem didn't think I was a completely despicable person.

"When did you get this?" The light from the screen reflected in her eyes as she stared down at the message and mouthed *Wednesday, 9.16 p.m.* "You waited this long to tell me?" Hurt cut through her voice.

We'd always told each other everything. Clem had an ability to slip into any group but had always called them *proximity friends*. People she was friends with because they happened to be near, who would be distant memories a few years after we left Heybuckle. They never knew her properly, not like me.

"I didn't want to upset you even more," I said. "I didn't want to do the wrong thing and make it worse…"

Clem hugged me suddenly, gripping me tightly. After a few seconds she let go and swallowed. "Go tell the police, Jess." Her voice was firm, not inviting argument. She handed the phone back to me, and I took it uncertainly.

"Er – now?"

"Yes. Now."

I headed straight to the police. You'd think they would have been super willing to speak to someone who said they had some information about the murder they were trying to solve. Instead, I waited for ages outside Mrs Greythorne's office, which they had commandeered for their investigation. I guess because Mrs Greythorne's office was the biggest in the school: a dark panelled room adorned with comfy armchairs, an enormous oak desk, deep bookshelves, and windows which had a great view of the school fields and the countryside in the distance.

But also because I bet the police wanted to assert their dominance. *This is our school now. We're in charge here.*

I sat on a wooden bench with a velvet green cushion that was, for some reason, hard. The golden clock mounted on the polished panelling ticked rhythmically and I tapped my finger against the bench in time.

Tick. Tick. Tick.

I was beginning to wonder if they had forgotten about me, when Mrs Greythorne's door opened and Inspector Foster stuck her head out.

"Come in," she said.

I had only been in Mrs Greythorne's office a few times before – once when I started at Heybuckle, and she did the whole *welcome, we hope you'll make us proud here, and end up as one of our school's many, many successes*. Another time, a few weeks later, when she wanted to check if I was okay because I only had one friend (Clem) and she was concerned I was *failing to thrive*. And once more when I was trying to throw a javelin in PE and my aim was so bad I hit Coach Tyler, and Mrs Greythorne had to open a formal investigation in case it had been an intentional rage incident, like what had happened with Millie a few weeks prior.

Mrs Greythorne sat beside me, and it was reassuring to have her there. She'd been the one to interview me for my place at Heybuckle and had taken the time to give Mum and me a proper tour around the web of never-ending corridors, the classrooms with freshly polished desks, the state-of-the-art science labs, the enormous swimming pool, the tennis courts. I'd heard rumours about how some of the school board, consisting of parents who had come to Heybuckle themselves and couldn't seem to let go of the good old days, had wanted to reduce the money going into the scholarship scheme. But instead, under

Mrs Greythorne's reign, the scheme had been expanded.

"You say you have some information for me, Miss Choudhary?" said Inspector Foster, as she picked up a pen and pressed the nib to a fresh page of her notebook. Her face was carefully blank, giving nothing away.

I wondered how many students had come forward with false information and wasted her time.

I explained about the short story I had written for G&T, telling her as much detail as I could remember about it. Then I showed her the message.

I expected her to scream *Eureka! You've helped us crack the case!*

She didn't even take any notes. Instead, she took my phone and asked a few more questions about the assignment, and what exactly Summer had contributed to the story, and who else had been in my Gifted and Talented class, and when I had received the message.

And why I hadn't come forward with this information sooner.

"Now, now," said Mrs Greythorne, pressing her fingers to her temples. "That's hardly relevant. She was probably scared. They're all scared, Inspector. These are just children you're trying to get to confess to murder."

"I'm not trying to get anyone to confess to murder," said the inspector, interlocking her fingers. "I'm simply trying to get to the truth."

"Did Summer also get a text?" I asked, leaning forwards. I wouldn't feel so bad if she had also received a text.

"Well, if she did, she hasn't come forward," said the inspector. "I would prefer it if you *didn't* tell anyone about this text message

– or discuss this further with anyone. Not even with Summer."

Well, that would hardly be a struggle. I guess she thought Summer was my twisted friend, and we got together on the regular to write murder stories in the hope one would actually come true.

I agreed to keep quiet.

The inspector tilted her head, her black eyes fixed on me. "From the autopsy, as well as circumstantial evidence, we estimate Hugh Henry Van Boren was murdered between 7 p.m., when he was last seen leaving dinner and heading back to his bedroom, and 10 p.m. Where were you at that time?"

I blinked, my stomach swooping. Was she trying to pin the murder on me? I'd have been the world's worst killer if that was the case, coming forward with this odd tale about the short story. I looked at Mrs Greythorne for reassurance.

"You can answer the question, dear," said Mrs Greythorne gently. "You're not in any trouble."

I told the inspector where I had been: the library, drowning in maths prep.

The inspector waited just a beat too long before she nodded. "Thank you, Miss Choudhary. I'll be right back." She left the room, taking my phone with her.

Mrs Greythorne and I sat in silence until she returned, half an hour later.

"Here's your phone, Miss Choudhary. Thank you."

Inspector Foster slid it across the desk. I stared at it, waiting for her to suddenly stand up with handcuffs and announce I was under arrest, that she'd thought long and hard about it and there was no other explanation – the murderer had to be me.

"You mentioned your short story was set in a forest. Can you tell me a bit more about why you chose that scene?"

I glanced over at Mrs Greythorne, unsure about the relevance of the question but not wanting to seem difficult by not answering.

"Because…" I stopped, because the actual reason for the forest setting made me sound super immature. Summer had wanted to set the story in an office, and I couldn't imagine anywhere more boring, so I told her she could choose between a forest setting or the victim dying in a freak accident where a satellite fell from space. She chose the forest scene, exactly like I thought she would, and also tried to educate me on why the satellite-from-space death was not physically possible. "It just seemed like a nice setting."

"There were no…deeper meanings to the forest setting? Like a code?"

"Er, no," I said, not following.

I looked at Mrs Greythorne again, hoping her face might give away some explanation. She was frowning slightly as she stared at the inspector.

"And do you know anything about the graffiti by the gallery?" said the inspector. "I've been told it was done by, er…a Regia Club?"

"No," I said. "I've got no idea what that's got to do with anything."

The inspector sucked in her cheeks. "Hmm," she said. "I've just checked with Miss Summer Johnson – she confirmed she worked on that short story with you."

"Both our names were at the top of the paper. Why'd you need to confirm with her?" I spoke without thinking and I immediately wished I could un-ask the question. Mum's words echoed in my head. *Keep your head down. Respect everyone at school. Remember, they can take it all away from you.*

The inspector tilted her head, the wrinkles around her eyes deepening as she squinted at me. "Well, that's the issue I'm having, Miss Choudhary. Because I also spoke to your teacher, a Mrs Henridge, about this short story, and she had absolutely no idea what I was talking about."

"What do you mean?" I asked. "It was an assignment."

"Oh, she didn't deny the existence of the assignment. In fact, she was very much looking forward to reading it – I understand it wasn't due for a few more days, and you were handing it in early?"

I nodded. It was yet another one of the pitfalls of working with Summer. Anything handed in on time was late.

"Mrs Henridge is *still waiting* for that assignment," said the inspector.

I didn't understand.

"We handed it in – Summer put it on her desk in Gifted and Talented. I saw her…"

But the inspector was shaking her head. "Mrs Henridge said her desk was clear at the end of that Gifted and Talented class."

It took me one more beat to get it. Summer had handed in the short story – she had made me scan through it, and then she had put it on Mrs Henridge's desk. But if Mrs Henridge said her desk was clear at the end of the lesson, it meant the short story had been taken *during* class. Someone in G&T had stolen our short story and used it for inspiration.

Which meant one of them had killed Hugh.

9

Mrs Greythorne walked out of her office with me, clutching some papers.

"I'm more than happy to accommodate the police, but it's not the most convenient thing in the world, having them camped out in my office," she said, keeping step with me. "Listen, Jess..."

She hesitated, coming to a stop in the middle of the corridor and looking around. Apart from several stone busts of glaring former headmasters lined up in a row, the corridor was empty. Still, Mrs Greythorne didn't speak. Instead, she nodded at a vaulted green door behind me. I pushed it open to reveal an empty office, smaller than hers.

"This is Miss Bilson's room," said Mrs Greythorne, closing the door behind her. "Jess, I just wanted to say that I know you're an excellent student – your English grades in particular are exceptional..."

I didn't even have time to digest the compliment and turn red before she pressed on.

"But the school board are obviously very concerned about

the impact this whole thing could have on the school's... reputation." She lingered on the last word, and I could tell she wanted to add something else. "I will speak to the police about making sure to keep the link to your short story from the board – and the thank-you text you received...that *only* you received, even though Summer was a co-writer. It might affect the ongoing investigation if they knew." She rubbed her forehead.

I nodded, my throat tightening, as if something had got stuck inside. I didn't like the way the conversation was going.

"I tell you this because the school board holds a lot of power." Mrs Greythorne's pursed lips told me all I needed to know about what she thought on the subject. "I can't forget that."

From the moment I'd started at Heybuckle it had been clear the teachers answered to a higher power. For the most part, the students were well behaved. Their parents were paying a lot of money for them to come here, and the world expected a lot from them. That meant they expected a lot from themselves. At my old high school, which I'd gone to for two years before coming to Heybuckle, the world ignored us, or else threw around words like *disadvantaged* and pitied us. All we had were supportive families, who pushed us to do better.

But the parents of the students at Heybuckle were a different beast. They paid incredibly high fees and that meant they expected a *service*. Ultimately any decisions the school made weren't for the students – they were for the parents. How to keep them happy. How to keep the money rolling in.

I knew what would happen if the school board, consisting of the pushiest parents, found out about my short story, and the thank-you text. Mrs Greythorne would have to choose between appeasing them and defending me. Even if she wanted to, she couldn't pick me. Heybuckle came first.

She was warning me. The longer it took for the police to solve the case, the more likely it was that the school board would find out I was connected to Hugh's murder – and they would probably take swift action.

"You're a very good student, Jess," said Mrs Greythorne. Her smile was sad as she left the room, like she was already preparing herself to say goodbye to me.

"You need to stop panicking," said Clem. "The police have a good lead – someone in G&T did it. That means they've got a super narrow suspect list." Her eyes flashed with intensity.

We were sitting in my bedroom, Clem sprawled out over my bed while I hunched up in my desk chair. All bedrooms were pretty much the same, with two beds, two desks, two wardrobes, two armchairs and two chests of drawers, although some were bigger than others.

People tried to personalize them by putting pictures up on the pinboard above their bed. Clem had a huge collage of family and her *proximity friends*, with at least ten photos of the two of us in the centre. Hattie had some family photos and weird works of art she had printed, along with pictures of places she had hiked to.

Annabelle had photos of her friends as well, and one family photo, though it was right in the corner of her board. Arthur stood in the centre of the photo in prime position, with his parents on either side of him, their hands on his shoulders.

Two Applewell girls stood beside their mother, two beside their father, although they were slightly away from the three in the middle.

For years, Annabelle hadn't had any family photos up at all, but then Arthur told his parents. It led to a huge row between Annabelle and her mother on the phone. I tried not to listen, pressing my head into my pillow, but it was impossible. Her mother was yelling so loudly I could hear every word.

"Arthur has dozens of pictures of us, Arthur clearly loves us much more than you do, how could you be so ungrateful, we've done everything for you, you're at the best boarding school in the country because of us, we've come from nothing and you're ashamed of us…"

And Annabelle had yelled back that she *was* ashamed, that nothing she ever did was good enough and that she had no idea why her parents loved Arthur more, because he was a horrible person. She screamed that she hated Arthur for snitching on her, and she would *never* put up a family photo because families weren't supposed to be like hers. But the next day the photo appeared on her notice board, and I heard her calling her mum to apologize, whispering *I'm sorry, I'm sorry* down the phone. *Please still love me.* If she confronted Arthur about ratting on her, I never saw it – they continued to ignore each other, like they weren't even related.

I had a few pictures of me and Clem, and me and Mum, and one of Dad. The rest of my board was blank, but at least my decisions on how to decorate my own bedroom didn't lead to massive drama.

"The police have a narrow suspect list that *I'm on,*" I pointed out, swinging around in my chair. "*I* know I didn't kill Hugh – and they can't possibly think I did either, because I was in the library all evening, but they might think I'm an accessory or something." I didn't want anyone to be in any doubt of my innocence, especially after Mrs Greythorne's warning. I'd be an easy target for rumours and if those made their way into the newspapers, they would stick to me like tar. Unlike other students, I didn't have rich, powerful parents who could make any bad stuff disappear.

"It's still a lead," said Clem.

"It's a stupid one. Think about who was in that classroom – me and Summer were the ones who wrote the short story. We had no reason to steal it. And whoever stole it was just casting suspicion on themselves – and why even bother to recreate my murder scene anyway?"

Summer's words floated back to me. *What kind of murderer kills someone and sticks around long enough to gather a bunch of twigs and spell out the words "help me"?*

I hated to admit it, but she'd been right. My story hadn't exactly been the most realistic of tales; I'd wanted to show off my imagination.

"There might have been a clue somewhere in your story," said Clem, sitting up and crossing her legs. She was wearing neon green socks patterned with bumblebees, instead of the expected grey ones. It was one of her favourite games, seeing how far she could make it through the day wearing non-uniform socks without a teacher telling her to change. "Something the killer realized implicated them. Do you remember everything in it? Can you recreate it?"

"Nope." My memory was good, but not that good. I remembered facts, dates and formulae if I sat down and tried to learn them. I did not remember everything I had ever written or read.

"Well, is there a copy somewhere?" Clem tried again.

"No," I grumbled. "It was handwritten."

"Okay, well even though Summer helped write it, she's still a suspect," said Clem. "She might have had a reason to steal it back that we don't know about yet. We can't count her out."

"I feel like you're reaching."

"Well, let's move on. Who else was in the room?"

"Hugh obviously. And Arthur and Annabelle. And Tommy."

"Right, so the police have four suspects. Summer, Arthur, Annabelle and Tommy," said Clem. "Five if we count you. Six if we count Mrs Henridge."

"Mrs Henridge is a *teacher*," I said.

"Teachers can kill too," said Clem in a wise voice.

I frowned. "She was running detention that evening."

"Fine," pouted Clem. "Let's say the police focus on those four. They would need motives for all of them – and to find out if they've got alibis." She was starting to look animated, more like her proper self. "Let's think logically about this – or at least, I will. You can be like my little sidekick. The Robin to my Sherlock."

"Watson," I corrected without thinking. "Robin is Batman's sidekick." I was happy to be the nobody. Hopefully the police would see me that way too.

"Whatever," said Clem. "Look – what if *we* do a bit of investigating too? You know, to help the police on their way – the quicker they solve this the better, right?"

"And our help's really going to make that happen?" I asked, though my stomach gave a flutter at the thought we might be able to make what felt like a horrible nightmare go away.

"Well, we need to do *something*," Clem said. "I can't *stand* this, Jess – sitting around, just *waiting*. I keep trying to remember the last thing I said to Hugh, and I can't. It was something stupid, probably, a joke maybe. And I just keep going round and round in my head…" She ran her fingers through her hair, making all the ends stick up. "Look, worst case scenario we don't find anything and the police solve it on their own. Best case scenario… We actually make a difference. People will be cagey around the police – they're much more likely to want to chat with us, let things slip. It's…all I can do for him now. Plus…the murderer *texted you*. You're now the person in the school with the biggest link to them."

I took a deep breath. Clem was right – I really needed my name not to be associated with Hugh's death.

"Look, let's take each suspect in turn – here." Clem tossed me a pen and notebook that had been lying on my desk. "Make notes. Right, so let's start with the person I like the least, because that's more fun. Summer. What reason did she have to kill Hugh?"

I wrote down Summer's name and underlined it. Clem was looking expectantly at me, like she was waiting for me to come up with a suggestion. It made sense, seeing as though I was the one who was supposed to have the imagination – an imagination so great a murderer had decided to copy me.

"Well…the bake sale?"

At the beginning of the year Summer had organized a bake sale to raise money for some good cause or another. It had been overshadowed by Hugh organizing a fundraiser talent show that same day. He wanted to raise money for the school's sports bus to be upgraded to an even newer model, which had screens built into the seats, and surround sound, and way more space. I didn't think for a moment that was a real reason for Summer to kill Hugh, but Clem nodded.

"Write it down!" she said encouragingly. "That's good stuff!"

I uncurled from the desk chair – my legs were starting to cramp. "That's…well. It's a bizarre reason to kill someone. Yeah, he sucked for doing what he did, but waiting months and months and then offing him?"

"Summer's a tightly wound kind of girl. People like her always snap," said Clem darkly, in a way that suggested she had many experiences of her rigid classmates suddenly deciding to kill her boyfriend. "And, look – it's a stupid reason, but we're hardly dealing with a smart murderer here. They could have just…well…you know, with a knife…" She trailed off, her voice starting to shake, and for a horrible moment I thought she was going to start crying again. But she seemed to recover herself, because her eyes got a glint of steel in them. She spurred on. "And the text – why send the text?"

I shrugged – it didn't make sense. But Hugh's family had influence – and money. They'd keep digging until they found an answer.

If they were going to get away with it, the killer needed to be smart.

But so far, nothing about this murderer seemed clever. Why bother to thank me for the help? Why take the time to arrange the twigs next to Hugh's body?

"Summer hated my suggestions for the short story," I said. "And if she hated them so much, why would she decide to use them in the real thing?"

"Remember that detective book I read because you said it would be great, only I couldn't figure out who the killer was and there was, like, no kissing or anything?" said Clem, getting off my bed and starting to pace.

"You need to be more specific," I said, because I had recommended several books to Clem when she went through her *I need to improve my mind by reading books instead of watching trashy reality shows* phase. I hadn't realized she'd actually read any of them.

"It had loads of red herrings!" said Clem triumphantly. "And I bet you anything that Summer was trying to throw you a red herring, to get you off the scent because she knew you would be suspicious." She went over to my wardrobe and started rooting around in my clothes, eventually pulling out my long winter coat. "You don't have much of a selection, but imagine this is a trench coat. And I just need a hat with a feather in it and a cigar and I would be like a proper detective. I just solved something, right? Summer was tossing out a red herring."

I wasn't convinced. I didn't like Summer, but that didn't mean I thought she was a murderer. "Right, so that's Summer," I said. "Annabelle?"

"Hmm…" said Clem as she stopped pacing and flopped to the floor, my winter coat fanning out around her. "Annabelle has always liked a gossip. But…that doesn't mean she's a bad person, right?"

I nodded. Annabelle didn't really fit in with the idea of

murder. She always struck me as the kind of person who considered other people as entertainment for herself. The thought stuck in my mind – could she have stood behind the scenes, pulling the strings while someone else did the dirty work of actually killing Hugh? But that didn't sit right either. When she had a problem with someone, she would have a nice gossip behind their back – but she would quite happily say her insults to their face as well.

"Did she have any reason to hate Hugh?" I asked as I tried to cast my mind back. I couldn't even think of a time I had seen them speak more than a few words to each other. Hugh had always made a point to only talk to his small group of friends, who largely consisted of those whose families knew his family from way back, and who came from generational wealth; Regia Club types, which Arthur and Annabelle weren't, seeing as their parents had only recently earned all their money.

I didn't think it said much about Hugh, that he was so determined to only stick to the super rich kids. I had once tried to point this out to Clem, but she glossed over it, saying he was shy – and, after all, he'd been interested in her, and she didn't come from generational wealth. One time though, she had got a faraway look and said he had a hard time trusting people, because his parents had never met a promise they couldn't figure out how to break. I believed that more than the shyness thing.

"I mean…" Clem frowned, her eyebrows furrowing. Her nose twitched, like it did whenever she was thinking. "Hugh used to say all that stuff about Annabelle's family. You know – how they were the worst kinds of lawyers, belonged in the gutter, *nouveau riche*…"

"But people gossip about other people all the time at Heybuckle," I said. "People say loads about Annabelle – remember, Millie called her *gaudy*, like that was the worst insult in the world, so Annabelle called her *trust fund trash*? Why would Annabelle single out Hugh and kill him for being a snob about her family? It's just…a stupid reason."

"Well, let's face it, whoever did this had some stupid reason because there's nothing – *nothing* – in the world that could justify doing what they did." Clem pressed her lips together, her cheeks flushing. She shrugged my coat off, and got to her feet, starting to pace again.

"Okay, okay," I said, in my best calming voice. "So that's Summer and Annabelle. What about Arthur?"

But though we tried, neither of us could come up with a reason Arthur might have killed Hugh beyond the stuff he'd said about the Applewell family – which seemed to have affected Annabelle more anyway, as she was the one who always talked crap about Hugh in return. In fact, neither of us could come up with *anything* about Arthur. He was such a…*nothing* person. A body in the room.

But then again, Arthur had definitely been off when he told Clem he was sorry for her loss. He'd been acting. Plus, he'd had that weird conversation with me, where he seemed almost excited by the idea of murder.

"Which", said Clem, as she flopped back on my bed, "is suspicious in itself." She bit her bottom lip. "Right – and is there any reason for Arthur and Annabelle to team up and do it together? Twin killers is an angle we haven't explored."

Arthur and Annabelle didn't even act like siblings – they

barely spoke to each other. I couldn't imagine them getting on long enough to plan a murder together. But we needed to consider all angles, so I nodded.

"Let's put that as a possibility," I said. "And then there's Tommy." I tried to keep my voice casual, but if Clem picked up on my secret yearning for Tommy, she didn't say anything.

"That's a more straightforward one," said Clem. "Jealousy. Hugh is the golden boy and Tommy has always been in second place. With Hugh out of the way, he's finally number one."

I wrote it down, though I didn't believe a word of it. I looked down the list again.

Summer Johnson.
Annabelle Applewell.
Arthur Applewell.
Tommy Poppleton.

Summer. Annabelle. Arthur. Tommy.

Kids I had gone to school with since we were thirteen years old.

One of whom had killed Hugh.

10

G&T was the class where I most noticed Hugh's absence. Not just because it was the smallest – since most people had chosen volunteering, there were only six in my G&T group, as opposed to the usual twelve in a class. But because I suspected one of the people in the room had murdered him.

Tommy had switched seats. Instead of sitting at the back alone, he sat next to me. A few days ago, I'd have been delighted at the chance to finally speak to him. Now, however, I was just uncomfortable – I'd never thought my in with him might be that I suspected him of murdering his best friend.

"Mrs Henridge said you needed help with chemistry," Tommy said. "I came top of the class last term."

Summer was sitting in the row ahead of me, but she was apparently listening because she twisted around in her seat and glared at Tommy.

"By *one* point – and only because I had a cough that day."

"Sounds like an excuse, Johnson," said Tommy with an easy smile.

Summer pursed her lips and swivelled back around.

I think he'd said his gift in the G&T application was "all the sciences". Arthur was good at music, Annabelle at art, Summer at maths and physics and debate. I didn't know what Hugh's "gift" was – his parents were one of Heybuckle's biggest donors, so of course the school would magically discover he was gifted, if he decided it was what he wanted to do for his forced extra-curricular. Amazing how having rich parents made it so much easier to be talented.

Summer, thankfully, didn't turn around again, immediately getting stuck into tutoring a reluctant Annabelle in maths. Arthur had brought a guitar along, which he was gently twanging as he stared blankly into space.

Out on the field, lacrosse practice had just started, and though Millie and Clem weren't arguing, I'd already seen some pretty aggressive tackles from both of them. Like the inevitability that I would always suck at complex maths questions, they would always hate each other.

"So, why'd you talk to the police the other day?" Tommy said abruptly.

I shrugged and tried to focus on listening to Summer telling off Annabelle ("Never ignore the decimal point! Never!"). My cheeks were going hot under his gaze.

"Eddy said he saw you going into Mrs Greythorne's office," said Tommy.

I tried to buy myself some time and turned to stare out the window again, just as Millie took an enormous dive that brought Clem down with her.

Tommy was still waiting, drumming his fingers on the desk.

Maybe he was the murderer and was trying to find out how much I knew.

Clem's words came back to me: *with Hugh out of the way, he's finally number one.*

And it was true. Eddy, who had once circled Hugh like he was the sun, now boasted to everyone about how he was such good friends with Tommy, whose family owned several businesses and were all gazillionaires. I didn't know how Tommy could put up with someone who collected people like trophies to show off – but then again, Tommy had been friends with Hugh, who hadn't exactly been pleasant.

Maybe Tommy wasn't as nice as he appeared. Maybe that was why he could so easily be friends with objectively terrible individuals.

"The police have spoken to loads of people now," I said at last. "Including you." I didn't mean for the words to sound accusatory, but Tommy raised his eyebrows.

"I was Hugh's best friend," he said. "They had loads of questions for me."

So where were you the evening he was killed? I had the question ready to ask – after all, Clem and I had agreed to try and solve the murder, and this was the perfect opportunity to quiz him. But I couldn't get the words out. I felt tongue-tied, wrong-footed by him sitting next to me and trying to start up a conversation. I'd liked Tommy for years and had barely been able to speak to him, becoming the most boring person alive whenever he was around. I thought he was good-looking, charismatic, funny and confident – and now all of a sudden, he was potentially a threat.

"Why do you let Eddy follow you around?" I blurted instead. "How can you be okay with the way he…boasts about people?"

"Boasts about people?" Tommy frowned.

"You know," I said, wishing I'd kept my mouth shut. "The way he *always* knows someone who's better than you, like their achievements are his."

Tommy squinted at me. "He's never been like that around me."

I forced down a snort.

"I mean we've always got on well," said Tommy with a shrug. "He's a laugh – although he was more Hugh's friend than mine – we only really played football together… To be honest he's a bit lost without Hugh."

The lacrosse team was taking a break, which meant I had nothing to watch outside. Summer had dragged her chair around the table so she could work opposite Annabelle, rather than next to her.

Every so often she would look up at me, her eyes narrowed.

Obviously, Summer now knew about the short story thing – the police had questioned her as well. She kept glancing over at me, either because she was guilty and knew I would be on to her. Or because she was innocent and thought the whole short story thing was a sure sign of *my* guilt.

The bell rang, and Summer got to her feet and left. She always packed up a minute early, so she could be ready for the next lesson.

I stuffed my books in my bag as quickly as I could, so I could catch up with her and find out what she knew – if she was guilty, or whether she thought I was. We all had a free period next,

94

and Summer, at least, would be heading to the library. I could quiz Tommy later, when I had properly steeled myself to ask him all the hard questions I'd prepared.

Tommy blocked my way.

"Sorry," I mumbled, trying to go around him. I don't know why I apologized to him – *he* was the one standing in *my* way. Force of habit, I suppose. Apologizing always seemed like the path of least resistance.

"You didn't answer my question, you know," he said.

Mrs Henridge had also left, and Arthur and Annabelle too, so we were alone.

"Why did the police want to speak to you?" He tucked his hands into his pockets, and his tie dangled loosely around his neck.

I got a whiff of that musky smell, and my knees, as always, went a little weak.

"The police told me I couldn't say anything," I said.

I needed to get moving – Summer would be power-walking to the library, to get one of the best desks, which had a computer, and a plug socket, and loads of space to spread out, as well as being by a window so there was a view to look at when your mind had a small wander. The desks around her would fill up fast.

I tried to skirt past Tommy, but he was quicker than me, still blocking my way.

"You're hiding something," he said. "Where were you when Hugh was killed?"

I stared at him. "*What?*"

"My parents are friends with the Van Borens. My mum told me that Hugh's parents have hired a private investigator because

95

for some reason they're convinced the police won't be able to solve this case...and they won't say why." Tommy's face was grim. "I don't know whether hiring a private investigator will even make a difference. My mum said they normally help do stuff like find your lost pet, or figure out if your partner is cheating – not solve murders. But whoever did this to Hugh can't get away with it, so I figured I'd ask around, do a little digging."

I balled my hands into fists. Clem and I had decided we would investigate, but our aim was to nudge the police along quicker. If Hugh's parents were right, then the police would *never* get to the solution, even if we were shoving them there. Except, what he was saying didn't make any sense – why would Hugh's parents be so sure the police couldn't solve the case? Unless Tommy had misunderstood, and they'd hired a private investigator out of an abundance of caution rather than a deep belief in police incompetence.

"I was in the library all evening," I said as the thoughts raced through my head. "You could probably check with about ten different people." Him broaching the subject of alibis first made my next question easier to ask; it felt like a natural follow-up. "And where were you?"

He stared at me, his eyes unreadable. "I was, er...alone in my room."

Generally, only kids in their final year got their own room, unless you were on the school council, or a prefect, or a sports captain. Summer was a prefect, so she didn't have a roommate – neither did Millie, Hugh or Tommy. Millie was part of the school council (she got elected after promising she would get more flattering lighting put into the school bathrooms). Hugh had been a sports captain, as well as on the school council. Tommy was his second for both those positions. Now, obviously, he was the top dog.

I folded my arms. "Seriously?" Surely, he couldn't expect me to buy that he was in his room – he'd hesitated, which made it obvious he was lying. Plus, it wasn't even an alibi. If he'd been alone there was no way I could check.

"Yeah," he said, stepping aside, his back pressed against the door so I could pass without having to touch him. "Seriously. And thanks, Jess. This has been a really interesting conversation."

11

On my way to the library, I mentally moved Tommy up to first place on my ranking of suspects. I had got three useful bits of information from him: the Van Borens didn't trust the police, he didn't have an alibi – and he was hiding something. He definitely needed to be investigated further.

But even though I'd made good progress with Tommy, it had set me back with Summer: there was absolutely no way I would get a seat next to her in the library now. The best seats went in minutes because there was a committed group of students at Heybuckle who were just as scarily keen as Summer. They practically sprinted to the library the moment the bell rang to secure their spot.

The library was a large space, set out over two floors. I quickly passed through the ground floor, which had hundreds of books and big red chairs gathered together for group work. It was normally quite noisy, but it was where Clem preferred to study. She hated silence.

I mounted the staircase, heading up to the quiet floor, where only whispering was allowed and where I would likely find Summer.

I spotted her immediately, because she had spread out on one of the big tables in the centre of the room. She must have stopped on her way, because she had loads more textbooks than she could possibly have been carrying in G&T. Her detour meant she wasn't at the best tables by the window – which meant there was room for me.

Across from her at the big table was Arthur, and Eddy was sitting at a separate desk by the window. Arthur and Eddy were roommates, but they were probably about as close as me and Annabelle. Other than those two, I didn't recognize anyone else in the room.

Arthur kept looking up at Summer, his expression unreadable. All the same, a shudder passed through me, and I couldn't put a finger on why.

I shouldered my bag, took a deep breath, and sat down next to Summer.

She didn't look up, remaining hunched over a book and occasionally stopping to scribble notes on a blank page in her enormous blue binder.

I reluctantly pulled out my maths assignment. I'd already done all the easy questions, where I just plugged numbers into formulae, and they spurted out the answer. I was stuck on all the other ones, where some actual understanding was required.

"What're you doing here?" Summer had noticed me, her pen dangling in her hand. Her hair was tied up even higher than normal. I wondered if it hurt.

"What's it look like?" I whispered back, gesturing at my maths paper.

"No – why're you sitting next to *me*?" She nodded at the few empty spaces on the other tables.

No one else would have asked that question so bluntly. For all Summer knew, I could have been lonely and trying to make a new friend.

"You motivate me," I said brightly, turning back to my maths. I already had her rankled, and I hadn't even asked anything yet. Inwardly, I grinned.

"I know why you're here," Summer hissed. She had put her book down. It had to be serious if she was giving up the chance to do more work in order to talk to me. "The police said we weren't supposed to discuss anything." She kept her voice low, making sure anyone in earshot wouldn't hear.

"Why'd you think that is, Summer?"

Of course, she had taken the inspector's insistence on not talking to each other about the short story – or about my text – as law. She was probably expecting the police to scale down from the ceilings and arrest us.

"Because they don't want it getting out – and, quite frankly, neither should you." Summer pursed her lips.

"What's that supposed to mean?" I said, forgetting to lower my voice.

At once three people looked up and gave a collective *shush*.

"Whisper, you heathen," said Summer, pushing her books away. "I *meant*, if anyone else finds out the murder scene was arranged like the one in *your* short story, everyone will think you had something to do with it. And the scholarship committee won't like that at all."

I wondered if Mrs Greythorne had given her the same warning as me.

"It was *our* short story," I whispered back, trying to convey anger in my tone. But it was hard to whisper angrily – probably why people who were having an argument normally chose to yell. "You were involved too. You need to be worried about the scholarship people as well."

"But *you're* the one who added all those random details – that stupid trophy and those bloody twigs spelling *HELP ME*," said Summer, her voice rising. Wow, she really wasn't going to ever let that go. "And I made sure to emphasize that to the police when they asked me about it."

"Nice," I said through gritted teeth. "Sell me out at the first opportunity."

"Let me make this very clear," said Summer, balling her hands into fists. "Just because I slightly tweaked *your* short story and a *murderer* copied it—"

"—*our* story – that you basically rewrote—"

"—doesn't mean we are on the same team. I *cannot* lose this scholarship."

She whispered it with such passion it made me stop and think. The scholarship meant so much to her – maybe that meant she wasn't Hugh's murderer. After all, it was clear she would never risk her place at Heybuckle. Although…if *Hugh* had somehow threatened her position at school, who knew what she might do to remove him as an obstacle.

Summer leaned back. "It's weird though – why would your

story, that I added a few lines to, be used? Why us?" Her eyes narrowed as she looked at me. "You were really insistent on the murder weapon being a trophy…"

"So now you think *I* had something to do with it?"

Summer shrugged. "It'd be a very…*silly* crime. Although…" Her expression turned thoughtful.

"What?" I leaned forward. "*What?*"

"I mean, the murder would certainly fit in with your character profile."

I decided to gloss over the fact that she had called me *silly*. "I had no reason to do it," I said. "You, on the other hand…"

Summer snorted. "Don't be absurd – I had absolutely no reason to kill Hugh."

"The bake sale," I reminded her, and was rewarded by her entire face flushing scarlet like a sunset at the end of a hot, mid-July day. Her face looked like her name.

"The police don't think I had anything to do with it."

"Doesn't mean you didn't," I replied. "Where were you between the hours of 7 p.m. and 10 p.m. last Tuesday?"

"You're being ridiculous," snapped Summer, and it was a testament to how annoyed I'd made her that she didn't even bother to lower her voice.

The expected *shush* came quickly.

"So, where were you?"

"Alone, doing schoolwork in my room."

It was the same excuse as Tommy. Why the hell was everyone coming up with the uninventive alibi of being in their room alone that Tuesday night?

"So, you don't have an alibi?" I said.

"Yeah, me and everyone who doesn't share a room. That means everyone in the year above, and all the prefects and school council members, and sports kids. We're in a *school*. There are hundreds of students – anyone the police are investigating would have to be particularly suspicious." Summer started shuffling all her papers into her bag, stacking her textbooks neatly in a pile. "And apart from being forced to put my name on that absolutely awful short story with *you*, there is quite clearly nothing suspicious about me."

The police hadn't told her that Mrs Henridge had never received our assignment, which was pretty smart of them now that I think about it. If Summer was the killer, she didn't yet know that the list of suspects was narrowed down to our G&T class, rather than anyone who could have had access to Mrs Henridge's office – that being everyone. It meant she wouldn't be on her guard as much, so might be more likely to slip up.

A thought occurred to me, and I tilted my head. "So why weren't you in the library?" I asked.

Summer paused her attempts to shove a particularly bulky textbook into her bag, staring at me. "What are you talking about?"

"The police might not think it's suspicious that you say you were in your room alone, working, but I do," I said. "Because I've known you since we were thirteen, and you spend every evening working in the library."

Summer turned on her heel and marched out of the room without another word.

12

An enormous sense of guilt had started to weigh me down. I hadn't killed Hugh, but I had helped set the stage for his death. A murderer had been inspired by *me*.

And also, a second issue was now worrying me, besides my fear of the school board: Clem. She'd had a meeting with the private investigator hired by the Van Borens, and had come to her own conclusion that he was rubbish. She said he'd asked a bunch of completely pointless questions, like how often she played lacrosse, and what was her impression of Hattie, her roommate, and did Hugh ever get mad at Eddy.

So, when I told her what Tommy had said about Hugh's parents not trusting the police, she had immediately wanted to go marching into Mrs Greythorne's office and demand they share all their information with her so she could take over. From what I could tell, losing faith in the police lit a fire underneath her: she devoted hours to making lists and coming up with theories on what could have happened to Hugh. Thinking about the case seemed to help her. She wanted to feel like she was *doing* something, even if it was just an illusion.

Millie, on the other hand, seemed to be coping just fine. She pranced through the hallways, her blonde hair bouncing, waving her fingers at good-looking boys and rolling her eyes at everyone else. She'd ditched the mourning clothes, most likely when she noticed the interest in her was starting to wane, but somehow seemed lighter. Happier. Like Hugh's death was something of a relief to her.

She had a little band of followers, which Eddy had recently joined. It looked like he'd got bored of Tommy, and needed someone to devote his attention to. Millie lapped it up. He even carried around all her books.

Millie had also taken to throwing things at Clem in class. Nothing that would hurt – bits of paper, or rubber she'd ripped from her eraser. Just enough to be annoying.

And she'd also started slipping notes under Clem's door. A typical one would read: *your a slut*.

"Seventeen years old," sighed Clem, as she slapped the latest one down in front of me at breakfast (*your a tramp*). "Seventeen years old and she still doesn't know the difference between 'you're' with an apostrophe and 'your'. In fact…" She got out a pen and corrected it, then wrote a big F underneath the sentence before getting up. I could tell what she wanted to do – go over to Millie's table, put it down in front of her and start yet another argument.

"Maybe you should leave it," I said, grabbing her sleeve. "It's not worth it."

But no one could ever get Clem to change her mind once she had decided on something. She shrugged me off and marched towards Millie.

"Need to work on your spelling there, sweetie," said Clem as she dropped the note in Millie's cereal.

Millie's mouth became a thin line as she got to her feet. "Get me another bowl," she said to Eddy, without taking her eyes off Clem.

"What are you going to do?" said Clem. "Pour your cereal over me? I'm getting bored of this, Millie. It's always the same – the attacks in lacrosse, the notes, the talk behind my back. I literally don't care what you do."

"Good," said Millie with a smile. "Because it's going to get a whole lot worse."

Her eyes slid from Clem to me.

The fact the murder weapon was a trophy spread through school. Coach Tyler and Miss Bilson discussed the missing trophy at dinner, and two gossipy third formers who overheard immediately made it their priority to tell everyone they could.

Theories flew wildly about, but none hit the mark, because the fact my short story was the inspiration for the murder remained knowledge only a few people had.

I figured I wasn't going to make any progress by questioning Summer or Tommy further – I'd put them on their guards, and it would be a lot harder to catch them out. Since neither of them had an alibi and both seemed to be hiding something, I thought they were equally suspicious. But Clem had latched onto the idea that Tommy was the murderer.

"It's the motivation," she said. "I think it's way more likely that he killed Hugh because he was jealous – rather than

Summer with the whole bake sale thing. And I'm going to prove my theory right, just watch."

I decided to speak to Annabelle next. I checked with her friend, Lucy, who had been in our room with her right after dinner on the night of the murder. They'd been having an argument (about something trivial, according to Lucy, though she didn't meet my eyes and she didn't expand on it) – hence why I'd had to relocate to the library. If Lucy said she'd been with Annabelle until bedtime, I could have crossed Annabelle off the list. But Lucy said she'd gone off to her book club meeting at 7 p.m., and Annabelle had been asleep in the room when I got back, which meant there was a good chunk of her time unaccounted for.

Clem had eagerly offered to help me interrogate suspects, but I was worried she was too close to the case. Plus, I figured people would be more likely to let something slip with me. I loved Clem – but she wasn't exactly subtle.

I didn't want to wait in our bedroom for Annabelle, because there was a possibility she might not be back for hours and then wouldn't want to chat to me. Instead, I decided to track her down.

There were two places you could generally find Annabelle Applewell – either in one of the art rooms, or in the common room gossiping with her friends.

I found her in the smallest art room, which had a few large wooden tables stained with paint and boxes of supplies stacked against the wall. Annabelle was sketching a self-portrait with charcoal. She had got all the shading perfect, capturing the exact way her bottle blonde hair fell around her face, her little chin dimple. But it was the expression that really made the portrait – she'd drawn her lips downturned, the frown minuscule, barely noticeable. Yet enough to make the entire thing look unbearably sad.

On paper, Annabelle had the perfect life. But I knew from overhearing the arguments with her mother that things weren't as rosy as they seemed. The conversations seemed to be about how Annabelle was doing *this* and *that* wrong, and how her hair needed to be better and her clothes weren't good enough, and how she should be thinner and all sorts of rubbish. It was constant sniping and I wondered why Annabelle even picked up the phone when she saw her mother calling. She already knew what her mother would say. At least Mr Applewell never rang, so Annabelle didn't have the critical comments from both sides.

"How's it going?" I said to Annabelle as I sidled into the room.

Annabelle looked up at me, and her expression immediately turned to one of confusion. I didn't blame her – I wasn't exactly known for being chatty.

After an awkward silence she grunted, "Fine," before turning back to her drawing.

"Er…that's a really good portrait," I said, nodding at it, wondering how to broach the subject of whether she had killed Hugh.

"No it's not," she snapped. Without warning, she ripped the sheet of paper from her easel, scrunched it up, and chucked it in the bin. "I want to make art people stop to think about."

I had no idea what she was talking about. "Like…er…with modern art, when you have to try to work out what's happening?"

108

I thought back to a school holiday when Clem had come to stay with me. I'd been self-conscious about how tiny my house was, a little two-bed terrace in one of the poorest areas of London. Especially since Clem, like most people at Heybuckle, had several houses – the enormous country mansion, the London town house, the summer home abroad. But she'd slotted right into my minuscule bedroom, which was smaller than the ones we had at school, with barely enough space for my single bed, a desk and a wardrobe. She had made my drab little house a thousand times brighter.

We'd gone to a few of London's many museums, including some art galleries, where we went up to random paintings and tried to guess what ridiculous things they were supposed to mean.

This single black line of paint that gets fainter and fainter down the canvas as the paint runs out, represents the meaninglessness of life, and how it's a predetermined path that gets weaker as you get older, until you die.

This chair, alone in the centre of the room, shows how some people are made to be supporting characters, objects that are used by other people to prop themselves up. (We discovered later, when we walked back through that room and found someone sitting down on it, that the chair had not been part of the display and was, in fact, just a chair.)

Annabelle turned her scrutinizing glare away from her now-empty easel and towards me. "Is there a reason you're here?"

"No… I, er…actually wanted to talk to you about…er…"

Annabelle had perfected the art of showing someone they were wasting her time with just a single arch of her eyebrow.

She'd probably turned it on waiters in restaurants, or boys trying to chat her up – and now she was using her talent on me.

"The night Hugh died – where were you?" I eventually blurted.

Annabelle's other eyebrow lifted. "Why?"

"I just…want to help Clem, you know? Figure out who…"

"You want to help Clem figure out who killed Hugh," said Annabelle, her voice deadpan, making me feel completely ridiculous. "And you bizarrely think it could have been me." She rolled her eyes. "Any reason for that or are you just clutching at straws?" She said it casually, but something felt off. She was trying a little too hard to act like I had said the most absurd thing in the world.

"You were in our room after dinner," I said. "But Lucy left you on your own. So where were you the rest of the evening?"

"Doesn't take a genius to figure it out, does it?" said Annabelle, as she turned back to her sketchbook. "I was in our room after dinner – and I was asleep when you got back. *Where* could I *possibly* have been for the rest of the evening?"

Although Summer had made a good point that half the school had probably been in their rooms at the time Hugh was killed, I was three for three on my suspects being "alone in their rooms". It was too much of a coincidence – at least one of them had to be lying.

"You're not much of a loner," I said, continuing to try and needle the point. Yes, she'd been asleep when I got back into the room, but she *never* went to sleep before me. So why that night? "At least not in the evenings, when you could be off having fun with people."

"I was sketching," said Annabelle. "It's something I like to do on my own."

"But—"

Annabelle got to her feet, and something in her expression made me take a step back. There was fury in her eyes – but it was mingled with fear.

"Leave it," she said through gritted teeth, and she dropped her fake posh accent, her real one spiking through. "If you know what's good for you, you'll stop asking questions about that night."

"I just…" I trailed off, suddenly filled with the certainty that I was about to become Annabelle's second victim.

"You've got no idea what you're doing," hissed Annabelle, jabbing me with her finger. "You're just blundering around – but there's still a chance you're going to stumble across something that gets the attention of the *wrong* people."

"What are you talking about?" I said, taking another step back. "What people?"

"The Regia Club," whispered Annabelle, her voice so low I barely heard what she said. "That graffiti showed up the night Hugh was murdered."

"Do you think there's a connection between them?" I said eagerly. "Was the graffiti a message or—"

"I don't know," snapped Annabelle. "It might have just been a coincidence. But I hear a lot of gossip – the Regia Club has always been everywhere in Heybuckle, controlling things… They gather up dark secrets to use as ammunition if anyone steps out of line. Why do you think that English teacher left so suddenly last year? She apparently pissed off someone in the club by giving them too many detentions and they sent an anonymous tip to the school board – who I'm guessing are *parents* of people in the Regia Club – that she'd lied about an old conviction for credit card fraud. The Regia Club finds out *everything*. And now I've heard the new leader…wants blood. So, if you're poking around the night Hugh was killed, you're going to get the attention of the Regia Club – as well as the murderer." Her words tumbled over each other so fast I almost missed what she was saying. It was like she'd been bottling the words up, just waiting for a chance to let them out.

I swallowed, but didn't want Annabelle to see she'd rattled me.

"Maybe I'll get lucky, and the murderer will be in the Regia Club. Less people out to get me that way."

Annabelle's nostrils flared as she glared at me. "You're going to get someone hurt," she said after a moment of silence, emotion rippling beneath her smooth skin. "And it damn well better not be me."

She left the room without another word.

13

I didn't know what to make of Annabelle's ominous words. I couldn't tell if she'd been warning me about the Regia Club, or trying to distract me from her flimsy alibi because she was hiding something. Or maybe, she'd been doing both. I also couldn't figure out how the Regia Club fitted into Hugh's murder – there were rumours, of course, about who was a member, but nothing was ever confirmed. The only person in my G&T class who fitted the requirements for Regia Club membership, other than Hugh himself, was Tommy. So that meant he should stay at the top of my suspect list.

But when I suggested that to Clem as we were discussing things in my room before dinner, she shook her head.

"Remember how I thought he was our biggest suspect, and I said I would do some digging into him?" she asked. She reached into her bag and pulled out a stack of paper, which she dropped on my bed, wiggling her eyebrows in a way I knew meant she was pleased with herself.

"What's this?" I asked.

"I hung around the admin office at lunchtime, hoping to

sneak inside and see, like…a file on Tommy. You know, like schools have in films," said Clem. "But apparently they're paperless now because there weren't even any filing cabinets. I thought I'd wasted my time – but when the admin staff all went for lunch, one didn't lock her computer. So, I had a quick look on the system for anything about Tommy…"

I couldn't stop my jaw dropping. "What if you'd been *caught*? You would have got into so much trouble—"

"But I wasn't caught," said Clem with a grin. "And look what I found." She shoved some of the papers into my hands.

I looked at the top sheet. It was a register…for a knitting club. Tuesday evenings from 7 p.m. to 9.45 p.m.

"What…" I trailed off as I looked down the list of names, one in particular jumping out at me.

Thomas James Poppleton.

"He's never missed a meeting," said Clem triumphantly. "Those registers go back months. And, *look* – here's the application he did to get in. I for one will never understand this school's obsession with making you apply for things that it's just going to let you into anyway, but there you go."

I scanned the application. Apparently, Tommy had wanted to join knitting club because his grandmother had loved knitting but developed arthritis and could no longer do it. She'd been devastated, so he wanted to make a sweater for her. That was over a year ago, so it looked like he'd enjoyed the club enough to want to stay.

"You're telling me that Tommy was *knitting* the evening Hugh was killed?" I said, still blinking at the registers.

"I confirmed it with, like, half the club," said Clem with

114

a satisfied nod. "They're all first years missing home and making…teddies and stuff. From 7 p.m. to 9.45 p.m. Tommy was working on a hat for one of his baby cousins."

"He told me he was alone in his room," I said. "Why would he lie?"

"Because it doesn't exactly fit into his cool reputation," said Clem. She frowned. "I wonder if Hugh knew about the knitting – he never mentioned it. Tommy might have asked him not to tell anyone."

"But Tommy could still be in the Regia Club though, right?" I said. "Maybe…I don't know, he ordered someone else to carry out the murder or something?"

Clem grinned as she pulled out another sheet. "I had a general root around his folder, just to see what else was in there – and look…" She handed me the paper. "It's a complaint from him to Mrs Greythorne about the Regia Club – it's dated around when we first started at Heybuckle. It says they tried to recruit him and he said no, so they cut up his football kit right before he tried out for the team and shredded his signed poster of… I can't remember the guy's name. He's a footballer or something? Menti?"

"Messi." I whistled as I scanned the sheet. "Looks like Tommy's off the list." I kept my voice as casual as I could, feeling weirdly relieved that I could go back to crushing on him from a distance without also worrying about him being a murderer.

Just over a week had passed since Hugh's murder, and we had made a tiny amount of progress – and that was only because of

Clem. So far, all I'd done was annoy my suspects. I tried to pick apart my conversations with Summer and Annabelle in case there was any useful information I'd overlooked.

Meanwhile another clue came from an observant second year, who noticed the only trophy missing from the trophy room was an old debate team one. At once, everyone swore they had noticed it was missing on the Monday, or the Sunday, or the Saturday before. Even though most people passed by the trophy room several times a day, no one ever actually paid attention to the trophies themselves, which meant the weapon in question could have been stolen ages ago and no one would have noticed.

"It's been missing since last year," said Arthur, in maths.

We'd just been given a problem to complete as a pair, and everyone had started talking about the task.

"Er – is that the solution?" I frowned at my algebra, trying to work out how X could have been missing for a year.

"The trophy," said Arthur. "It's definitely been missing since last year."

I gawped at him as my brain scrabbled to process that, like everyone else, he wanted to get in on the trophy theories.

"How do you know?" I asked, wondering why he was so certain.

"I mean, it was so big, wasn't it? Can't believe more people didn't notice. But then again – I see most things." He doodled on one side of the worksheet, ignoring the problem we were supposed to be solving.

If the trophy had been missing since last year, it meant the murder had been planned well in advance. But that didn't line up with the fact that the murder seemed to have been inspired last minute by the random addition of the details of my short story… Unless the killer had *always* planned to use a trophy and our choice of weapons was purely coincidental.

"Er…the trophy," I said delicately. "What did it look like again?"

"Big. Gold."

That sounded about right.

"And do you generally pay attention to the trophies in the trophy room?" I asked.

Arthur's pen paused over a doodle of a car. "I think I might be the only one who does – but come on, you must have seen it. Enormous, with red tassels."

I frowned. I had a vague idea of what the debate trophy looked like, except red tassels didn't factor in at all. But there *was* another trophy which had huge red tassels, which dangled down the front.

"You mean the football trophy?"

The football trophy had been taken from the display after a shocking defeat last season, when our school team came second to Flufferton School (an all-boys' boarding school where I think they wear straw hats and walk around with canes and cigars).

"Oh, yeah, that must be what I'm thinking of. My bad."

Arthur looked slyly to his left, where Tommy, who was now the captain of the football team, was glowering at him. I tried not to catch Tommy's eye. Ever since I'd found out he was innocent of Hugh's murder, and had taken up knitting to make his ailing grandmother happy, I felt like I wouldn't be able to look at him without combusting.

Arthur smirked, and there was something just a little bit wicked in his grin.

"So, you have no idea when the debate trophy was taken," I sighed.

I didn't think this was particularly important to the investigation, because polishing all the trophies in the trophy room was a punishment frequently dished out if you were late to assembly in the morning, so lots of people would have had access. But I figured it was better to have a complete picture of the situation.

Arthur looked at me out of the corner of his eye. "Annabelle said you asked her a bunch of questions about that night. Said you think she killed Hugh."

I glanced around the classroom. Arthur's voice was just a little bit too loud, and Tommy wasn't even trying to hide the fact he was listening in.

"I don't think you're right – about my sister killing Hugh," said Arthur, his voice matter of fact.

Of course he didn't believe his sister was a murderer. What did he think he would achieve by telling me that?

"And obviously, *I* didn't do it either. I was in detention."

I frowned. Arthur normally faded into the background. Why would he have got a detention?

Arthur seemed to sense my question. "I didn't agree with Mrs Henridge's mark on my last English essay." He shrugged. "Apparently I got a bit too heated arguing my point – but she was *wrong*." He clenched his fists – I could tell he wasn't over the perceived injustice.

He'd given me a good opening to find out his alibi.

"So, were you ever left alone in detention?" I asked, trying to keep my voice casual.

Arthur smirked, like he knew exactly what I was doing.

"Nope," he said. "I was *surrounded* by people." He seemed amused, like he knew something I didn't. "You want my advice? If you want to do a proper investigation, look at the teachers. I could see Mrs Greythorne getting really angry at a student for not listening to her rules and snapping, for example…"

Maybe I should have been grateful for the fact that Arthur had never spoken to me before everything happened with Hugh. The more I talked to him, the more I realized how much I disliked him. My skin was starting to itch and even though it wasn't out of the realm of possibility that a teacher might have done it, I didn't want to agree with him.

"You're ridiculous," I said.

"*What* did you call me?" he hissed, and I flinched back at the sudden venom in his voice.

I opened and shut my mouth, unsure what to say.

His nostrils flared. "*Never* call me ridiculous again." There was unbridled anger in his eyes.

I was confused – he'd never appeared to have a problem with Hugh spouting all sorts of crap about his family and yet he was acting like I'd said the worst thing in the world.

"Er… Sorry," I said, wondering if I had accidentally stumbled onto a deeply personal insult to him.

"Good," Arthur said, leaning back. "Now – X is forty-three." He gestured at the problem sheet and then lapsed into his familiar silence, like his sudden outburst had never happened.

* * *

"Jess – wait up," a boy called from behind me.

Tommy was hurrying along, pushing through crowds of people. I knew he'd said my name, but I still didn't register that he was talking to me. I was heading to the common room, where Clem was going to meet me after lacrosse practice.

I slowed down slightly but didn't come to a complete halt.

"I said *wait*," huffed Tommy, his bag swinging by his side. "Where're you going?"

"Common room," I said, keeping my eyes fixed straight ahead. I probably sounded like a robot.

"So, someone in my knitting club mentioned Clem was asking about me," said Tommy, as we turned into the common room.

I stumbled, slightly shocked he was bringing up knitting with me so casually when he'd gone to so much effort to keep it a secret.

The space was flooded with sunlight, which streamed in through the windows, and was largely empty. Throughout the winter term, outside of class time, it was nearly always full, but during the spring and summer terms it only really got busy in the evenings. Even if it was cold or raining, people would put on raincoats and their country boots and splash around in the drizzle. School could feel very confining after a while – most people preferred to be outside in the fresh air.

Tommy sat down on one of the comfy couches, lounging back. "So now you know my deep, dark secret." He smiled slightly. "Hugh was the only friend I told and he didn't even blink. Immediately asked if I could knit him a Chelsea football club jumper, and I said never. Arsenal all the way."

"Was Hugh…er, generally supportive of you?" I said, sitting down next to him – well, not exactly *next* to him. More like leaving a huge space between us, and perching right on the edge of the couch. I'd only known Hugh as arrogant, but that couldn't have been entirely who he was, not if Clem and Tommy had both cared so much about him. It seemed to me like he'd been good at wearing a range of faces: a different Hugh depending on who he was with.

"Yeah," said Tommy, his voice distant. "Yeah he was." He cleared his throat. "Look, I know you and Clem are doing a bit of investigating too – Clem isn't exactly subtle about things, is she? Anyway, have you found out anything?"

Yeah, that you're not the killer.

"No," I said, trying to keep the bitterness from my voice as I thought about the fact that the police didn't seem to be doing much either, beyond interviewing as many people as they could.

His face was now serious. "Well…the thing is, you're not being very careful."

The words sounded similar to Annabelle's warning – was he going to tell me to keep off the Regia Club's radar as well?

"What do you mean?" I asked.

He hesitated. "Just…watch out for Summer," he said. "She'll do whatever it takes to get what she wants. *Whatever* it takes."

I didn't get to ask what he meant because Coach Tyler arrived. He stood over us, clutching a clipboard.

"Oh, hello, Jess – I haven't seen you in a while. I hope you've been practising your aim."

I blushed, and Tommy grinned. Apparently, everyone had heard the javelin story.

"What's up, Coach?" he said.

"You haven't seen Eddy, have you?" Coach Tyler shifted his clipboard from hand to hand. "He's missed yet another homework assignment – if he keeps this up, I'm going to have to suspend him from the team."

Tommy frowned. "I'm pretty sure I saw him in the library earlier."

Eddy had been at the library when I questioned Summer. If he hadn't been doing prep, why was he there? He hated reading – he'd once failed an English assignment because he only watched the film version of the book we were working on.

More likely he'd been playing fantasy football or something. It was Eddy – he lived and breathed the sport.

Either way, the conversation didn't sound like it involved me.

"I'll see you," I said to Tommy, and rose from the couch.

"Wait," said Coach Tyler. His expression softened. "If you see Clem, tell her...tell her I'm sorry for her loss."

"Er... Will do," I said, edging towards the door.

"It's just – she was in *my* detention that night. To be scraping mud off balls while Hugh was...you know..." Coach Tyler trailed off, and I saw with horror that a single tear was sliding down his cheek. "She and Millie did such a great job too," he choked.

I locked eyes with Tommy.

"I'll look out for Eddy," Tommy said, and I used the change in topic to slip out, almost colliding with Clem.

I marched past her, down the corridor – no way was I going back inside.

"Where're you going?" said Clem, hurrying to keep up with me.

"Common room's packed," I lied.

"Sure… Listen, I have a new idea – about how we're going to keep up momentum on the investigation."

Clem's eyes glinted, and that was enough to get me to slow down. My stomach started to churn. I knew I wouldn't like whatever she was going to say.

"What?"

Clem grinned. "I know how we're going to get the dirt on Summer."

14

"I don't want to do this," I said, for what felt like the millionth time. I might as well have been talking to a wall, because Clem did not care one bit about what I wanted.

It was a Friday evening, which meant Summer was at debate club, one of her many extracurriculars. We were heading towards her bedroom to search through her things and look for clues. Well, Clem was going to. I was supposed to stand at the peephole in Summer's door and keep watch to see if anyone was coming. I'd tried pointing out that by the time I saw anyone through the peephole it would be too late for us to hide, but Clem apparently didn't care about minor details like that.

"We'll be in and out before you know it," said Clem in her breezy voice.

Easy for her to say – if she was caught, she'd get a slap on the wrist from school. If I was caught, Mum would kill me. And who even knew what would happen to my scholarship.

None of the bedroom doors in school had locks, as it was apparently a fire hazard. We weren't supposed to have valuables, but everyone brought laptops since no one wanted to use the school's slow computers. Most people kept their phones on them, and our house-parents were meant to look after our pocket money, though everyone in the oldest two years (not including me) smuggled in extra to spend in the village near school.

Lucy, Annabelle's best friend, had the room next to Summer's. She was just coming out, closing her door behind her.

"We should go!" I hissed at Clem, as Lucy looked up.

Clem ignored me.

"Hey," she said to Lucy, like it was completely natural for us to be down this corridor.

Lucy frowned at us. "What're you two doing here?"

"Looking for Kate," said Clem, and she pulled her phone out of her pocket. "She forgot this at lacrosse."

Lucy rolled her eyes. "Kate is *always* leaving stuff lying around. Anyway, see you later." She wiggled her fingers at Clem as she left.

I waited until she was gone before I wheeled around to Clem. "We've now got a witness putting us at the scene of the crime! Why aren't you *panicking*?"

"Crime! You're so dramatic," said Clem, as she pushed Summer's door open. "We're on the side of justice."

My heart jumped into my throat as we went inside. Summer's room was, unsurprisingly, incredibly neat. She even had a flower-patterned throw over her bed, with all the corners tucked in. On her notice board, she had plastered what looked to be all the certificates she had ever won. She'd run out of space, so had had to start pinning some on top of others.

I winced as Clem started rattling through Summer's desk drawers.

"Put everything back exactly the way you found it," I said, closing the door.

"It'll be *fine*," said Clem, as she sifted through piles of papers. "Oooh, jackpot. Laptop."

She fired it up while I glanced through the door's peephole. I could see a bit of the corridor if I looked through at the right angle, but we definitely wouldn't have time to hide if the need arose.

"Any luck?" I said, because Clem had gone quiet.

"Not unless you know how to hack a laptop," said Clem, as she slammed the lid down. "Password protected – what does she have to hide?"

"Everyone password protects their laptop," I replied, as I looked through the peephole again. "*You* password protect your laptop."

"Because I have stuff to hide – no one needs to see my attempts to write English essays," said Clem, as she opened up the wardrobe. "She's followed the suggested clothes list exactly – shirts, skirts…*wow*, there's a lot of plaid in here."

"Focus," I said through gritted teeth.

"Relax. We've got loads of time. Debate doesn't finish for another half an hour." She switched on her phone torch and dropped down to her hands and knees.

I tried not to groan as she army-crawled underneath Summer's bed.

"What're you *doing*?" I said to her legs, which were the only part of her I could still see.

"This would go a lot faster if you helped me look," came her muffled reply.

I bit my bottom lip. We *would* be in and out much faster if I helped. I still hovered by the door, checking the peephole once more. The corridor remained empty.

"Okay, fine," I said, even though fear of getting caught had made my entire body weak.

Clem had given up on the rest of Summer's desk drawers when she found the laptop, so I half-heartedly pulled open the bottom ones. It felt so wrong, going through Summer's stuff.

In the bottom drawer was a scrunched-up piece of paper lying on top of some notebooks. I frowned, because it stood out as the only *not* neat thing in the room.

I unfolded the paper, smoothing out the creases. It was a handwritten…short story, from the looks of it. It was only a page and a half and as I started to read my blood ran cold.

"Er…Clem. I found something." My voice came out as a squeak.

"Not as big as what I've found!" said Clem as she slid out from under the bed, waving a piece of paper above her head. "What have you got?"

I handed the paper over to her, watching her mouth drop in shock as she read.

Together, Summer and I had written a short story in which a man called Bob was killed. It was set in a forest and there were twigs spelling *HELP ME* and the murder weapon was a trophy.

But Summer had written another version of our short story, set in a classroom – where the victim's name was Hugh.

15

Clem stared at the paper, her face a mask of shock. "Surely not," she said. "Surely…there's no way…"

"This short story is rubbish," I said. "It's completely boring – the main character is just plain old stabbed…"

"Summer's not creative," said Clem. "She needed your help to plot the murder – *she thanked you for the inspiration.*"

"What did you find?" I said, my stomach still lurching.

Clem passed me a piece of paper that said *Tell the police what you did, or you'll end up just like Hugh.* The words had been printed out in large Times New Roman font.

I frowned at the message, but before we could discuss, noises came from the corridor.

"I *didn't* forget the note cards. I meant to leave them in my room!"

It was Summer's voice.

Clem's eyes went wide. "Hide here!"

She dragged me into the wardrobe, closing the door just as Summer entered the room. There was a gap where the wardrobe doors should have met but didn't. I angled myself to see Hattie, who was also on the debate team, standing in the doorway with her arms folded. Summer went to her desk, moving around the stacks of papers.

"They're here somewhere," she said, as a few pens rolled off her desk. "I've got a lot on my plate at the moment, that's all. Ah!" She grabbed a stack of flash cards.

My stomach swooped and I clamped a hand over my mouth to stop myself gasping. I'd left the bottom drawer of the desk open.

Clem crouched beneath me, peering through the gap in the wardrobe doors as well, and a second later she sucked in a breath.

Please don't let Summer see. Please don't let Summer see.

"What the…" Summer stared down at the open drawer.

"What's wrong?" said Hattie impatiently. "Do you have the notes or not?"

"Yeah, but…" Summer dropped the flash cards and started rooting around in the bottom drawer, flinging papers in every direction. "I had…" She got to her feet. "Someone's been in my room."

I dug my nails into my palms. This was a nightmare. This wasn't happening.

"What do you mean?" Hattie frowned.

I could barely hear over the sound of blood pounding in my ears.

"Someone's stolen…" Summer swallowed.

"What?" said Hattie. "What's been taken? Your laptop?"

Summer pulled open another drawer and shook her head. "No, not my laptop."

"Then what?" said Hattie, with fear in her voice.

There had been the odd occasion in the past where small things went missing, but on the whole stealing at Heybuckle wasn't really an issue.

"I – nothing." Summer closed the drawer, taking a few deep breaths as she picked up the flash cards. She looked around the room, and her eyes locked on the wardrobe. I twitched back. For a second, it seemed like she'd been staring straight at me.

My entire body shook.

Leave. Don't check the wardrobe.

After a pause, she swallowed. "Come on. Let's get back to debate."

They left, and for a moment neither Clem nor I moved. Then, together, we both tumbled out of the wardrobe.

"I can't *believe* you left the drawer open!" said Clem at once.

"Don't blame me," I snapped back, though of course I was cursing my carelessness. Adrenaline still pumped through me. "I didn't even want to do this."

Clem took a picture of the story and the note.

"I'm going to put them back now," she said, as she opened the drawer and dropped the crumpled paper inside. She shoved the blackmail note back under Summer's bed.

"Won't that short story popping back up freak Summer out?" I asked. "She's just seen it wasn't there."

Clem shuffled some of the papers around. "There, now she'll think she just missed it."

"But—"

"We need to get out of here." Clem talked over me, determination in her voice.

She charged into the corridor and I followed, closing the door behind me. My heart rate didn't settle until we were safe in my room. Annabelle was out doing whatever it was Annabelle did in the evenings. Probably shooting pheasants to make herself seem super posh (or peasants, she wasn't picky).

"I can't believe we just did that," I said, collapsing onto my bed.

"What does that note mean?" said Clem, wheeling around to face me.

In all my worry about getting caught, as well as the shock of finding Summer's short story, I'd forgotten what the note said.

Tell the police what you did, or you'll end up just like Hugh.

Dead, like Hugh.

"Does… Does this mean that Summer killed Hugh?" I asked. "And someone else knows and is threatening to…to kill her because of it?"

She *must* have killed Hugh. She had written a murder mystery with his name in it. But I couldn't wrap my head around it. Summer. *Summer.* Sure, the girl was incredibly intense. She'd do anything to get what she wanted, and she had a ruthless, cutting tongue. But did she have a dark side? Should we be scared of her? I didn't want to believe it – but we were investigating a murder, and she was one of my top suspects.

Plus, Tommy had warned me about her. Did he know Summer was Hugh's killer? But then if he knew, why hadn't he turned her over to the police? Why just tell me to be on my guard?

Clem sat down at my desk, shrugging her blazer off and flinging it onto the floor.

"Well, clearly Summer…Summer's done something bad.

Maybe something really bad." She shook her head.

We stared at each other.

"I just…what reason could Summer have to kill Hugh? Is the bake sale thing really that big of a deal?"

I was starting to get the impression that Hugh's murder was going to result in us peeling back the golden, elite layer that Heybuckle presented to the world, to reveal a tangled web of darkness beneath the surface.

Clem looked at me, her gaze intense. "Do you think Hugh was killed because of something really bad he did?"

I didn't know the right answer to her question. I didn't want to say anything that might upset her.

"I… Of course not." My voice sounded unconvincing, even to myself.

"You never liked him," said Clem, shaking her head. "But be honest…" Her voice was slightly pleading. "We've always been honest with each other."

"I didn't even know him," I burst out.

He'd never bothered to talk to me. Did she not see how wrong that was, that her boyfriend didn't want to get to know her best friend?

A single tear dripped down Clem's face.

"I keep wishing it isn't true," she said. "I keep wishing none of this was happening. I wish we could go back to last year. Everything was better then."

I decided now wasn't the time to remind her that last year she was sneaking around behind Millie's back, having a secret relationship with Hugh. I got up and hugged her, and she leaned into me, and began to sob.

"Maybe," she hiccupped, pulling away from me and wiping the snot dripping from her nose with the back of her hand. "Maybe Summer wrote the Hugh short story *after* his death? As a way to...I don't know...process her grief? And maybe there's a separate blackmailer who is riding on the coketails of the fear surrounding Hugh's death to scare Summer."

"Coat-tails," I said as I frowned. The theory actually made sense. "So there's someone who killed Hugh and then there's someone else who is using that to scare Summer? Why?"

Clem shrugged. "I mean...no one likes Summer."

"Does this mean Summer *didn't* kill Hugh?" I said.

Clem hiccupped again. "No. We can't rule it out... Plus..." Her eyebrows knitted together. "She hasn't told the police about that blackmail note."

"How d'you know?"

"Well, the fact that the blackmail note is under her bed seems to suggest the police don't have it," said Clem. "And that doesn't exactly scream *I'm innocent*."

"She might be planning to tell the police," I said. "Otherwise, she'd have just thrown it away."

Our conversation was cut short by Annabelle and Lucy bursting into the room. Clem hurriedly turned away, rubbing at her eyes. When she turned back around it looked like she hadn't been crying at all, flashing Annabelle and Lucy a dazzling smile. It was a talent of hers, an ability to hide how she was really feeling from people she wasn't friends with. My stupid face told everyone exactly what I was thinking.

"See you around," Clem said as she headed towards the door.

"Did you find Kate?" said Lucy, as she dumped her bag on the floor.

"What?" said Clem, freezing.

"Kate – remember, you had her phone? You were outside her bedroom?"

"Oh – yeah," said Clem, widening her eyes at me like I was the one who had forgotten the excuse she had given Lucy. "Yeah, we did, thanks. Honestly, that girl – we should strap her phone to her palm or something."

Lucy turned her back on Clem, who used the opportunity to grimace at me.

Close one, she mouthed, then scarpered from the room.

Annabelle frowned at me. "I just saw Kate, and she had her phone."

"We, er, probably gave it back just before you saw her," I said, nowhere near as smooth as Clem.

I could feel Annabelle's eyes boring into me as I lay back on my bed, scrolling through my phone while my cheeks burned.

I kept my eyes on the screen. There was one message from Mum, which I flicked open.

Are they feeding you k?

Annabelle had started gossiping with Lucy, though her eyes kept flicking over to me, full of suspicion. I did my best to ignore her as I tapped out a reply (No, they are starving me).

Very funny, came the response.

Then, typing. Typing. Lots of *Mum is typing*.

Mum is typing.

134

Mum is typing.

Mum is (still) typing.

Oooh, Mum stopped typing. Maybe she gave up.

No, it had started up again. *Mum is typing.*

The message finally came through.

Ill make saag when you home.

(Lots more typing ensued in between each individual message – she never could just send everything at once.)

Andlot of roti.

You need properr food.

How Clem.

Mum is not illiterate, in case that's how it comes across. She was just very slow with her phone, and it meant she could never be bothered to correct mistakes.

Not good, I tapped back.

I woke up at 7 a.m. the next morning to Annabelle's snoring (she always vehemently denied she snored, and I hadn't yet gone as far as recording her to prove it, something Clem had been suggesting I do for ages).

Saturdays normally meant I could get up much later because breakfast went on until 10 a.m. We didn't have to wear uniforms at the weekends. When I first arrived at Heybuckle, I was worried everyone would walk around decked head-to-toe in

135

designer stuff. But most people seemed to slouch around in casual clothes (which were still probably horribly expensive), with the exception of people like Millie, who dressed up no matter what, and Annabelle, who always made sure everyone knew her clothes were designer.

I lay in bed, snuggled down all toasty and warm. Eventually I got bored and reached over to switch my phone on.

It buzzed with all the expected messages from Mum – but then came one from a blocked number.

My blood ran cold. I thought about not opening it, about pretending it didn't exist.

But I needed to know what it said.

My fingers shook as I clicked on it.

Just like last time, it took me a few seconds to process exactly what I was reading.

Hugh Henry Van Boren did something terrible and deserved to die.

Confess what you did last year, or you'll be next.

16

What the hell?

At least the last message thanking me for the inspiration and acknowledging they couldn't have killed Hugh without me had made some sort of sense…

This one…

This one…

I sat up in bed, rubbing my eyes and trying to think. The tiredness cushioned me from freaking out too much – my brain felt like it was coated in cotton wool.

But there was no denying it. I had woken up to a death threat.

A death threat *that didn't make sense.*

The murderer knew what I had done last year. They wanted me to confess, or I would be next. It sounded like they were on some sort of crusade, like they were trying to kill all the bad kids in the school. Hugh was one. Summer was one.

I was, apparently, another.

Except I *wasn't.*

I hadn't done anything bad last year. Well, I mean I wasn't

perfect. I had done lots of things that weren't great. Like the whole javelin incident with Coach Tyler.

But nothing *murder*-worthy.

This was like one of those teen-slasher films, where the characters all had dark, deadly pasts. It made complete sense that Hugh would have done something terrible in his past, probably while drunk at one of the wild parties his two older brothers threw. Summer came across as someone who would do whatever it took to stay ahead, so it wouldn't surprise me if she had a guilty conscience.

But *me*?

I was Jesminder Choudhary, and I had grown up in a little terraced house in north London, and I had earned a scholarship to one of the most prestigious schools in the country. I was definitely not the type of person who should be targeted by a wild vigilante.

Maybe they had the wrong person.

I imagined texting something back like, Hi, sorry, wrong number. Maybe you put an 8 instead of a 7. Please go and threaten to kill the next person on your list.

But I couldn't, of course. I just stared at the message, wondering what it could mean.

Clem was at her Saturday morning lacrosse practice, after which, the team would go out for lunch in the village. It meant I had no one to tell that I had been threatened with death.

The more I thought about it, the angrier I got.

I was being accused of something so heinous, so absolutely

awful, someone wanted to kill me for it – unless I confessed what I had done to the police.

But I couldn't confess to the police, because I hadn't *done* anything, so I guessed I was just supposed to suck it up and get murdered. And even if I did go to the police, what if they didn't believe I really hadn't done anything bad?

Plus, according to Tommy, they were crap at their jobs. And I hadn't seen anything that proved otherwise. They hadn't arrested anyone. In fact, it looked like they weren't making any progress at all. And who even knew what the Van Borens' private investigator was doing, apart from occasionally interviewing people and asking them random stuff – he'd apparently asked Eddy what his last grade in chemistry was.

It was becoming clearer and clearer to me why, even if she was innocent, Summer hadn't said anything about her note – why she had left it crumpled up under her bed.

After a while, I figured my time wasn't being well spent lying in bed and worrying. Plus, my stomach was rumbling.

I headed down to breakfast, and for the first time I properly considered how creepy it was that the school was filled with people – and yet could appear so empty. As the death threat properly sank in and I slipped alone through endless corridors, I really wished I had company.

Because even if the text didn't make sense, there was still apparently a murderer out to get me. Hugh hadn't been safe – why should I think I was?

I quickened my pace, the floorboards creaking. A prickling sensation crept down the back of my neck and every time I turned a corner, I flinched, half expecting someone to leap out at me. The knot in my chest loosened as I finally headed into the dining room, with the faint, reassuring sounds of the kitchen staff coming through the hatches. It was still only 8 a.m., so though there were a few early risers sitting at the tables, the room was mostly empty.

I ignored all the hot food and got myself some cereal, sitting right in the middle of the room, where the kitchen staff could see me. I was almost done when Tommy slid in opposite. He was wearing a plain white T-shirt, which showed off his muscular arms. His hair looked damp, like he had just taken a shower, and he had a plate loaded with scrambled eggs and bacon, mushrooms and grilled tomatoes, toast dripping with golden butter.

My stomach flipped at how cute he looked and flipped again at the fact he'd chosen to sit with me.

"Morning," he said, shovelling down some toast. His normal musky smell peeked through the scent of strawberry shower gel.

"Er... Hi," I said, trying to sound casual. "Why are you up so early?"

"Couldn't sleep," he said, his cheeks bulging with food. "You?"

"Same," I said, as my brain finally woke up and pointed out that he'd never chosen to sit with me before. I knew he wasn't Hugh's murderer and wasn't part of the Regia Club. But surely him sitting with me randomly on the same day I got a death threat couldn't be a coincidence? He'd warned me about Summer – but maybe that was a red herring he was throwing out to cover something else up.

He stopped chewing. "Why're you staring at me like that?"

"I got a text message this morning," I said, carefully watching for his reaction.

"Oh – er – good for you?"

I took out my phone and slid it across to him. His mouth fell open, his eyebrows raised in shock. Either he was a really good actor, or else he had never seen the text before.

"It could be from Hugh's murderer – or the Regia Club pulling a horrible prank... Or it could be from someone else..." I said, watching him carefully.

He looked up from my phone. "*I* didn't send you this," he said in disbelief, pushing my phone back to me. "But also... what did you do last year?"

"Nothing," I said through gritted teeth. "I did *nothing*. And what did *Hugh* do, that's the real question? What's the terrible, awful thing he did? What secret did he have that was *so* bad someone killed him?"

Tommy's gaze dropped away from me, towards his food. His cheeks flushed red.

"You know something," I said at once. "Is it to do with the Regia Club?" It was a wild guess, me clutching at straws, but the text had me flustered and I wasn't thinking properly.

"No, I'm not..." said Tommy. But he was hesitating, his eyes drifting back to my phone. "I said the whole Regia Club thing was basically bullying...but..." He took a deep breath. "But Hugh was in it – we were both asked to join when we started at school. I said no, he said yes. He was almost its leader, I think, but someone else got voted in a few weeks ago – not sure who. Hugh never said much about it, but I know it made him really angry."

It didn't surprise me at all that Hugh was in the Regia Club. My heart hammered in excitement – it felt like I was close to a breakthrough.

"Who else is in the club?" I leaned forwards, lowering my voice.

But Tommy was shaking his head. "I asked Hugh loads of times – he wouldn't say. And it's a *secret* society – I shouldn't even have known about Hugh being in it." He bit his bottom lip. "I always thought there was something off about it – a group of people putting pressure on everyone else to pull pranks they might not want to take part in. How could a bunch of students have so much power that the school actually listened when they demanded a half day for everyone last term, just because they wanted one? But ex-members grow up – they become the parents making donations. They get onto the school board. People talk about the Regia Club running Heybuckle – but that isn't a joke, Jess. They really do. And I don't think there's any limit on what they could do."

17

I texted Clem to tell her we had to speak as soon as possible. She couldn't have known Hugh was in the Regia Club – she would have told me, even if he had sworn her to secrecy. But maybe together we could figure out how it fitted in with everything else. I kept checking my phone for her reply, but I knew she wouldn't be looking at her messages while she was with the lacrosse team. I decided to grab my book so I could read outside, in a nice exposed area of the fields where multiple students would be passing by.

I knew something was wrong the moment I walked into my room. Despite the brisk breeze blowing in through the open window, there was a strange, sickly-sweet smell hanging in the air.

I froze as I noticed my bed. What appeared to be all of my clothes – even my underwear and socks – were laid out neatly on top of the covers. They looked wet, as though they were coated in something sticky.

Near my pillow, someone had left a poster of an Indian actress. They had taken a photo of my face and scratched the eyes out, sticking it on top of the actress's head, and added a speech bubble that said *STOP LOOKING AND MIND YOUR OWN BUSINESS*. The letters had been crudely cut from magazines, like an old-fashioned ransom note you'd see in films. Underneath someone had stuck a printed note that read *ENJOY THE HONEY – NEXT TIME I WON'T BE SO SWEET XO*.

My heart started pounding as I stared at my clothes. It was honey, I realized. They were covered in honey.

I tried to tell myself it could have been worse, but angry tears threatened to spill out as I looked around, praying my bed was the only thing that the intruder had targeted. I pulled open my desk drawers, to find more honey poured all over my books, my laptop case, my prep, the black ink smeared. I yanked my laptop out of the case, my heart beating fast – if it had been ruined, I couldn't afford a new one.

Thankfully the case had protected it. But the rest of my stuff – my hairbrush, my photos, prep I had spent hours doing – was all destroyed.

"What's going on here?" said a voice behind me.

I spun around to find Millie standing in the doorway with her arms folded. Her room wasn't anywhere nearby – how had I got so unlucky that she of all people stumbled onto the scene just as I discovered it?

Millie's eyes widened as they slid to my bed, her mouth dropping open in shock.

"*Wow*," she said, and for a brief moment I thought she was angry for me. But instead her shock slowly morphed into a smile as she came forwards, her eyes scanning hungrily over my clothes. "This is amazing," she said, picking up the poster.

"What?" I said, my voice coming out strangled as I blinked back my tears. I would not cry in front of Millie.

"It's a Regia Club prank!" she said, pointing at the corner of the poster, where someone had scribbled *S.R.* in capital letters. "But it looks so, so good." She pulled the picture of my face off the poster, exposing the actress underneath. "This woman even looks like you."

There was no resemblance between us, apart from the fact we were both Indian, and for some reason that knowledge cut even deeper than the stupid honey all over my stupid stuff. Even when they were trying to break me, people still didn't see me properly. All they saw was my skin colour.

"And the *honey* works brilliantly," said Millie. "It's so perfect for you."

"What does that mean?" I said, blinking at her.

"*You* know," she said. "*Honey*. Like your skin?"

I gaped at her, as she started laughing.

"Oh man, I *have* to text Eddy about this," she said. "He's going to find it *hilarious*—"

"What the *hell*?" Annabelle came into the room, wrapped in a golden dressing gown. Her hair was darker because it was wet and she looked a lot better for it – the fake blonde made her appear slightly ill. She stared at all the crap on my bed.

My cheeks started to burn. They were all treating this like I was some sort of entertainment.

"Oh, Annabelle, *look* at this," said Millie, holding up the poster as she laughed. "It turned out so well! And her face is on this actress and—"

"You're sick, Millie," said Annabelle, to my complete shock.

The smile dropped off Millie's face almost instantly. "What did you just say?"

"This isn't something to laugh about – this is horrible. Jess, I'm going to get Miss Evans and she can help us sort this out." Annabelle turned on her heel, still wearing her dressing gown.

"No," I said weakly. "No, just…can you help me get this stuff into the wash? And all my bedsheets as well?"

I didn't want Miss Evans, our house-mother, to find out about this – I didn't want *any* adult to know. I was too embarrassed. Because it felt like there was something shameful about being bullied like this, because I was already the different kid, the scholarship kid, the poor kid – the Indian kid. And now someone had poured honey over everything I owned and Millie was acting like this was the funniest thing she had ever seen.

Annabelle shook her head. "We need to tell her," she said, her voice getting gentler.

I nodded, unsure why she was being so nice. Millie was getting her phone out, presumably to take photos, and I wanted to tell her to stop, but I was afraid I was going to start bawling in front of both of them and I couldn't think of anything worse.

"Millie – go away," said Annabelle, her face scrunched up with disgust. "You've done enough now – why are you even here?"

Millie's lip curled as she looked at Annabelle, her eyes flashing. "I actually was here to see you – to tell you I saw that story about your parents getting sued by one of their old clients for being terrible lawyers—"

"Oh, piss off," said Annabelle, her real accent coming out in full force. She sounded better with it, more powerful.

146

Millie tossed back her curls, her lip curling. "You're pathetic, honestly. Always gossiping about everyone else and you're the biggest story of all – with your horrible hair and your terrible fake accent, and your tacky need to show everyone you have a little bit of money. Where'd you actually grow up – next to Jess in a council estate?"

Something inside Annabelle seemed to snap as she stepped forwards. "Why did you do this to Jess?" She pointed at my bed, and I wanted to cower in a corner because she seemed like she was seconds away from raking her nails over Millie's face. "You're obviously in the Regia Club and now you're here to see Jess's reaction to this awful prank because people's misery makes you so happy—"

Millie raised her hand.

"Go on!" yelled Annabelle. "Slap me, you two-faced cow – just like you slapped Hugh a week before he was killed—"

Mille's slap was probably heard all around England. Annabelle stared at Millie, her chest slowly rising and falling, the handprint a red outline on her pale face.

"You're just jealous," said Millie, and she looked over at me as well. "Because people like you could never be in the Regia Club. They don't take *new* money. And they don't take the poors."

She flicked back her golden hair and stalked out of our room, and I had never hated someone as much as I hated her – and the worst thing was, she could be the most horrible person in the world and yet she would have *everything* in life handed to her, all because she was accidentally born into the *right* family and looked a certain way.

Annabelle was still breathing heavily. "She's an utter cow," she said. "A two-faced prick. A bell-end." She continued to list all sorts of insults she would never normally utter, insults someone like Millie would call *common*. "I'm going to get Miss Evans, but if you don't want to talk to her, I can tell her I found your stuff like this and we'll sort it out for you, yeah? Get it all cleaned up?"

I nodded, feeling like a bobble-head. At the very least, my complete despair had been replaced by shock at Millie and Annabelle's argument.

Annabelle took off her dressing gown and grabbed a plain T-shirt and joggers from her wardrobe. With her damp hair, no make-up or big earrings, no flashy designer clothes she was only wearing to impress other people, she looked a lot younger... a lot nicer.

She left, and I waited a few seconds before I picked the poster up and tore it into tiny pieces. I didn't want to throw the shreds into the bin in my bedroom and know they were still there, festering near me until our bins were next emptied. I grabbed a blanket and my book and took the remains of the poster, chucking them into one of the big bins in the corridor. Then I went out into the grounds, stumbling around until I found a good location in view of other people, yet far enough away they wouldn't see me trembling, before I allowed myself to cry.

18

I didn't end up reading my book. I couldn't focus. Annabelle texted me to let me know Miss Evans and the cleaners were sorting out my stuff – chucking all my clothes into the wash, scrubbing the honey away. I would go back later and assess the damage, but not yet. I currently couldn't stand the thought of going back to my bedroom.

There were loads of people in the grounds, lounging on the grass or going for walks. A few boys were playing football, and there were screams of laughter from the tennis courts.

Everything was as it normally would be on a weekend afternoon in late spring. The school woods were no longer cordoned off by police tapes, but we had all been warned about going in and gawking at the place Hugh's body had been found.

That hadn't stopped people going in. Annabelle had gone with her friends, and told me, "There really wasn't much to see. It was just the woods – as boring as ever."

I don't know what she'd been expecting. Blood-spattered tree trunks? An indent of Hugh's body on the ground? Traumatized squirrels?

But for most people, what had happened to Hugh was something tragic they could gossip about and then set aside while they got on with their lives. I wished I could forget about Hugh. I wished I could be like everyone else, happily laughing with their friends, with nothing to worry about but mock exams in June and our finals next year, and university applications, and whether we'd be picking Oxford or Cambridge.

But I had to be honest with myself. Even if I hadn't had that death threat, I wouldn't have been sitting on the sweeping lawns of the school grounds laughing with my friends. I'd still be sitting alone on the hill.

I was feeling very sorry for myself when Clem eventually showed up.

"Budge over," she said. "You're taking up all the blanket."

I scooted, and she sat down next to me. She opened her mouth, I guess to launch into the latest part of the Clem Chronicles. Before she could, I told her about the prank, and the message telling me to stop looking, and the death threat text, and the fact we knew about one member of the Regia Club – Hugh – and it looked like we could make a very good guess at a second member – Millie. She had been waiting near my room, and looked proud of the prank rather than surprised by it, which indicated she had known about it and thought it was a great idea.

Clem blinked a few times. "Well, it's been…an eventful morning for you." She continued to blink, then got to her feet, pacing in circles. "Sorry, I'm just trying to process… Someone put *honey* all over your bed? And Millie came in and laughed?" She rolled up her sleeves and looked like she was going to go charging over to the school.

I held out my hand, too tired from all the crying to get up properly, praying that for once she would just listen to me.

"I've been thinking more about this whole thing and…isn't it really weird? One anonymous text is telling me to *confess what I did* and the other message is telling me to stop looking. Don't you see what that means?"

Clem nibbled her bottom lip. "The poster is from the murderer and the text is from…someone else?"

I shook my head – I'd already thought all this through. "The first text I got, thanking me for the inspiration – that was from the murderer, right? Very obviously. So, it follows that the second text is from the murderer as well – they killed Hugh for something he did and now they're…they're going to kill me." My throat closed up, but I managed to get the words out. I coughed. "Right, and the poster… Someone is worried that our murder investigation is going to dig up…something. I guess about the Regia Club? So, what if it's multiple people involved in this…thing. Like…all of the Regia Club? And they're sort of at war with each other? Maybe Hugh and Millie are on one side – and our murderer is on the other."

Clem pressed her knuckles against her mouth. "I didn't know," she said. "About Hugh being in the Regia Club. He told Tommy – but not me."

There was a catch in her voice.

"Tommy was his best friend," I pointed out.

"And I was in love with him," said Clem, shaking her head. "But… Did I even know him? He and Millie were in this horrible club together. He had a whole other life I didn't know anything about."

"I just don't understand," I said. "Why was I the only one to get the first text, thanking me for my help with the short story? Why didn't Summer get one as well?"

"Because…because…" Clem scratched the end of her nose. "Because the murderer likes you best?"

"Be serious here, Clem – someone wants to *kill me*."

"Well, they can't if you tell the police," said Clem, in what I guess was supposed to be a calming voice. I'd heard her use it on her horses at home whenever they got rattled. "I know Hugh's parents don't trust them to solve his murder, but maybe this could help the police with their investigation? I mean…this text says a lot about who the murderer is."

"Does it?" I whipped my phone out and reread the message (even though by that point I'd already memorized it).

Hugh Henry Van Boren did something terrible
and deserved to die.

Confess what you did last year, or you'll be next.

"Am I looking for a code or something?" I said, squinting at the screen. "Like every other letter spells out the words *Hi, I'm your murderer-friend. My name is Stabby-Mc-Stabface?*"

"Well, *that's* not what I meant," said Clem.

"Well, I don't know," I said, frustrated. "What's this text say about the murderer, then, if you're so smart?"

"It tells us *why* they're doing this, of course," said Clem, like it was the most obvious thing in the world. "They're going after people who've done bad things."

"Except they're not," I reminded her. "Because I haven't done anything."

"Okay, with the exception of you," said Clem. "Maybe they were having an off-day when they went down their list of Bad People and misread and got your name instead."

"So, I'm going to the police with this?" I sighed.

It was, of course, the most sensible thing to do. I had nothing to hide – and maybe they weren't as bad at their jobs as Hugh's parents thought. If they solved the case then obviously who ever had sent me the death threat wouldn't have time to follow through.

But still – what if they didn't believe me?

What if the school began to think I was more trouble than I was worth? That it was easier to just send me home, for my own safety? Expulsion, but under another name.

Clem had already made up my mind for me. "Yes, you're going to the police."

"And what about the whole *stop looking* Regia Club thing? Do I tell them about that?" I asked. "You know what happens to people who rat on the Regia Club."

Well, actually neither of us did know, because no one had ever done it. Plus, if my tattling got back to any ex-members on the school board, I'd be kissing my scholarship goodbye.

"Millie's probably told the whole school by now," said Clem. "So it's not like it's a secret."

Another issue occurred to me. "What about Summer's short story, and *her* death threat? Do we tell the police about that? If we tell them how we got that information, we might get into trouble." I hated this, having to second guess whether or not

I could speak to the people in charge, the people who were supposed to be looking after me.

"Maybe…we should tell them," said Clem, rubbing her forehead.

"Or we could wait," I said. "Summer could easily say she wrote that short story *after* Hugh was killed… Like you said – as a way to process her grief. We'd be getting into trouble for nothing."

Clem nodded. "Right. Well, let's just stick to telling the police about your death threat then."

Since the police weren't a constant presence in the school any more, we couldn't just march right up to Mrs Greythorne's office and ask to see them. Instead, I had to tell Mrs Greythorne, and she had to ring up Inspector Foster and inform her that I had a new lead for her.

Then Mrs Greythorne told Clem to wait outside.

"I'm supporting Jess," said Clem stubbornly.

"And you can support her *outside*," said Mrs Greythorne.

Clem scowled, but made to leave.

"I'll be in my room," Clem told me pointedly.

I knew what that meant – go see her straight after I was finished with the police and tell her exactly what they'd said.

"So, Jess," said Mrs Greythorne, once Clem had gone. "You need to ring your mother."

I'd convinced Mrs Greythorne that the first text thanking me for the inspiration didn't mean I was in any sort of danger. Judging from her grim face, I wouldn't be able to make the same argument twice.

I dialled the number for home. Mum picked up on the third ring.

I told her what had happened.

She started screaming, then immediately said she was going to pull me out and bring me home *right this very instant*.

I pointed out that Heybuckle was much safer than the corner of London we lived in.

She said she didn't care, because at home she could protect me.

I pointed out that leaving school – and such a prestigious one too – in the middle of my penultimate year would be unheard of. And nowhere else would be able to take me at such short notice. Schools didn't generally tend to let in sixteen-year-old dropouts in the middle of the year, especially ones who'd left under a cloud of death threats.

Eventually, Mrs Greythorne had to join the call and persuade Mum it was better for me to stay.

"Do I need to come up?" said Mum, her voice crackly down the line. "I can drive. I can be there in a few hours. I don't like the idea of my daughter speaking to the police without me."

Mum hated driving on motorways, and she couldn't just leave her job without warning.

"Not necessary at all, Mrs Choudhary," said Mrs Greythorne in her calm voice. "I can assure you that I'm here to look after Jess and I'll be right by her side when she's talking to the police."

We finally persuaded Mum she didn't need to race up to Heybuckle and Mrs Greythorne gently put the phone down. She sighed as she looked at me. Her face was like a freshly-washed shirt, full of creases and wrinkles. Much more, it seemed, than the last time I had seen her.

"I hope you have kept these messages you're receiving to yourself?" she said after a long pause. "And that Clem is sworn to secrecy?"

I nodded. I wasn't an idiot. The last thing I wanted was this leaking into the rest of the school, especially since I would already be on everyone's radar after the Regia Club prank.

We'd been on the phone to Mum for so long, Inspector Foster had arrived. She hovered by Mrs Greythorne's chair, until my formidable headmistress gave up her seat. Inspector Foster sat at the desk, leaning back as she tapped her fingers together.

I recounted my story, flushing as I explained I had ripped up the poster. At least I could show her the text. She squinted at my phone, took a few notes, and asked all the same questions she had before (about whether I was *sure* I didn't know anything more). Finally, she gave a small sigh.

"This information will help us catch this killer," she said confidently. "And once we've solved this, you'll be as safe as ever – especially since it's my professional opinion that this threat is just that. A threat. You're not in any danger."

But she continued to scribble in her notebook, and she didn't meet my eyes.

I knew I should have felt safer having told Inspector Foster about the message, but I didn't. I walked out of the office with Mrs Greythorne, nerves prickling through me. She turned down a different corridor, leaving me to head over to Clem's room.

I was halfway there when I realized I'd left my phone on Mrs Greythorne's desk.

I sighed as I swivelled and headed back to the office. The door was open a crack and Inspector Foster's voice echoed into the corridor.

"There's definitely something odd about this – I've been trying to investigate Hugh's past, to see if there's anyone who might have had a grudge against him, and I keep getting pushback from the higher-ups…"

I peered through the crack. Inspector Foster was pacing back and forth, her phone to her ear.

"Yes, there's *something* that they don't want getting out about that… Yes, exactly… If they don't want me to look into it, what can I do? It's a key part of this investigation, I'm so sure of it – but my hands are tied…"

I pulled back, hardly daring to breathe as the inspector lowered her voice. I had to strain my ears to hear what she was saying.

"You're right, you're right…" She muttered something I didn't catch. "And *yes*, the Regia Club… I don't like it – you're right, of course… Yes, the family's hired a private investigator. He sounds bloody useless, he won't find anything – vultures the lot of them, probably just preying on the family's grief… Yes – I'd better go."

From the sound of it, she had hung up. I waited a minute before knocking on the door, not wanting her to have any idea I'd been listening.

"Sorry, Inspector," I said, trying to keep my voice steady. "I just forgot my phone."

I grabbed my phone and hurried from the room. The police weren't investigating properly and the private investigator was crap.

There was no one but us to find the murderer before they followed through on their death threat.

19

Somehow, Annabelle had stopped Millie from telling everyone about the honey prank. Annabelle and I had to temporarily sleep in the attic, in a room which was small and hot. Annabelle grumbled about the switch, but she didn't blame me, even though I was the only reason we were up there. Something in our relationship had shifted after she stood up to Millie for me.

I couldn't sleep. The walls felt like they were closing in on me as I sifted through the implications of what I'd overheard Inspector Foster saying. She'd said the police weren't allowed to look into something – and then mentioned the Regia Club. What if some ex-members were in the police, stopping Inspector Foster investigating Hugh's connection with them?

I'd never seen Clem go as quiet as she did when I reported back Inspector Foster's conversation.

"Bloody hell," she'd said after a long pause. "What kind of conspiracy are we living in? I just thought the police were a bit crap. I didn't think they would be actively *trying* not to solve the case."

Her words didn't reassure me.

I lay staring up at the slanted ceiling. Every gurgle of the pipes and every time the wind whistled at the windows, my heart thudded. My entire body was tensed for the moment someone opened the attic door, murder-trophy held aloft. Annabelle's snores were half reassuring to me, because they meant I wasn't alone – and half not. She'd stuck up for me, but she had no proper alibi for Hugh's murder. If she was the killer though, it wouldn't make sense for her to stab me when everyone knew we were alone together. But if she *wasn't*, maybe the killer would be able to take us both out…

My mind went round and round in circles, until at last I must have fallen asleep.

When Sunday morning arrived, I hurried down from the attic, relieved that Annabelle and I would be back in our own room that evening. I waited ages for Clem to get up, and after breakfast we headed to the common room. We passed the trophy room on our way. At the back of one of the cabinets was a large, empty space where the debate trophy had been.

"Whoever took it would have been risking a lot if they lugged it all the way back to their room," I said, nodding at the cabinets. "Or even direct to the crime scene."

Heybuckle only had CCTV at the entrances, which I'd found weird after my old school, where there was CCTV everywhere.

"I mean, we're not dealing with a risk-averse person here, are we?" said Clem. "This is someone who literally killed a guy – oooh, Mrs Greythorne is coming. Quick!" She shoved me towards the door, and we burst into the weak sunshine. "She'll tell me to take all my earrings out." Her feather-hair couldn't hide the whole line of earrings she had in, and even at the weekend there was a dress code her piercings were breaking.

The morning was crisp and the air filled my lungs, taking away some of the tension I still felt after sleeping in the attic. I found myself walking towards the woods. Clem was silent as we went. Although both of us had heard about the crime scene from various people, neither of us had actually been there since *it* happened.

We passed several people on our way. The trails were clearly marked, wide and well-used. Some of the athletic students used the paths to run on, early mornings and in the evenings, and the school had installed floodlights every so often, so the paths were always lit.

On the other side of the woods was a huge dip, which led down to the school boundaries. If you stood at the edge of the treeline though, you had a stunning view of the open countryside.

I expected Clem to break down when we got to the clearing in the heart of the woods, but when we reached it, she kept going.

I came to a halt, and Clem looked back.

"Why are you…? Oh," said Clem, her eyes widening. "Is this it?"

I nodded. It was a large space, with a few logs that people sat on. The tree branches locked in a canopy of green, meaning it was largely private – except for the odd person randomly walking through. Using it as a murder scene would have been very risky during the day – but less so in the evening. The school, though not far away at all, was blocked from view by the trees. There were no windows overlooking the area; absolutely no chance that anyone would see.

"What I don't get," I said, spinning slowly in a circle, "is what Hugh was doing out here."

He'd gone to dinner, then afterwards maybe hung out in his room for a bit…then something had made him choose to go outside, into the woods. And that fateful decision led to his death.

Clem shook her head hopelessly.

"Maybe we should try…" I trailed off. I'd been about to suggest we should try to recreate what had happened. But the thought made me shudder.

"Try re-enacting the crime?" Clem asked. She took a deep breath, but nodded. "Anything to figure this out."

"Do you, er…" I didn't know how to ask whether she wanted to pretend to be Hugh or the murderer in this scenario. Either option didn't scream *great!* to me.

She saved my awkwardness by plopping down on the log, facing the school.

"Right, so in this scenario, I'm walking towards you." I went a little way down the path and found a large twig lying on the ground. "And let's pretend this is the trophy. I'm walking… I'm walking… Hi there, friend!"

Clem reached the same conclusion I had. "This wouldn't make sense – you and the twig-slash-trophy. Hugh would have thought that was really weird."

"But if he was meeting someone he trusted in the woods, he wouldn't have been on his guard yet," I said, swiping the

162

twig through the air. "He'd have found it odd, but it's not like he'd have thought, *Okay, this trophy is going to be used to kill me.*"

"Right, so you have the trophy, and I ask, *Why've you got that?*" said Clem, squiggling on the log.

"And I say… *It's a prank. I'm stealing the trophy as a prank.*"

"Rubbish prank, but okay," said Clem. "So, what happens next? Do you sit or do you stand?"

There were two logs, but it wouldn't have made sense for me to go for the other one, which was right on the other side of the clearing. I sat down next to Clem, still clutching the twig.

"This is weird," I said. "This is a weird set-up – maybe if we were standing?"

We both stood up, but it was still weird.

"It would help if we knew where the trophy actually hit," I said. "Like, was it from behind or…in front."

It was something the police would know, but we weren't privy to that information.

"Let's try the other way," said Clem. "Let's pretend he was facing towards the woods."

I could sneak up behind her quite easily, my footsteps muffled by the soft ground.

"But it wouldn't have been natural for him to sit this way," I said, biting my lip as I considered the scene. "With his back to whoever it was he was meeting."

"Unless…" said Clem, looking thoughtfully at the path, which continued to wind on into the woods. "Unless he was meeting someone *coming through the woods.*"

"What do you mean?" I said, frowning. "So, someone who'd been waiting for him…in the woods?"

"No. Not someone from school. An outsider."

"How could they have got in?" I asked. "Over the school wall? Is that even possible?"

"Let's go have a look," said Clem, bouncing up enthusiastically. She seemed to think we were on to something.

Somewhere else, along a different path, floated the ghostly echoes of other students laughing.

We reached the end of the woods, where the ground fell away into a steep drop. At the bottom was the school wall. No one had ever bothered to attempt to sneak out from this side because the slope was so sheer, but I supposed it was theoretically possible to climb up from the bottom if the murderer used a ladder on the other side of the wall – but then how would they have got back out?

"But surely it couldn't have been an outsider," I said. "What about my story? If someone from outside school snuck in – how'd they get my story?"

We had hit another wall.

20

Clem had a lacrosse home game in the afternoon, so after I'd done all my prep, I went down to the playing field to watch. Even though it was now May, the grey clouds threatened to burst with rain. I stood a little away from everyone else, on a hill with a good viewpoint.

The opposing team all looked really preppy, their hair tied into buns, their burgundy kit freshly washed.

Like for most sports games here, a big crowd had gathered; there was a lot of school pride. I compared the fever to the tepid interest in sports teams at my old school in London. Grades were the most important thing there, not extracurriculars, which were poorly funded anyway.

Clem and Millie were both warming up, but Coach Tyler had seen the sense of making sure they didn't go on at the same time; Millie was a substitute.

The game began and I tried to feign interest, clapping whenever the ball was passed to Clem. The players hurtled around the pitch, their sticks slashing. My eyes glazed over.

"Hello there." A man who looked to be in his mid-thirties

stood next to me. He was wearing faded jeans and a raggedy hoodie that looked older than me. He had short brown hair, and the sort of face you'd look over if you passed him in the street. "I'm Andy Willet, private investigator."

The crowd gave an enormous groan; Kate had been brought down in a tackle, and the other team had used the opportunity to score a goal.

I stared at Andy Willet. I wondered if he'd heard all the disparaging comments floating around about him. He didn't look like a private investigator, who I thought should be someone tall and super old, wearing a suit, with a monocle or something – the type of person Mr and Mrs Van Boren would approve of.

"I believe you're Jess Choudhary?" he went on, his north London accent reminding me strongly of home.

"Yeah...how did you know?" I asked.

He smiled, then looked down at the sea of faces surrounding the lacrosse game. "Process of elimination."

Fair point. He was looking for an Indian girl watching the game – it wouldn't have taken that much investigating to find me.

"I hope you don't mind me asking you a few questions?" he carried on. "Mrs Greythorne gave her permission, and I ran it past your mother as well."

I had a feeling Mum wouldn't have taken him that seriously. She'd probably been surprised private investigators weren't just something Hollywood had made up for films.

"Yeah, that's fine," I said, feeling slightly nervous.

A shrill whistle blew; one of the opposing team had body-checked a Heybuckle girl. Clem lined up to take the penalty, and a singular *boo* hissed out from the cheering crowd, coming from Millie.

"Why aren't you doing interviews in Mrs Greythorne's office?"

Mr Willet's mouth twisted into an amused smile. "The police have insisted that space remains available to them – I do encounter a lot of hostility in my line of work, though I don't know why. Now, *I* was wondering why you're not on the lacrosse team, like Clem." He nodded at the field, where Clem, having scored the penalty, was dancing around.

"I'm not great at sports," I said.

"Lack physical coordination?" he asked.

"Something like that." I shifted from foot to foot. "Is this relevant to Hugh?"

"Well, actually, it is," he said. "See, Hugh was hit on the back of the head with the trophy..." He trailed off. "The police don't want you to know that, of course. They're treating you all like kids. But I don't like their approach – keeping information from people isn't the best tactic, I think. I find a lot of the time everyone knows *something*. Something small, you see. A single puzzle piece, that doesn't make sense on its own. But when you put it all together – ah, then you see the full picture. So, the question is, what little thing do *you* know?"

He paused, and there was a moment of silence as the whistle blew for half-time. People ran onto the field with orange slices for the players, who were all red-faced and smiling; the score was currently tied.

"Oh – er... Do you want me to respond?" I asked, as the silence stretched on.

"No, no," he said with a small smile. "Let's get back on track. The trophy in question was quite heavy. It would have required a lot of strength to lift it, even – as I suspect was the case, though of course I can't be sure – if Hugh was sitting down when he was struck."

"But why would he have been facing away from the school?" I said without thinking. "If he was waiting for someone, he'd have been facing towards it."

Mr Willet nodded, and his smile grew wider. "I can see you've considered this. Yes, if he was waiting for someone, he most certainly would have been facing towards the school."

His tone suggested…well, *something*, but I didn't know what. He moved on.

"So the first thing we have to consider about all this, is your short story," he said. "It's a massive shame there was only one copy. Quite unusual for it not to be written on a laptop, because then we would have an electronic version."

"It's Mrs Henridge's policy around creative writing. We have to handwrite it all," I said.

The whistle blew for the second half of the game.

He nodded. "Yes, I checked in with her. She's had this policy for years, through all the schools she's taught at, so that was nothing particularly new. A rather mundane but very convenient fact for our murderer. The fact that your story went *missing* is another thing."

"So it means someone in my Gifted and Talented class killed Hugh, right?" I said. For some reason, I wanted to show him that I had thought things through. "I mean, that's the logical conclusion. If Summer put it on the desk at the beginning and

168

it was gone at the end, and no one else came into the room all lesson, that means someone in my class took it and stole the details when they murdered Hugh."

"That's the *obvious* answer," said Mr Willet. "But I don't think it's the correct one." He didn't say it in a way that made me feel bad for not seeing whatever it was that he saw. It was almost like he was a teacher, who acknowledged that I didn't know everything, but that was okay, because he would help me get there. "Did you and Summer treat your writing of the short story as a secret? Where, for example, did you work on it?"

"Erm… Well, I wanted to just write my bits, and then slot them all together, but Summer wanted to actually discuss things." I tried not to roll my eyes. "She said that was the point of the assignment – for me to work with her and teach her something. So, we'd write sections and then talk about how they were all going to fit together – we worked on the ground floor of the library. It's the best place to talk and hash things out."

"And all the special details and things – the twigs and such – they were all your idea?"

The crowd reached fever-pitch as Clem scored a goal. When the cheering died down, Millie gave a loud boo again. The girls from the other school all looked at each other and smirked.

"Yes," I said, shifting again. My palms were sweating a little, like they did whenever someone brought up the short story link. "But I only added those details at the last minute. We had one final meet up before we handed it in."

"And you had this meet up in the library – where anyone could have been listening?"

I nodded. "Summer kept picking at my contribution – she really wanted me to take all that stuff out."

It was beginning to dawn on me what he was getting at: whoever had taken the details of my short story didn't necessarily have to have *read* the whole thing to be able to steal the key parts of it, especially since we'd discussed it in public several times.

Clem and I had been too narrow in the suspects we had considered.

"You'd been working on this project a while, yes?" Mr Willet went on.

"About two weeks."

"And, say…Hattie Fritter. Was *she* around when you were working on it?"

What did Hattie have to do with anything?

"Not really… Well, I mean, I'd – er – talk about it with Clem, and Hattie would be in the room." I mainly brought up the assignment with Clem to moan about Summer, but I didn't want Mr Willet to know that.

Mr Willet nodded, like he'd been expecting that answer from me. "On to the texts," he said. "And one note – Summer's."

"How do you know about that?" I asked without thinking. "Did the police tell you?"

Mr Willet smiled slightly. "I have my sources." He paused, his eyes sweeping over me, like he was trying to work something out. "As far as you know, Summer hasn't done anything… particularly *bad*, shall we say?"

"No," I said. "I mean…" I hesitated. Clem and I had decided not to tell the police about Summer's short story with Hugh as the main character. But Mr Willet wasn't the police. "There's an earlier version of the short story... Well, I don't know if it's an earlier version. Another version, where the character who gets killed is called Hugh." I was gabbling, getting flustered. "And I didn't think Hugh had done something bad – but it looks like he was killed for whatever he did. So...I guess Summer could have done something bad too?"

"Yes." Mr Willet tilted his head. "It's interesting you don't think Hugh did anything bad. You see, when Hugh's room was searched, an anonymous note was found amongst his belongings. It was printed from a computer, so of course analysis of handwriting wouldn't help us figure out who left it – no fingerprints on it either."

"What did it say?" I said, my heart starting to hammer. I didn't even need to ask – I already knew what he was going to tell me, because *what else* would a mysterious note to Hugh say?

It was possible Mr Willet saw the dread on my face, because he quirked an eyebrow.

"Essentially the same thing as the text you were sent," he said. "*You did something bad, and if you don't confess you deserve to die.*"

21

I gasped, my mind racing. My first thought was a selfish one – whoever had sent me the death threat had *followed through* with Hugh. Inspector Foster had said my death threat was an empty one, and I hadn't believed her – and I was right. I didn't know how much time had passed between Hugh getting the note and being killed – I didn't know how much longer I had to solve the case. The idea that the murderer could decide at any moment to try and kill me was worse than having a clock to race against – I could never let down my guard.

I forced away my initial panic, to focus on what this new information meant for the case. If Hugh had done something bad, then surely it was linked to his membership of the Regia Club – maybe it was something they'd made him do. And *that* was why they wanted me to stop looking – whatever it was, they wanted it all to stay secret. Maybe that was why they were putting pressure on the police as well.

"So, you see my issue here, yes?" went on Mr Willet, oblivious to the connections being made in my mind.

A collective groan rose from the field below – the other team must have scored.

"We have these texts and printed notes. Summer is adamant her blackmail message means nothing, same as you. You've told me about her own version of the short story, so now, I'm going to ask you a different question – *do you think Summer is lying?*"

"I…er… I don't think Summer has done anything so bad it's worth being murdered over." I worded my answer clumsily, because I still didn't know what to make of Summer, or why Tommy had warned me about her.

He definitely picked up on my weird wording, if his next question was anything to go by. "You wouldn't say you're friends with Summer, would you?"

"No," I said.

"Your best friend is Clem Briggs?" He nodded at the lacrosse field, where Clem's copper hair was easy to pick out amongst the blondes and brunettes.

"Yes."

"Who had been seeing Hugh since around May last year?"

"June."

"Just so. And they were serious?"

"Well, yeah." I might as well have said *duh*. My tone probably wasn't very polite. I tried to cover it up by explaining a little more. "Clem was, like, in love with him."

"How'd they first get together?"

I shrugged. "A party. Hugh's older brothers take it in turns to throw them, in their London house, and Hugh would invite people from school who were nearby."

That had included me, but I think the invitation was only extended because I was sleeping over at Clem's London town house that night. I spent the party in a corner on my own, hating the loud music, and the huge crowd of drunk people pressed together, their faces invisible in the dark. I tried dancing for a bit but felt absolutely ridiculous, so I sat in a corner until Clem stumbled over to find me and said the taxi had come to pick us up.

"But Hugh was also seeing Millie Calthrope-Newton-Rose – he only broke up with her a week before his death?" asked Mr Willet.

"*She* broke up with *him*," I said.

"Ah, yes. And I, ah, get the sense Millie and Clem don't like each other?"

The question was perfectly timed, as Millie was being told off by Coach Tyler for heckling Clem. His yells of "You need to be a team player!" were heard even over the roars of the crowd. In response, Millie tried to snap her lacrosse stick over her knee. She howled when it simply bent, then chucked it to the ground.

All in all, Mr Willet's comment was the understatement of the year.

"That's right," I said. "They definitely do not like each other."

"Do they have anything in common?"

"Erm…" I squinted at them both: Clem essentially skipping around the field, Millie standing with her arms folded and a huge scowl on her face. "They both do lacrosse?"

"No, no, I mean…personality wise."

"Well…they're both fairly confident, I guess."

"And Hugh's best friend was Tommy Poppleton?"

"Yes," I said.

"Who is also quite confident?"

"Er – yes, I guess." I didn't understand the point of these questions. Surely, he already knew the answers to all this stuff.

He seemed to sense my confusion. "It's important, in these sorts of things, to *know the victim*. Get a sense of who they were – after all, they lie at the heart of everything. And you can tell a lot about a person by who their friends are, who they choose to hang around with. Please do bear with me."

"Okay," I said, shifting again. I didn't like not knowing what was going on. Mr Willet made me feel like I was two steps behind him.

"Tommy's well-liked, isn't he?"

"Er…yeah," I said. "He's really popular."

"And who would you say were Hugh's closest friends? Besides Tommy?"

"Eddy," I said at once.

He was standing near Millie, offering her a bottle of water. She swiped, and the bottle of water crashed to the ground, next to her lacrosse stick.

"And what can you tell me about him?"

"Not much," I said. "He basically follows Millie around like a little minion."

"And has he always done that?"

"Well, no, he always used to hang around Hugh. He latches onto people." I said the words without thinking, as I watched him pick up the bottle.

"Why does he do that?"

I shrugged. "He likes to pretend he has powerful friends? Makes him feel like he's more powerful? I don't know, we hardly speak."

"Edward Japledove is an interesting one," said Mr Willet. "From what I can tell of him, he puts on a show of confidence... but underneath he's deeply insecure."

Eddy was now attempting to heckle Clem on Millie's behalf. His booming *"You SUCK!"* reached us over the sounds of the crowd.

"I don't think he's insecure," I said with a snort.

"His family has always been extremely wealthy – and they make even more money by making connections with those more talented than themselves and piggybacking on their success." Mr Willet tapped his fingers together. "What sort of student is he?"

I shrugged. "He's a weird one. I've seen him in the library quite a few times, but he always misses homework assignments and I've heard him being told off for putting in basically no effort."

Mr Willet's eyes glittered. "Has it ever occurred to you that carrying Millie's books is not the only thing he's doing? Maybe when he's been in the library, he's also been doing her homework?"

"But his grades are awful," I said. "Why would Millie even *want* him doing her homework?"

"Perhaps his bad grades are intentional – perhaps he knows he won't come top of the class... So why bother at all? Why *not* ask stupid questions in class, get a laugh out of people?

He knows he wants to go into the family business – which is simply investing in those with better ideas. *That's* what he's learning how to do."

This all seemed like a bit too much thinking for a boy currently trying to distract Clem by squirting water out of his bottle whenever she ran past.

Mr Willet half closed his eyes. "And your roommate, Annabelle – you're not close to her, are you?"

"No." I frowned. "What does that have to do with Hugh?"

"Humour me," said Mr Willet. "Why would you say you're not close to her?"

"Well, we don't really have much in common, I guess. She's erm…" I paused, not wanting to say anything too bad.

"You won't get Annabelle into trouble," said Mr Willet with a smile. "I'm not a teacher."

"She's a bit…er…loud." I figured that was the safest way to sum up Annabelle.

"A bit forceful, shall we say?" said Mr Willet.

"Yeah, I guess," I said.

"I see."

He got out a little notebook and wrote something down. I tried to look without making it obvious, and managed to get a glimpse of a few words before he snapped it shut: *Jess is not confident.*

Great. Just great. He'd interviewed me for twenty minutes and all he thought was noteworthy was *Jess is not confident*, an obvious but pointless observation. Maybe Inspector Foster *was* right about him: he might genuinely be useless. It seemed like he'd woken up one day, read a bunch of books on how to be a private detective, and then started his new career. It felt like he had gone from dropping hints that he knew lots of information to just flinging questions at me in the hope that *maybe* one of my answers just *might* reveal something.

It was a good thing I wasn't relying on him to save my scholarship, or figure out who was targeting me. Because if I was, I'd be a goner either way.

22

"It's not fair," said Clem as we pored over our books in the library. For a moment I thought she was talking about all the work we had to get through – me, a huge pile of questions for biology, her, an essay for history. "Why'd he tell you all that stuff and not me?"

She was referring to my conversation with Mr Willet. I'd, of course, told her everything we'd talked about.

"I don't think he was trying to help us," I said. "In fact, I think he might have confused himself. He had a theory Eddy might be smarter than he lets on."

Clem blinked a few times. "Eddy? The guy who asked our history teacher if it hurt to get hit by a cannon?" She shook her head. "Okay, but let's say that Mr Willet isn't completely useless. He was really interested in Eddy. We weren't looking at him before because we were focused on the murderer being in your G&T class, which now that I think about it, wasn't smart of us. We never even considered that might be a red herring."

I could hear the frustration in her voice, which mimicked how I felt. We weren't any good at solving this murder because we weren't *supposed* to need to be. It wasn't our job.

"Okay, Eddy's on the list," I said. "But…what about the Regia Club? We know they're involved somehow – they warned me off investigating, they're putting pressure on the police. How do we figure out for *sure* who's a member?" I bit my lip. We suspected Millie was involved in the club, but even guessing that hadn't helped – we couldn't do anything without proof.

Clem was shaking her head. "I don't know."

Hugh's memorial was going to be on Wednesday afternoon in the school hall. I heard rumours that Hugh's family didn't want the school to hold a memorial for him; that they didn't want anything more to do with the place where he'd died. Their reluctance explained why the memorial was happening so long after his death; his funeral had been a while ago, held at his country home. Only his family and a few of his closest friends attended. Clem had not been invited. She thought it was because his family didn't approve of her, but I gently pointed out they had likely not even been aware of her existence. As far as they knew, Millie had been his only girlfriend.

The memorial had put focus on Clem again. She skipped lunch, saying she wanted to be alone. I decided to sneak a sandwich from the dining room and take a walk in the grounds. It was an overcast day, with a few spatters of drizzle, the threat of rain in the air.

"Hey, Jess, wait!" Tommy ran up beside me. "Where're you going?"

I shrugged, swallowing a mouthful of bread. "Just on a walk."

"I saw you talking to Mr Willet at the lacrosse game," he said. "I was wondering if you could tell me what you spoke about? Be helpful to, you know...piece stuff together."

There was no reason for us not to pool our knowledge. He hadn't murdered Hugh, he wasn't in the Regia Club, and yet we were still skirting around each other. I was glad he was also on the case – I needed all the help I could get to figure this out. I kept looking over my shoulder, expecting to see a looming figure holding a trophy aloof while screaming, *You didn't confess what you did, Jess Choudhary! You must die!*

And Tommy might be really useful. Mr Willet had said it was important to know the victim and Tommy was his best friend. I had asked Clem about Hugh, of course, but apart from the one time she mentioned he had a hard time trusting people because of his parents, she always gave me the same sort of crap. *He was sweet, he was loving.* I hoped I never got to the point in my life where all I could spout was mushy stuff about my boyfriend. I couldn't reconcile the Hugh Clem talked about with the Hugh who had cheated on his girlfriend of three years, or the boy who had seemingly done something bad and been killed in the woods.

Then there was my own impression of Hugh, which clouded things as well. As I said, I never liked the guy. I resented the fact that he treated me like I was nobody. Sure, everyone else did as well, but at least they bothered to learn my name. I knew a huge part of it was that I wasn't from his world. I wasn't posh, I didn't come from money. My family's net worth was negative two, and that meant I wasn't worth his time.

I needed a third party's opinion, and it made sense to turn to

Tommy. He'd never really spoken to me either, but he'd never ignored me. He was *nice* to people. I could tell he didn't look down on me. He was just a person, and so was I.

"Only if you tell me about Hugh," I said, forcing myself to sound as assertive as I could.

His eyebrows went up in surprise. "Okay, sure."

We went past the tennis courts, where a few people were having a quick game. Their laughter followed us as we went. Because we were walking away from the main school lawn, the gravel paths were largely deserted.

I filled him in on my conversation with Mr Willet. He sucked in his cheeks thoughtfully, not making any comments until I finished.

"I can't find anything about him online, which means he hasn't had much success solving things before," he said. "Which is weird – I'd have thought the Van Borens would pay for the *best* detective, not someone who seems like he's never solved a case. Did *you* have a stalk of him?"

"No," I said, as I crumpled up the paper my sandwich had been wrapped in. "Was I supposed to?"

"Detective rule number one – always stalk the person questioning you," said Tommy with a grin as he swiped my rubbish off me and tossed it into the bin nearby. "Score." He shot me a quick look out of the corner of his eye. "What – no praise? That shot was amazing."

"You were practically in the bin when you threw it," I said. "I'd have praised you if you'd managed to miss it."

He clutched his chest, feigning hurt. Then his smile broadened. "Tough crowd."

I grinned back – his smile was infectious.

"So, what was that information worth?" he said. "What do you want to know about Hugh?"

"Hugh was your best friend," I said. "It might help me figure things out if I knew a little more about him."

Tommy stopped walking. I thought I'd upset him. Instead, he took his blazer off.

"Er – what're you doing?" I said.

"Let's sit," he said, placing his blazer on the grass beneath an old oak tree and sitting.

I made to take mine off, but he shook his head.

"It's fine – we can both fit."

So I sat beside him, feeling super aware of everything; the hairs on his arms, his large hands resting so close to mine, our fingers were almost touching.

We were behind the storage hut, where the sports equipment was kept. It was secluded, away from everyone else. Apart from the faint sounds of noise from the tennis courts – and further still, screams of laughter from the main lawn – we could have been the only two people in the world.

"What can I say about Hugh?" Tommy shook his head. "I'm giving a speech later at the memorial service, so I guess you'll hear all the good stuff then. But I've known Hugh since we were kids – our mums are in the same circles..." He stared ahead. "Were. Sorry – I can't get used to it. Talking about him in the past."

He swallowed hard, and without thinking I put my hand on his and gave it a little squeeze before letting it go again.

"His parents really screwed him up," Tommy continued, not

acknowledging my touch. "I think it would have been better for everyone if they'd just got a divorce – but image is everything to them. They didn't want people to talk." He looked at me, his green eyes sad. "Bet this sounds like every cliché you've ever heard, right? Poor little rich kid. But I was there through it all – I saw what they did to him. He had a small group of friends – he only trusted a few people. And once you were in, you were in. He'd do anything for you. He'd randomly give you gifts – it didn't need to be a special occasion, he just thought loads about his friends and wanted to make them happy. And the gifts were always so well thought out, so absolutely perfect for you as a person."

"What do you mean?" I asked.

"Well, when I went through my comic-book phase, he spent months trying to source a first edition Spider-Man I really wanted." Tommy's voice was soft as he reminisced. "When I started knitting, he bought me personalized knitting needles and more yarn than I could ever possibly need. A few months ago, he got me this set of books on football – and a joke one on rugby, because I'm embarrassingly shocking at rugby." Tommy smiled faintly. "He wasn't much of a joker, but that was him trying something new, I guess. He knew I'd never touch the rugby one, but it was a reminder of how well he knew me. He cared so, so much about the few people he let in. Sometimes I think he cared a bit too much…"

"How?" I said, as Tommy went quiet, running his fingers over the blades of grass beside him. I didn't want to upset him – I was aware of standing on some sort of cliff edge, with the rock beneath me in danger of crumbling away if I made the wrong move.

"Like with Millie. He really did love her, but he loved Clem as well. He wanted to keep them both. He didn't want to hurt Millie, I know he didn't. That's why he stayed with her, even though he was cheating – he could never have the tough conversations." Tommy furrowed his eyebrows. "I kept telling him it was wrong, but I also kept making excuses for him."

He paused, and I waited for him to go on.

"He just…he did loads of really *stupid* stuff. Like he'd get so drunk at his brothers' parties, and he'd break into his neighbour's house, or steal someone's car, or…" He shook his head. "And then he'd be so sorry about it all, and he'd be crying and apologizing – to me, to everyone. He was scared he'd do something so bad that one day his friends would leave him. And then it'd just be him, alone, in those giant houses with his parents."

I found my eyes welling up with tears, at the pain in his voice. But I also felt terrible, because I still didn't feel sorry for Hugh. He sounded as entitled as ever, making bad choices over and over and then apologizing after as if that fixed everything.

"Look, I grew up with Hugh and he was my oldest friend, my best friend, but I don't think I ever really knew him," said Tommy. "He had…well, he had something dark about him. This other side to him that I would always sort of excuse."

"I…don't understand," I said.

"That note he got." Tommy swallowed. "The one that said, *You did something bad.* Mr Willet told me about it when he was questioning me, just after you told me about yours." He gulped. "Hugh's was basically identical to your text, and that reassured me a bit. Because I just *knew* whoever sent yours was wrong.

So I thought they had to be wrong about his…"

Tommy put his warm hand on top of mine, gazing at me.

"But I've been thinking more and more about this and…" Tommy was breathing quicker now. "He did so *much* stupid stuff when he was drunk. I was there most of the time – I could look after him. But sometimes I wasn't around and… He asked me about committing crimes, once. How the police catch people, and whether older unsolved crimes are less serious than newer ones, and all this other stuff. I thought he was just asking, you know? Like a thought experiment."

"Did he ever say why he wanted to know about crimes?" I asked. "Was there any *specific* crime or…"

Tommy shook his head. "He never said." His eyebrows pinched together. "The only stuff he wouldn't tell me about was Regia Club stuff – said he swore an oath and all that. Like I said, he was loyal…"

"So could the crime have been something to do with the Regia Club?"

"I think there's a good chance of that," said Tommy.

I nodded along. "Did you tell Mr Willet this?" I said, knowing there was no point asking if he'd told the police, not if they would just hush it up because of the Regia Club connection. I wasn't even sure if there was any point asking about Mr Willet.

"Yeah," said Tommy, as he balled his hands into fists. "Mr Willet said he already knew that Hugh had committed a crime and it was all under control, but I think he was putting on a bit of an act – seems to me like he just wants to…wait for the murderer to slip up." He shook his head. "I feel like it's my fault Hugh died. He was in trouble, and I didn't see. I could have *helped*." A single tear dripped down his cheek. "I could have helped – and now… Now the only thing I can do for him is make sure his murderer doesn't get away with it – and I'm failing at that as well."

I didn't know how to comfort him, so I decided to focus on the investigation. "Er…Eddy's one of our suspects," I said. "Do you know where he was the evening Hugh was killed?"

"I can't believe Eddy's a suspect," said Tommy, wiping the tear away and sitting up straighter. "He was one of Hugh's closest friends – they never argued, not once."

"Mr Willet was interested in him," I said. "There has to be a reason. Eddy will be more likely to tell you what he was doing that evening than me."

Tommy nodded. "Okay…I'll ask him."

"Good," I said. "See? We're making progress."

He smiled.

23

Going into the school hall for Hugh's memorial service was the weirdest thing in the world. The whole school shuffled inside, speaking in muted whispers. There was none of the usual jostling and chatting, no shushing from the teachers. The podium was covered in a black sheet, and an enormous picture of a smiling Hugh was projected onto the back wall.

Clem was in the gallery, along with Millie. I bet they were sitting at opposite ends in stony silence. Even Millie wouldn't start an argument at a memorial service. I had briefly seen her on her way up the stairs to the gallery, dressed once more in head-to-toe black like she was a widow mourning her husband of eighty years. She seemed to pick and choose when to remember that she had broken up with Hugh a week before his death. Pretending that what he had done couldn't erase the years they had been together. I didn't believe anyone but Millie herself could ever really be sure what she was thinking.

I sat in the second row from the front. Annabelle was in the seat in front of me, gossiping with her friend Lucy.

"*I* heard Millie wanted to speak at this memorial," Lucy was saying, pushing her raven-black hair out of her eyes. "But given how it all ended between her and Hugh...well, you can see why they said no."

"That cow would probably expect a standing ovation after her speech," said Annabelle in response.

"It is a bit of a shame, though," said Lucy. "You have to admit that. They were together for so long. Now we all know she didn't kill him, I feel like they're sort of...brushing her to the side."

Annabelle snorted. I also felt no sympathy for Millie. I couldn't get over the way she'd tried to take pictures of the Regia Club's prank on me. Like she was *proud* of it.

"I'm not saying we should like her," Lucy continued. "But she's been through a crap time too."

I asked Clem, once, if she felt guilty about cheating with Hugh, back when they were still hiding their relationship from everyone else. We were sitting in the common room after dinner one night, chatting. I think I specifically said, *Don't you feel bad for stealing him?*

"I didn't *steal* him," said Clem. "If Hugh was happy with her, he wouldn't have wanted to be with me. And..." She'd blinked. "All I did was fall in love. And it got messy."

Hugh had walked in at that exact moment and though he didn't say a word to her, his face lit up when he looked in her direction. As he walked past, he casually dropped a note in Clem's lap. She glowed as she read it, then passed it over to me.

I spoke to my dad about your Save the Forest campaign.
He's donating some money to that charity you mentioned.
And also, you're incredible.

The handwriting was immaculately neat, of course. Like everything about Hugh.

Clem had smiled like a smug cat as she folded the note up along his precise lines, so the edges perfectly lined up.

"I only mentioned this charity once – in passing. Ages ago. I'd completely forgotten about it – and he remembered."

Despite everything else, it was clear Hugh had loved Clem. But if I was Millie, I wouldn't care about facts like *people can't be stolen*. I would hate Hugh and Clem with a burning passion.

Mrs Greythorne took to the stage, and everyone went silent. She had some cards, which she placed onto the podium in front of her.

"Welcome, all, to this most tragic assembly," she said. "In all my time as a teacher at this school, I have never borne the sadness of saying goodbye to a student. I spoke very briefly before of Hugh, and how he was a star of this school. As one of the youngest captains ever of our football team, he shouldered lots of responsibility. He contributed much to this school. I remember meeting him at thirteen and being impressed by his stoic determination to succeed. So many of his friends came forward to contribute tonight – to read poems, to tell stories about how he touched their lives. First up is Edward Japledove."

Eddy read a passage from a book.

I watched him carefully. His voice shook as he spoke and he kept having to pause to take deep gulps of air. If he was Hugh's murderer and was *acting* devastated, he was doing a really good job.

More people came up to speak, but it was Tommy I was waiting for.

He came onto the stage last. His face was pale, but he looked determined, like he'd been preparing for this moment. He was holding a few sheets of paper; even from a distance I could see they were covered in his sprawling handwriting. Carefully, he placed his notes on the podium, and cleared his throat.

"Hi, everyone," he said. He scanned the crowd, and his eyes caught mine. I nodded, in what I hoped he knew was an encouraging way. His eyes went back to his paper. "Hugh Henry Van Boren was my best friend. I've known him for fourteen years, and... And..." He swallowed. "I'm sorry. I can't do this." He looked up. It was like the entire hall was holding their breath. "I spent ages preparing this speech to give, all about how great Hugh was and what an amazing friend he was and how I'm going to miss him so, so much."

He bit his bottom lip.

"But I can't do this. I can't just...read from a piece of paper, like a few pages is enough to sum up what Hugh was to me. He wasn't perfect. He had his faults – we all do. And he had secrets too – he had regrets." Tommy took a deep breath. "But he was a person. He was the most loyal friend in the world. He would stick by you, even when you didn't want him to. Even when you just wanted him to *go away*, he wouldn't." The corner of Tommy's mouth tugged upwards.

Mrs Greythorne, standing on the side of the stage, was dabbing at her blotchy face with a handkerchief.

"You know, a lot of the time this doesn't feel real. I'll be playing a game of football and I'll watch Eddy miss an open goal and I'll just want to look over at Hugh and laugh." There were a few chuckles in the crowd. "Or I'll hear something funny, and

store it up to tell Hugh later. And for a brief moment, I forget…
I forget that I can't tell Hugh later. That there's never going to
be a later." Tommy's throat bobbed, and his voice got harder.
"And someone out there, maybe even someone in this room,
right now, knows exactly what happened to Hugh Henry Van
Boren, my best friend. Because someone in this room is the
reason he's never going to have a later."

Tommy was gripping the podium now, standing with his
legs apart like he wanted to make sure he was as grounded as
possible.

"Someone in this room decided that my best friend was
never going to get to go to university, or have his first job, or buy
his first car. And I can't stand the fact that whenever people
think of Hugh, *that's* where their minds will go. They're not
going to remember he was a person. They're not going to
remember he was the best, most loyal friend you could possibly
ask for. They're not going to remember he hated peas, and
thought Mondays were the best day of the week. They're going
to remember him as the boy in the woods. So don't let Hugh's
end blot out the rest of his life. Please. Take a moment right
now, and don't think about what happened that Tuesday night.
Just…think of Hugh as a person."

The memorial was over. Everyone was getting up to leave. I was
held up by the fact that I was right in the middle of the row,
so I had to wait for everyone else to filter out before I could go.

And then someone's phone buzzed. And so did someone
else's.

"It's a blocked number," someone said.

My blood ran cold. It was Annabelle, speaking to Lucy.

"I got a message too," said Lucy.

"Me too," said someone else.

"And me."

"Is it from the Regia Club?" asked someone.

"No – it's not signed by them."

There were whispers, as more and more people whipped out their phones. I got mine out, but I hadn't received a text.

"Who the hell is Jess...?" someone said.

I twisted around, trying to pinpoint who had spoken.

"Jess," said Annabelle, a bit too loudly. What felt like hundreds of heads all swivelled in my direction. "Is this true?"

I don't know how I found the strength to speak. "Is what true?"

Wordlessly, Annabelle passed me her phone. It was a text, from a blocked number.

I killed Hugh Henry Van Boren.
But I couldn't have done it without the help of Jess
Choudhary and Summer Johnson.
Their short story provided all the inspiration I needed.
So, thank you, girls. Thank you from the bottom of
my heart.

Bile rose in my throat. I probably would have thrown up right then and there had Mrs Greythorne not barked at everyone to get moving. The school started shuffling out, but I was locked to the spot. My legs didn't work any more.

My phone screen lit up.

One new message.

Blocked number.

With shaking fingers, I opened it.

You still haven't told the police what you did.

Consider this a last warning.

Tell the truth, or the next memorial will be for you.

24

It felt like time had stopped. Everyone was staring at me, their whispers rattling around my head. Mrs Greythorne appeared at the end of my row and gestured at me to follow her. I did so numbly, and everyone recoiled like they thought I had something contagious. The whispering continued, like leaves rustling in the wind.

I brushed past Arthur and he gripped my wrist. I was in too much shock to do anything but look at him.

"You and Summer teamed up together?" he breathed. "Best friends, aren't you? I *knew* it."

His cold blue eyes were piercing as he dropped my wrist and I felt so numb from shock I continued to shove through the crowd without saying anything. I turned around to see if he was still watching me, but the crowd swallowed him up.

Summer was already waiting in the corridor, and we followed Mrs Greythorne in silence to her office.

The office was lit with dim lamps that cast everything into shadow, the poor lighting reflecting my mood quite nicely.

The expression of shock on everyone's faces as they read

the message was burned into my mind.

Who's Jess?

It wouldn't be long until their parents found out as well. And who knew what would happen then. There would be an uproar, probably. Parents who didn't like how the school had handled the case, who felt like the world had spun out of their control, would finally have someone to pin the blame on. Summer and me being involved would feed into their sense of rightness – brown kid, poor kids, *problem* kids.

Mrs Greythorne made us ring our parents and once more I had the glorious task of telling Mum I'd had a death threat. A *second* death threat. This time it took even longer for me to calm her down, and by the time I was done reassuring her that I would be fine, I wanted to burst into tears. I kept looking at Mrs Greythorne's grim face, wondering what she was thinking.

The school board holds a lot of power. I can't forget that.

All the parents would know about the short story by morning and even though this scandal wasn't my fault, I knew it might not make any difference. I felt like I was letting Mum down. Everything she had worked for, everything she had sacrificed for me, would all be for nothing if they took my scholarship away. The late nights working so I had enough money to buy a laptop, all the Saturdays she had spent walking with me to the library so I could pick up as many books as I could carry. The times she had cried quietly in her bedroom when she thought I couldn't hear, worrying about whether she was going to be able to pay the mortgage that month. Dad had passed away when I was so small, I couldn't even remember him, so she'd been my mother and my father, doing everything for me.

I told the police I didn't *know* anything, that I had nothing to confess. I wanted reassurance from them, that they had some inkling of who was behind the messages, that they would be able to stop the nightmare.

But they couldn't give me any reassurance. They kept repeating empty words about how they were looking into every avenue and they were sorry I had received another threat. But the entire time Inspector Foster's words from before were ringing in my ears: *if they don't want me to look into it, what can I do?*

When I got back to my bedroom, it was to find a crowd of girls standing outside, chatting quietly. Annabelle was there, with Lucy, and Kate from lacrosse.

Millie was with another group of girls. Like everyone else, she went silent the second I arrived.

"What's going on?" I said, trying to avoid looking directly at Millie, as if she was Medusa and would turn me to stone.

"Miss Evans is going to be here in a second," mumbled Annabelle. She looked shocked, and her eyes were fixed on the ground. Lucy had her arm around her.

I walked to my bedroom and they all parted, leaving a clear path to the door.

I stepped in and switched on the light.

"What the…?" The words caught in my throat.

Someone had painted *MURDERER* on the wall above my bed in red paint, the edges of the letters dripping down towards my covers. At least I hoped it was paint. Surely it was paint…

I took a step back, colliding into someone. Miss Evans, my house-mother, was behind me, her mouth hanging open as she took in the graffiti.

"Regia Club?" I heard someone whisper.

"Yeah," someone else said. "They've signed it underneath."

"Wow."

"Yeah."

"Is it true though? That she's the one who killed him?"

I didn't want to hear any more.

"Girls, please go to bed," said Miss Evans.

The other girls continued to hover, as Millie folded her arms.

"I'm going to be speaking to my parents about *her*." Millie nodded at me. "I don't feel safe with her in my school – not after everything else that has happened. With…with Hugh." Her voice cracked on the last word and she covered her face with her hands. One of her friends hugged her, but as she pulled away, she flashed an enormous smile right at me before once more pretending to sob.

My blood started to boil, because she *knew* something. She *knew* who had written on my bedroom wall – hell, she was probably more than just a member of the Regia Club. She was probably its brand-new leader.

"Please go to your room, Millie, and I'll come and speak with you in a moment, okay?" said Miss Evans, her voice soothing.

Millie nodded, and now there were actual tears rolling down her face. Everyone looked really concerned and I didn't understand how they couldn't see she was faking it.

Miss Evans waited for the corridor to empty, leaving me and Annabelle behind.

"I'll...I'll get maintenance to paint over it and I'll speak to Mrs Greythorne about this. Bullying is intolerable—"

But I didn't want it going any further. I didn't want to be blamed for any more scandals, even though none of this was my fault. Whoever had walked into my room and written this on my wall absolutely wouldn't get caught. Even if they *were*, they would just hide behind the Regia Club.

They could get away with murder if they wanted to.

Wherever I went the next day there were whispers and people craning their necks to stare at me. I felt like I was on display at the zoo.

In maths, Arthur didn't say anything to me, which could only be a good thing. The tightness of his grip around my wrist as I left the memorial remained lodged in my mind. I didn't understand his anger – he hadn't even been friends with Hugh.

"Hey, murderer," whispered Millie in chemistry, as she walked past me to take her seat. She looked back at me and winked, clicking her tongue against her teeth as she smiled. "This is why people like you don't belong at Heybuckle. I've always said we shouldn't have to mix with the...poors." She lingered on the last word, and I wondered if she wanted to say something else.

Clem kept telling me to ignore everyone's staring, glaring at everyone who was whispering as we went by. But she couldn't say anything to make me feel better.

We were already inside the dining hall for lunch, when Clem remembered she had a lacrosse match at another school that afternoon, and was supposed to be with the rest of the team getting ready to leave. She swore and sped off, leaving me standing alone with a jacket potato on a tray and the eyes of what felt like the entire school on me.

I considered tossing my food and hurrying from the room, but I figured that would probably draw more attention. Instead, I scanned the polished tables, hoping to find some dark hole I could crawl into.

My eyes landed on Summer, sitting apart from everyone else. For the first time in my life, relief surged through me at the sight of her. Before, every interaction between us had been tainted by the fact that we were both scholarship students. In some way, I think Summer took that as competition. She needed more than just the validation of getting a rare scholarship to one of the most prestigious schools in the country. She needed to be the absolute *best* of us.

That might have been why she was so critical of my short story. She didn't have much of an imagination and wanted to shoot down my suggestions, knowing she couldn't come up with anything like that herself. I had wanted to show off what I could do. Even with someone who I should have seen as my equal, I was *still* fighting to prove my place. Maybe Summer and I had more in common than I thought.

And now, she was the only person in the world who knew what I was going through. I'd been so shocked by the text yesterday, I hadn't even considered she would also be worried about losing her scholarship.

Maybe, together, we could finally figure out who had killed Hugh and was also so intent on messing up our lives in the process.

I took a deep breath, swallowed, and summoned up all the courage I had. As I marched across the room towards her table, I ignored the muttering following me. I kept my back straight, my head held high, and sat down next to Summer.

I expected her to tell me to get lost. Instead, she blinked at me, and offered a tiny, tight smile.

"You know, if we sit together, everyone is definitely going to think we plotted something," she said. "And we'll let them. I heard about someone painting *murderer* on your wall."

I nodded, looking around as she spoke just in case anyone was listening in. But we were sitting far away from everyone else, and the only person looking in our direction was Arthur. His eyes met mine for a second, before he turned back to his food.

"They're all stupid," said Summer. "As far as I'm concerned, everyone in this school can take their gossip and stick it up their overprivileged arses."

I tried to hold back a smile, but Summer caught on.

"I could say a lot worse, you know – especially about *certain* people." She turned around and glared at Hattie, who was sitting at the next table over.

"What's, er, going on?" I said, as I took a bite of food.

"Hattie and I broke up again," said Summer unconcernedly.

I almost choked on my potato. "I didn't know you two were together?"

"Third break-up in three months," said Summer, and she almost sounded proud. She peered at me. "You did know I'm gay, right?"

No. "Er – yes." The truth was, before all this mess with

Hugh, I'd probably paid as much attention to the other students as they had to me. "So, why'd you break up?"

Summer gave a small chuckle. "Well, in case you haven't heard, there's this short story I helped write..."

She started laughing, and I couldn't help it – I laughed as well.

And, just like that, I became friends with Summer Johnson.

25

Once afternoon lessons were finished, Summer and I sat together in the common room. We weren't a band of two for long, however. Tommy came and sat down next to me. My heart fluttered as he grinned at me. How did everyone else manage to speak to him without wanting to throw up?

"How's it going?" he said, ignoring the curious looks he was getting from the rest of the room.

"Er…" I said, trying to keep my voice level. "Things could probably be worse."

"Everything is great," Summer said, her voice coming out unnaturally bright. She squirmed slightly in her armchair, and tension crackled between her and Tommy.

Watch out for Summer.

Tommy's eyes lingered on Summer as she determinedly looked down at the ground. He seemed to be debating saying something to her, but then decided against it and turned to look at me. "I wanted to see if you were okay earlier, but Clem said you wanted to be left alone."

I could have killed Clem. Sure, she was just looking out

for me, but also *Tommy* had wanted to speak to me.

"So, I guess Summer's on the team now?" said Tommy. He leaned back, resting his arms on the back of the couch. His arm went past me, but he didn't seem to have noticed. "To try and crack the case?"

His words seemed to make Summer relax, which I thought was interesting. She'd been expecting him to talk about something else – not about the investigation.

"Well, apart from the fact that we have absolutely nothing in terms of leads or theories," said Summer, her voice sounding much more normal now. "None of this makes any *sense*. It's not logical at all – it's literally like Jess's short story. Everything seems wildly thrown in. If I could only crack the code, everything would slot into place."

I took a deep breath. If I was going to trust Summer, properly trust her, I needed to confront her about her alternative short story with Hugh as the victim – and the death threat she'd received. I needed the truth from her.

"Summer...you know you received a death threat?" I began as casually as I could.

Summer's eyes locked onto me.

"Yes," said Summer. "I got one, you got two."

"Er..." I cleared my throat. "Why did you wait to tell the police about it?"

"Because—" Summer's eyebrows twitched together. "Wait, how do you know I didn't tell them straight away?"

"You also wrote a short story," I said carefully, deciding to ignore her question. "With a main character called Hugh..."

Summer's hands tightened around the arms of her chair.

"It was *you* in my room. How intrusive. What were you *doing*—"

"So my methods aren't the best," I interrupted, thinking I should probably leave out the fact Clem had also been with me. "But you were a suspect – and that short story with Hugh's name doesn't make you sound innocent…"

"What short story with Hugh's name?" said Tommy, looking from Summer to me.

Summer kept her eyes locked on mine.

"We had the assignment for Gifted and Talented, and I wanted to get working straight away. And all the books I read on how to write creatively said I should try and draw inspiration from real life – and I didn't like Hugh, so I used his name in a murder story."

Summer shrugged, but her red cheeks betrayed her. "You know – cathartic. I'd never have done it if I'd known what was going to happen to him." She paused. "And then you did the second draft of the story and added in all those details like the trophy and stuff. I did tell the police everything, you know. Eventually."

"So why'd you wait?" I pressed.

"Why'd you think?" snapped Summer. "It would have made me look guilty as hell and I didn't exactly have a great alibi for his murder…" She sucked in her cheeks. "You know. Because I was alone in my room."

I still didn't believe Summer had spent the evening in her room studying when she could have been in the library, but I was more convinced than ever that she hadn't killed Hugh.

"But why did you hate Hugh so much?" I asked.

To my surprise, Summer turned to look at Tommy.

"Go on," she said. "Tell her."

He raised his eyebrows.

"We need to work together on this," said Summer. "And we can't do that if you both think I'm a murderer. So go on, Tommy. Tell Jess my deep dark secret. It's a good one."

Tommy drummed his fingers on the table. "The science fair last term. I spent months working on my project and it was decent—"

"It was incredible," interrupted Summer. "You absolutely smashed it, like you do with all science stuff."

"But the night before the competition, someone completely destroyed my project and I came dead last," Tommy continued, waving off Summer's compliment.

"And I won," said Summer, her eyes flashing.

It took me a second to work out what she meant.

"Summer... You sabotaged Tommy's project?" I gasped, looking from her to Tommy. "And, Tommy – you *knew*? Why didn't you report it?"

"Because he's a good guy, isn't he?" said Summer, narrowing her eyes in a way that suggested she didn't think that was true. "I hadn't done so well in my English exams, and I was worried the scholarship committee might start thinking I wasn't...you know, exemplary enough. I thought doing well in that science fair would make up for it, show them my strengths really do lie in other areas."

A flash of understanding passed between us. Even before this whole murder thing, we had the same pressures on us. Heybuckle was an incredible school and coming here was a huge opportunity for us. But they had never made it easy for scholarship kids to stay. We had a much bigger burden on us, greater expectations compared to everyone else – and so much more to lose.

I wished I had become friends with Summer sooner. I might have felt less alone. All it took was a murder to bring us together.

"Anyway," continued Summer. "Like I said, Tommy is a *good* guy. Just the best. All his friends trust him and he trusts all of them." Her voice was deeply bitter, and Tommy's eyes narrowed at her. I was missing something.

"I don't get it," I said.

"Tommy didn't tell any of the teachers about what I did, but he couldn't just keep it to himself," said Summer. "He told Hugh. And the little git tried to blackmail me—"

"Oi," snapped Tommy, glaring at Summer.

"*Sorry*," Summer said theatrically and held up her hands. "The *delightful little twerp* started asking me to do his homework. Knew that if he ratted on me, I'd lose my scholarship. Tommy, how did you not know the type of person Hugh was? How could you have been *friends* with someone like him?"

"He was a good guy, underneath it all," said Tommy, his voice cracking slightly. "He's always been there for me, no matter what. We grew up together, we were basically brothers."

"That's your problem, Tommy Poppleton," said Summer. "Just because things are easy for *you* doesn't mean they're easy. Just because people are good to *you* doesn't mean they're good. You can't close your eyes and then claim ignorance – people who *let* bad stuff happen are just as bad as the people who *do* bad stuff."

Tommy stared at her, and I thought he would argue back. Instead, his shoulders slumped.

"I know," he said. "I hated the Regia Club and even though

I knew Hugh was in it, I let him tell me it wasn't as bad as I thought – that's what I wanted to hear. But honestly, I never thought I was shutting my eyes. It wasn't until Jess asked me how I could be okay with the way Eddy boasts about people, and I told her he'd never boasted around *me*, that I realized what I was doing. I'm trying to be better, I am."

He looked deflated, his eyes fixed on a point on the ground. I shook my head. We'd got off track. I turned back to Summer.

"All you've done is tell me exactly why you had a motive to kill Hugh – you still haven't told me what you were doing the evening he was murdered." I folded my arms, wondering what sort of game she was playing, if she was trying to distract us on purpose.

She sighed.

"If I tell you what I was doing…you can't tell anyone. Not the police or Mr Willet or any of the teachers." She raised her eyebrows. "Promise?"

Just how many secrets did she have? I didn't want to promise before I knew what she was going to tell me, but Tommy was already nodding and I felt like I had no choice but to agree as well.

"I wanted to get Hugh back. And I just *knew* he was part of the Regia Club—"

"How'd *you* know that?" I interrupted. I'd needed Tommy to tell me and she'd figured it out on her own.

"How could he not be?" said Summer, rolling her eyes. "If you think about it logically, there's a finite list of people in school who *could* be members – there's not actually that many people who come from generational wealth and whose families are still super rich now. Plus, you also have to be pretty smart to be a member – smart enough to make sure you're not caught. And the most important members will be the older ones – it means I could discount people in the younger year groups." She counted off the points on her fingers. "All that put together meant Hugh was a shoo-in for the club, but obviously I had no actual *proof*. And that's the genius of the Regia Club – they've got defined rules for membership, you can narrow down the list to certain people all you want, but without any *proof*, what do you have? Just gossip and rumours. You can't bring down an institution that's hundreds of years old with that."

I exchanged a look with Tommy, wondering where exactly Summer was going with her story.

"Anyway, I was trying to get Hugh back by exposing his membership," said Summer. "I did my research, looking over archived stories about the Regia Club in the school newspaper from years and years ago. They were a bit laxer back then, I think – no social media to make it easier to catch people. One of the stories said the club kept minutes of their meetings, which set out exactly what pranks they pulled. I knew if I had the minutes, I would have actual, concrete proof I could leak to the press – think of the scandal. Exposing the super elite and how all the powerful ex-members across the country got their head starts by pulling wild pranks in school. It would've been shut down in days. I thought Hugh was the leader and assumed he would have the minutes book, so I..." She trailed off, flushing red.

"You were looking through Hugh's stuff the evening he was murdered?" I said, and I whistled because if you tried to imagine the worst possible thing Summer could have been doing, that was probably up there at number one (beyond being the person who actually killed him). But at the same time, I could see exactly why she had lied about her alibi, and also that I could definitely trust her. She wouldn't have told me or Tommy about any of this if it wasn't the truth because it made her look awful.

Tommy nibbled his bottom lip as he looked at Summer. "And did you find anything in Hugh's room?" he asked.

She shook her head. "If he wasn't the leader, it makes sense that he didn't have the minutes book. The leader would have it."

"It's Millie," I said. "It has to be – they were together for years. A twisted couple."

"Okay, so let's focus on the murder," said Tommy. He lowered his voice. "I asked Eddy where he was that evening. There's about half an hour unaccounted for – he says he was in his room, calling his mum. The rest of the time he was hanging out in the common room... Loads of people saw him."

"Do we think he had enough time to get to the woods and back in that half hour?" I asked.

Tommy grimaced. "At a push...yes. But he'd have had to be *sprinting* – it would have been really, really tight. And he's not much of a runner – it's why he sucks at football."

"Wait, why are we interested in Eddy?" asked Summer. "There's no motive, surely?"

"Mr Willet asked a few questions about him," I said. "And he's *supposed* to be the expert, so there has to be a reason for that."

Summer snorted. "He asked me how long Millie's been in the drama club – I think he just likes asking whatever random question pops up in his head."

I thought back to other things Mr Willet had said. He'd mentioned it was important to get a sense of who the victim was.

My issue was that five different versions of Hugh were currently floating around in my head. There was the arrogant Hugh I knew, who never paid me any attention. There was the Hugh Clem knew, who had been sweet and loving. There was the Hugh Tommy knew, who'd cared so intensely about his friends. There was the Hugh who'd secretly been part of the Regia Club and blackmailed Summer by threatening to get her scholarship taken away. And there was the Hugh who'd been killed.

I sat back – something wasn't right with the image of Hugh I had painted in my mind. It was an instinct, a *feeling* of something wrong, something I couldn't explain. It was the same instinct that helped me in English class, which got me re-reading passages in books to analyse them more closely.

Hugh had been hiding something about a crime from Tommy. It wouldn't have been unusual for someone to hide that they'd committed a crime, except Hugh had told Tommy everything – even the fact he was in the Regia Club: something he wasn't supposed to tell anyone.

He knew Tommy. He *trusted* Tommy – he *surely* would have told Tommy.

Maybe…he'd wanted to tell Tommy but hadn't for some reason…

"He could never have the tough conversations," I whispered.

Tommy frowned at me.

"What?" he said.

"You told me that Hugh could never have tough conversations with people," I said. "That's why he didn't break up with Millie – he waited until she found out about his cheating on her own

211

so *she* would break up with *him*. So maybe he couldn't just *tell* you about the crime he'd committed – maybe…maybe he gave you something so you could find out on your own, without him having to tell you?"

"Like what?" demanded Summer. "Did Hugh give you a diary or something, Tommy?"

"Er…I think I would remember," said Tommy, scratching his head. "Hugh gave me loads of stuff…"

"Did you keep it all?" I asked.

He nodded. "Yeah. It's all in my room."

"Let's go have a look," I said.

Tommy had his own room, since he was a sports deputy (now captain, after Hugh's death). The room, though pretty much identical to everyone else's, was somehow super boy-like. A football sat in a corner, and on the wooden board above his bed he had posters of various football players, alongside a few pictures of his friends at football games, as well as photos of his family – there was one of him with an old lady, who I guessed was his grandma. Football scarves hung from the walls, a half-finished knitting project was piled up on his desk.

The room was messy too; papers scattered over his desk, his armchair hidden under a pile of clothes. Ironic, that Hugh had been so focused on tidiness, yet his best friend and Clem were both huge slobs.

Tommy had lined up his books and comics against the wall – from the looks of it, the books were a mixture of sports biographies and thrillers.

"Hugh gave you that Spider-Man comic," I remembered. "And knitting needles…and that rugby book as a joke."

"Hugh didn't make jokes," snorted Summer. "He wouldn't know a good joke if it slapped him in the—"

"Right," I interrupted. "Tommy, where's that rugby book?"

He looked confused as he selected a thin volume from his collection and opened it up. It was a little tired; a few of the pages were dog-eared, and Tommy wasn't particularly gentle with the rest of them as he flicked through.

"Er – what am I supposed to be searching for?" he said. But then he stopped, frowning. "There's a random newspaper article paperclipped in here…" He lifted it out, and as his eyes scanned the page, the colour disappeared from his face.

"What's wrong?" I gently prised the clipping from his fingers.

Summer stood next to me, looking at the article.

The headline jumped out immediately.

WOMAN KILLED IN HIT AND RUN

I scanned the article. *The incident happened in Richmond, London, in the early hours of the morning of 16th July…*

Hugh's London home was in Richmond.

He'd get so drunk, Tommy had said. *He was in trouble, and I didn't see.*

Tommy and I were wordlessly staring at each other.

We had discovered why Hugh was asking about crimes before his death: he had killed someone.

26

We immediately did an internet stalk to see what we could find out, which wasn't much. The woman who had been killed was called Katherine Smith, but it was such a common name we had no luck trying to track her down on social media. There was a small, grainy photo of her in the article, but that didn't help.

"Woah," said Summer, squinting at her phone. "I think I've found something...weird."

"What?" Tommy and I said in unison.

"Someone wrote an article about unexplained murders. One of those clickbait things, but Katherine Smith is mentioned – hit-and-run in London, the date matches up. It has to be her. Says a few weeks after her death, someone left a book at her grave with a bunch of love poems – and inside the book, someone wrote *I promise you, I'll avenge you.*"

"Intense," I muttered.

Tommy's face had been pale since we'd found out about Katherine Smith, but he looked at me and his mouth twitched slightly.

"It must have been someone in love with her," said Summer.

"So, an adult. What if they tracked Hugh down to Heybuckle and killed him? What if the Regia Club *doesn't* have anything to do with the murder – but they're putting pressure on the police to not investigate properly because it might come out that Hugh was a member, and they don't want him associated with them?"

I remembered how I had briefly considered the possibility that an outsider had snuck in and out of school to murder Hugh.

"The security here is really tight – there's no way a random person could just waltz in," I said. "And there's the issue of our short story inspiring the murder."

"It doesn't need to be a random person though," said Summer. "It could be any of the teachers…"

"Doesn't need to be an adult," I said, scanning the article again. "Katherine Smith was in her mid-forties. She could have a son or daughter at Heybuckle – the love poems don't have to have been romantic ones."

We went around in circles a few times, before working out we weren't going to get any further on our own – but this had to be the key to cracking the case. We had to tell someone. I wanted to skip the police and go straight to Mr Willet with the information. But when we asked Mrs Greythorne to contact him for us, she said we should tell Inspector Foster first, since she was already in school for her own investigation. Mr Willet would come and speak to us tomorrow.

Inspector Foster took the newspaper article off us. Her eyebrows flicked up in surprise for the briefest of seconds, but other than that she didn't give away what she was thinking.

Mrs Greythorne made Summer and me stay behind in her

office after the meeting with Inspector Foster. The door closed behind Tommy with a gentle thud.

"The school board are itching for something to be done about this whole situation," Mrs Greythorne said as she sat behind her desk. She interlocked her fingers, resting her hands on the varnished wood. "I've told them again and again that you two are also victims, but the terms of your scholarship state you must maintain exemplary behaviour and they're really not sure being linked with this whole affair is…exemplary."

"What're you saying, miss?" said Summer. "Are we being kicked out?" Her voice was oddly calm, which was good, because I couldn't have managed a word. She sounded like she had been preparing for this moment.

"The school board wants action," said Mrs Greythorne. "They're not so worried about answers. They'll be convening just before half term in a few weeks to discuss your places at this school."

Something inside me snapped. *I* had found something out about the case. I had figured out Tommy might hold a clue. The school board had money, which meant they thought they were better than us, but it wasn't *money* that had made the breakthrough, or the police or Mr Willet. It was me.

"We got these scholarships because we deserve them, and *no one* is going to take them away from us," I said. It was the first time I'd ever said that out loud: *I deserve my scholarship. I deserve to be here.* Because why the hell *didn't* I deserve to be here? Why should anyone have the power to tell me I didn't? "We're going to figure out who did this. The school board isn't blaming us. I won't let them."

My heart fluttered and I panted, like I'd been running. I half wanted a round of applause to follow my big speech. Instead Summer stared at the ground and Mrs Greythorne blinked at me.

"Miss Choudhary, I'm sure the police are grateful to you and your friends for your help, but perhaps you should leave this to the experts. They'll figure everything out and when they do, the school board will back off…"

I didn't listen to the rest of her soothing speech about how amazing the police were. Rage boiled inside me. My scholarship came with vague terms, like *must continue to maintain exemplary behaviour*. I hadn't realized that made it easier for the school board to use me as a scapegoat if they needed one.

Summer and I nodded, and we left her office without another word.

There was half an hour before dinner. Clem should have been back from her lacrosse match by now, but none of my messages were delivering to her so I guessed she'd been delayed and was currently somewhere with poor signal.

I lay down on my bed, careful to avoid looking at my freshly painted wall – the school hadn't been able to source the exact shade of cream as the rest of my bedroom, and they'd needed to go over the bright red MURDERER several times before it disappeared. It meant there was now a dark patch next to my bed, forever reminding me of the word that had been painted beneath.

My rage at the school board had given way to cold fear,

twisting my insides. I had nothing to do with this murder and yet I'd been dragged into it against my will. And now we had just under three weeks to solve this case before the school board gathered – worse still, I might not even *have* three weeks left if the murderer was serious about their death threats.

My phone bleeped. I flipped it over to find a message from an anonymous number. My stomach swooped as I clicked it open, expecting to see another death threat.

Hello Jess,
Time to do the Regia Club proud – wear a paper mask
of dearly departed Hugh Henry Van Boren's face
to dinner.
S.R.

I frowned as I sat up, rereading the text. This anonymous message wasn't like the *thank you for the inspiration* text, or the death threats. It was a classic Regia Club prank – with a dark twist.

Well, screw them.

If I was only going to be at Heybuckle for a few more weeks anyway, I didn't care about forfeiting the dare.

My righteous anger carried me to dinner with my head held high, my back straight as I scanned the crowds of Heybuckle students, trying to see if anyone was paying me any special attention. It was hard because I was still the subject of gossip and rumours and loads of people turned to look at me before going back to their conversations.

I ate quickly, waiting for the retaliation for my failed dare.

When it was clear nothing was going to happen in the dining room, I went back to my bedroom. Time to find out what the forfeit was. My scholarship had already been threatened – and my life. How would the Regia Club step up?

My phone bleeped, and I got it out to look at the message flashing up.

Dare failed.

My phone bleeped again.

Jess Choudhary has forfeited a Regia Club dare.
As punishment, we can reveal that she and her family are so poor they've had to use food banks. You can take the girl out of the slums...

I stared at the screen. Obviously, this message would have gone to every single person in the school. But *this* was how the Regia Club punished people who forfeited pranks? A bubble of laughter burst out of my throat. I might have felt inadequate compared to everyone else at Heybuckle, desperate to blend in and prove I belonged. But I was never *ashamed* of where I came from. I never pretended to be anything other than a scholarship student from a poor area of London.

All this text did was say more about the sender and what they valued than it did about me – especially the slums comment.

Could the Regia Club be capable of murder if *this* was their forfeit? Or had they simply misjudged the impact it would have on me?

What exactly was their goal?

The door to my bedroom opened and Annabelle walked in, clutching her phone, her hair puffed up with hairspray like one of her favourite celebrities, her eyes outlined with thick, black eyeliner. I expected her to make some sort of catty remark, but instead she looked slightly shocked.

"You *forfeited* a Regia Club dare?" she said, blinking at me. "How could you *forfeit* a dare?"

My feeling of righteousness was back. "Because they can't tell me what to do."

I waited, expecting Annabelle to make a remark on the food banks thing. But she didn't. She just shook her head again, still blinking rapidly.

Clem came to find me in my room, just before lights out. She was spattered in mud and dripping with sweat. Annabelle had gone for one of her long, hot showers about ten minutes ago, but I bet she had been caught up gossiping with someone.

"What's this stuff I heard about the Regia Club?" Clem said, very out of breath. She'd clearly run from the lacrosse team bus to my bedroom.

"How was the match?" I asked.

Clem waved her hand. "Got called off because it started pouring and we were all basically sliding around in mud – and the bus broke down on the way back and we had no phone reception and we had to hike miles and miles. When I got back everyone said…"

I filled her in and she shook her head, a smile slowly

spreading across her face.

"That was amazing of you, Jess. Like, properly."

She looked like she wanted to give me a hug, and because I didn't particularly want to be smeared in mud and sweat, I took a sharp step back.

"You know, besides the whole drowning in a torrent of rain thing, it was a productive afternoon. I got invited to the Helker party in the holidays. I can die happy," she said with a sigh.

My stomach lurched. With the Regia Club message, I had forgotten that she didn't know about Hugh's hit-and-run.

"Er… There's something I need to tell you."

She must have caught the gravity of my tone, because she sat up, looking concerned. "What's wrong?"

I showed her a photo of the article on my phone.

"It was Hugh," I said softly.

I'll never forget the expression on her face as she read, all the joy sucked away.

"How did you…how'd you find this out?" she said, her voice shaking.

"Hugh slotted a newspaper clipping into a book he gave Tommy," I said carefully. "I think he wanted Tommy to know, but was too ashamed to tell him outright…"

Clem closed her eyes and took a deep breath. "It's not true. It's not… It's not…" Tears poured down her cheeks.

I forgot all about the mud and sweat as I stepped forwards to hug her and she sobbed into my shoulder.

We sat together in silence for ten minutes before Clem pulled away. "Let me see that article again," she said. She stared at it, then frowned as she zoomed in. "It's weird…I…I feel like

I've…like I've *seen* this woman before."

"Katherine Smith?" I asked, leaning forwards.

Clem nodded, rubbing at the tear tracks on her cheeks. "Maybe she's got one of those faces or something… But I don't know – I think I've seen her picture before. Somewhere in school?"

"Like on a teacher's desk?" I said eagerly. "Or in someone's room?"

Clem was shaking her head, looking frustrated. "I don't know – I'm *sure* I've seen her photo somewhere – but maybe it's just someone else who looks a bit like her or something?" She continued to stare at the article, her eyebrows drawn together and a troubled look on her face.

I squinted at the article, but Katherine Smith's face was unfamiliar. Where would Clem have seen her in school that I hadn't?

27

Mr Willet arrived at school the next day and asked to see Clem and me after lunch. I guess he knew Clem wouldn't want to speak to him on her own.

Clem hadn't said much since she'd seen the newspaper clipping. I didn't know what to say to cheer her up, and I think it would have been worse if I'd tried.

In Clem's defence, she handled the revelation that Hugh had killed someone better than Tommy, who skipped all our morning classes. At least Clem turned up, even if she did just sit in the corner and stare into space.

Millie dropped a banana and an apple on my desk.

"Doing my charity for the year," she said with a glint in her eyes.

I stared back at her in silence, and it seemed to unnerve her. For a moment her smile flickered, as she looked across at Clem. If she wanted a reaction, she wasn't going to get one: Clem was still staring blankly ahead, not registering Millie at all.

* * *

Mr Willet had commandeered a disused classroom near Mrs Greythorne's office for the purposes of the meeting. White sheets covered the majority of the furniture, but he had dragged out three dusty chairs and arranged them in a circle in the middle of the room. He was wearing yet another faded hoodie and jeans, this time paired with trainers that might once have been white but were now a dirty grey. He had stubble all over his face, looking slightly more unkempt compared to the last time I had seen him.

"I spoke to Millie earlier," Mr Willet said, launching straight in. "She said she had no idea about Hugh's...accident. Did you?"

"No," said Clem. She got up, paced around the room once, and then sat back down again. "I just don't understand...the Hugh I knew..."

Mr Willet gulped from a bottle of water, before placing it on the floor. "I once worked on a case where a husband and wife had been married for something like fifteen years. They were perfectly happy, until one day the wife went down into the husband's man cave – as he called it – because she was looking for something. And, to her horror, she found the chopped-up bodies of, well...I *think* they were strangers. The husband had this fascination, you see, with killing. He described it as like an itch..."

Both Clem and I gaped at him. Was there a *point* to this horror story, or did he just wait for any excuse to whip out the husband-chops-up-strangers-and-hides-them-in-his-basement tale? A vision of Mr Willet at a dinner party flashed across my mind, with him calmly telling this story over mini burgers and quiches and things small enough to spear on a stick, while everyone else ran away screaming.

"I suppose that case taught me that people can have all kinds of secrets, even the people you think you know well," finished Mr Willet. "And it also taught me that people are capable of doing the most terrible things. Even those we love." He spoke gently, his kindly eyes fixed on Clem.

"Er... Sir," I said, deciding it was high time to do my duty as a best friend and step in so Clem wouldn't have to speak. "What questions did you have for Clem?"

Mr Willet tilted his head. "Tommy has helped me with my investigation so much, with all the titbits he shared about Hugh. As we've seen with this newspaper article, Tommy knew something even if I didn't figure out what. The question is..." Mr Willet frowned at Clem. "What do *you* know?"

"If I knew that, you don't think I would have told you?" snapped Clem, her eyebrows furrowing together. "I don't know, okay? I don't know anything – I don't know who killed Hugh, and it looks like I didn't even know Hugh."

"I think you do know something," said Mr Willet. "And when the right time comes, you'll be able to figure out exactly what that something is. There's some knowledge in that head of yours that'll help us crack this."

Clem scratched her head, her nose wrinkling as she looked over at the open window. She frowned, her back straightening. "Did you see that?"

"See what?" I said, sharing a concerned look with Mr Willet.

Clem got to her feet, flinging the window wide open. The classroom was on the ground floor, overlooking the school playing fields. A gym class was taking place, with students dribbling footballs across the grass.

Even from a distance, the shrill sound of Coach Tyler's whistle echoed around the room. I thought that maybe Clem had seen a particularly great manoeuvre from one of the kids on the playing field and wanted to get a closer look. She stuck her head out the window. When she leaned back into the room she was shaking.

"There was someone listening to us," she said, clenching her hands into fists. "I saw someone looking in the window."

"Er…well, if someone was listening, they wouldn't have heard anything useful," I said.

All we'd discussed was that Clem had to know something about the case. But all the same, a shudder went through me – someone was following us. Someone was *watching* us.

And we couldn't get away.

Tuesdays didn't get enough credit for how incredibly crap they were as a day. With Mondays, sure the weekend was over and that sucked, but a brand-new week stretched ahead again, full of possibility. Wednesdays meant the week was halfway over; Thursdays meant Friday was around the corner – Friday to Sunday were self-explanatory.

But Tuesdays? They were the worst. All the shiny sheen of Monday had worn off, to reveal that *yes*, this week would be just as long and boring as the last.

And like I said, Hugh Henry Van Boren was killed on a Tuesday. So whenever one rolled around and I sat down in

G&T, I always thought about the last time I had seen him properly. We had looked out the window and seen Clem and Millie fighting over him, two girls who had loved him, and two girls whose hearts had been broken by him.

Only during this G&T class, I looked out of the window and saw Millie barking orders at her teammates – no Clem. I frowned, wondering where she was, but the sound of Summer and Tommy having a heated discussion about who they'd want on their teams in a zombie apocalypse distracted me. (Summer: scientists, so she'd be the first one to be given the cure; Tommy: trained military; me: no one because there was always a risk someone would turn into a zombie and eat me.) Annabelle was occasionally butting in with cutting comments, like she didn't want to get involved but couldn't seem to help herself from presenting an opinion. Arthur was sitting by himself as usual, though his cold eyes constantly flicked over to us.

Mrs Henridge was sitting at the front of the class, marking papers. I guess she thought if we weren't too loud, she didn't need to tell us to get on with our work – or else she thought the zombie discussion was a good use of our apparent talents.

The door opened and Mrs Greythorne's assistant peeked in. "Is Jess Choudhary in here, please?"

"Er…" I raised my hand.

She nodded at me. "Please could you go to Mrs Greythorne's office?" she said.

"What's it about?" said Summer.

"Not your concern, Miss Johnson," said Mrs Henridge without looking up.

I swung my bag over my shoulder. My heart thudded a little, my imagination going into overdrive. Had the murderer tried to poison my bedsheets or something, and been thwarted before they actually managed to kill me? They were still after me – they could follow through on their death threat at any time.

Or else…maybe Heybuckle had decided to take my scholarship away. We hadn't even had the *chance* to make further progress – I still had two weeks left before the school board's meeting.

I wondered what questions the police had for me now, but as I entered Mrs Greythorne's office, it wasn't to find Inspector Foster waiting for me. Instead, in a strange turn of events, Mrs Greythorne was sitting at her own desk.

"What's wrong?" I asked, as I sat down opposite her.

Mrs Greythorne's face was bloodless. "Mint?" she said, as she held out a small metal tin with shaking hands.

"No, I'm all right," I said, as she prised the lid open and popped one in her mouth. She sucked on the mint, still staring at me in silence. "Er – is everything okay, miss?"

"Clem," she said, as she swallowed what must have been a still fairly large mint. "It's Clem Briggs."

There was a roaring in my ears. I was glad I was already sitting down, because the ground seemed to be swaying beneath my feet. I didn't like the way Mrs Greythorne's voice trembled.

"What's happened?" I gripped the chair. My knees shook and every single terrible possibility flashed through my mind, the roaring in my ears getting louder and louder, so I barely heard what Mrs Greythorne said.

I had to ask her to repeat it.

She did.

I shook my head. It wasn't true – it wasn't—

It was.

Someone had tried to kill Clem.

28

Clem was on her own, collecting the equipment for lacrosse practice from the sports shed, when someone attacked her from behind. They'd smashed the back of her head with a bat.

"They probably would have finished the job," said Mrs Greythorne with a shaky breath, "had Kate not arrived to help with the equipment."

"Is Clem going to be okay?" I said, my voice stuttering.

Mrs Greythorne nodded. "Thank goodness Kate arrived when she did. But with a head injury… You can never be certain of what's going on with a head injury… She's at the hospital now, getting checked."

I closed my eyes, but the image of my fiery best friend lying in a hospital bed made me snap them open straight away. I couldn't think about it, about how close Clem had come to…

Heybuckle wasn't safe.

Clem had been attacked a day after Mr Willet had said she knew something, so there had definitely been someone out in the grounds listening in on our conversation. The murderer was getting desperate: they must have heard Clem repeatedly say she didn't know anything – but that hadn't stopped them. They had to think we were on to something – if only we knew *what*.

"Did Kate see who did it?" I said breathlessly.

If Kate had seen, then this could all be over.

"No – from my understanding, Kate was speaking on the phone when she got to the sports shed and – er – making quite a bit of noise."

I cursed.

"The attack was timed well," said Mrs Greythorne. "Lots of the older students have free periods on Tuesday afternoon. There are a huge number of people who could have done it."

But, at least I knew now that it wasn't anyone from my G&T class, given we were all sitting inside at that point – specifically, not Arthur or Annabelle.

"Can I visit Clem in hospital?" I asked after a moment of silence. I wanted to hug her and swear we'd get to the bottom of everything. I wanted to make sure she knew how much I loved her, and how I was certain it would all be over soon.

"Her parents are currently with her. I don't think they want any visitors," said Mrs Greythorne. She got up, peering out of the (closed) windows, with her hands behind her back.

"Are they...?" I wanted to ask if they were angry at the school for letting this happen, but I already knew the answer.

Clem's parents wanted the best for Clem – and by the best, I mean the best clothes money could buy, and the best jewellery, and the best school. Heybuckle, despite everything, was still the best.

I'd met her mum and dad a few times, though I didn't visit

Clem at her parents' home often since she was always either on holiday, or staying in one of their other houses. Her mum and dad were nice enough. But they were sort of…dismissive. I guess because they were so successful. They treated everything like a task that needed to be checked off their list. Make another million before breakfast – check. Invest in this company – check. Chair three board meetings at the same time – check. Speak to our daughter – check.

I think this was because for them, money was a measure of happiness. The more they had, the happier they were. And I think they felt like Clem would measure happiness in the same way.

"I noticed you haven't signed up for counselling," said Mrs Greythorne, turning back to me. "Remember the option is always available to you, if you need to talk about anything… I know this year has been very stressful for everyone."

I nodded, taking her words as my cue to leave. I didn't want Mrs Greythorne pushing the counselling thing – I know it sounds bad, but I really didn't think I needed it. Sure, my classmate had been murdered, and my scholarship was threatened, and the whole school turned on me, and someone had said they wanted to kill me – twice, and then someone *actually* attempted to off my best friend, and I was now walking about with a constant, tight knot in my stomach and the feeling I might throw up at any time…

But I thought that was normal. I thought it was *normal* to feel constantly worried and on edge. My life currently seemed like a giant test, whereby if I passed, everything would be okay, and if I failed, I would die. And it sounds dramatic, but that's also how I felt about exams. The world would end if I flunked maths, because that would mean I was in danger of losing my scholarship and I had fought so *hard* to get to Heybuckle. Mum had fought so hard. All my family too. I wasn't here just for me. I had the weight of all their dreams on my shoulders.

"And – Jess," said Mrs Greythorne, as I opened the door. She had an odd expression on her face – kindness mixed with… fear? "I know this is hard on you. If you ever need to talk to me…about anything – my door is always open."

Great. If her door was always open, then our friendly murderer could *always* listen in.

"Thanks, miss," I said.

I left, wondering if she genuinely cared, or if, like Mr Willet, she suspected I held a piece of the puzzle that I hadn't yet realized.

29

The rumour mill did its job quickly. Soon the entire school knew what had happened to Clem.

Whispers followed me in the corridors. Even now, when I'd so obviously had nothing to do with Clem's attack, people backed away from me. It was like they thought I would suddenly snap, whip out the trophy I kept up my sleeve, and just go full killer on them. If the school board had anything to say about the latest development, I didn't hear of it, though of course all the other students had shared the information with their parents. Maybe Clem's attack had taken some of the heat off me.

I did my best to keep the details from Mum, but she read about it in the papers anyway. Hugh and everyone around him were being painted as tragic heroes. People on online forums talked about how they would never want to be like *those kids*, not for all the money in the world.

"Stay safe," Mum said. I could hear her worry through the phone.

"The school board are pushing to find out who's doing this," I lied. "They really care."

"That's good – but you look after yourself too, okay?" said Mum.

The only reason I managed to walk around without bursting into tears was Summer, who was now my firm friend. Once I got past her abruptness and inability to filter anything she was thinking, I discovered she was actually all right. She had a toughness about her that I admired. She didn't take crap from anyone and gave no mind to people's opinion of her.

She took a direct approach towards the students leaping out of our way in the corridors, marching up to people and demanding to know what their issues with her were, before listing all the reasons why she was completely innocent. I said that made her seem even guiltier, but she didn't care. At one point, Eddy asked her what *really* happened that Tuesday night. I genuinely thought she might prove everyone right and murder him right there in the common room.

"Well, Eddy, I did in fact kill Hugh and attempt to murder Clem and it makes *complete* sense for me to confess all that to you in public," said Summer as she flicked through a book.

"Just thought I'd ask," said Eddy, holding up his hands. "Please don't kill me next."

"Baiting someone you think is a murderer is hardly the smartest decision in the world," said Summer, as she snapped her book shut. "But then again, you *are* the person who once plagiarized your homework for Mr Greenburg *from an internet source he'd told us about*, so you're not the *best* decision-maker."

"Yeah, well…" Eddy's face contorted, probably with the effort of thinking. "You're a killer."

"And you once drove one of the school's golf buggies into the lake on a dare because someone convinced you it would float like a boat," said Summer. "I know who I'd rather be."

Eddy was no match for Summer's sharp tongue. He stalked away, shooting her venomous looks over his shoulder. Well, at least if someone tried to murder Summer next, we definitely had one person with a rock-solid motive.

Hattie, who was sitting nearby, laughed. Summer turned her back, making it very clear she was ignoring her.

"You're still fighting?" I asked, as Hattie pursed her lips and started talking again to the group of friends she was with.

"I have a basic rule that I don't date people who think I'm a murderer. I feel it's a pretty low bar," said Summer, tossing her book to one side.

Tommy entered the common room, and his face lit up when he spotted us. He made a beeline to our seats in the corner, ignoring his friends calling for him to come join them. His reputation had not been tarnished in any way by his association with us. I guessed the difference between us and him was that everyone liked him. I'd always been invisible, and Summer had always been known as *difficult*. It would take a lot more than him hanging out with the school weirdos for people to turn their backs on Tommy Poppleton.

He plonked himself down next to me, even though there was a free armchair. I'm not saying this meant he was in love with me, but there's really no other way to interpret that gesture.

Who was I kidding? Tommy definitely only thought of me as a friend – if he even thought of me at all. I was a means to an end, a way to find out what had happened to Hugh. And once we figured that out, he'd be gone.

"I've been thinking – if Hugh was killed because of his hit-and-run, then that discounts the Regia Club as his murderer," he said. "They wouldn't be linked to that; it happened during the summer holidays."

"Agreed. And I'm not convinced they're killers," I said. "The forfeit they gave me for not doing their prank was so low stakes…" I bit my lip. "But they're involved *somehow*. The police aren't investigating properly because of them, and they keep cropping up."

Summer sighed. "No matter what angle we look at this from, we come up short. Let's just hope we figure things out before Jess and I are kicked out." She paused. "Or the murderer makes good on their threats and tries to kill us next. Worst case scenario, we're kicked out *and* killed." She stood up. "Anyway, I have prep to do. You're both welcome to join me in the library."

"Wait – wait. You're going to casually bring up our potential expulsion and murder and then just *leave*?" I squawked.

"This was certainly a fun chat," said Summer, shouldering her bag. "Let's do this again."

She marched off, her blonde hair swishing behind her.

I turned back to Tommy, who was grinning at me.

"What's so funny?" I demanded.

"Nothing," said Tommy. "I saw you were reading *A Chariot of Flames and Empires* the other day."

"Yeah," I said, settling down. I had no other place to be, and also I wanted to spend time alone with Tommy. Even if he did just think of me as a friend, at least I had the opportunity to really get to know him and find out whether I'd been one-hundred-per-cent right to have an enormous crush on him for the entirety of my time at Heybuckle. "It's a terrible book – you should definitely read it."

A Chariot of Flames and Empires was a fantasy book about a world where everyone had a turtle dove which followed them around, only the doves were spies for the king and order could only be restored by a red-headed Chosen One who was Not Like Other Girls. I had been hate-reading it for a while.

Tommy's eyes glimmered. "I read it a while ago – and it was absolute rubbish. The ending? Well – I won't spoil it for you, but let's just say it was one of the worst things I have ever read."

"I don't think it is," I said. "It's such a happy ending."

"You've already finished it?" Tommy raised his eyebrows and gave a low whistle. "Impressive."

"No, I haven't – I'm still only on part one."

"Then how do you know the ending?"

"I read it first," I said with a shrug.

"*What*?" spluttered Tommy, and then we got into a whole debate about whether it was acceptable to read the ending of a book first, and *then* we started arguing about the actual ending, and whether the turtle doves should have won.

It was probably counterintuitive to argue with a boy I liked, but Tommy would never think of me that way so I figured it wouldn't really matter – it was a change to speak to him about something that wasn't murder related. Plus, I so rarely felt comfortable with anyone, it was nice to just…be myself. Not be aware of everything I was saying and how I was sitting, and not stumble over my words.

Before I knew it, we'd got to 10 p.m. and it was time to go to bed. Tommy walked me back to my room, which I was grateful for. Even though there were plenty of other students in the corridors, heading for their own beds, I was on edge after Clem's attack. She hadn't even received warning threats like I had, the attack had come from nowhere.

Annabelle glanced up as I entered, and her mouth hung open as she looked past me.

"Hi...Tommy," she said. Her eyes bulged like a cartoon character's.

Tommy waved at her, then grinned at me.

"Night, Jess," he said, and he put his hands in his pockets as he strolled back down the corridor.

"You and Tommy Poppleton are a *thing*?" whispered Annabelle. She'd warmed to me since I'd refused to do the Regia Club dare, but generally still kept her distance. That clearly didn't matter now: the apparent gossip took precedence.

"No, we're just friends." Even that felt weird to say, because in my entire school career, I'd just had the one friend: Clem.

"Sure – a friend you want to sneak out to the woods with," said Annabelle, wiggling her eyebrows at me. This was bizarre – it was like she was teasing me. "Anyway, Tommy is literally the *fittest* boy in school – but did you know, Eddy and Hattie were a thing? For like three days? And then Hattie broke up with Eddy to be with Summer, and Summer broke up with her because she killed Hugh – only Hattie's one hundred per cent in love with Millie now. And Eddy's also in love with Millie – he offers to do loads of stuff she doesn't want to do, and she always just lets him – takes advantage of him, *I* think. She's never once turned down his help." Annabelle's face seemed to light up as she recounted all the gossip, like she was on familiar ground.

I had to repeat it to myself three times before I worked out what she was saying.

"Summer didn't break up with Hattie because she killed Hugh," I said. "Summer didn't kill Hugh—"

"Not *Summer*," said Annabelle. "Hattie killed him."

"What?" I spluttered, sitting down on my bed.

"Because she's in love with Millie, and she wanted to get Hugh out of the way. Millie told everyone – well, she told Lucy in confidence, and Lucy obviously told me, and *I* told everyone." Annabelle gleamed with pride.

I didn't believe a word of Annabelle's theories, but I was massively confused by what was happening – this was the most Annabelle and I had talked since…well, since *ever*.

I got ready for bed and climbed in, to find something hard under the sheets. I pulled out a thin brown book with gold lettering on the front.

S.R.

The Regia Club. They'd been in my bedroom again. Was this a second punishment for forfeiting their dare?

"Er…Annabelle," I said. "How long have you been hanging out in here?"

"About ten minutes – I was in Lucy's bedroom, painting my nails." She wiggled neon green nails at me. "Why?"

Our bedroom had been empty all evening. Anyone could have walked in.

"Never mind," I said. "That's a nice colour. For your nails."

"Thanks," said Annabelle, smiling as she clicked the main light out. "Night, Jess."

I got under my sheets and pulled out my phone, using the

torch for light. My hand trembled as I opened the book to find pages and pages of handwriting. I frowned, squinting at the pages. They were…minutes of meetings. Minutes discussing potential dares. My heart almost stopped. This was what Summer had been looking for the night Hugh was killed – and someone had deposited it in my bed for me.

I scanned the pages. Members had numbers for names, obviously to anonymize everyone. I read a few pages, before noting the date in the corner of the page was from a few months ago. I flicked on to the more recent dates and stopped at a page with nearly all the words blacked out by a thick pen, so only a short paragraph was left.

Number Two wants it to go on the record that he does not agree with the decision to make Number Thirteen the new Number One, and hence the new leader of the Regia Club. He has stated he will do whatever it takes to get them removed, and that the Van Boren family is highly influential.

I sucked in a breath. All the other names were blacked out or anonymized, but whoever had been taking the notes – or given me the book in the first place – had forgotten to hide Hugh's last name. Or else they'd left it in on purpose, so I would know that Hugh had been angry at the decision to instate the new leader.

I flicked on – there were the minutes about the prank in the dining room a week before Hugh was murdered, where the boys mooned the teachers. It was suggested by Number Two – Hugh. At the end of the page, it was stated that the current

Regia Club book of minutes was almost full, and a new book would be used. There were a few blank pages, and right at the back of the book there were a series of numbers and tallies that I couldn't make sense of at all.

I bit the inside of my cheek, then went back to the start of the book and began reading through the other pages. There were only a few months' worth of minutes because the book was so thin, and it didn't take me long to read through them all. In the passages, there were random words blacked out and it became clear to me that those were all names or details that might reveal members of the Regia Club. Whoever had left this book in my bed had been trying to help me figure out... *something* about the Regia Club, but they hadn't wanted to betray them completely.

The only relevant item seemed to be the short passage where Hugh had said he would do whatever it took to get the new leader removed. But that would only help me if *Hugh* was a murder suspect and had killed the leader. It was the wrong way round.

And I hated to admit it, but Hugh had been right about the new leader. They had taken the Regia Club pranking to new heights. Maybe Number One had really hated Hugh's questioning of them being in charge and had wanted revenge.

I'd been given this book of minutes for a reason – and I needed to figure out why.

30

Clem still wasn't back at school. At the behest of Mrs Greythorne, she was having a short "holiday" away from everything.

It was a few days before her parents let her have her phone back, and she called me at once.

"You're *sure* you're fine?" I said anxiously.

"Yeah…" she said, though she sounded uncertain. "I keep running over what happened. I was just walking along…and then next thing I know, I'm on the ground and my head's in splitting pain. Jess…do you think…do you think that's how it happened for Hugh?" Her voice wavered.

I was silent, not knowing how to reply.

"I think I might have heard footsteps," she carried on. "Someone running towards me? I'm not sure – it's a blur…" I could hear her ragged breathing on the other end of the phone. "I have no idea who it was, Jess. I haven't got the faintest clue."

"And…do you know *why* they attacked you?" I asked. "Like…what they possibly think you could know about Hugh that might lead us to his murderer?"

"I wish I knew," Clem said. "I've been going over everything in my head – not like I can do much else, my parents are *insisting* I stay on bed rest – and I can't come up with anything I know that might make someone think they need to kill me." Her voice was small now.

"You will come back, right?" I said, a slight pang of worry shooting through me, that she might be too scared to return to Heybuckle. It was selfish, but I didn't know what I would do without her – I was already missing her, spouting all her ridiculous theories and getting common phrases wrong, and talking about how she was going to launch an appeal to Save the Forests (not a specific forest or anything – just all trees). Plus, the fact the killer had actually attempted a second murder, that once more they had got away without being seen, sent shudders through me. Clem being around made me feel braver.

"Oh, yes," said Clem, her voice firm. "No attempted murder is going to scare *me* away – just like those death threats didn't scare *you*. I'm going to be back soon and then we're going to figure out who is behind this – we're not running. Plus…" She lowered her voice. "I'd rather be at Heybuckle than with my parents. They're trying to expand the fruit business and from what I can tell, it is *not* going well."

While Clem was away, the only thing I could do was keep trying to figure things out. I told Summer about the Regia Club minutes, but she seemed as baffled about them as I was. She looked at the back page with all the numbers and the tallies and frowned.

"I think it's some sort of code," she said. "But for what?"

We were sitting together in the common room. It was Friday morning, the space largely empty because the weather was excellent and anyone with a free period would be outside walking the grounds. Only Arthur was nearby, strumming on his guitar, so we were keeping our voices low to make sure he wouldn't overhear.

"Can we leak this to the press?" I asked. "That's what you wanted to do originally with the minutes, right?"

Summer nibbled her bottom lip. "These minutes would expose the fact that the Regia Club *exists*, but it doesn't give us proof of who's actually in it, except for Hugh, which we already knew. Plus…the code at the back – I want to crack it. What if it leads to something bigger?"

"You know what's weird," I said, frowning. "The Regia Club is so big on anonymity – they've even numbered all their members. And yet there's actual names in the minutes that someone had to black out."

"It's arrogance," said Summer. "I bet they never thought someone outside the club would get hold of these minutes." She bit her bottom lip. "From our year group, the people most likely to be members, apart from Millie, are Eddy, Kate and those boys in the drama club who've started wearing pirate hats everywhere to promote their play… Tommy obviously fitted the bill because they tried to recruit him. Hey, maybe we should suggest to Tommy that he tells them he's changed his mind about joining so he can go undercover?"

I rolled my eyes. "I'm sure they'd forgive Tommy for complaining about them and accept him in no questions asked."

We lapsed into silence, and I watched Arthur as his fingers

flew over the strings of his guitar. He seemed to sense that I was looking at him, because he glanced up.

"How's your little murder investigation going?" he asked, his lip curling as he put his guitar to one side.

"None of your business," replied Summer curtly.

Arthur's eyes narrowed. "You two are so pathetic," he sneered. "The way you got all involved in this because of your rubbish short story. With the little twigs spelling *HELP ME*. How ridiculous."

A bolt of electricity went through me. "How do you know about the twigs?" I said, staring at him.

He grinned in reply, but it wasn't a nice grin. "I heard you talking about it. In the library."

He'd been there when I first confronted Summer about it, sitting opposite her – and, clearly, listening in.

"And I bet you two think you're *so* smart," Arthur went on. "Smart little scholarship girls – as if you two are going to be the ones who figure out what happened to Hugh and Clem."

He seemed to be gearing up for a rant, even though I had no idea why he hated us so much. It looked like he was seconds away from launching into a master villain monologue about how he was the murderer the whole time.

Summer and I didn't say anything, and that seemed to rankle Arthur even more.

"I don't even know why you're pretending to care so much," Arthur said. "At least *I'm* not fake. I never pretended to like him. But you two – such hypocrites." He was half spitting the words out. "You both hated him."

"I did not," said Summer.

Arthur raised an eyebrow. "I always knew you were a liar. Remember that last G&T lesson? You called him Hugh Henry Van Boring."

Summer flushed. "Yeah, we argued a bit, but that doesn't mean I don't want his *murder* to be solved."

"As far as I'm aware, unless you were *also* having a secret affair with him and met up with him later that evening, that was one of the last things you ever said to him."

Summer was staring at Arthur, her face going redder and redder. I thought she might be getting angry, but there was a sheen to her eyes. I decided I needed to step in, because the last thing in the world someone like Arthur needed to know was that he had the power to make Summer cry.

"He didn't seem that fussed about the insult at all," I said. "As far as I remember, he was super cheerful at the end of class because Millie and Clem were fighting over him."

Arthur rolled his eyes. "He wasn't *that* happy they were fighting over him. I bet Summer's insult really got to him. You'll have to live with that knowledge for the rest of your life, Summer." His mouth was twitching, like he was *enjoying* watching Summer getting steadily more upset at his words.

"He was happy," I insisted. I didn't know why I thought this was the hill to die on, to prove to Summer that she didn't need to feel guilty. But I just couldn't stand the thought of Arthur being right. "I remember after we went back to our seats, I turned around and he was just…triumphant."

"But *surely* if he was happy about them fighting over him, he'd have, I don't know, actually watched the whole thing?" said Arthur. "You were all pressed up against the window, watching the lacrosse fight, and he didn't seem fussed, just wandered around."

Something about what he'd said seemed to snap Summer out of her misery. "I didn't see him wandering around. Did you, Jess?"

I shook my head – but then again, I had been completely focused on Clem and Millie, hoping they wouldn't hurt each other.

Arthur shrugged. "Unlike you, I notice things. I stayed at my desk, instead of watching those sad little girls fight."

The way he kept calling us all *little girls* rankled me, like he was so much older and wiser than we were. Smug prat.

But Summer didn't seem to care about being patronized. All the blood had left her face. "Wait – Hugh wandered around. *Where did he go?*"

And it clicked for me as well. I gasped, almost missing what Arthur said next. He scrunched up his face, and I bet the only reason he didn't make up a stupid lie and was actually helpful was because Summer's question had caught him off guard.

"I don't know. Just a wander. Your desk – Mrs Henridge's—"

I didn't even hear the rest. Summer and I were staring at each other.

"Hugh took the short story," I said.

31

I could tell exactly why Hugh had taken the short story: sometimes, people could be massive dicks.

"He wanted to get you into trouble," I said to Summer, half-forgetting Arthur was still sitting in front of me. "*That's* why he was triumphant – it was nothing to do with Clem and Millie fighting. You'd just insulted him, and he thought he had got you back. We'd have got a right telling-off from Mrs Henridge if our assignment was late – of course, she didn't end up punishing us because—"

"Hugh was killed," said Summer. Her whole body trembled, but we couldn't discuss it any further in the common room because Arthur was obviously listening to everything we were saying.

"Let's go," said Summer to me as she gathered her stuff.

Arthur licked his lips as he looked at Summer, like her reaction had been some kind of treat for him.

We hurried from the common room, not speaking again until we were three corridors over and well out of earshot. We stepped into a little alcove and were alone, but even then I didn't want to discuss what we'd just discovered. Heybuckle's wood-panelled walls were closing in on me. The eyes of the portraits followed me. We were peeling back the golden surface Heybuckle presented to the world and finding not just darkness – but rot.

"Hugh stole the short story that inspired his own death," I breathed.

"What does this information tell us?" asked Summer. "That the short story going missing in G&T was irrelevant? We already knew that."

"Maybe…" I bit my bottom lip as I thought. "If the murderer was Hugh's friend, then *Hugh* might have told them about the short story after he stole it…and *that* could be when they got the idea to copy it. We never crossed off Eddy as a suspect – sure, he only had about half an hour to get across to the woods and it would have been tight but…"

"But Eddy fits the membership requirements for the Regia Club, and we know Hugh was also a member," finished Summer. "And we have that book of their minutes – it all must link together somehow. Maybe Eddy's the new leader."

We stared at each other.

"Let's speak to Mr Willet," I said after a pause. I still didn't know how good a private detective he was, but maybe he was smarter than he let on, or might accidentally say something that gave us a nudge. "He might know something."

"If he does, he won't tell us," Summer said darkly. "He'll just act all cryptic and drop a few hints that mean absolutely nothing."

* * *

To sum up our conversation with Mr Willet, he dropped a few cryptic hints that meant absolutely nothing.

"Did you ever think," he said, when I told him about Hugh taking the short story, "that you might be looking at this the wrong way around – just like you've looked at everything else the wrong way around?"

Gee, Mr Willet, did *you* ever think that if you said exactly what you were thinking in a way people could understand, you'd be, like, ninety per cent less likely to be murdered by an irate student like me?

I didn't say that out loud, of course. I just shook my head. "I didn't consider that point," I said.

Summer and I were in Mr Willet's disused classroom. A police officer had popped her head in and told Mr Willet that he couldn't use the space, but Mrs Greythorne had shown up and said it was fine, before hurrying off to deal with some students who had decided it would be a good idea to try and abseil down the side of their dormitory building.

Summer was standing, staring at Mr Willet intently. Before, I would have assumed she was hanging onto every single one of his words, in order to suck up to him as much as possible. Now, I knew that was how she looked at everyone. Her two settings were intense, and even more intense.

"There are still one or two things that aren't clear to me," Mr Willet said, leaning back in his chair and thrumming his fingers together. His burgundy hoodie had a mustard stain on it, and he'd swapped the faded jeans he'd been wearing last time I saw him for tracksuit trousers. His stubble was now turning into the beginnings of a beard. "But for the most part, I think

I have everything largely worked out – though I am expecting the murderer to…" He trailed off. "No, perhaps it's better if I keep this to myself, for now. Let's just say I'm expecting one final thing to happen – and when it does, I'll know exactly who we're dealing with. But, in the meantime, take heart from the fact that I'm closing in on our killer."

"Well, could you close in faster?" said Summer. "The school board meeting to decide whether Jess and I get expelled for writing the short story is in *ten* days – because despite everyone's *best* efforts to crack this case, we're apparently still the only two people in the school with any actual link to the murderer – who, by the way, might very well kill us before you work this out."

Mr Willet frowned. "Well, that's not very fair – neither of you could have attacked Clem, for example. So, it follows neither of you are the murderer…"

"Welcome to my life," said Summer, rolling her eyes. "It isn't fair."

"So, what about Eddy?" I asked, trying to steer the conversation back. "There's a thirty-minute window that evening where no one knows where he was – he says he was on the phone to his mum."

"And according to his mother, he was," said Mr Willet with a shrug.

Well, there it was – Eddy had a solid alibi. I bit my bottom lip, feeling deflated that we would have to cross him off the list.

"I *do* think Eddy has a secret," continued Mr Willet. "Just not that he killed Hugh. As I said, take heart. I'm close to solving this case. Very close."

Summer waited until we were out of the office and down the corridor to offer up her opinion on Mr Willet. "He's got absolutely no clue," she said. "He's completely bluffing. He's hoping we'll tell everyone that he's onto the murderer, and then they'll get spooked and slip up and he can act like he knew what he was doing all along."

It sounded like a fine plan to me, but clearly Summer was of the opinion that detectives needed to solve everything using their brains, rather than the gullibility of their murderer.

We entered the dining hall, got our trays of food and sat down together. It was still an odd feeling, having more than one friend. Normally, if Clem wasn't at dinner, I'd have been sitting alone and eating as fast as I possibly could. Now, I could sit with Summer like it was the most natural thing in the world.

It wasn't just us two for long. Tommy, who normally sat with a gaggle of friends, sat down on my other side.

"Mr Willet tell you anything good?" he asked.

I was about to answer him, when Clem slid in at the end of our table, with a plate of peri-peri chicken and a stack of chips.

"What's up, everyone?" she said with a grin, as she dug into her food. She had dark circles underneath her eyes, but apart from that she didn't look like she'd almost been killed. All her earrings were in, and she had several badges saying stuff like CAN'T KEEP A BAD GIRL DOWN pinned to her blazer, completing the look with multicoloured socks that went high above her knees. Several people were staring our way. I guess Clem surviving a murder attempt made her pretty interesting.

"You didn't say you were coming back today," I said, gaping at her. She hadn't even messaged me.

Clem shrugged, as she glugged some apple juice. "It was a last-minute decision – as in, I couldn't stand a second more of my parents pretending to care about me. My mum tried sitting by my bed for a bit and spent the whole time screaming down the phone at someone from work."

"So, Clem, that attack," said Summer, launching right in. "You're sure you didn't get any sort of glimpse of who it was?"

I kicked Summer, because Clem didn't deserve to have everyone almost immediately jumping down her throat about what had happened.

"No, I didn't see who it was," said Clem, still cramming in her food like she hadn't eaten in weeks – and knowing the weird healthy food her parents served, like cottage cheese with sides of kale and broccoli, it had probably been a while since her last decent meal. "But I'd rather not talk about it, if that's okay. What were you guys speaking about?"

More people were looking our way, and the buzzing was getting louder.

"What Mr Willet said to Jess and Summer when they told him Hugh was the one who took the short story," said Tommy.

Clem's mouth hung open, revealing half-eaten chicken. "*Hugh* took the story?"

Her face summed up my own feelings on the matter.

"Mr Willet says he knows who killed Hugh – there's just a few things that don't make sense to him that he's got to figure out. You know, maybe we were being super pessimistic about him. Maybe he might not be as useless as the police."

As I spoke, Summer and Clem's eyes slid to something

behind me. I spun around, to find Millie hovering at my shoulder. Her face was pale.

"Mr Willet knows who killed Hugh?" she whispered.

"Er – yes," said Summer, shifting. "Do you want something?"

"I came to… To…" Millie blinked a few times, like there was something in her eye. "I came to speak to Clem, actually."

"To *me*?" said Clem, pausing from her attempt to break the world record in eating dinner the fastest. She clutched a chicken leg in each hand, her mouth smeared with sauce. "Why?"

"I wanted to say that I forgive you," said Millie. Her voice grew surer, like she'd rehearsed this. "I forgive you for breaking all my trust in men and being a complete slut. When I heard Kate found you lying on the ground…" She trailed off and reached into her bag. She got out a wand of lip gloss, dabbing it against her lips as though she were dabbing tears with a tissue.

As always, everything Millie did had to be extra. The last argument she and Hugh had (before the break-up in the dining hall), she took all of his shirts and hid them in random places around the school grounds. He had to recruit about six of his friends to help him find them, and even then he'd been heard complaining about how he'd had to ask his folks to send him more because they'd been *ruined* by "filth".

It had to be exhausting to be Millicent Cordelia Calthrope-Newton-Rose, consistently providing so much drama.

"Is there anything else you want to say?" said Clem, her voice deadpan. "Or is *I forgive you for being a slut* the gist?"

"I just… When I heard someone tried to kill you, I realized that life is fleeting and…I just don't want a repeat of what happened to Hugh, okay?" said Millie, as she popped her lip gloss back into her bag. The sheen of her lips reflected the lights. "I had an argument with him and then he died and I've just got to let go of the fact that you two were both disgusting arseholes because otherwise it's going to mess me up."

I didn't know whether to be impressed that she was trying to move on and forgive Hugh and Clem for the terrible thing they had done to her, or impressed that she had managed to take Hugh's death and Clem's near-death and make them both about her.

"Well – er – that's big of you," said Clem. She looked very uncomfortable, still clutching her chicken legs.

"And now let's focus on the really important thing," said Millie. She folded her arms and tapped her foot. "Mr Willet knows who killed Hugh? Why hasn't he made an arrest?"

"Because he's not a policeman, you idiot," said Summer.

Either Millie didn't hear – and I don't know how she wouldn't have, given the fact Summer hadn't even attempted to be quiet – or she pretended she hadn't.

"And he's absolutely *sure* he knows who killed Hugh?" said Millie. She was speaking directly to Clem, though her eyes flicked to Tommy a few times. I guess because they were the only two people at our table who she didn't consider beneath her.

"Well, he can't be absolutely sure," said Clem. "Or else he'd have accused the murderer and called the police and this would all be over."

"But I bet he knows," cut in Tommy, shooting Clem a look. Maybe he thought it would be insensitive to tell Millie that

Mr Willet probably didn't have a clue. "Mr Willet is the best in the business. He won't stop digging until he has an answer."

Millie sucked in her cheeks. "This is good to hear," she said.

But she didn't look happy at all. In fact, she looked rather scared.

32

"Millie knows something," I said quietly to Tommy after dinner.

Clem had decided to go to sleep early. She said the day had worn her out and I didn't blame her. If people kept coming up to me and asking me to recount the time someone almost killed me, I'd have been exhausted. In a shocking turn of events, Summer said she was going to the library.

"How d'you know?" said Tommy, as we headed to the common room. He was supposed to have an evening football session on the floodlit pitches outdoors, but it was pouring with rain and practice was cancelled. His teammates were hitting up the gym, but he said he wasn't in the mood.

"Her expression when she heard Mr Willet was close to figuring things out," I said, as we entered the common room. It was absolutely rammed, in the way it only was when the rain was so heavy even the hardiest of people didn't want to go outdoors.

"Come on – let's hang out in my room," said Tommy, turning on his heel before we were properly inside. "Now, if Millie knew something…why wouldn't she tell the police? Or Mr Willet? Why would she keep it to herself?"

I was distracted for a second by the cymbals crashing in my head over Tommy's offer to hang out in his room. Alone. Just me and him.

"Maybe she's protecting someone – like, she knows who the killer is, and she's absolutely fine with what they did." I kept my voice steady, determined to focus on the mystery. Tommy didn't think about me that way. "Or…she's scared. If she's not the leader of the Regia Club, she might be terrified of whoever is."

Even as we continued to investigate, the Regia Club remained lurking in the shadows. They had perfected the art of never getting caught and the only bit of proper evidence we had on them was the book of their minutes anonymously given to me. I thought back to the list Summer had made of potential Regia Club members. I couldn't imagine Millie being scared of Eddy or Kate.

But I leaned towards my first suggestion as being the correct one. Millie had a steely coldness about her, and Hugh really had screwed her over. Even if she wasn't the one to kill him, I bet she would have cheered on whoever had.

Okay, so maybe my personal dislike of Millie clouded my thoughts a little bit. But *still*, there was definitely something odd going on there.

We entered Tommy's room. Technically, boys and girls weren't allowed into each other's rooms, but teachers only really patrolled at night. Tommy sat on his desk chair, spinning around, leaving me to perch on the edge of his bed.

"I've been thinking about that newspaper article," said Tommy, once he stopped spinning. "And that note he got – *you did something bad, and if you don't confess you deserve to die…* Maybe it was a threat by a relative or friend of the woman who died in Hugh's car accident. The person who left that book of poems."

"*I promise you, I'll avenge you,*" I said, quoting the note on the woman's grave.

Tommy rubbed his chin. "There are many reasons for someone to kill Hugh," he said. "So many threads. Either they're a relative of Katherine Smith, or they were in love with her, or they're the leader of the Regia Club and held a grudge against Hugh for questioning them as leader, or else they have some sort of vigilante complex. We still don't know anything about the murderer… Apart from the fact that they then tried to kill Clem in the middle of the day. That was risky – clearly they thought Clem knew too much…about *something*…and wanted to stop her. Something they think she's going to figure out soon? It's not like she has any breakthrough information for us right *now*."

A horrible thought occurred to me. "So the closer we get to solving this murder, the more likely it is someone will try to kill us?" I'd received two death threats – there hadn't been a time limit on them, but that just meant the murderer could strike at any point. Even in broad daylight, where anyone could potentially see them attacking.

Tommy's gaze was intense as he looked at me. "We're going to be fine, because we're going to outsmart them. We can do this, Jess – together."

* * *

The next major event that happened was Millie's breakdown. I suspected she was jealous of all the attention Clem was receiving.

It happened at lunchtime on Sunday. I was sitting with Summer. Tommy was with his friends, and Clem's normal Saturday morning lacrosse practice had been moved to Sunday because of the rain. The rescheduled practice had clearly overrun.

Clem didn't really like the fact that I was now friends with Summer. It was an odd shift in the dynamic of our friendship, because before I'd just had her. Now, I had my own friend too – and Clem and Summer did not get on at all.

Clem still called Summer *plain rude.*

Summer, meanwhile, didn't like Clem's cavalier attitude to everything, as well as her disregard for school rules.

"I think," Summer said to me, as she tucked into her lamb hotpot, "that you should try tutoring me in English again."

"No," I said.

We'd tried it the night before, to take a break from discussing murder theories. I'd been getting tired, and even though I knew the school board's big meeting was only a week and a half away and the killer could follow through on their death threats whenever they wanted, I needed to pause on thinking about murder. I knew me tutoring Summer was a bad idea almost immediately, when Summer had insisted that my interpretation of the text we were reading was wrong. I tried to explain to her that in English, there *was* no wrong answer, which she simply couldn't wrap her head around.

"The author was thinking *something* when they wrote it," she kept saying. "And whatever that was, is the right answer."

In exchange, Summer had offered to tutor me in maths – but her mind was so quick, she couldn't understand why I didn't catch onto everything as fast as she did. We gave up when she tried to take me through the answer to a complicated problem for the seventh time and got so frustrated she broke her pen. In the end she turned to the minutes of the Regia Club and continued attempting to crack the code.

Clem banged her tray down next to me. "Millie is literally an alien sent from Mars to torture me," she said.

"Figuratively," corrected Summer.

Clem glared at her.

"You know what Millie did at practice today?" Clem rolled up her sleeve, to reveal a stunning bruise.

I whistled.

"*And* she—"

"Hang on," interrupted Summer, as she set down her fork. "I thought she forgave you."

"Yeah, well, she lied," said Clem. "She's just as angry as ever."

Speak of the devil and she shall appear – at that exact moment, Millie entered the dining room. I inwardly groaned because I already knew what was coming. Millie's eyes narrowed as she marched towards us.

Everyone turned to look, and a few people were already smirking. Annabelle and Lucy swivelled around on their bench – I'm guessing they wanted to watch more comfortably.

"You left me to put all the lacrosse equipment away on my own," Millie said to Clem, her hands on her hips.

"Yeah, well, I was recovering from your attack on me," said Clem, holding up her arm. "Remember doing this?"

"You're a troll," said Millie, raising her voice.

"Wait," said Summer, pushing her plate away. "You said you forgave her. Not that I'm disagreeing about the troll thing, but what changed?"

To probably everyone's surprise, tears welled up in Millie's eyes. "I hate you," she said to Clem, her voice wobbling. "I hate what you did to me – and I hate Hugh too… Only I loved him as well, okay? I loved him so much, and all anyone ever thinks about when they talk about him is how *you're* feeling."

Normally, when people cry, they don't look their best. Millie, on the other hand, seemed to get even prettier. Tears gathered on her long lashes like jewels.

"And the longer time goes on…the more I regret…" Millie trailed off, staring at Clem, who was breathing heavily.

"What do you regret?" prompted Summer.

I kicked her and she winced.

"Everything," said Millie. Her bottom lip trembled. It looked like she was on the verge of saying something.

The tension mounted as we waited, and I knew – I just *knew* – that she was going to tell us exactly what had happened to Hugh.

But then Eddy sidled up behind Clem.

"What's up, Mill?" he said with a grin.

Millie's face, if possible, went even paler. "Nothing." Her nostrils flared, and she hurried off, her head bowed.

Eddy followed her like a shadow who couldn't leave her side.

A thought flashed across my mind – *Millie was scared of saying something in front of Eddy.*

263

But what?

Tommy slid in next to me. "What the hell was that?" he said.

I stared after Millie, trying not to feel too disappointed. "Not sure," I said.

"She's close to cracking," said Summer. "Whatever it is she knows – and she definitely knows something – she's going to share it."

33

Clem and I discussed it in English class the next day. Arthur sat in silence, which was just the way I liked him.

Mrs Henridge had put on the film version of the book we were reading. She sat at her desk, marking prep, and didn't seem to mind us all talking in whispers.

"Millie's protecting someone," I theorized. A few people whistled because the lead in the film had just taken his shirt off. "Maybe someone killed Hugh for her."

Clem shook her head. "I don't think she wanted him dead. I think she really did love Hugh." She shifted uncomfortably as she said this.

I know it sounds bad, but I don't think either of us had really appreciated the fact that Millie genuinely might have been in love with Hugh. Up to that point, she'd been his dramatic ex-girlfriend, the one everyone suspected of murdering him, until it became clear she hadn't done it. Then, we'd sort of…cast her to the side. We hadn't really considered that Millie might be a gold mine of knowledge, having dated him for years.

Tommy had said Hugh really did love Millie, despite the

cheating. The whole thing was a twisted triangle, a web of lies that had spun out of control.

Who else could have been hurt by what Clem and Hugh had done? Had Clem been attacked just because she had dated Hugh, and not because she knew something? Was there someone else, other than Millie, who was jealous of their relationship and wanted to kill them both?

I pushed that thought aside. "We've been in Millie's class since we were thirteen," I said slowly. "And what do we know about her?"

"She's violent?" said Clem, rubbing at the bruise on her arm.

"And she's *dramatic*," I said. "But after that one confrontation with Hugh in the dining room, she didn't do much about him cheating on her—"

"Hang on," interrupted Clem. "Do you not remember the stuff she posted about me online? And the gossiping and…"

"She could have been a lot worse and we both know it," I replied. "So why wasn't she?"

Clem's mouth twisted; there was guilt all over her face. "I don't know?"

"Because maybe *she was cheating on him too*," I whispered, thinking about the gossip Annabelle had shared with me, about how Eddy was in love with Millie. "With one of his *best friends*."

"*Eddy?*" said Clem.

It sounded ludicrous when we said it out loud. Millie treated Eddy like a servant, not a potential love interest.

"Maybe not him," I said. "But maybe there was someone else…someone who knows how to keep their identity a secret… Like…someone in the Regia Club?"

* * *

At lunch, I went for a walk on my own. Now that I had more than one friend, I found I didn't have a lot of time to myself – and, as it turned out, I quite liked the alone time. I kept to the main path, in sight of other people playing on the main field.

Behind me came a rattling of stones, and the back of my neck prickled. I spun around.

Millie was sprinting down the path, her eyes fixed on me. There was something almost manic in her gaze. Terror rushed through me, followed by adrenaline. I was poised to run when she skidded to an abrupt stop a few metres in front of me. Her eyeliner was smudged and her hair was flying wildly around her face.

"I need to talk to you," she said, panting. "About the Regia Club...and about Hugh. I know who killed him."

Blood rushed to my ears. "What—"

She spun around, gazing back at the school. "Everyone can see us," she said. "We need to talk later – alone."

"I don't—"

"Meet me outside the trophy room at midnight," she said. "And don't tell *anyone*, okay? Rumours spread too fast in this school. Nothing stays a secret."

"I—"

"Promise?" she said, and the manic light in her eyes shone brighter. "Jess, you need to promise me that you won't tell *anyone*. It can't get around – and it will, I guarantee you."

It might have been the first time she had ever referred to me by name, and that alone was enough to break me out of my shock.

"There's a murderer running around school, why would I meet you in the middle of the night—"

267

"I can tell you *so much*," said Millie. She looked left and right, even though there was no one around. "*I'm* the leader of the Regia Club," she whispered. "And I can tell you *exactly* what its goals are – the mystery isn't *who* is involved but *why*. Now, promise."

I gaped at her. I'd suspected, of course, that she was the Regia Club's leader, but it was different having her admit that she was the one who'd orchestrated pouring honey all over my stuff and blasting a text to everyone telling them I had grown up in a slum. I wanted to walk away and never speak to her again, but I needed her information, so I forced down my revulsion, wanting to gag like it was three-week-old sour milk. "I promise."

"Good," said Millie, and she turned on her heel and walked away.

"But – wait," I began, as Millie sped up.

"People can see," she said. "They'll think it's weird I'm talking to you – and the rumours will start…"

"Why me though?" I said, starting to get out of breath as I tried desperately to keep up. Millie was a lot taller than me, and her strides were longer. "Why'd you come to me about this?"

Millie whirled around to face me. "You haven't got a clue," she said with a derisive snort. "But you're the perfect person to speak to."

"Why?" I asked.

"Because that text we all got sent after Hugh's memorial said *you* helped the murderer," said Millie. "And my only other option is speaking to Summer, who is an absolute cow. Process of elimination."

With that, she strode away.

34

I kept my word to Millie. I didn't say anything to anyone about our planned meeting. She was right: the only thing that had stayed secret in the school was the identity of the murderer. Everywhere else, there was always someone listening – Clem and me listening in on Summer in her bedroom, Arthur eavesdropping on Summer and me in the library, the murderer themselves listening in on Mr Willet telling Clem he was sure she knew something.

The day ticked by slowly, and though I passed Millie in the corridors, she didn't acknowledge me at all. I half started to worry that I had somehow made up our entire chat. Or else she was playing some sort of weird practical joke on me and at the stroke of midnight she would appear and throw a bag over my head and then take me to a lake and make me chant the school song backwards as part of a twisted Regia Club prank.

"You okay?" asked Clem at dinner. "You're oddly quiet."

"Yeah, I just have a headache," I said, as I ate a second helping of cake. Sweet stuff always calmed me down. "Might go to sleep early. Here – have my chips."

It was the easiest thing in the world to distract Clem. She dug into my chips with the eagerness of a dog burying a bone. I headed up to my room, where I scrolled through my phone and exchanged a few texts with Mum.

Mum: Saw a nice dress today
Me: okay
Mum: It was £100 – who spend that much on a dress
Me: rich people are idiots
Mum: I bought you a dress for £5 – bargain
Me: thanks
Mum: Clem ok
Me: Yes
Mum: Good

I hesitated over the chat. Mum had told me to keep my head down, to stay safe. Right at the beginning of all this, she had even said not to go anywhere in school after dark. But so far, the attacks hadn't been after curfew. Hugh had been killed between dinner and bedtime – Clem had been clubbed over the head in the middle of the day. The killer was consistent in that they didn't attack after the 10 p.m. lights-out rule. It was risky, betting I would be safe because the killer appeared to follow this apparently sacred school rule, but the observation gave me a bit of comfort.

I said bye to Mum and locked my phone, feeling more determined than ever. I had to do whatever it took to solve this before the murderer turned their focus on me – and before the board meeting next week. Mum had worked so hard to get me to Heybuckle – I couldn't let her sacrifices go to waste.

Annabelle came in just before ten. I was already tucked up in bed, pretending to sleep. She shuffled around the room in what I assumed was supposed to be a quiet way, before switching her bedside lamp on and flooding the space with light. It was lucky that I was such a deep sleeper, or else I probably would never have got much rest.

She normally texted for ages before going to sleep, and I started to worry that she would do the same tonight and wouldn't be asleep before twelve.

Half an hour later, however, her light clicked out and the room was left in darkness. Ten minutes after that, our bedroom door was gently pushed open and light from the hallway filtered in. Through my lashes, I watched as Miss Evans, our house-mother, peered in. She stayed long enough to check there were bodies in both beds before moving to the next room.

My eyes started to grow heavy and I sat up – if I got too comfortable, I would fall asleep and miss my meeting with Millie. I still didn't understand why she wanted to come to me, or why, if she knew something, she didn't go straight to the police. Maybe, like me, she didn't trust the police to actually do something with the information.

Annabelle started snoring, and I heaved a sigh of relief.

Eventually, my phone showed 11.45 p.m. and I got out of bed, slipped on my shoes, and put on a jumper over my pyjamas to keep myself warm from the draughts whistling through school.

The corridor outside was dimly lit and the neon green of the fire exit signs made everything look sickly. At night, I had only ever gone as far as the bathroom, which was at the end of our corridor; we shared it with four other girls.

I entered the largest corridor of the bedroom section and slipped out and into the main body of the school. Creeping through the school after hours alone would have been unsettling at the best of times, with the constant fear that a teacher might suddenly appear to haul me off to Mrs Greythorne's office. But now, of course, I knew there might be a murderer lurking in the shadows. Shapes loomed out of the darkness, sending my heart racing, and only when I got closer did I see they were the statues I walked past every day.

I wished I could use my phone torch, but I didn't want to make myself too obvious. If someone suddenly appeared down a corridor, I wanted to at least give myself the opportunity to dart inside a classroom.

As I crept down the hallway, it occurred to me to wonder why Millie hadn't asked me to meet inside her room – after all, she didn't share with anyone. I didn't get why she wanted to meet outside the trophy room. Maybe it was because the trophy room was right across school, and there would be no one around – there would be no possibility of being overheard, even if there was a higher chance of getting caught.

I reached the trophy room just before midnight. I shivered as I waited. The jumper I'd chosen wasn't enough to keep me warm.

It had almost reached midnight when a soft tapping started.

Someone was knocking on the front door.

I'll make this very clear: I am a coward. My first instinct was to leg it out of there and forget whatever it was Millie had so mysteriously wanted to tell me.

But someone was coming down the corridor, with a torch. It might be Millie, or a teacher – or the murderer. I slipped into an alcove, pressing myself up against the corner and hoping their light wouldn't shine into my hiding space – which wasn't really a hiding place at all.

There were harried voices, and Mrs Greythorne and Mrs Henridge appeared, wearing dressing gowns and heading towards the front door as they muttered.

"I don't know what we do," Mrs Henridge was saying. Her voice was thick, like she had been crying. "I just don't understand – how could this be happening? We're supposed to *protect* them."

"It'll all be fine," said Mrs Greythorne, but she didn't sound convinced.

The knocking started again.

If either of them had turned around, they would have seen me there, eyes wide like a terrified rabbit. Blood pounded in my ears, and my heart beat so fast a music producer probably could have made a club banger out of the sound. I clutched my phone, thankful I'd at least had the sense to keep it on silent.

Mrs Greythorne fiddled with the enormous padlock on the front door. Before, there had simply been a standard lock, but after Hugh's death I guessed they had decided to *extra* lock the door to show parents we were *extra* safe. In the light of the torch Mrs Henridge was holding, she was deathly pale, like a sheet of fresh snow.

What were they doing? Who were they letting into the school? All my suspicions about Katherine Smith's family came rushing back to me – Mrs Henridge had only started at Heybuckle in September. She could have infiltrated the school.

Mrs Greythorne – Mrs Greythorne… I struggled to come up with a reason for why Mrs Greythorne was involved. Clem would have been able to. I wished she was here with me – or Summer, or Tommy. Heck, I would have been happy with Annabelle.

Finally, Mrs Greythorne untangled the padlock from the door, the chains rattling as she set them down on the floor. She undid all the bolts and heaved the door open.

Inspector Foster stepped inside.

My mouth hung open in horror. Was this some sort of conspiracy? Were all the adults I had ever encountered involved? Had Heybuckle School turned into some sort of cult, where teachers killed their students and the police helped cover up the crime?

Or…I shuddered as the breeze from the front door reached me. Or, had someone else been murdered?

Inspector Foster said nothing as she followed Mrs Greythorne and Mrs Henridge down the corridor. They headed in the direction of the dormitories.

Everything in me was screaming to wait, to stay hidden until the risk of being caught by them was gone. But I also knew I couldn't miss the chance to find out what was going on.

I crept after them, straining my ears to hear snatches of their voices echoing down the corridor.

"…this is your fault, Inspector – if you weren't so damned *slow*," said Mrs Greythorne.

"It's Hugh's parents' fault – their bloody money has been their own undoing," replied Inspector Foster. "Arrogance. That's what's caused this mess—"

"Corruption," came Mrs Greythorne's hiss.

"*I'm* not corrupt – I've been trying to solve this with half my normal resources, working against orders in spite of what the higher-ups have said—"

"Now is not the time for arguing," said Mrs Henridge. "Hush. We're near the students' bedrooms."

They all fell silent as they entered the main dormitory corridor. I couldn't risk following any further – lots of the corridors led to dead ends and there weren't any places I could hide if they turned around. We were close to my bedroom – I slipped along, gently opening and closing the door and diving into bed. I pulled the sheets right up around me. Annabelle was still snoring away.

I kept awake for ages, tensing for any sound of the teachers. Frustration gnawed my insides, that I hadn't got to speak with Millie, and I hadn't been able to hear more of Inspector Foster's conversation with Mrs Greythorne.

Millie must have been very lucky to not run into them. She must have been late meeting me – or else decided against it.

But when I was pulled out of class the next morning, to speak to Mrs Greythorne, it turned out Millie wasn't lucky at all.

Because she was dead.

35

Millie's body was found at around 11 p.m. A first-year student with a ground-floor bedroom said she heard something *thud* onto the concrete outside, waking her up. The first year was half of the mind that the noise had been nothing. But with everything that had been going on, she decided it would be best if she just had a quick look outside.

Millie was lying on the ground, legs bent at an odd angle. The first year ran straight to Mrs Greythorne (without screaming, which would have been my first instinct).

The police asked to speak to people in our year group, one by one. They set up several simultaneous meetings with students, to get through everyone as quickly as possible.

I'd already decided I wouldn't be telling them about my arranged meeting with Millie. I didn't know if withholding this information from the police was a crime and I didn't want to google it, in case they could check my search history. Maybe it was only a rule that you couldn't lie to a judge in court, and I was getting my information from television shows mixed up. But I had no real alibi for the time of Millie's murder – sure,

I had been in my room with Annabelle at 11 p.m. But Annabelle had been fast asleep, and if I told Inspector Foster I had been able to sneak in and out without Annabelle knowing, there was absolutely no reason why I couldn't have snuck out at 11 p.m. and not 12 a.m.

Plus, they were corrupt – Mrs Greythorne had said as much to Inspector Foster, who replied that *she* wasn't. But who knew if she had enough power to go against her superiors?

It was way, way too much of a coincidence that Millie had been killed just an hour before she was meant to meet me, to tell me what she knew. *I* hadn't told anyone about our arranged meeting, just like Millie had asked. We'd only talked briefly on the school fields before, and I didn't think anyone had been nearby to listen in. I considered the possibility that someone had somehow bugged all of us (listening devices on our phones or something) before I remembered we were all students at school and not part of MI5.

Which meant *Millie* had told someone about our meeting – someone she trusted. Someone else in the Regia Club? Or perhaps the murderer. But the whole reason she had wanted to speak to me alone at night was to tell me who killed Hugh. Why would she decide to turn on that person and then *tell* them about her betrayal?

I had one of the earlier interview slots with the police, and was waiting outside Mrs Greythorne's office for my turn when Eddy exited the room. He must have been booked in directly before me. Tears streamed down his face, and he barely looked at me, his shoulders heaving with sobs as he walked away. Mrs Greythorne followed him out and sat beside me.

"The police need a few minutes between each student," she said, her voice heavy. Her hands were curled into fists as she stared into space.

"Have Millie's parents been told?" I asked eventually, partly to fill the silence and partly because I genuinely wanted to know.

"Yes," said Mrs Greythorne. "Well, her father has. Her mother is currently shopping in Paris and is out of reach. We've left a message with the hotel."

How horrible would that be? Returning from the shops laden with designer clothes, and the receptionist at the hotel running after you, flapping a piece of paper with the news that your daughter had been killed.

"Millie's father has asked for discretion around this," said Mrs Greythorne. "Her family were distraught by all the press surrounding Hugh's death." She glanced at me. "We're keeping it from the school board as best as we can."

Which was much better for the school too. Two deaths and an attempted murder at Heybuckle would be a massive blow to its reputation. Even if Heybuckle eventually recovered from all this, I bet some parents would have started pulling kids out if they heard about the latest death. But then again, private schools had scandals all the time and people still sent their kids to them. I guess it was mainly tradition: for people like Tommy it was a legacy – his father had come to this school, and his grandfather, and his great-great-grandfather. Okay, so maybe the scandals didn't usually involve murders. But Henry the Eighth had killed, like, two of his wives and the royal family had recovered fine.

Inspector Foster stuck her head out of the doorway. "I'm ready for you," she said.

Mrs Greythorne and I went in and sat down, and in response to all of the inspector's questions I said I didn't know anything.

And that was the moment when good girl Jess, who only a short while ago would never even have *considered* lying to the police, officially went rogue. I didn't trust them to protect me – not when they had done so little for Hugh and Millie.

Not when Clem had been attacked in broad daylight.

Not when I'd had two death threats and they'd done nothing to show me they were anywhere near catching the murderer.

After my interview with the police, Mrs Greythorne told me that Mr Willet wanted a chat with me.

"This is all my fault," he said as I walked into his disused classroom. He looked like he hadn't slept, his eyes wild, his beard messy, and his clothes looked even more crumpled and faded than normal.

"Er – how so?" I asked.

"The police have been sitting on evidence," said Mr Willet, rubbing his eyes. "That's why Hugh's parents hired me – they trusted *me* to solve it. And I haven't, not fast enough. And now another student is dead."

"*What*?" I said. "What evidence?"

Mr Willet took a deep breath. "That hit-and-run. When Hugh killed Katherine Smith, his car was caught on CCTV – so he told his parents about it. The police wanted to arrest him, so his parents paid some senior people to hush it up – investigating officers were told to keep quiet, evidence was buried, files were made confidential… Ironic then, that when Hugh was killed under a year later, the fact that he had murdered Katherine Smith was one of the biggest leads as a motivation for his death – but the police could never link to it, of course, because officially Hugh *never killed her*. They believed admitting otherwise would expose their own corruption. Hugh's parents knew this – they thought their money had solved a problem – but it led to an even bigger one down the line. That's why they hired me, to look everywhere the police wouldn't. Even if my investigation couldn't lead to Hugh's killer's arrest, they wanted the truth – and I still don't have it." He kneaded his cheeks with clenched fists as he sighed. "It's hard as a private investigator – I just don't have the resources. I'm in a paddleboat fighting against a current alone, while the police are in a motorboat with an engine they just don't want to switch on."

That was why the police had been so crap, why it looked like they hadn't made much progress. I thought back to the phone call I'd overheard, where Inspector Foster had said her hands were tied because there was something *they* didn't want getting out. She'd mentioned the Regia Club a moment later and I'd linked the two together in my mind. Except the police weren't being slow because they'd been infiltrated by the Regia Club, but because they were dragging their feet while they tried to work out a way to make sure they weren't brought down with the killer. So how did the Regia Club fit in with everything, then? *Did* they fit in? They had to *somehow* – Millie was going to tell me something about them, and then she was killed.

"Have you told Mrs Greythorne about the police being paid off?" I said, remembering the argument I had overheard between Mrs Greythorne and Inspector Foster the night before.

"Yes. I needed an ally. She's been filling me in on anything the police share with her."

Mr Willet looked so forlorn, I wanted to lift his spirits.

"Inspector Foster said she's been looking into things anyway," I said. "Even though her bosses said not to."

"Well, then she'll be running into the same issues as me," said Mr Willet. He looked at me and sighed. "I suppose I could ask you all the usual questions. Did you notice anything unusual about Millie's behaviour? Anything…erratic?"

"Well – she said she forgave Clem and then got super angry at her again and then declared she still loved Hugh." I rubbed my head, trying to think of a way I could give him the clearest picture of who Millie had been as a person. "But she was always like that. No one ever knew where they stood with her."

"Mmm…" Mr Willet stroked the bottom of his chin, his eyebrows briefly drawing together. "But that would mean – but that's – ridiculous… And yet…" He trailed off, his eyes flicking to me like he had only just remembered that I was still in the room.

"Do you…er…know how she died?" I said, with morbid curiosity. "Only, Mrs Greythorne didn't say…"

He pursed his lips. "She fell from the roof," he said. "Students aren't allowed up there, of course, but when have rules and locked doors ever stopped people like Millie? It's a perfect place to talk about things without being overheard – if indeed there was someone else up there with her. The police might settle on the explanation that Millie chose to jump – her ex-boyfriend is dead, she's been behaving erratically…"

"She didn't jump," I said loudly. Of course she hadn't jumped – she'd been planning on meeting me an hour later. Would the police just brush off her death without properly investigating whether it was a murder? Did they just want to wash their hands of the whole issue?

Mr Willet rubbed his forehead. "Usually, the most straightforward explanation is the one most favoured – whether or not it's the right one. The police will want this to be over as soon as possible – they'll latch onto the obvious win." He shook his head, then sighed again. "You can leave now."

"Really?" I said, gaping at him. "Already?"

Mr Willet shrugged. "I don't think there's anything more I can ask you – I was hoping you might be able to tell *me* something. Clearly, I was wrong."

The tension in my shoulders lessened, and I got up to leave.

"But – Jess," said Mr Willet, as I was about to open the door. I turned.

"Be careful," he said. "I wasn't in time to warn Millie, but I have enough information to figure out that you're in danger as well."

"I know," I said, my hand still hovering over the door. I didn't know why he was acting like this was some sort of revelation. "The death threats I got gave that away."

"No, previously a *number* of you were in danger. Summer also received a threat – Clem was attacked. Even Tommy was probably at risk. But this killer is getting desperate – the initial murder was well thought out, the scene all neatly arranged.

In comparison, Clem's attack showed desperation, and Millie's death was sloppy – no time to lay out twigs spelling *HELP ME*. The murder might even have been impulsive." Mr Willet pursed his lips. "And though a desperate killer is more likely to be caught... Well, they're the most dangerous kind. And, I'm afraid, they seem to have something of an...obsession with you, shall we say."

"What do you mean?" I said, trying to keep my voice measured and not give away the fact that inside I was screaming at the thought that a murderer was obsessed with me.

"*You* received the first thank-you text," said Mr Willet. "Summer got a death threat too, but only *you* received a follow-up. Just watch out, Jess. We know this murderer is willing to kill again and again. And if I was going to guess their next victim...well, I'd guess you."

36

Obviously, I was not killed. This isn't one of those she-was-dead-the-whole-time type things, where I'm writing this story from, like, beyond the grave, as a way to deal with my Trauma and therefore Move On into the next world (though add in some singing and a lot of dancing and that would make a *great* Bollywood film).

I am very much alive. But Mr Willet was right. I did come very close to dying. I had, in fact, already been very close to being killed without realizing it. And we hadn't yet come to the end of all the tragedies, because—

Well, wait. Let me just keep going.

Clem, Summer and Tommy were with the police, having their interviews, so it meant I sat on my own during the rest of morning lessons. Summer knocked on my door at lunchtime. She entered my room, followed by Tommy.

Clem texted me, as Summer and Tommy crowded into my room.

Clem: Millie

Clem: Omg

Clem: Wtf

Me: Come round to my room – Summer and Tommy
are here

Clem: Am going to talk to Mr Willet in a sec

Clem: I can't believe this

Clem: I don't understand

Clem: I feel sick

"This is…ridiculous," said Summer, her face a mask of shock as she sat down at my desk. "Millie and Hugh are…"

I nodded glumly. It was hard to comprehend. For the entirety of my Heybuckle life it had been Hugh-and-Millie, the inseparable pair. Even when Hugh and Clem got together, in my head it had still been Hugh and Millie. They were the perfect couple, basically models. They had everything – all the money in the world, and futures where they could do anything. They went to their expensive houses at weekends, and they had all the designer clothes they could possibly ask for – and they had each other, of course.

And now they were both gone.

"I need to tell you all something," I said. I quickly relayed what Mr Willet had told me about the police.

Tommy whistled as he leaned against my door with his arms folded. "That definitely explains why Hugh's parents hired Mr Willet then."

Summer's mouth hung open. "This is incredible," she said. "We need to tell the press – get them to run an exposé – this is *exactly* the sort of thing that exposes the super elite and the sort of crap they pull. I can see the headlines now – one law for the rich, another for the poor – the price of buying off the police is lower than you think—"

"With what evidence?" said Tommy. "Newspapers wouldn't run a story like that without a huge ton of proof."

"There's something else," I said, because I could tell Summer was gearing up to argue and I didn't want to hear any more of her long-winded headlines. While the whole police corruption thing was mindboggling, discussing it wouldn't help us solve the murder. "I didn't tell the police this, but I was supposed to meet Millie last night. She said she was the leader of the Regia Club and that she knew who killed Hugh."

That distracted Summer.

"And she was killed before she could tell you?" She swore, loudly and repeatedly. "Of *course* she was, because why would we ever get a break?" She scrunched her face up, clearly frustrated. "Well, it makes sense for Hugh to have been angry about Millie becoming leader – he didn't want to be upstaged by his ex? Or…his girlfriend at the time?"

"So Millie knew who killed Hugh…and didn't do anything about it apart from suggesting a midnight meeting with you?" said Tommy. His voice was angry, disbelieving. "What else did she say?"

I thought back. "She said she wanted to talk to me about the Regia Club, and that she knew who had killed Hugh. And she said she could tell me what the Regia Club's goals are – that the mystery isn't about *who* is involved but *why*."

"What the hell does that mean?" said Summer.

"Was she *trying* to speak in riddles?" groaned Tommy.

It was the refrain we kept coming back to. Even with all the tiny breakthroughs we had made – *it still didn't make sense*.

Things were different to when Hugh died. For one thing, there was no big assembly about Millie's death. The school tried their best to hush it up, just like Millie's parents wanted. Obviously, it got out anyway – Millie had been such a big presence and the first year who'd found her body told half the school her story. But even with the death out in the open, it was all just whispers.

Whispers that Millie was behind everything and, consumed by guilt, had decided to jump from the roof.

Whispers that it was all over.

I knew those whispers to be completely untrue. At the very least, however, everyone started treating me normally again. The school had bigger things to talk about.

It meant I could focus properly on the important issue of Mr Willet warning me that I would be the murderer's next victim. I hadn't told Summer and Tommy that part – it was stupid, and I'd known about the threats to my life previously, but Mr Willet confirming that he thought I was next made it too real. I was worried that saying the words aloud would make them come true.

"I don't want to talk about what happened to Millie," said Clem, when I finally saw her at dinner – she had skipped classes for the rest of the day and her eyes were red. "This whole thing is just – rubbish. And Millie is… I didn't like her, but she was the only person who really knew how I felt about Hugh... Who got it..." She ran her fingers through her hair, which stuck up in clumps, and I could tell things were really bad because she hadn't touched her pizza.

Just like when Hugh died, I didn't know what to say to make her feel better. Her expression of sadness, however, quickly changed into one of confusion.

"Since when's that a thing?"

I turned around. Hattie and Summer were holding hands as they walked into the dining room.

"Oh – they're back on," I said with a smile. "That's great."

"*Back* on?" spluttered Clem. "Hattie doesn't date. She just goes on long mopey walks by herself."

"Well, she and Summer have been on and off again for a while. And now they're back together."

Summer and Hattie were laughing really loudly as they walked past us. It was the most carefree I had ever seen Summer look – and Hattie as well. I wondered how they had made up. Summer had been really mad at Hattie over how she'd acted about the short story thing.

Clem watched them thoughtfully. "They make a cute couple – maybe Hattie'll put some pictures up of them, so she'll finally have something on her board in our bedroom, besides pictures of walks..." She trailed off, and her eyes went wide as she stared after them. "Oh no... Oh no... I've just realized something." She put a hand over her mouth. "Oh no – Jess..."

"What's wrong?" I said, worried by how flustered she looked.

"Let me see that article about the woman who Hugh... About the hit-and-run."

I got my phone out, scrolled through my pictures and showed her. All the colour was sucked from her face, and she was trembling, almost dropping my phone on her pizza. I took it back from her slack fingers.

"Jess, remember when I said I'd seen a photo of this woman before?" Clem spoke fast, breathing heavily. "And I couldn't quite place it?" She was shaking her head. "But it *can't* be – but if it is... No... I'll have to tell... Oh, but I *can't*..."

"Clem – tell me what's wrong," I tried again, starting to get really worried. I'd never seen her look so flustered. Dread replaced the acid in my stomach, churning my pizza in circles.

"I need to go," said Clem, sliding out from the bench.

I didn't even get a chance to follow her. She practically sprinted out and I looked around, terrified someone might have heard us speaking. The room buzzed with noise, and there was no one near us. Still, the back of my neck prickled.

Clem wouldn't tell me what she'd figured out, even though I texted her and asked again and again.

Police said I can't say yet, was all she replied.

After dinner, I went and sat in the common room with Tommy and we had one of our heated non-murder-related discussions, the conversation flowing freely. We were chatting for a while before Summer burst in. Her tie was askew, and one of her socks had fallen down. Her hair was loose around her face. She sat down opposite me and Tommy, and buried her head in her hands.

"What's wrong?" said Tommy.

"The police…have taken someone into custody," Summer said, and when she looked up, tears were dripping down her face.

We sat in silence as she told us Hattie Fritter had been arrested on suspicion of the murders of Hugh Henry Van Boren and Millicent Cordelia Calthrope-Newton-Rose.

37

I tried to shield Summer from all the curious eyes as we got up to leave the common room.

"Let's go to my room," said Tommy, and I nodded.

Arthur blocked the exit. "Is it true?" he said to Summer, his eyes flashing. "Your girlfriend killed Hugh?"

The common room went silent and out of the corner of my eye I saw Annabelle and Lucy leaning in. Or, at least, Lucy was leaning in. Annabelle looked uncomfortable, her cheeks flushing red.

"Get out of the way, Arthur," said Tommy, trying to push past him. Tommy was a lot taller and stronger, but obviously didn't put a lot of force into his push because Arthur stood his ground, shaking his head as he looked at Summer.

"How did you not know?" he said, his lip curling. "How'd you miss that – if you were dating her, you were supposed to be the closest person to her, surely?"

I didn't think Summer was in any state to respond, given the fact that tears were still streaming down her face, but she looked up at Arthur.

"She didn't do a damned thing," she said. "The police are wrong." But she hiccupped as she spoke, which lessened the impact of what she was saying.

Arthur looked Summer up and down, with an expression in his eyes that I couldn't read – he looked…angry? Hurt?

Why did he care so much? He was never friends with Hugh.

"Leave them alone, Arthur," said a quiet voice at my shoulder. Annabelle had got up and was standing beside me. "You're causing a scene."

Only then did Arthur seem to become aware that the entire common room was watching him.

"You could never hack being the centre of gossip," he said to his twin as he stood to one side.

Annabelle's shoulders rose and fell, her cheeks flaming crimson red and her hands curling into fists – I wondered if she was going to punch her brother. Something seemed to be bubbling beneath the surface, threatening to rise to the top. I thought back to the way she had screamed down the phone to her mother that she would never put a family photo on the board in our room, because she thought her parents loved Arthur more – an argument Arthur had started by ratting on her. I wondered just how much resentment was festering inside her.

Arthur winked at her. "Stay quiet, little sister." He walked past us and back into the common room.

Annabelle stared after him, her nostrils flared. I wondered if I was supposed to thank her for sticking up for us. But then she went back to Lucy without a second glance.

Summer half ran from the common room, and I hurried to

keep up, trying to push the weird Applewell twins from my mind. Once we were inside Tommy's room, Summer took us through what had happened. She'd been hanging out with Hattie, and the police had come to make the arrest, along with Mrs Greythorne. They wouldn't answer any of Summer's questions and took a shocked Hattie away.

I couldn't make sense of the arrest – Hattie hadn't even been on my radar as a suspect. She'd just been the person unlucky enough to find Hugh's body.

"She looked so scared," sobbed Summer. "She had no idea what was happening."

Tommy gave her a little pat. I stood awkwardly by the door, trying not to look at Summer. Crying in front of people would have been my worst nightmare, so I figured the nicest thing I could do was give her some space.

She only took a few minutes to calm down. "Do you have any tissues?" she sniffed at Tommy.

"Er…" He reached into a blazer hanging on the back of his armchair and pulled out a scrunched-up tissue from the pocket. "It's clean," he said, as Summer wrinkled her nose.

Summer proceeded to dab at her face, and when she was done, she looked like the steely Summer we all knew and (now) loved.

Tommy sat on the floor, then looked at me and raised his eyebrows, nodding at the space beside him. I sat down.

"The police are going to do everything they can to charge Hattie with this arrest," Summer said. "They won't care that she's innocent – they can close the case before anyone figures out how corrupt they are."

"Are you *sure* she's innocent?" said Tommy.

I elbowed him.

"Ow," he said to me. "You've got bony elbows."

"Of course she is!" snapped Summer, balling up her tissue and throwing it into the bin.

"I saw her that night," I said, thinking back to the Tuesday of Hugh's murder. "Coming out of the common room. She walked with me back to my room."

"They think she killed him sometime after dinner and then washed up and went to the common room like she was some sort of cold-hearted…some sort of cold-hearted…"

"Murderer," I muttered to myself. Summer was awful with similes. "Why'd they think she did it?" I said a bit louder. This had to have something to do with what Clem had figured out earlier.

"I've asked her parents," said Summer, waving her phone. "They said they'll let me know what the police say."

"I mean…I heard a rumour she was in love with Millie," said Tommy. "I guess she could have killed Hugh for breaking Millie's heart, and then killed Millie when she said she didn't love her back?"

Summer and I turned to him.

He shrugged. "Millie told Eddy, who told me."

"Millie thought *everyone* was in love with her," wailed Summer. "Hattie is in love with *me*." She got to her feet and paced as she scrolled through her phone. "Why haven't her parents texted me back? What could they be doing? Do you think I should give them a call—"

Tommy gently prised the phone from her hands. "I'm sure

they're still catching up with the fact that their daughter has just been arrested," he said. "They're most likely not even *thinking* about anything else."

"This is *so unfair*," said Summer. "The police are wrong! They're *wrong*!"

But the police had a damning case against Hattie. They found a strand of her hair on the stairs leading up to the roof where Millie had stood before she was killed, even though Hattie insisted she'd never gone near that part of the school, and certainly not that night. She said she'd gone to sleep early, but so had Clem – she easily could have snuck out without Clem knowing.

Then Clem had finally worked out why she recognized Katherine Smith, the woman Hugh had killed: she had seen her in one of the family photos that Hattie had on the board in their room. She hadn't put it together before because she never properly looked at Hattie's family photos, Katherine Smith's face lodging in her subconscious instead.

Inspector Foster checked out the connection between Hattie and Katherine Smith – I guessed her superiors wouldn't have wanted her to, but she felt as guilty about Millie's death as Mr Willet. She found out they were second cousins.

Everything else seemed to fall into place. Hattie had overheard me telling Clem about the short story when I was hanging out in her room – and Summer had shared bits of it with her (i.e. Summer had complained about my contribution).

"But I don't understand why she was sending texts to us," I said to Summer.

It was breaktime, and I was sitting with Summer, Tommy and Clem in a private corner of the school grounds. It was overcast but warm, and though the grass was damp, Summer had brought out a big blanket for us all to sit on. "And how would Hattie even have known it was Hugh who killed Katherine Smith?" I asked. "Not even Tommy knew about that."

"I don't know – she could have overheard him talking about it with his parents or something," said Summer in a dull voice. "People are always being overheard at Heybuckle."

"But why thank me for the short story inspiration?" I pressed. "Why would Hattie threaten to kill me and Summer and try to kill Clem and *actually* kill Millie?"

"Millie was on to her, apparently," said Summer. "And Clem obviously saw the photo with Katherine Smith in it – it was tacked onto her board in their room for a while."

Clem flushed, avoiding Summer's eyes. No one, not even Summer, blamed her for handing the evidence in.

"And as for the texts," continued Summer, "Hattie was apparently angry at me, because of a big fight we'd had. But if she'd targeted just me it would have been obvious – so she disguised it by texting you as well." I had never seen her look so lost and defeated.

"But—" There were a thousand other things that still didn't add up, and I wanted to go through them all, one by one.

"Mr Willet said they'll find an explanation for everything even if they don't have answers now," said Tommy. "They've got physical evidence – the strand of hair. And a motive – Katherine Smith was her second cousin and it sounds like they were close—"

"Not that close," interrupted Summer. "They only met a few times—"

"Close enough to kill Hugh out of revenge," said Tommy, before shrugging. "In the eyes of the police at least."

I wasn't convinced. I didn't believe it was Hattie – it was my instinct again, telling me things still weren't quite as they seemed.

I knew I should just leave it – if the police were right, everything could go back to how it was before. I'd no longer be a murderer's target – I'd be safe again. Nice and invisible. The school board's big meeting was less than a week away, so the arrest had come in the nick of time for me and Summer. They'd finally got the action they wanted, and we were off the hook. Our scholarships were safe, and I felt like a heavy weight had been lifted off my shoulders.

Except I didn't want to let Hattie take the fall. I knew what injustice felt like. We needed to keep digging.

"I've got to go," said Summer, getting to her feet. "I want to give Hattie's parents another call – see if they have any updates. Bring my blanket in when you guys are done, okay?"

"We should have a brainstorm session later," I said, turning back to Clem and Tommy as I rolled up my sleeves. "The police aren't looking for the killer any more, so it's down to us and Mr Willet now… If we can convince him the police are wrong."

"Mr Willet won't be allowed to carry on," said Tommy with a frown. "He was only allowed on campus because Hugh's parents really wanted him here, and Mrs Greythorne couldn't go against their wishes. Hugh's parents will be happy that the police have found the killer – they won't see a need for Mr Willet to keep investigating."

Clem looked confused. "What do you mean? Why would we have a brainstorm session later? Hattie is the killer. It's over."

I gaped at her. "You can't really think she did it?"

"Yes, I do," said Clem, jutting her chin out, though her voice shook. "The police have all the evidence – they said it's her and I believe them. I *have* to believe this is the end. Jess – Millie was *killed*. Someone tried to kill me as well… And I slept in the same room as Hattie. She knew I was dating Hugh – she knew what he'd done. And she didn't say anything…" She took a deep, shuddering breath. "She had Katherine Smith's picture on our wall."

But my instinct said that Hattie was innocent. That our killer was still at large and people could still be in danger.

I turned to Tommy. "Do you think Hattie's guilty?"

Tommy shrugged. "I mean…the evidence against her doesn't look good. And, er…she's the one who found Hugh's body, isn't she? They say the person who finds the body is the one who most likely killed them."

"That doesn't apply here though," I argued. "For one thing, she found him the next morning."

Clem pressed her fists against her eyes. "This needs to be over," she whispered. "I need it to be over. Hugh's gone and Millie…" She shook her head. "But I trust you, Jess, and if you think we need to keep looking, then…" Her entire body trembled, and I knew even if she thought Hattie was the murderer she would keep going, for me, even if it broke her – and she was very clearly close to breaking.

I couldn't do that to her.

"No," I said gently. "I just…I just wanted to be the one to solve it."

Clem sucked in a breath, and I could tell she was debating whether to press on or leave it.

"Okay," she said after a large pause. "Okay…" She nodded, and gave me a hug, squeezing tightly before she pulled away. "I'll see you inside," she said, looking from me to Tommy before she headed back to the school.

"Better get this blanket folded up," I said to Tommy. I was disappointed he agreed with Clem, but at the very least I still had Summer to figure things out with. Clem didn't need to know I was going to carry on searching.

"Look, I want this to be over as much as Clem does," said Tommy, as he stood up and started folding. "It sounds bad, but I really want it to be Hattie, because that means Hugh will have got justice – and that's the only thing I can do for him now." He took a deep breath. "So did you mean that stuff about just wanting to be the one to solve it, or do you genuinely think we still need to keep looking?"

"We need to keep looking," I said without hesitating.

Tommy stared at me for a second, his eyes unreadable. Then, he nodded. "I trust you, Jess. I trust your instincts. And if you don't think Hattie did it…then I believe you. And I'll help you keep looking for answers."

38

I obviously didn't tell Clem that I was still investigating. When Saturday arrived, she went off for lacrosse practice in the morning.

"I'll join you after lunch?" she said as we put our trays away after breakfast. "The team wants to go into the village, so I might be a while."

She probably felt bad for leaving me on my own, but little did she know, this time I wouldn't be by myself. I would be with Summer and Tommy, trying to solve the mystery and clear Hattie's name.

I headed up to Tommy's room, where Summer was already waiting, sprawled out on the floor with sheets of A3 paper in front of her. Tommy was on his bed, his legs crossed as he looked intently at the papers. He was tossing a stress ball back and forth between his hands.

Summer had clearly been hard at work. The papers exploded with colour, and Summer had all her pens laid out, and was currently sucking on the end of a red one.

I squatted down to look more closely at everything.

"We've been here for ages," said Summer, without looking up.

"Sorry – I had breakfast with Clem," I replied, as I decided that squatting was super uncomfortable. "Toss me a pillow, Tommy."

He threw one at me, and I propped it on the wall, so I could lean against it.

"Don't apologize," said Summer, in her bossy voice. "Women apologize too much."

"Sor—" I began, then stopped myself.

Tommy caught my eye and grinned.

The papers were filled with all the details we'd gathered about the case: Katherine Smith was killed in the hit-and-run, Millie was the leader of the Regia Club, the Regia Club had told me to stop looking into the murder...

Summer was working on a timeline, which she was drawing with a ruler. The first event was Hugh and Millie's fight, then our last G&T class with Hugh, then the murder, and so on.

A third paper was headed *HUGH*, and was largely blank, though there were a few words written in Summer's perfect handwriting. I read upside down:

Rich
Neat
Cheated on girlfriend
Cared about friends
Liked football
Killed woman

It was certainly an eclectic list.

"We're approaching this logically," said Summer. "Timeline – everyone that could possibly be involved – anything we know." She yawned so widely I thought she was trying to suck in all the air in the room.

"Maybe you need a break..." said Tommy.

"No, I don't," said Summer, yawning again.

"Did you not sleep?" I said, raising my eyebrows. That explained the huge circles under her eyes and the strange, slow way she was talking.

"I won't sleep until Hattie's name is cleared," said Summer through gritted teeth.

"Which is an admirable goal," said Tommy, still tossing the ball back and forth. "But with no sleep, you probably won't be thinking clearly."

Summer dismissed Tommy's concerns with a twitch of her nose.

"How're you, Jess?" asked Tommy, his green eyes fixing on me.

"Been better," I said, as Summer started muttering to herself. "Look, Summer, we can help too. I'm sure between the three of us—"

Summer finally looked up at me. Her eyes were bloodshot, strands of hair falling out of her ponytail, which hung limply at the back of her head like a dog's tail when the dog in question was in trouble.

"We can't figure this out," she said. "Because I've gone through this in every possible way."

"Well, our page about Hugh as a person is pretty empty," I said, trying to be helpful. "What else did we know about him?"

Summer frowned, then picked up her pen, writing *loved Clem, hated Millie*.

"He didn't hate Millie," I said, frowning. "He really did love her." I looked to Tommy for confirmation.

He nodded. "That's right. He cared about them both."

"When a guy cheats on you, it means he doesn't care about you very much," said Summer, explaining slowly like I was five.

"I know that," I said. "But Hugh was an…an odd person." I know you're not supposed to speak ill of the dead and all that, but I guess *odd* was the best way to describe him.

We rehashed everything again, all morning.

We took a break for lunch – well, Tommy and I did. We brought food back from the dining hall for Summer.

We carried on.

I thought Clem might message me, to ask where I was, but she didn't. From her posts on social media, she was still hanging out with her teammates. I guessed that as it was their first proper time together since what happened to Millie, they would probably stay out all day. Which was fine with me, because I could keep going with the others.

We went round and round in circles, always hitting the same dead ends.

There was no reason for the murder to be based on our short story.

The texts to us generally didn't mean anything.

Millie had been killed before she could tell me something about Hugh and the Regia Club – *the mystery isn't who is involved, but why*. What did that mean?

And so on, and so on.

I started to get frustrated. "None of it makes sense," I wailed. "Hugh was this mix of people...did anyone even know him at all...?" I trailed off, because something had just occurred to me. All the events flashed through my mind like lightning, a highlight reel of what had happened.

My story – Hugh snatching it – the texts – the notes – Clem's attack – Millie's death – Hugh being a good friend – Hugh caring so much – Hugh being weirdly neat...

Hugh being weirdly neat.

His textbooks were always pristine. He cared about his books.

"What is it?" said Tommy, almost falling off his bed in his eagerness to stand up.

"I think I've figured something out," I said in shock.

39

"Hugh was super neat," I said, my voice trembling as I got to my feet. "And he cared about his friends."

"You're just repeating what we already know," Summer said, stabbing her pen at those two statements on her poster.

I didn't want to tell them what I was thinking, just in case I was wrong. That would have been embarrassing. In fact, I wasn't even sure if my hunch would lead anywhere – I worried it might just be a coincidence, me making a big deal out of nothing. But it was the only thing I had at this point.

"Tommy – your last present from Hugh. The rugby book – where is it?"

His collection of books was no longer lined up against the wall. I trembled as I thought back to the first time I saw the book – how I'd registered it as tired-looking, how a few of the pages had been bent over.

Tommy said he hadn't touched it, so *he* hadn't bent over the pages. The book could have been second-hand – except Hugh was rich: that information was right at the top of our list about him. He wouldn't have bought anything second-hand.

Plus, he was neat and tidy. Folded-over pages really didn't seem like his style – especially if it was a gift. He would have treated it well, particularly since it was the place he'd hidden the information about Katherine Smith, his biggest secret.

This all added up to something odd about the book – even after we'd found the newspaper clipping.

"I put it in the wardrobe," said Tommy, hovering behind me. "Seeing it all the time…was making me sad." He slipped past and reached into his wardrobe, rooting around at the back. He emerged a second later with the book in question. "There aren't any more newspaper articles in here or anything," he said.

"I'm not expecting there to be," I replied, taking the book and gently turning the pages, scanning for…something. I wasn't even sure what. Except if there *was* going to be another clue from Hugh, he would have given it to Tommy – he'd trusted him above anyone. And there *had* to be another clue, because otherwise I didn't know what we were going to do. We hadn't even properly looked through the book – Tommy had stopped when he got to the newspaper article… Which had been carefully clipped in so as not to harm the pages… The already bent-over pages…

There. Right on the second to last page, Hugh had—

"Doodled?" I said, looking up at everyone. "He's drawn a doodle here." It was some sort of puppy, with squiggles around the edges.

"Hugh didn't doodle," said Tommy firmly. He held out his hands, and I passed him the book. "This is…bizarre," he said.

Summer took a look, frowning as she peered closer at the page. "This doodle's in pencil," she said. "Really hard pencil, drawn over and over…and I think there's something underneath… Get me a rubber."

Tommy tossed her one and she rubbed at the page.

"There's pen underneath, really faint…" she said. "*H*… That's a lowercase actually…*h*…*V*…*B*…" She carried on muttering to herself. "*hHVB!%17/07*. What does that mean?"

Tommy and I looked at each other, shrugging at the exact same time.

"Fat lot of use you two are," she said, as she frowned at the page. "I think…maybe it's a password? Mixture of upper and lowercase letters, numbers and symbols?"

"Well, what's it a password to?" I asked. "His laptop?" I bit my lip. The police would have that – or else his parents.

"Or maybe to his personal cloud account," said Tommy, pulling his laptop out of his drawer. He flicked it on, and the screen lit up at once. My ancient laptop would have taken about three weeks to load up. "I can try logging into his account – his username would have been his email."

We all hovered behind him as he brought up the login page.

"Surprised he had such a strong password," said Summer. "I'd have taken him for a *Password1* type of guy."

"HHVB…" I muttered. "His initials."

"What's 17/07 mean?" asked Summer, as the screen finished loading.

We were staring at a list of all Hugh's files. Tommy started scrolling. Most were school assignments, though there were a few pictures as well.

There was a folder labelled *Science Fair*. Summer growled as Tommy scrolled past that one.

"Snake kept the evidence," she muttered.

I ignored her as a thought struck me – the password. "Go to the seventeenth of July," I said.

Tommy scrolled down through what felt like hundreds of files until he got to files uploaded on that date. There was just one – a video named *Tommy*. We all looked at each other.

"Open it," said Summer, her voice trembling.

Tommy was hesitating, his mouse hovering over the video. I placed my hand on his shoulder, and he looked up at me. There was fear in his eyes, but I tried to wordlessly tell him that it was okay, that we were here too – that *I* was here too. I didn't know if he'd got my silent message, but then his other hand reached up to squeeze mine, once. It was so brief I almost missed it, but I got the meaning: he was grateful for my support.

He swallowed. "The hit and run was on the sixteenth of July."

Hugh had made this video the day after he killed Katherine Smith.

I moved my hand so it was on top of his, over the mouse. And together, we clicked.

40

The screen was dark for a second – then the camera panned up to Hugh's face. He was sitting at a desk in what looked like an office space, with just a lamp on. The light was weak, and behind him was darkness.

"That's his house in Richmond," said Tommy, tensing.

"Hey, Tommy," said Hugh, looking right at the camera.

It was like he was talking directly to us. I still had my hand over Tommy's. He was trembling.

"I don't know if you'll ever watch this – I don't know if you need to see this…"

Hugh hesitated. A part of me wanted to throw up, because here was a boy who I thought I'd never see again. This Hugh had absolutely no idea what was lying in wait for him. This Hugh had no idea that in less than a year he would be dead.

"I'm doing something bad," Hugh said, his voice cracking. "And Eddy…" He trailed off, rubbing his head, his blond hair sticking up in tufts. "I don't even know what I'm saying. Tommy, you're my best friend – you'd forgive me, no matter what, right?

Even if I did the worst thing in the world… Loyalty – that's the most important thing…"

Hugh's face was troubled. He licked his lips. "Millie is… I know you've never liked her. She gets me, like no one else does – she's been through everything with me…but you know she'd kill me if she found out about me and Clem." I did the maths: by mid-July last year, Hugh and Clem had been seeing each other for a few weeks behind Millie's back.

"Well, someone else killed you before Millie could," muttered Summer. I elbowed her automatically. "Ow."

"I know Eddy is in love with Millie and he feels really guilty about it," said Hugh. He was slurring his words and there was sweat dripping down his forehead. "But he doesn't know… He doesn't know… I can't lose her, I can't…"

The camera shook as the video clicked off. We all sat in silence.

"That's *it*?" said Summer. She collapsed to the floor. "That's *it*?" she repeated.

I knew exactly how she felt – I'd been expecting some sort of big revelation. Not a jumbled mess of words that barely made any sense.

"He was thinking clearly enough to upload it," said Tommy, standing back. His voice was desperate, grasping at straws. "And he was thinking clearly enough to change his password to the date he uploaded the video, and hide it under that doodle…"

"He didn't tell us anything we didn't already know," said Summer. "Everyone knows Eddy was in love with Millie – that's why he did so much for her."

"I know we knew… But shush," I said, my mind whirring.

I was such an idiot. I'd heard Millie arguing with a guy on the same night Hugh was killed. Telling him he needed to stop – and he'd been pleading with her, asking her what had changed. Saying he'd do *anything* for her.

I hadn't even registered it as an important conversation, because at the time I had no reason to be suspicious. Then Hugh's death drove everything else from my mind.

"What if Millie made it very clear to Eddy that she wanted Hugh dead?" I said. "What if she said she wanted to kill him as a joke and Eddy took it seriously?"

"And then she wanted to protect him," said Summer. She jumped to her feet, like something had shocked her. "Or else she was scared of him. She went back to letting Eddy do everything for her. But that wasn't enough for him. When it was clear she didn't love him back…"

"He killed her," I finished.

"But there was only half an hour of Eddy's time unaccounted for that night," said Summer. "And Mr Willet said his mum confirmed he was on the phone to her…"

"She could have lied," I said. "The police might not have bothered to check phone logs… They might have just taken her at her word. Eddy's family is really powerful…"

We all stared at each other. My heart was thudding, like I had just run a marathon.

Tommy swallowed. "Let's go speak to him."

Eddy was playing football outside with a big group.

"How's it going?" said Tommy, as he intercepted a pass.

The other boys whooped.

"Are you going to play? Come join our team!" one called. Another looked at me and Summer. "You can come too!"

I could see how Tommy might not have actually known Eddy very well when Hugh was alive, if all they did was play football together. The boys didn't seem to care too much about *who* they were playing with, as long as they could have a good match.

"Actually, I need to talk to Eddy," said Tommy with his easy smile.

The boys shrugged, carrying on playing their game while Eddy followed us to a quieter patch of grass.

"Why do you always hang around with *them*?" said Eddy, running a hand through his spiky hair as he nodded at us. He must have put a tub of gel in his hair because it was all shiny.

"I need to ask you about the night Hugh died," said Tommy.

I dug my nails into my palms. This was it. This was the moment of truth.

"You were in the common room for most of the evening – except for about half an hour. Where were you?"

Eddy frowned. "I told you – I called my mum." His eyes flicked to the ground as he spoke – he was lying.

He'd done it.

He'd killed Hugh for Millie. Which meant he'd tried to kill Clem because she argued so much with Millie – and then, finally, killed Millie as well. I balled my hands into fists. My entire body shook. He'd been one of Hugh's best friends. He'd been in love with Millie.

312

I wanted to back away slowly and tell Mr Willet. There was no point confronting Eddy. We had no real proof, and I didn't want to anger a murderer even further. But Summer had other plans.

"Hugh trusted you," Summer said, her voice croaky. "The night he died, he went out to the grounds to meet with you. He wouldn't have been suspicious at all, because you were one of his closest friends. And you killed him, and tried to kill Clem – and then…and then you pushed Millie to her death."

Eddy was staring at Summer like she had grown three heads. "What the hell are you talking about?" he said. "I didn't kill Hugh. Or…*her*." His bottom lip trembled and he suddenly looked a lot younger.

"You wanted to help Millie with something," I said, though my confidence in the theory was ebbing away like a turning tide. "I overheard you and her, in the stairwell, a few hours before Hugh died. You wanted to kill Hugh for her and she didn't want you to take it that far—"

"I wanted to do Millie's detention!" Eddy was half yelling. "Because I was in love with her and I'd have done anything for her."

Well, at least we'd been right about something.

"But she wouldn't let me," continued Eddy. "I even… I even went over to the sports shed that night. *That's* what I was doing when I told everyone I was calling my mum. Clem was cleaning the balls and Millie was chucking them around to annoy her. And I told Millie I would help, and then she called me a… a loser." His voice shook. "And while I was chasing after her, someone was murdering Hugh." His gaze locked onto Tommy.

313

"I betrayed Hugh and I thought it would all be worth it, if it meant I had a shot with Millie. And now... And now..."

Tears poured down his face.

"She's gone," said Tommy gently.

Eddy stared at the ground. "They're both gone. And the police couldn't save Millie – and neither could that stupid private detective." To my surprise, he spat a huge glob of spit onto the floor.

"What've you got against Mr Willet?" I said in surprise.

"Always acts like he knows exactly what you're thinking," said Eddy. "Thinks he knows it all, but he *doesn't*. You know, he tried to tell me I was wrong about Millie, that she never actually liked me?"

"Shocker," muttered Summer.

"But he does know stuff, that's the worst bit," said Eddy. "I saw him, you know, like, a week before Hugh died. In the village near school."

"What?" I frowned.

"I asked him about it when he was questioning me," said Eddy. "And he said he was following a hunch...like *he already knew Hugh was going to be killed*."

"So, you think Mr Willet is a psychic," said Summer, sounding decidedly unimpressed. "My friends, I will say this – this has been a complete waste of time."

"Well, that was a good lead gone up in smoke," said Summer, as we started walking back up to school for dinner. "I mean, Eddy could have been lying, but he was really convincing."

314

"But why was Mr Willet near school *before* Hugh died?" I said, scrunching my face up.

"Maybe he's super hard up for money and killed Hugh so he could be paid to not solve his murder," said Summer.

Tommy and I stared at her.

"What?" she demanded. "Maybe *he's* related to Hugh – *his* second cousin. And they were actually really close, and Hugh stole the short story and told him all about it, and then Mr Willet was like *ah, it's so unfair, my side of the family is so poor compared to Hugh's, this short story actually gives me a great idea.* Maybe that's why the Van Borens hired him – keeping the investigation in the family. Maybe his name's not even Andy Willet, but something like Andrew Stevenage-Clay-Reynolds the Third of Shropshire."

"Er…" Tommy began.

"Or *maybe* Mr Willet is pals with the killer, and they gave him a heads-up that things were about to go down so he came to Heybuckle early to be ready for the murder." Summer's face was getting redder. "Come on – if the police can think of stupid reasons for why Hattie killed Hugh, we can do it for Mr Willet. We can make anything fit if we want to." She was breathing heavily – I could tell she was tired, frustrated, angry… And all that meant she had finally unlocked her imagination. If she'd shown this amount of creativity when we were writing the short story, who knew what sort of murder scene the killer would have had to copy.

"But this is genuinely a new clue," said Tommy.

I guessed he was trying to be encouraging.

"Except it doesn't *tell* us anything," said Summer. "That Mr

315

Willet got tipped off that someone was going to murder Hugh? He can't have killed him – how would he have snuck into school to do the murder? How would he have stolen the trophy in the first place, or heard about our short story, or found our numbers to send the murderer's messages?"

We sat together in the dining hall, still discussing Mr Willet and going back over Hugh's video in case we had missed anything.

"Maybe it really was just Hugh rambling because he was drunk and feeling guilty about killing Katherine," said Summer, shaking her head.

After we'd eaten, Summer mumbled something about wanting to be alone. But then she told me she'd be taking the minutes of the Regia Club back to her bedroom, and I figured she wanted to carry on trying to crack the code at the back of the book – Hugh and Millie had both been members of the club, and Summer didn't think that was a coincidence. She hadn't said it explicitly, but I think she had a new theory that the Regia Club was trying to kill off all its own members. She'd gone past the point of grasping at straws; I knew all she could think about was Hattie, sitting alone in a cell – or wherever she was.

I didn't even have a theory for how the Regia Club fitted in with the murder any more – it was like they belonged to a different puzzle. Someone had taken a big risk to get the book of Regia Club minutes to me, but I had no idea who – or why.

Tommy and I remained sitting, with Tommy staring at me.

"Did you really think I did it?" he said. The question came out of nowhere. It was like he had taken a leaf from Arthur's book, by launching into a conversation and expecting me to catch up. "Early on?"

"Well…" I wanted to say *No of course not, I would never suspect you.* But I didn't want to lie to him. "Yeah. I mean, I didn't really know you, before. You never talked to me."

"Yeah, that's true," said Tommy, and his expression was earnest. "But that's only because—"

"Awww, you guys are so *cute*," said Lucy, as she slammed her tray down beside us.

Kate sat on my other side, and Annabelle sat opposite, looking a little bit reluctant.

"We were sitting at the next table over, but we just *had* to come and join you. So, how long have you actually been dating? It's been a while now, right?"

"We're not," I said, my face flushing. "We're just friends." *Even though I am in love with you, Tommy Poppleton.*

Tommy flashed one of his dimples as he smiled. "Yeah, that's right," he said, his eyes full of amusement.

"Ah, I was wondering why you were on a date with Summer as well," said Annabelle. She actually sounded a little bit sad. It might have been because she wanted gossip, but also maybe… maybe in her own way she actually wanted me to be happy.

"Why aren't you with the other lacrosse girls?" Tommy said to Kate, as I squirmed with embarrassment.

"I'm banned from leaving campus because I got too many tardies," said Kate, rolling her eyes.

Lucy launched into new gossip, and Kate gasped at the right moments. I looked over at Tommy and he seemed to understand my silent plea to leave, because he got to his feet.

"Jess and I were supposed to meet a few people. We'll see you later," he said.

Annabelle was looking at me. "So, are you done with your investigation then?" she said. "Hattie did it, case closed, it's all over?"

"What's it to you?" I said, feeling suspicious at once. I'd never got to the bottom of the fact that Annabelle had no alibi for the night of Hugh's murder.

Annabelle shrugged. "I just didn't take you for a quitter," she said. She seemed…almost disappointed in me.

I stared at her, not knowing what to say. "What's that supposed to mean?"

"I just thought *you*'d uncover the truth," she said, putting a weird emphasis on the word *you*. Like she expected something way more from me. "After all, you were forced into this whole mess – and the Regia Club came after you as well. I don't know… I just don't see Hattie Fritter being involved with them. And I really thought they were part of it all somehow."

"Why are you so sure?" said Tommy, frowning at her.

Annabelle bit the inside of her cheeks as Lucy stared at her, her eyebrows furrowed like she wanted to say something.

"I just thought that maybe while doing everything else, you'd bring down the Regia Club too."

Tommy and I left the dining room together. Tommy had his hands in his pockets, walking slowly by my side. I think he was going to walk me to my room, when a group of his many friends stopped him.

"We've got a game of table tennis set up in the games room," said one of them. "Come join!"

And he was dragged off.

"Speak to you later, Jess!" Tommy called over his shoulder.

I smiled, as I headed back up to my room.

Clem had messaged me, to let me know she was only just coming back from the village and would see me tomorrow. We would hang out for the day, just us. I smiled.

I read a book for a while, then rooted around in my desk drawer for a notebook. I hadn't written anything since that stupid short story. It hadn't even occurred to me.

But now, I felt…lighter. The words were coming back to me.

I picked up a pen, and I wrote.

41

"*Jess*," someone was hissing. "*Jess*."

I thought I was dreaming, so I rolled over. The voice kept going.

"Jess."

I opened my eyes to find a dark, hulking shape looming over me. Panic snapped through me – the murderer had come to kill me. My hand went up of its own accord – maybe to throw a feeble punch.

"What are you doing?" the figure hissed at me.

"Summer?" I whispered, and the enormous monster looming above me morphed into Summer's familiar shape.

"Let's speak outside," she whispered. "So we don't wake Annabelle." Without another word, or any sort of explanation as to what she was doing in my bedroom in the middle of the night, she turned on her heel and stalked out.

I hesitated a second before getting out of bed, throwing on my jumper and some trainers and grabbing my phone, memories of the last time I had snuck out in the middle of the night flashing back to me – Millie had ended up dead. A shudder passed through me as I slipped into the corridor and gently closed the door.

"Why are you here?" I asked, rubbing the sleep away from my eyes and checking my phone. It was just past midnight. In the dim lighting, I could see she was dressed head-to-toe in black; black jeans, black shoes and black hoodie. "Why are you dressed like that?"

"Why did you try to punch me?" she said.

"I thought you were trying to kill me!"

"Why would I wake you up and *then* try to kill you?" she replied, rolling her eyes. "And I'm dressed like this because we're going on a mission."

"You what?" I said stupidly, blinking at her.

"I figured out the code in the Regia Club minutes!" she said, pulling the little book out of her hoodie pocket. She flipped to the back page. "When I cracked the code, I figured out I was looking at *dates* and *times*. For meetings."

I could see where this was going. "And let me guess – there's a meeting tonight."

Summer nodded. "At half past midnight."

"But surely they wouldn't *still* hold a meeting?" I said. "Not after what happened with Millie?"

"This might be their last one!" said Summer. "Come *on*." She tugged at my sleeve.

"So, what – you want to go around the entire school looking for a secret meeting?" I demanded. "We're never going to find where it is, even if we do know when."

Summer smiled triumphantly. "That's what I thought. But – look." She flipped to the back page of the minutes book, where someone had written *Cellars*.

I frowned. "I'm sure the last page was blank before."

Summer brushed aside my concern. "Let's go," she said. "It's probably going to take us ages to find the right cellar."

The cellars were off limits to students, a warren of rooms below Heybuckle, carved into the stone. We could easily get lost. I pointed that out, but Summer was obviously prepared. She held up a piece of chalk.

"We'll mark our way with this. And if we get lost, we can just go back and rub off the wrong marking and try a different way."

"And what are you going to do when you get there?" I asked. I was determined to be smarter than I was when I went to meet Millie, and ask all the sensible questions first. "Burst in on the Regia Club and...what? Tell them you're going to the press?"

"Accuse them of being the murderer," said Summer triumphantly. "I think they're killing off members who broke the rules by telling people they were in the club. Hugh told Tommy when he shouldn't have. Millie told you."

"So why was Clem attacked?" I asked, raising my eyebrows. "Why were we sent death threats?"

"I haven't figured it all out," snapped Summer. "But I think it's a plausible theory. So, are you coming or not? Because if not, I'm perfectly capable of going by myself."

I could tell she was serious, and I also knew there was no way I could let her go on her own. "Fine," I said. "We'll go and have a look."

She smiled at me, and some of the tension in her shoulders dropped. Despite her big words, it was clear she really hadn't wanted to go alone.

322

I didn't even know where the entrance to the cellars was, but that wasn't an issue for Summer.

"I did a report on Heybuckle when we first started," she said. "For a bit of extra credit. I saw the cellar door on a map. It's near the kitchens."

We went down one of the back corridors, where students normally didn't go. The corridor was much narrower than the main ones. Summer had to put her phone torch on, because there weren't any lights, and the small windows set into the thick walls weren't much help, as outside was pitch-black. The narrow beam of light revealed the corridor was dingy, dust on the floorboards and cobwebs hanging above us.

"Here's the cellar door," said Summer, stopping outside a plain wooden door.

I half hoped it would be locked – surely it would be locked... But Summer tried the knob and it turned easily.

"Excellent," she said. "The Regia Club must have a key."

I wanted to point out the fact that if they had a key and we didn't, they could very easily lock us down there. No one else knew where we were, and I bet there wouldn't be any phone signal.

If we went down, we might not come back up.

I shook my head, forcing the thought away. Quickly, I got out my phone and texted Tommy to let him know where I was going, so that way if we didn't appear in the morning, he would be able to sound the alarm.

Summer had already gone through the door, and I followed her, my heart thudding. I switched on the torch on my phone as well, but both of our beams did little to penetrate the thick blackness, barely lighting the few steps leading down from us.

We reached the bottom and found ourselves in a small room with boxes. I peered inside one.

"It's just school supplies," I said, feeling slightly relieved. I don't know what I was expecting. Skeletons? Monsters? The murderer?

In the darkness, it felt like anything could jump out at us.

Summer went into the next room, taking her light with her and leaving me with the weak beam from my phone. I hurried after her, not wanting to be left alone. She was flashing her light over the walls, revealing five empty doorways leading off in different directions.

"This is stupid," I whispered, not wanting to break the silence weighing down on us. "We're going to get lost even with your chalk."

But Summer had gone up to the middle doorway, peering at something on the wall. "Jess, come look at this," she said.

Reluctantly, I sidled up behind her, looking longingly back at the first room with the school supplies and the exit. I glanced at the wall she was so interested in. "Yes, that's a lovely patch of stone. Shall we go now?"

Even in the darkness, I could tell she was rolling her eyes.

"Look!" she said, jabbing at the wall. I squinted, and there was a faint *S.R.* etched into the stone. "It's going to lead us to the Regia Club!" she said as she entered the next room.

There was an *S.R.* marked on the wall on the other side as well, to help us find our way back. We found ourselves in a corridor, with doors leading off like gaping mouths, appearing in the light of our torches and disappearing the next second. We flashed our phones over the walls, and I found the next *S.R.* This one led into a large round room, again with several doors leading off. It really was a maze, none of the rooms matching up with the school layout above.

"The cellars down here are actually bigger than Heybuckle," whispered Summer. "There used to be a castle with cellars and dungeons, but part of it got burned down and they made the rest of it into a school."

I could tell that presenting me with historical facts helped to relax her as we flashed our torches over the walls, searching for the next marking.

I slowly passed my light over the walls, and something glinted at me. Terror flooded through my body – I thought I had seen someone's *eyes*.

I passed the torch back, sidling up to where I thought I'd seen the eyes. There was a gap in the wall, just big enough for someone to look through. The doorway nearby wasn't one of the marked ones, and I shone my torch into the room to find it was empty. But there were more gaping doors leading off.

The back of my neck was prickling, but I shrugged off my fear. I was tired and scared, and I had probably imagined the eyes. But all the same, I hurried back to Summer, who had just found the next marking.

We entered the next room: a long corridor with a few doorways leading off. The way forward was easier this time, because there was a faint light spilling from one of the doorways and voices floated towards us.

We edged forwards, and as we did so something crunched

behind us. I grabbed Summer and we stopped, but footsteps behind us carried on.

There was someone following us.

I spun around, flashing my torch over the dark room, but the beam was narrow and the room too large. There were too many cracks and crevices.

"Let's just go," whispered Summer, nodding towards the light.

I nodded as well, because the Regia Club seemed like the lesser of two evils. At least we knew it would just be other students waiting for us in the next room, rather than...

I shook my head. I was being stupid, letting my imagination run away with me. Heybuckle wasn't haunted. All its issues came from human sources.

We switched off our phone torches and entered the lit room, to find ourselves standing on a stone balcony running around the wall. The balcony looked down on a depressed bowl in the ground, where there were around twelve people sitting in a circle, clutching torches and wearing grey cloaks with hoods drawn over their faces.

What the hell? I'd imagined the Regia Club sitting on couches and sipping mint water as they discussed ways to rule the school, not wearing weird robes like they had stepped out of the fifteenth century.

Summer and I crouched down, peering through the narrow gaps between the ornate stone pillars of the balcony.

A few of the students had their hoods pulled down and my stomach swooped as I recognized two faces: Eddy and Kate. The others whose faces were visible were only vaguely familiar, students in the year above me who I passed in the corridors.

326

"How has your first meeting been?" a boy was saying to Kate.

"Good," she replied, but she looked nervous as she stared at the person sitting opposite her, on a slightly raised stone. They had their hood pulled up, their face hidden.

"Nice to have someone to represent the lacrosse team again – you know, after what happened with Millie."

Kate nodded, still looking uncomfortable. I guessed we had missed most of the meeting, if they were having a chat about how Kate's experience of it had been.

"Write up the minutes," said Eddy. He was sitting to the right of the hooded person. "And stagger your leaving times. Number One, you should go first."

Number One. With Millie gone, they had already picked a new leader.

Without saying a word, Number One got to their feet and slipped up the stairs leading to the balcony. I tensed, but they didn't come to our doorway. They went through a different one, swinging their torch.

I knew what Summer was going to want to do, and I shook my head at her to stop her. But she was already creeping along, to follow the leader to wherever they were going. Except they'd gone through an unmarked doorway, and if we lost them, we'd be screwed.

How had the Regia Club already replaced Millie? How could they be so cold-hearted?

I had no choice but to follow Summer. We didn't switch our torches on again, relying on the Regia Club leader's thin beam of golden light. All sorts of wild possibilities were flashing

327

through my head – that Number One was Tommy, that Millie wasn't really dead, that Millie *was* dead and we were following her reanimated corpse, that Hugh had a twin…

The leader turned down a side passage, taking their light with them. We fumbled along until we saw their beam of light down a different corridor. There was scuffling behind us and I knew Summer had heard it too. She got her phone out.

"I'm just going to flash the torch quickly," she muttered. She passed it over the corridor and the doorways, and my heart almost stopped as the beam caught a white face standing in a doorway, which flinched back from the light.

"Oh no, oh no," I murmured. A horrifying thought flashed across my mind, that there were people *living in the cellars beneath the school*.

"Who was that?" whispered Summer, and I could tell she wanted to investigate.

But I glanced back towards Number One – they had gone further along the corridor and were just slipping inside a door. If we lost them, we might never get another chance to see who they were and ask them about the murders.

Blood was pounding in my ears as I made a decision.

"Let's follow the leader," I said.

We hurried to the door Number One had gone through. It led to a set of stone stairs, leading up – out of the cellars. This had to be a secret exit that Summer didn't know about. We tiptoed up them, our footsteps quiet on the stone as we reached ground level. But Number One was still climbing – I could hear them above us. They weren't bothering to be quiet, huffing as they went.

I looked at Summer, and she nodded, pressing a finger to her lips. I rolled my eyes, not needing her reminder to be as silent as I could. Together we followed – up to the bedroom level. The fear flooding through me lessened, because we were back in the relative safety of the main school – except it wasn't really safe, because two of its students had been murdered, and another one nearly killed…

The stairs led to a closed door, which we went through. I closed it behind me, and the door disappeared into the dark wooden panel. A secret door – a secret passage. I wondered how many there were across the school.

We were in one of the boys' bedroom corridors – not Tommy's. Ahead, one of the doors was just closing.

Summer and I looked at each other.

"We've come this far," said Summer.

I nodded.

Together, we went to the bedroom, which was flooded with light.

Inside, Arthur Applewell was waiting.

42

"I thought I was being followed," Arthur said mildly, as he took off his grey cloak and folded it, placing it into a drawer.

Eddy's bed was empty, of course; he was still down in the cellars, waiting to come up.

"*You* took over leadership of the Regia Club from Millie?" I said, unable to process what I was seeing.

"Millie was never leader of the Regia Club," said Arthur, looking confused. Then his expression cleared and he chuckled. "Oh, did she tell you she was? And you believed her? She was always a liar – though she did enjoy the new responsibility I gave her, of coming up with ideas for *proper* pranks."

"But you can't be the leader," said Summer. "You don't come from old money."

Arthur's fists clenched. "That's exactly what Hugh said, why he was so against me becoming leader – but the rest of them wanted to prove that they could be…*progressive* is the word they used." His nose scrunched up, like there was a bad smell hanging in the air.

"But Millie herself called you…*gaudy*," I said, the stupid

insult feeling unnatural in my mouth. "Tacky."

"No, she called *Annabelle* gaudy," said Arthur with a shrug. "Never said anything bad about me."

It was true: Annabelle was the one obsessed with celebrity and flashing money, the one who drew attention to herself. No one had ever insulted Arthur; he faded into the background, a loner.

"Hugh didn't approve of the direction I wanted to take the club," Arthur continued. "I think he knew I was trying to get it shut down."

"You were *what*?" I said, sure I'd misheard.

"I knew if we started doing stuff like damaging school property, Mrs Greythorne would have no choice but to do a proper investigation – that's why I suggested the graffiti prank. The rest of the Regia Club were too thick to work out what I was doing." He rolled his eyes.

"But why did you want to get it shut down?" said Summer. "Surely you would have been happy you were the leader?"

"They're snobs," said Arthur. "They look down on people who *don't come from old money*." His voice was mocking as he quoted Summer. "How amazing would it be if someone like me – whose family is *tacky* – was the one who had all the power? All those years and years of them keeping it going and I come along and destroy it. Show them who's really in charge."

"You could have just gone to the press to shut the club down," said Summer. "You were the leader, you had all the evidence. Why would you go to all that trouble with those awful pranks?"

Arthur rolled his eyes. "If I went to the press, I'd have been

331

exposed right alongside them, and I like my anonymity, thanks. Plus, this way was more fun – slowly destroying their reputation without them even realizing. Showing the school what monsters they *really* are – and letting them know their power isn't infinite."

Summer's mouth fell open in horror. "So did Hugh find out what you wanted?" she asked. "Did you order someone in the Regia Club to kill him so you could lead the club to its ruin without being challenged?"

From Arthur's bemused expression, it was clear he had no idea what she was talking about.

"What? No one in the club would commit *murder* for me."

"Then you killed him yourself?" pressed Summer.

"For the millionth time, I was in detention all that evening," said Arthur, sounding irritated.

I rubbed my head. "You – and the Regia Club – really had nothing to do with Hugh's death?" No wonder I'd felt they belonged to a different puzzle – because they did.

"Nope," said Arthur cheerfully. "Although it was very inconvenient that Hugh *was* killed that evening, considering that was when Annabelle was doing the graffiti of the school logo and she didn't have an alibi – I couldn't have done any of this without Annabelle, of course."

The bedroom door opened and closed. I spun around to find Annabelle standing silently behind me, her expression unreadable as she looked from me and Summer to her brother.

"Annabelle definitely *wasn't* part of the Regia Club," said Summer. "Surely not—"

"Of course she wasn't," said Arthur, like that was the most

obvious thing in the world. "Doesn't mean she couldn't be the one to carry out all the pranks."

I stared at Annabelle, a spike of betrayal shooting through me. I thought she'd been sticking up for me after the honey prank – but she was the one who'd carried it out, who went along with using my ethnicity as a punchline. She was the one who'd written *murderer* on our bedroom wall. I thought we'd been getting closer, becoming something like friends, but she'd been lying the whole time.

"It was very irritating when you started your little... *investigation*," he said, his voice still mocking. "Asking about alibis, snooping – I was worried you might accidentally come across a grey cloak, or something that would give you actual *proof* of who was in the Regia Club. *I* wanted to be the one to get it shut down."

Of course it had been Annabelle. She had the easiest access to my bedroom. Millie had kept popping up, but Annabelle had been there every time too. I shot another glance at Annabelle, then quickly looked away. I didn't want to show her how hurt I was. Even if we *weren't* friends, we'd been roommates for years. Surely, I deserved to be treated better than this.

"I can understand the *STOP LOOKING* poster," I said, trying to keep my voice from shaking. "Annabelle worked out I was looking through Summer's things and told you, and you thought my investigation might dig up Regia Club stuff, so wanted to warn me off. But what about the graffiti calling me a murderer – the prank telling me to wear a mask of Hugh's face?"

Arthur's mouth became a hard, straight line, his eyes full of hatred. "Because you became friends with *her*." He nodded

333

at Summer, who looked baffled.

"What's that got to do with anything?" said Summer.

"I asked you out and you said no," he said, like it was the most obvious thing in the world. "I don't know why you think you're too good for me – you're not, obviously. I wanted to punish you – I suggested that Hugh blackmail you, after you sabotaged Tommy Poppleton's science fair project. And I wanted to punish your friends – of course, you didn't really have any until Jess came along." Arthur smiled at me, and I shuddered.

"I'm *gay*," said Summer. "I was never going to date you. But even if I wasn't, you're not…entitled to go out with me just because you want to."

That was the right word for Arthur. Even if he didn't come from money, like he kept saying, he was entitled, like he thought the world owed him something – like he thought women owed him something. Maybe that was why he'd reacted so angrily when I called him ridiculous in maths. Plus, he'd only become hostile towards me after he saw me with Summer – when he thought I was friends with the person who'd rejected him. Before that, he'd been not *friendly* exactly, but on good enough terms with me to strike up a conversation.

"Why'd you never target Hattie?" I said, the thought suddenly occurring to me.

"I didn't know about Summer's murderer girlfriend until it was much too late – I wanted to plan something special for her, but of course she got arrested." Arthur's face lit up as he said that. "One thing I don't understand is how you knew about the meeting tonight."

334

"I told them," said Annabelle quietly.

I flinched: she had sidled up so that she was standing next to me and I hadn't realized.

"I left them a book of Regia Club minutes."

Arthur stared at his twin, the twinkle gone from his eyes. "You did not," he said. "You're forbidden to. *I* forbid you to—"

"I blanked out all the other names," said Annabelle, carrying on as if her brother hadn't spoken. Her words seemed confident, but her voice trembled. She'd lost the fake posh accent, her voice mirroring her brother's. "Apart from that meeting, where Hugh said he didn't like you. I wanted to make sure they thought the Regia Club had a connection to Hugh's murder, so they would stop you doing horrible pranks – and forcing me to help. I knew Summer was great at maths, so I thought she would crack the code easily." She paused to look at Summer. "It took Summer longer than I hoped, so I thought I would move her along and write *cellars* at the back so she wouldn't have to break the entire code."

Summer looked slightly affronted at the suggestion she'd needed help.

"But why?" I croaked to Annabelle, unsure how I should feel about her. What she was saying didn't change the fact that she'd betrayed me, had pretended to be sympathetic about the honey poured over my belongings, had written *murderer* on my wall at one of my lowest points. At least Millie had always been honest about exactly who she was. "You helped Arthur do all that stuff to me."

Annabelle looked at me, and to my surprise she had tears in her eyes. "My parents always wanted a son – to carry on the

335

family name. They started with nothing, but I guess they turned into huge…snobs. Forgot their roots or whatever. Arthur and I were their last chance at a son – and they were so happy when *he* came along. Their golden child."

The smile was back on Arthur's face, and his chest was puffed out.

"Arthur could do no wrong," continued Annabelle. "And I was always under his thumb. I wasn't brave enough to get away – if I ever tried, he'd rat on me to Mum and Dad and I'd get into trouble. They always made it clear that I was second best – that all my sisters were as well." She took a deep breath. "Lucy tried to tell me not to do the first prank, the graffiti of the school logo, because she knew it was eating me up. She couldn't understand why I *had* to. But then…but then you stood up to the Regia Club, Jess, when you refused to wear that mask of Hugh's face. You stood up to *Arthur*. And I thought maybe you'd help me – that you'd take the club down, take him down, and he'd no longer be the golden child – and I'd finally be free."

"Why didn't you just *say*?" I said, still not understanding. "Ask for my help?"

"We were hardly friends," said Annabelle. "How was I supposed to trust you to help me – especially if you knew the Regia Club didn't have anything to do with Hugh's murder?"

Arthur's fists were clenched as he stared at his sister, his face red with anger; fury radiated off him like heat.

"But even when I gave you those Regia Club minutes, I wasn't brave enough to betray Arthur properly…" Annabelle shook her head. "I tailed you down into the cellars, I thought maybe you might…snap a few photos or something, send them off to a newspaper. No one would ever know I'd been involved. But then you followed Arthur out and I realized I might have put you in danger…" She was quivering as she looked at me and Summer. "I'm sorry – I'm sorry I've been so cowardly, I'm sorry for helping with the pranks, I'm sorry I tried to trick you into saving me… I thought I didn't have a choice."

Her voice cracked, and any anger I was feeling towards her vanished. I knew what it was like to feel backed into a corner, with no way out.

Summer stared at her. I could see disappointment on her face – she'd really been hoping the Regia Club would help prove Hattie's innocence. But then she took a deep breath, throwing her shoulders back and thrusting her chin forward. "Don't apologize," she said, her voice steely. "You've got nothing to apologize for – because no matter what, Jess and I would have wanted to take the Regia Club down – right, Jess?"

I nodded. "Absolutely."

"You can help us if you want, Annabelle," said Summer. "But if you don't, that's okay too."

Arthur snorted. "She won't do anything of the sort. You've already gone too far, Annabelle. Just wait until Mum and Dad hear about this – they'll kick you out, you know. They'll stop paying for your education. Your word against mine—"

"Amelia has a good job now," said Annabelle. "I could live with her."

"Like you'd have the guts," said Arthur, his lip curling.

The Applewell twins stared at each other, locked in a silent battle of wills. How sick, how twisted, had their relationship become – where one twin was raised to feel superior to the other?

I could sense Annabelle teetering on the edge of something, and willed her to know she wasn't alone, that Arthur wouldn't have any power over her if she didn't let him.

The door opened again, and Eddy walked into the room. His eyes widened as he took in the scene.

"What's going on?" he asked.

Annabelle looked at me, and I nodded. I tried to put a lot into the nod – that I understood, that I would be behind any decision she made.

She smiled at me. "What's going on," she said, as she straightened her back, "is we're ending the Regia Club." She shoved past her brother and pulled up a loose floorboard. From the space underneath, she pulled out stacks of books identical to the one she had given me. "Take as many as you can," she said to me and Summer. "None of these minutes are anonymized – they all name Regia Club members."

I didn't hesitate. Arthur tried to block our way, towering over us and holding out his arms, but Summer and I charged together, shoving past him and grabbing a huge pile each.

"Stop them!" shrieked Arthur to Eddy, but he stood to one side and let us go.

"I'm not touching them," I heard Eddy yelling to Arthur, his voice echoing down the corridor as we ran. "I'm not a cartoon henchman!"

We sprinted around a corner, still clutching all the books.

"What are we going to do with them?" puffed Summer.

Annabelle answered by opening a random bedroom, sliding a book inside, and closing the door.

"Bit of morning reading for the school," she grinned. "Can't have a secret society if it's not secret any more."

So that was what we did – running along the corridors, opening bedroom doors and lobbing random books of Regia Club minutes inside. A few people stirred, asked what was going on – but we were gone before they registered what was happening.

We ended up back at mine and Annabelle's bedroom, panting hard. The three of us were smiling widely at each other. Summer's face was flushed, her hair a mess. I bet I didn't look any better.

"Well…this has been a fun night," said Summer. She shook her head, her shoulders slumping slightly. "You know, I really did think the Regia Club was trying to kill off its own members." She smiled sadly as she left.

"Thank you," said Annabelle. "I…wouldn't have had the courage to do this without you."

I collapsed onto my bed, adrenaline still racing through my veins as what we had done hit me: the Regia Club had reigned over Heybuckle for hundreds of years, lurking in the darkness and pulling the strings of everyone in school. In the span of a few hours, the three of us had dragged it into the light – where, hopefully, it would wither and die.

43

I woke early on Sunday morning, and lay there for a while, staring up at the ceiling. Last night felt like a good dream. My sheets were cosy and warm, and Annabelle was snoring comfortingly in her bed. In a weird way, I would miss her next year when we all got our own rooms. She'd betrayed me, but I could understand why. Maybe...we were on our way to becoming proper friends.

The pipes gave a gurgle, and Annabelle's alarm clock was ticking. All familiar sounds, on a normal Sunday morning at school. It really did feel a bit like a second home – after next year was finished and we all left for university, I knew I would look back on my time at Heybuckle fondly. Except the murders...

The nightmare was starting to fade a bit. That was the reason I could look beyond, to next year, when everything would be back to normal. We'd unmasked the Regia Club and it looked like Hattie really was behind everything. Tomorrow, I would get ready to go home for half term and I didn't need to worry about the school board's meeting. And yet...

And yet…

Something still didn't feel right. Deep down I knew Hattie wasn't guilty.

Leaning over, I pulled my notebook from my desk and reread everything I'd written the night before. I winced, because most of it was absolutely terrible. There was a lot of rambling, of going off topic. I would definitely need to edit it – word choice was so important…

My stomach lurched. I sat up properly.

For a second, I didn't know what was wrong. It was like the part of my brain doing all the work couldn't figure out a way to let the rest of me know.

Hugh's video to Tommy – his choice of words was very odd.

I'm doing something bad.

Random bits of conversation floated around in my head. All of us exclaiming again and again that nothing made sense – there were a thousand trails, and they all seemed to lead nowhere. Summer – even me – pointing out that it was just like a story I would write.

And then came the brainwave: none of it made sense *because it wasn't supposed to make sense.* It was all designed to confuse, for us to latch onto the wrong information.

It didn't matter that the murder was based around my short story.

It didn't matter that I had no secret to share with the police.

None of the clues mattered.

Well, none of the ones that had been laid out intentionally for us. Anything we had discovered ourselves, that wasn't presented to us by the murderer, was important.

I got ready for the day slowly, still thinking. Annabelle gave a little grunt as she turned over.

"What time is it?" she said, squinting at me.

"Half seven," I replied.

She groaned, burying her face in her pillow. "Do you always get up this early?" Her voice was muffled.

"No – I'm just going for a walk."

She grunted again, and a second later she was snoring. I slipped out of our bedroom, and down the corridor.

As usual for a Sunday morning, the school was quiet. I passed maybe one student, heading in the direction of the dining room, where the tantalizing smell of sizzling bacon was already drifting out.

I went out to the grounds. The sun was shining in a cloudless sky. It was already beginning to get warm; it was going to be a perfect day. There were one or two people in the distance, going for a morning run.

I found myself walking to the clearing where Hugh's body had been discovered. It had been a morning much like this one, when Hattie decided to go for that fateful walk. Grass and mud stuck to the bottoms of my trainers; it had obviously rained at some point last night – not that we would have noticed.

I entered the woods, and at once was thrust into a perpetual state of dim light. The trees were so tall there were only very brief glimpses of the blue sky above. A gentle breeze blew, rustling the leaves. The air was clear and fresh after a night of rainfall.

Eventually, I reached the clearing. I still couldn't reconcile it with the site of a violent murder. It looked completely normal, the place where kids came to hang out, away from the hustle and bustle of school. Sunlight dappled across the open space, and somewhere above me, birds chirped in the trees.

I'm doing something bad, Hugh had said in that video to Tommy.

Not – *I've done something bad*. Which would have been the more normal way to phrase that you had mowed someone down in your car and left them to die. It was a very odd choice of words.

I sat down on one of the logs, facing in the direction of the school – though of course the building was hidden by the trees.

Mr Willet's voice floated back to me: *If he was waiting for someone, he most certainly would have been facing towards the school.* But the most likely scenario was that Hugh had been facing *away* from school, because that made it easier for the murderer to sneak up behind him and hit the back of his head.

Something else Mr Willet had said came back to me: *Did you ever think that you might be looking at this the wrong way around?*

He'd been right: we'd started off our investigation on the wrong foot, by thinking that someone in my G&T class had killed Hugh because of the missing short story – we'd taken a red herring as fact.

Maybe that wasn't the only fact we'd got wrong.

There was one key assumption we'd made right at the beginning of the investigation... And if it wasn't correct...

A shudder passed through me.

I'd thought I didn't know anything about Hugh beyond the basics – *he was rich, he was neat, he cared about his friends, he cheated on his girlfriend.* But then I'd had that conversation with Tommy, in the school fields. He had told me everything I needed to know about Hugh.

Sometimes I think he cared a bit too much.

And, just like that, I knew who had killed Hugh.

For a moment I was rooted to the spot, too overwhelmed to move.

Somewhere nearby, a twig cracked. Someone was walking down from the school.

I got to my feet, my entire body trembling.

They were getting closer – their footfalls getting louder. They rounded the bend.

"No," I said, shock freezing me to the ground. "*No.*" It couldn't be—

But my protests didn't change anything.

Hugh's killer stood in front of me, holding a knife.

44

"I wish you'd just left it alone," said Clem, in a completely conversational tone, like we were having a gossip session over breakfast. She was dressed in a white T-shirt that said *HERE WE GO!* and bright red jeans, with multicoloured trainers to complete the look. "Hattie got arrested – it was all over."

"How'd you know I was out here?" I said, keeping my eyes fixed on the knife as shock continued to pound through me.

The knife caught the sunlight peeking through the branches, sending out a brilliant reflection.

"I was up early today. Saw you walking across the school fields from my window and I decided to follow. You really should have just left it."

"How'd you know I was still digging?" I whispered, thinking about screaming but knowing no one would be able to hear – we were too far from school.

The leaves on the trees rustled in agreement.

"Lucy mentioned you were with Summer and Tommy at dinner yesterday." Clem raised her eyebrows. "No other reason for you to be with those two."

"Summer's my friend," I said, my voice getting a little bit surer. "Tommy is as well."

"No, they're not," said Clem, her mouth twitching as she twirled the knife lightly between her fingers. "*I'm* your friend. But anyway, I carried on chatting to Lucy – she does love a gossip. And she said you were discussing a video that Hugh recorded for Tommy... Really, *nothing* stays secret in this school. There's always someone listening in. You know – I've been looking for that video for ages. Can't believe *you* found it."

"The video didn't say anything," I said, swallowing hard. "Hugh just said he was doing something bad – it was the day after his hit-and-run..." I could hear myself rambling, but my brain refused to stay still, because that would mean I'd have to accept the horrible truth: *Clem.*

The funny thing was, she didn't look any different. There was no sudden evil malice in her eyes, she hadn't sprouted devil horns. She looked the same as ever – because she had *always* been this Clem.

"It wasn't his hit-and-run," said Clem, still clutching the knife.

All at once it clicked. *Hugh* hadn't been the one who killed Katherine Smith.

Clem had.

"He was in the car with you when you hit her," I said. My lips were dry and cracked. "The CCTV that the police had only picked up that it was *Hugh's* car – not who was driving it."

Clem raised her eyebrows to acknowledge what I'd said, but kept quiet.

"It was probably after one of his brother's parties. You're like

346

him – you do really stupid, wild stuff when you're drunk."

"It's the reason I fell for him in the first place," said Clem, her mouth twisted. "We were the same in a lot of ways."

"*You* were driving the car – and *you* killed Katherine."

"I wanted to forget about it," whispered Clem. She was shaking her head. "I wanted to just move on – it was a mistake that could ruin my life."

I thought back to Tommy's comment on Hugh. *He'd do anything for you. Sometimes I think he cared a bit too much.*

"Hugh took the blame for you by saying he was the one responsible for the hit-and-run," I said. "His parents paid the police off."

Had no one cared about the woman who died? She was just a problem to them, something to sweep under the rug.

The cool amusement slipped from Clem's face as a single tear dripped down her cheek, but I didn't know if she was genuinely upset or if she was still putting on a show.

"I loved Hugh, but I didn't want us to be together in public. I knew the police had buried any evidence about it, but I kept worrying about that night, about people finding out that I was the driver. I didn't want any links – I wanted to keep us a secret. But Hugh was weighed down by all the lying to Millie – and after a while I guess he started to feel guilty about that woman who died." She shook her head. "Our relationship was complicated. I loved him, but sometimes I hated him too. How much he cared, how far he was willing to go for me. Sometimes I would lash out in stupid ways. I got his bag muddy once, because he hated dirt, but he just laughed it off. I could never do anything wrong in his eyes. It was a bit pathetic, really."

Horror flowed through me. "But what about Katherine Smith's family? They never even found out who killed her."

"It's done now," said Clem in the dismissive voice that she sometimes used – which I now realized I hated. "She's dead – and me turning myself in wouldn't make any difference. I'm not going to prison, Jess. I like my freedom too much."

I couldn't believe I'd considered her my best friend – what did that say about me?

"They wouldn't put you in prison – you'd go to, like…a young offenders' institute or something…" I just needed to keep her talking. Maybe she would forget about the knife and come to her senses. "Your parents—"

"Care about their bloody fruit business," snapped Clem. "Nothing else. They wouldn't have done for me what Hugh's parents did for him. They don't care about me – just money."

I felt a small flash of sympathy for her – but she was still twirling the knife in her hands. The hands of a killer.

"But why'd you kill Hugh?" I asked.

"Hugh wanted a clean start," said Clem. "A few months ago, he told me that he wanted to apologize to Katherine Smith's family. He said the guilt was getting to him, he was worried someone in her family would find out what we'd done and come after us." Clem shook her head. "I couldn't let him do that. I convinced him that he needed to wait, to think about what he was suggesting we do. But I knew eventually his stupid conscience would get the better of him and I couldn't let that happen. Even if we somehow managed to avoid prison – doubtful, because we'd committed a whole host of crimes – my reputation would have been in tatters, my career plans over.

What company would want to pay millions to a girl to be their spokesperson, if that same girl had been all over the news for killing someone? All my stupid charity campaigns – doing that podcast to save those ugly frogs and that thing about the trees – would have been for nothing. My image would have been ruined." Her eyes flashed. "I couldn't kill him on my own – I read that detective book that you gave me and it made it clear I needed an alibi that would fool everyone. So, I told Millie about Hugh and me. She hated me, of course – but I think she respected that I had the guts to tell her. She loved anything dramatic, even if it wasn't in her favour."

And there it was, the key assumption I'd made right at the beginning of the investigation – the *wrong* assumption, that Clem and Millie hated each other. Because if they had hated each other, they would *never* have worked together.

"You teamed up to kill him," I whispered.

"After she found out he'd cheated on her, killing him seemed like the natural thing to do for Millie." Clem shrugged. "She really was dangerous."

"Millie got you both into detention by tackling you on the lacrosse field... Coach Tyler literally always sets the same detention – clean the sports balls – so you knew exactly what you'd be doing. And Millie normally took advantage of Eddy. She'd get him to do all sorts of stuff... But she wouldn't let him do her detention that night, because you both needed the alibi." My gaze was still fixed on the sharp point of the knife, my legs wobbling with fear as I went through everything aloud. "But that detention should have taken all evening – how did you manage to finish early to go and kill Hugh?"

Clem rolled her eyes. "I've done that exact detention before – Coach only signs you in and out… He doesn't bother to check you've actually cleaned everything. Then by the next day, there's no evidence you didn't."

Coach Tyler had *said* Clem and Millie did a great job that night – but he'd also been feeling guilty because he thought he'd kept Clem from being with Hugh. He wouldn't have admitted he'd never even bothered to check his detention was done properly.

Plus, Eddy told us he'd seen Clem and Millie there, but we hadn't thought to ask him *when* he went. He could have gone soon after dinner, while they were still working. Millie had been rude to him because she wanted him gone.

"I told Hugh to come meet me out here, for some fun," Clem went on. She looked pleased with herself, her chest puffed out. She had always loved showing off – I bet it had been killing her that no one knew just how *clever* she had been. "He sat right on that log, talking to me." She gestured at the log I'd been sitting on. "Then Millie snuck up and hit him with the trophy from behind – Millie was very strong. From all the lacrosse – it's a great sport."

"The whole performance Millie put on about hating you – it was just for show, so people wouldn't link you guys together," I said, shaking my head.

Clem nodded. "She got really into it. She loved all the theatrics. Of course, she did actually hate you. Genuinely didn't like the poors." She said it in such a glib way, it was clear she didn't care one way or another about Millie looking down on me.

"But you were attacked," I said. Somehow, even though she had the knife, I still didn't want to believe it. "Someone tried to kill you…"

"That was Millie, and it was completely staged," said Clem with a grin. "It was just after you discovered that stupid newspaper article. I thought there was no way I'd ever be connected with the hit-and-run, not when the police had been paid off and all the evidence buried. My original plan was to send the police running in other directions that led nowhere – but I wasn't expecting *you* to get anywhere near the truth. Hugh's family never even knew we were together, and there were always so many people at his brother's parties, I didn't think any of them would be able to place me at his house that night. But *you* knew I went to loads of those parties – I was worried you'd guess I had been with Hugh in the car. But obviously you didn't, so my little fake attack was unnecessary. Not that I regret getting Millie to hit me with that bat – no harm in throwing suspicion away from me."

She talked about faking her own attempted murder like it was the most casual thing in the world. "But then…why'd you kill Millie, if you were working together?" I said, my voice cracking.

Clem had shoved Millie off the roof and hadn't even acknowledged it. She was talking about Millie like she didn't matter at all.

"Hey, I saved your life by killing Millie," said Clem, tilting her head. "See, Millie was getting worried, because Mr Willet said he was onto us. And I *said* he was bluffing, that he was a crap detective – but she wouldn't believe me. She'd got the gist of my method – throwing out a bunch of ridiculous clues to throw everyone off the track—"

"Like that first text to me," I interrupted. "You guessed you'd be a prime suspect. So you sent that message to me, then insisted I tell the police." She'd forced me to go to them – in fact, every time I'd gone to the police, she'd been behind it. She forced me to do loads of stuff I didn't want to – like go through Summer's stuff, where we'd found Summer's blackmail note – that Clem had obviously given to her. What *I* wanted never mattered.

Clem grinned. "You acted as a great red herring for me. It was the same with the threat to Summer – I thought she'd go to the police with it, but when she didn't, I had to use you again. You were a lot easier to manipulate. I wasn't expecting half of the other stuff we found – like Summer's short story with Hugh's name in it, and all the Regia Club stuff. They were really helpful in confusing the trail. Anyway, Millie was freaking out about Mr Willet possibly being onto us, and she'd also figured out how my method worked. So, she decided she would kill you—"

"*What?*" I spluttered. "She was going to *kill* me?"

Clem shrugged, looking completely unconcerned. "It was a good idea. At least, that's what I told her when she let me in on what she was planning to do that night. But she was too erratic – I knew eventually she'd screw up, let something slip. So I decided right then, she had to go."

I felt sick. Millie had wanted to lure me out by claiming that she was the leader of the Regia Club, and pretending she would tell me something about Hugh's murder.

Clem continued with her explanation. "Millie had served her purpose. She'd provided me with my alibi. I knew that as the closest person to Hugh, I'd be under suspicion – even if Millie hadn't staged that original fight in the dining hall, the news would have got out about me and Hugh. I obviously knew you would never say anything – but Tommy knew as well."

All the pieces were still falling into place in my head. "You killed Hugh in this clearing because you knew Hattie took an early morning walk this way. You knew she'd be the one to find him."

"I controlled everything I could," said Clem, puffing out her chest again. "And the universe was on my side. After Millie died, I knew I needed to wrap things up – people were starting rumours that she had killed Hugh and I needed it to be clear that that was impossible, because if Millie was a suspected murderer, that meant there was a good chunk of *my* time that night unaccounted for. So I knew I needed to get someone else arrested for the murders. I didn't actually know Hattie was related to Katie Smith—"

"Katherine," I muttered.

"Like it matters – anyway, I didn't know they were related, but I knew I recognized Katherine from *somewhere*. And then it clicked that she was actually on the pinboard in my bedroom and I knew I could put it all on Hattie. It was a nice coincidence that the murder weapon was a *debate* trophy – Hattie was in debate for years, though obviously no one made that link. I even stole some hair from her hairbrush – really easy to do, seeing as we're roommates – and went back to the stairs leading up to the roof and dropped it there. The pierce résistance."

"Pièce de résistance," I mumbled. I wanted to be sick. It felt like we were a million miles away from everyone at school. My death would probably be the thing that got the school shut down: three murders in the span of a few weeks.

This time, Clem wouldn't even be able to blame Hattie for my murder.

She'd obviously become cocky – and the worst part was, she was smart enough to get away with it. She'd concoct something ridiculous, and the police were rubbish enough to follow whatever trail she set out for them.

"But what about Hugh taking the short story? Us narrowing down our suspects to our G&T class? You *helped* me investigate. And after his death – you were distraught. You're not that good an actor."

Clem grimaced. "Hugh taking the short story was a twist I didn't see coming. I didn't want the suspect list narrowed down – Mrs Henridge leaves her office door unlocked, and if Hugh hadn't stolen that story to piss off Summer, anyone in the school could have read it and been inspired. So *anyone* would have been a suspect. And I helped you investigate because it would have looked suspicious if I didn't – I actually got quite into it. I wanted to make it look like I was *really* helping; that's why I made sure we crossed Tommy off. Hugh told me about his knitting club and I knew he'd never be a serious suspect, so I figured, why not act like I was doing a proper look into his alibi? And as for the whole sadness after Hugh's death…" She pursed her lips. "I really did love him, and it did keep randomly hitting me that he was gone. It truly is a shame that things had to turn out this way. But Hugh was too much of a loose cannon."

There was still something that didn't make sense. "But…
why me? I know you said you wanted to confuse the police.
Why send all those texts and things to me? Why threaten to kill
me? Being involved with all this – it almost lost me my
scholarship, it almost got me *killed* by Millie."

The twisted smile was back on Clem's face. "You're my little
sidekick. So *grateful* for my friendship. I knew you'd never
suspect me."

My eyes burned with tears. Clem had never thought of me as
a real friend – we'd never been on a level playing field, because
she'd always thought she was better than me. When she sat
with me, in the first few days of school, it wasn't because she
could see something in me. It wasn't even because she pitied
me. It was because she knew she could use me – that I was sad
enough to latch onto anyone who was nice to me. One friend
was better than no friends.

She hadn't liked it when I'd started getting close to Summer,
when I'd started expanding my circle beyond just her. That
meant I was slipping out of her control.

I'd believed her when she called everyone else proximity
friends. I had told myself that I was the only one who knew her
– justifications to myself, an explanation for why she never
tried to include me in the rest of her life. No wonder I had never
properly known Hugh; she hadn't ever cared what I thought.

And she hadn't even thought about what sucking me into her
scheme could mean for my scholarship, and Summer's too. She
hadn't cared how precarious our positions at Heybuckle were
compared to hers, never understood why doing well at school
mattered so much to me. She'd never bothered to understand.

She was like Arthur in a lot of ways. Entitled – assuming she was better than everyone else. Thinking she could use other people like they were nothing, tools to be used then discarded.

"I just really, really wish you'd given up when Hattie was arrested," said Clem, as she started edging forwards, holding the knife up. "I really didn't want to have to do this."

I backed away, holding up my shaking hands. My entire body was icy with dread. "I won't tell – I promise I won't." I really couldn't believe what was happening. I felt like I was in a nightmare – that soon I would wake up, nice and safe in my bedroom, the triumph from defeating the Regia Club still coursing through me, with Annabelle snoring across from me.

"Sorry, Jess – this needs to be done," said Clem, and she built up her speed towards me.

I acted instinctively, ducking out of the way.

And then I ran.

I had always hated exercise, but if I had known I might need to run in order to save my own life, I would have trained every day. I crashed through the woods, not even sure where I was going. Without a clear path, I had no sense of direction. I cut through the trees, jumping over roots which rose out of the ground. I couldn't trip – if I tripped, I would die—

My legs were getting heavier, like something had been tied to them, weighing me down. A stitch cut into my side, twisting between my ribs like a knife. My breath got caught in my lungs, and a fire burned around my heart.

Clem snapped twigs as she sprinted behind me – she was faster than me, so much faster—

I swerved to the side, taking a sharp turn. The sudden change was enough to help me gain a few extra seconds—

I plunged into the clearing again. I had done one giant loop. No time to stop, no time to think—

Clem slammed into my back, and I crashed to the ground. Adrenaline surged through me – I had heard about mothers suddenly having the ability to lift cars to rescue their children. Maybe my desperation to save my own life gave me the strength to immediately roll over. Clem was on top of me, her expression one of pure focus as she held up her knife – she plunged it down—

I grabbed her arm, the knife centimetres from my chest. My entire body shook with the strain – her eyes were focused on the knife, on pressing it down—

She wouldn't even look at me. She didn't want to see the desperation on my face, the terror. She would kill me and tell herself she *had* to do it.

My arms were already tiring – she was so much stronger than me—

Then someone grabbed her, pulling her back. She was wrestling with Tommy – and Summer was helping me to my feet, asking if I was okay.

"NO!" screamed Clem, her eyes full of frenzy. She leaped away from Tommy, stumbling backwards, holding the knife in front of her.

Tommy was panting, taking slow steps towards Clem. Scarlet-red blood beaded out of a gash down the side of his arm.

I remember watching a documentary about animals, and how they were most dangerous when they were cornered.

Clem was still holding out the knife, and a scream bubbled within my throat – I wanted to tell Tommy to stop, that she was going to pounce, that she would stab him – she would stab all of us if she had to.

I was not expecting what happened next.

Quickly – so quickly none of us had a chance to react – Clem spun the knife around so it was facing towards her.

And she plunged it into her own stomach.

45

I'm squeamish, so I won't go into too much detail as to what happened next. It's enough to say it involved blood and lots of screaming from everyone.

We were all taken to hospital, even though I insisted that I was fine. Tommy needed a couple of stitches, but apart from that seemed okay.

Shortly after we arrived, the police came to ask us a bunch of questions. They were led by Inspector Foster, and I resisted the urge to tell her that she should think about a new career.

We were eventually allowed to see each other, and sort of collapsed into a group hug in Tommy's private hospital room.

"How did you know I was out there?" I asked them, once we'd untangled ourselves.

"I wanted to have breakfast with you," said Summer, as she slumped onto the edge of Tommy's hospital bed. "But when I went to your room, Annabelle said you'd gone for a walk."

"And I was *at* breakfast, and I saw Clem sneaking into the kitchens and it *looked* like she was taking a monster knife," said Tommy. "I was trying to angle myself so I could see through the hatch. And then she just walked out, and you know…I thought that was odd, so I followed her. Ran into Summer on *her* way down to breakfast and we had just gone outside and seen Clem going into the woods, when Mrs Greythorne stopped us to chat. And then when we got to the clearing… Well, you know what happened then."

I felt a surge of love for them both. They'd really had my back.

As for Clem – well, it turned out stabbing herself was her last-ditch attempt to control the narrative. She had done loads of research when she was looking into how to kill Hugh, getting familiar with different murder methods. She learned the best places to be stabbed and *not* die, and, in the moment, had thought if she faked an attack from the three of us, she could elicit a bunch of sympathy from the fact that she'd almost been killed twice at Heybuckle. It obviously wasn't a well-thought-out plan – but Clem had been coming up with so many ridiculous ideas for so long, eventually one of them was bound to be a dud.

The police took her in, and it turns out her parents *did* care about her a little, because they immediately hired the best lawyer money could buy. Not that this made them good parents. They were partly the reason Clem turned out the way she did, leaving her to raise herself to think she was better than everyone else. They'd shown her the only thing that mattered to them was…*them*. So Clem turned out the same: the only thing that mattered to Clem was Clem.

But I don't want to talk about her any more.

* * *

Going back to school after half term was a weird experience. We walked into the common room and everyone crowded around us like we were celebrities.

"Jess! Tell us what happened! I heard you and Clem had a proper fight, action-film style—"

"Summer – I heard you hacked into the police system and that's how you solved it—"

"Tommy, I heard Clem wanted to get into the Regia Club and had to do a bunch of dares—"

"The Regia Club is finished, didn't you hear? Some minutes of the meetings turned up in my bedroom—"

"They were meeting in the school dungeons—"

"Oi! Back *off!*" yelled Annabelle, pushing them all back. "Give them some space. The truth is, Clem and Millie loved Hugh, and Hugh was in love with a *third girl* and—"

She launched into a version of events that bore little resemblance to what had actually happened, her real accent coming out strong as she caught my eye and gave me a quick wink.

"What happened to your accent?" said Eddy.

"What happened to your hair?" replied Annabelle without skipping a beat, as her eyes dragged over his gelled-up hair.

At least my fellow students had got one thing right: the Regia Club *was* finished. Clem had been inspired by the way the Regia Club sent anonymous texts and notes and the fact that two of its members, Hugh and Millie, thought they were so elite they respectively could get away with a hit-and-run and a murder meant it became a huge embarrassment to the school. No ex-member of the club wanted to step forward and publicly admit they were associated with such a stain on Heybuckle's reputation. Parents of students in the club said they were ashamed of their children's actions and thought Heybuckle was raising them to be better.

Heybuckle assured the world they were taking the shutdown of the Regia Club very seriously. Everyone associated with the club had to have a meeting with Mrs Greythorne, alongside their parents.

Summer and I waited with Annabelle outside Mrs Greythorne's office when it was her turn to have her interview. We sat either side of her on the hard wooden bench and I hoped just our presence would be enough to make her feel like she had moral support.

"You know, you weren't *technically* in the Regia Club," muttered Summer, tapping her fingers against her lap as she shot glances at Mrs Greythorne's closed door. "Like, you weren't listed as an official member. So theoretically, you shouldn't be in any trouble."

I doubted Annabelle would manage to weasel her way out of trouble on a technicality.

Annabelle pushed a strand of her mousey brown hair away from her face, sitting up straighter. She had dyed her hair back to its natural colour a few days after Clem's arrest, and said she only went blonde in the first place because her mum insisted it would make her prettier. I thought she looked a lot nicer now – finally comfortable in her own skin, not ashamed of who she was. She was Annabelle Applewell, and she liked flashy things and gossiping. She wasn't a doll for her mother to control.

A few minutes before Annabelle's allotted meeting time,

her sister Amelia showed up. I recognized her from one of the photos Annabelle had stuck up on her board in our room, but even if I hadn't, it would have been easy to figure out who she was. She was an older version of Annabelle, though she was dressed in a pair of worn jeans and a faded T-shirt that looked like it had been put through the wash one too many times. She had a pixie cut, and a nose piercing, and a tattoo peeked out from underneath her T-shirt sleeve.

"What are you doing here?" said Annabelle, standing up and rushing to her.

"I got your messages," said Amelia, crushing Annabelle in a hug. "And I'm here to act as your parent."

Just as she finished speaking, the door to Mrs Greythorne's office swung open. Mr and Mrs Applewell exited, with Arthur between them. Mr Applewell was wearing a dark grey suit that matched his thick grey moustache. Mrs Applewell was a tiny woman, whose thin lips were pursed, like she was sucking on something sour.

They both stopped in their tracks, eyes widening as they stared at Amelia Applewell.

"What are *you* doing here?" said Mrs Applewell, her nose wrinkling like she had smelled something disgusting.

Mr Applewell didn't acknowledge his older daughter, his eyes fixed on Annabelle. "Come on, Annabelle," he said. "It's your turn to speak to the headmistress. Arthur told me exactly what you did and let me tell you now—"

I expected Annabelle to try and argue with him. But instead, she and her sister completely ignored their parents and Arthur, marching straight past them, into Mrs Greythorne's office.

Amelia closed the door in his face.

There were some people you couldn't argue with, and it looked like Mr Applewell was one of them.

The first properly nice moment was when Hattie and Summer were reunited. Hattie slipped into the dining hall and Summer ran from her seat and they hugged and kissed and we all cheered, like we were in a film.

Meanwhile, Tommy and I got closer. We'd both had friends who had turned out to be completely different from the people we thought they were. We spent a lot more time together than before, going on walks whenever we took breaks from revising for end-of-year exams. Annabelle kept asking me if we were official yet, and I had to keep telling her we were just friends, even though my heart gave a little twang every time I said it.

I didn't hang out with Annabelle all the time or anything. But the atmosphere in our bedroom was a lot friendlier, and I was always welcome at her table in the dining hall if I wanted a gossip with her and Lucy and Kate, who apparently hadn't even wanted to join the Regia Club. She'd felt obligated to, just like everyone else felt they *had* to do the dares.

Annabelle had stayed at school over half term, and when summer term was over, she was going to move in with her sister, who would start paying her school fees instead of their parents. They would be living in a flat in London, not far from my house, so we would be able to see each other during the school holidays.

Arthur, on the other hand, was quietly removed from

Heybuckle by his parents shortly after his meeting with Mrs Greythorne. I didn't know where he'd gone, and I didn't care.

Mrs Greythorne and the rest of the school board asked to have meetings with all of us individually. I was worried about it at first, but then Summer told me they basically wanted to apologize to us and tell us we had all shown *great strength, worthy of a Heybuckle student*. I called Mum before my meeting, and filled her in on everything that had happened, including all the bullying from the Regia Club and the possibility of my scholarship being taken away from me.

"I wish you had let me know all this," she said. Her voice was crackly down the phone line, and I couldn't tell whether she was angry with me for not telling her everything. "These people…" She sighed. "When you go into that meeting, don't let them intimidate you. Stand up for yourself."

"But you told me to always keep my head down," I said.

"You kept quiet and were exactly the type of student they wanted you to be," said Mum. "But that still wasn't enough for them. I sent you to that school because I wanted you to have all the opportunities I never had. Make sure you take them all."

I repeated the words to myself as I waited for my meeting. The school board had been an anonymous cloud hanging over me, faceless people I'd never met who somehow had the power to take my scholarship – something I had earned all by myself – away from me. There had been two murders at Heybuckle and instead of focusing on that, they'd pegged getting rid of me as an easy way of avoiding scandal. I'd received multiple death threats and instead of feeling protected by the school, by the police, I'd been forced to try and save myself, terrified all the time I'd be booted out for something I had no control over.

They were worried about me letting them down – but *they* had failed *me*.

The minutes ticked past my allotted meeting time. On top of everything else, they were keeping me waiting – like my time was less important than theirs.

Anger started to simmer in me.

Twenty minutes late, I was asked to go inside. I discovered the school board consisted of three men and three women, who somehow all looked the same.

Mrs Greythorne gave me a small smile as I sat down.

"I'm glad to put this whole mess behind us," she said. "We're very sorry you had to go through all of this."

The school board murmured in agreement. None of them were looking at me; one of the men yawned, and one of the women checked her watch. They weren't sorry, not at all. The simmering anger turned to white hot rage.

"Sorry isn't enough," I said. For once in my life, I was going to say *exactly* what I was thinking. "On top of everything else, Summer and I had the threat of our scholarships being pulled away from us. We're held to higher standards than any of the fee-paying students. We have to get higher grades. We have to be *exemplary*—"

"How *dare* you speak to us like this?" interrupted one of the men.

"I'm not done," I said, trying to keep my voice from shaking. "You need to change the conditions of the scholarship. You need to make it so once we're in, we're just students, same as everyone else."

"We will do no such thing," said one of the women. "If you don't like the conditions of your scholarship, feel free to give all the money back. You should be grateful to be here."

I laughed. "Two of my classmates are dead. My former best friend killed them and tried to kill me. *Grateful?*" I slid back my chair, and got to my feet, copying one of Summer's power moves by looking them all in the eyes one by one. Then I hit them exactly where it hurt. "If you don't change the conditions of the scholarship, I'm going to the press and I'm telling them *everything*. Heybuckle's reputation is already falling apart – and that's all you care about, isn't it? Reputation? Well, once I'm done, you'll probably have to *beg* people to come here."

They all stared at me, their mouths opening and closing.

"*Now* I'm done talking," I said, and I walked out with my head held high.

46

Two and a bit weeks after Clem's arrest, I was chilling in G&T as I went through some maths prep that Summer had been paired up with me to work on. Maths didn't concern me as much any more, not now I had Summer to help me whenever I got stuck. She hadn't softened her tutoring skills or anything like that, but I knew her better. And, for her part, she was certainly less forceful about sticking to rules and things, which I guess had been her way of protecting her scholarship position.

But she didn't need to worry about that so much now.

We'd both received letters from Heybuckle saying the additional requirements which needed to be met by scholarship students had been reviewed and would no longer apply. I didn't tell Summer why the rules had been changed – I knew she'd berate me for my stupidity in being rude to the board – but the knowledge I had got the better of them filled me with a warm glow.

My blissful time with maths was interrupted by Mrs Greythorne's assistant, calling me to the headmistress's office.

My stomach swooped, and I immediately flashed back to the

days of the murder investigation. Then I shook my head. Clem was gone, at home on bail while she waited for her trial to start. It was all over.

Summer mouthed *Are you okay?* while Annabelle looked concerned.

"I'll find you after," said Tommy, and I smiled at all of them.

Instead of entering the office to find Mrs Greythorne, I was greeted by Mr Willet, lounging in an armchair and sipping a cup of tea.

"How's it going, kid?" he said. "With the police gone, I can finally sit in here. It's not as exciting as I thought it would be." He looked much better compared to the last time I had seen him; he was wearing what looked to be a freshly washed hoodie and jeans, and was clean-shaven once more.

I shot him the dirtiest look I could muster. It probably looked like I was constipated. I had never managed a good dirty look.

"All that money the Van Borens were paying you, and you didn't even figure out the right person," I said, as I sat down and crossed my arms, pursing my lips at him.

Mr Willet glowed red. "The thing is…well, I thought it was Clem and Millie for quite a while. They were the most obvious suspects – and your friendship with Clem made me question her even more."

I frowned. "Why?"

If he'd said it was because he didn't think I was cool enough for Clem, I would have started throwing things. I was not about to be insulted by a private detective who'd been beaten to the punch by a bunch of teens.

369

"Well – I asked you if you got along with Annabelle, and you said you didn't because she was a bit forceful. But *Clem* was forceful – you were always doing what she wanted. I wondered why that didn't bother you."

"Because people are multifaceted and Annabelle is, in fact, much more than 'a bit forceful'?" I offered.

"No," said Mr Willet. "Well, yes, I'm sure that's true. But I could see right then that there was something odd about your friendship. You seemed a bit, er…*oblivious*, shall we say, to any of Clem's flaws."

I knew he was right – I had seen Clem switch her tears off in front of Annabelle and Lucy as easily as turning off a tap, and instead of wondering how she could be so disingenuous, thought she was talented for being able to hide her feelings. I had berated myself for not having the same talent, turning a warning sign into a positive because I had so little confidence in myself.

"The friendship was a bit unhealthy, I think," said Mr Willet. "Where one person feels they are inferior to the other, to the extent that they *worship* the other – well, friends should never make you feel lesser. The dynamics of your friendship seemed to explain why you, in particular, were targeted by the murderer. Summer just happened to be roped in because her name was on the short story too. And, of course, Clem felt it would be easier to exploit you both considering your status as scholarship students."

"Clem was always so much more confident than me," I mumbled. For some reason, I felt like I needed to justify myself to him. "I liked that…"

"There's something to be said for quiet confidence," said Mr Willet. "Of which I see you're developing plenty, now you're away from her."

I cracked my knuckles, trying to stop myself from smiling at the praise. "Well, if you had all these thoughts about who the murderer was, why didn't you say something sooner?"

Mr Willet rubbed the end of his nose, clearing his throat. "In my role, I need to be one hundred per cent sure, to have all the evidence so the police can't question my conclusions. Then, when Hattie was arrested, the Van Borens threw me off the case."

"Right," I said, decidedly unimpressed with just about every adult who was supposed to have protected me. In a way, he was responsible for Millie deciding she needed to kill me. I paused, something occurring to me. "Eddy said something weird about you, you know. He said he saw you hanging around in the local village about a week before Hugh's murder."

Mr Willet sucked in a breath. Then he gave a slow smile. "Really, you can't keep any secrets at this school."

"So it was true?" I said. "Why were you hanging around the village?"

Mr Willet bit his bottom lip. "I *am* a private detective. And the Van Borens *did* put me on this case – after I asked them to. I'm one of the best in the industry, after all…" He tilted his head. "You don't believe I'm the best?"

Had my face given me away? I tried to smooth out my features. "There's just…er…no reviews of you online."

"I'm discreet," said Mr Willet. "It helps sometimes, if people don't know what I look like, or if they underestimate me. But I had a personal interest in this case…because of Katherine Smith."

The way he lingered on her name made the truth click into place.

"You left the book of love poems on her grave."

"She was my fiancée," said Mr Willet with a sad smile. "That was her favourite book. You see, after her hit-and-run I investigated… That's what I do, of course. I worked out it was Hugh, but my evidence was weak… I didn't want to trouble her family with what I'd found, not when I couldn't also give them justice. I went to the police with my suspicions and they wouldn't listen to me. Then I went to the press and they said the Van Borens would sue for defamation if they printed what was essentially a hunch. I figured out the Van Borens had paid the police off. I was…angry. Angry that money means you can evade justice. I began to get angrier and angrier – it was eating me up. I couldn't think of anything else. My family and friends were sympathetic at first but after a while people get tired. They wonder why you can't just move on. So I tried. I tried to forget about it and I just couldn't. I came to Heybuckle hoping to…to ask Hugh *why*. Ask him how he could just move on and act like it never happened…"

"And then he was killed," I said.

"And then he was killed," repeated Mr Willet, with a shake of his head. "I thought it was the universe finally giving Katherine – my dear Kat – justice. But I couldn't let it rest even then, you see? I knew the Van Borens had shot themselves in the foot by paying off the police, because they'd closed off a huge lead. I wanted all the truth to come out – especially if it was linked to Kat's death. I approached the Van Borens and told them who I was and that I would be much better than the police at solving the mystery. They were willing to throw any sort of money at me – money had always solved everything for them in the past, you see."

"So why did you come here today?" I asked.

Mr Willet let out a small sigh. "To say…thank you. I figured out that Clem and Millie had killed Hugh, but I didn't know *why*. I came to Heybuckle initially because I wanted to confront Hugh – and of course now I know it was actually Clem who killed Kat. I don't want to speak to Clem now – I've spent enough time with her to see what she's like; I know she won't feel remorse – she's got the deaths of three people on her hands and it won't mean anything to her. But I have answers now." Tears dripped from his eyes, and he dabbed them. "I have closure." He shuddered on the last word, and took a deep breath, getting to his feet with a sigh. "And hey, kid, if you find yourself interested in the world of private investigation… Let me know, okay?"

The rumour mill had done its job, with what felt like hundreds of different versions of the story floating around, and most of them nowhere near the truth. Eddy, as the former number two of the Regia Club, was front and centre, and was happy to give the inside scoop on the club to anyone who would listen. For the first time in his life, he was proud of something he had sort of "achieved" himself. I guessed that was progress for him.

He came up to me one day, while I was reading in the common room.

"Er… What's up?" I said, looking up from my book.

He sucked in his cheeks as he sat down next to me. "How's it going?" he said.

I stared at him.

"Right," he said. "Good." He swallowed. "Look – I joined the Regia Club to…fit in, I guess. It's where I got close to Hugh – and…and Millie. I just wanted to say…" He cleared his throat. "I'm sorry, Jess. For being involved in those pranks. Arthur was my roommate, and in charge, and I just didn't think too much about following him. I don't know, maybe I need to hang around better people or something."

I blinked at him. He looked nervously at me – waiting to see what I would say.

"Er – thanks for saying sorry," I said awkwardly, wondering if underneath it all, Eddy was actually a good person.

But then he grinned at me, the moment of nervousness gone. "No problem," he said. "And look, I know the *best* PR person – her rates are ridiculous, but I could swing it so you get a discount. You could make some really good money off this story, you know – get into the press, onto talk shows—"

Looked like some things would never change.

Summer had suggested Hattie try to sue the police for being "incompetent arseholes", but as we had no proof of their corruption and they'd actually had evidence against Hattie (even though it was planted by Clem), it was more of a pipe dream than a realistic idea. Hattie said the most important thing was that she had the truth about what had happened to

Katherine, though she still asked to switch rooms. She couldn't stand sleeping opposite Clem's old bed, knowing what she had done.

The final part of term raced by and after our exams were finished Heybuckle decided to put on a firework display. I guess because they thought we all needed to be cheered up or something. I was going in a big group to watch them – with Summer, Hattie, Annabelle, Lucy, Kate, Tommy and a bunch of his friends. The fields were floodlit, though these lights would be dimmed when the fireworks started.

This was probably the happiest I had ever been at school – and best of all, I didn't feel *grateful* that I belonged. I liked the company of my friends – and they liked mine. We were all equals. Instead of Clem for a best friend, who wanted me isolated and never properly listened to me and stole all my chips (and, you know, had murdered two people and tried to kill me), I had Summer. She was tough too, but she would always be there for me.

I finally understood that coming from money didn't make your life perfect. Mum and the rest of my family cared so much about me, loved me so much. Heybuckle had given me lots – but I'd given it a lot too. They were *lucky* I'd won that scholarship.

"Come on – the best view is going to be from the hill," said Summer, and she led the way across the grounds, to where most people were gathered.

I made to follow her, but Tommy caught my arm.

"Hey, Jess, walk with me?" he said, nodding in the direction of a quieter spot, away from everyone else.

"Going to kill me?" I joked, then grimaced.

Luckily, he smiled.

We were just outside the circle of light shining from the floodlights, standing in the golden glow coming from the windows of the main school building.

Tommy looked down at me. He was standing very close, and he wasn't smiling now.

"I'm really excited about the fireworks," I blurted, just to fill the silence.

"Listen, Jess – I just wanted to…" He trailed off, his throat bobbing.

I swallowed. He was standing so close now I could see tiny flecks of brown in his eyes.

"There's something I wanted to say…" He took a deep breath. "I like you – a lot. For quite a while, in fact. I always thought you were pretty cool, but Clem said to me once that she thought you weren't interested in dating, so I figured that was it – I trusted her to be looking out for you. And then all this happened, and we started getting closer – and I couldn't tell if you liked me back, because you kept telling everyone we were *just* friends…" He was speaking so fast that I could barely keep up. "And you really don't give anything away, Jess, even when I've been making it really clear how much I like you."

My heart thumped painfully hard with joy. I hadn't even considered the possibility that he might actually like me back. But then again, I'd initially put him on some sort of pedestal. It was only when I'd started treating him like a normal boy – a normal friend – that I could open up to him properly.

I realized I hadn't said anything. "I do," I said quickly, my voice coming out all weird and croaky. "I do like you. A lot."

For a second he just looked at me. And then he smiled, and it was like the sun had come out. He leaned down, and kissed me, really softly, his lips barely grazing mine.

And I kissed him back, and my hands were in his hair, and his musky smell was overwhelming. My knees were weak as I leaned into him. The kiss became more urgent, and his arms were round my waist, sort of moulding me to him.

I don't know if he pulled away first, or if I did. Either way, I was looking up at him again, and his breathing was ragged.

"Wow," he said, and he pushed a loose strand of hair away from my face.

"Yeah," I agreed. "Wow."

The fireworks crackled around us and as the colours burst in the sky, I grabbed him again and kissed him once more.

47

I could never get over how short Heybuckle's terms were; before I knew it, we had reached the end of the school year. The sports hall was dedicated to Hugh's memory. I heard from Annabelle that Millie's parents wanted the theatre to be dedicated to her, but considering she'd been a murderer, the school put their foot down.

I didn't tell Mum I was now dating Tommy – she'd always said I could only have a boyfriend when I was over eighteen. But we kept discussing what had happened with Clem. It was national news for weeks, the headlines churning out the same *PRIVATE SCHOOL KILLER* stuff.

Journalists hounded me, interested in my position of being best friends with a murderer. One even went as far as to find out my personal email address and send me a message asking for a quote on how I was feeling, along with a hefty price tag for my time. They were like vultures, and I knew even if I did sell my story, they would twist my words to fit a narrative I had no control over.

I wanted to put it all in the past, but I still had to give

evidence at Clem's trial. She was there, sitting in the dock, her eyes fixed on a point in front of her. She looked small, lost – I thought what she had done might finally be catching up with her.

But then it became clear what her angle was – her bullish lawyers gunned for a charge of manslaughter, twisting things to make it seem like Clem and Millie were both afraid of Hugh and had teamed up out of desperation. They said neither of his girlfriends had been *planning* on killing him, that they had only wanted to hurt him, to make it clear they wouldn't be intimidated by him.

Mr Willet told me the lawyers were trying to mitigate the sentence, get it reduced as much as they possibly could. My blood boiled as I realized Clem was putting on an act for the jury, of a scared girl who had no other choice. She was good at acting – she could present herself however she wanted to.

Everyone knew Clem had killed Millie as well, but unsurprisingly, given that they had bungled everything else and just wanted the case to be over, the police ruled her death a suicide and Clem had no charges there to answer for.

Katherine Smith never got proper justice. The police's buried evidence about the hit-and-run "mysteriously" turned up (and Inspector Foster was coincidentally shipped off to another position), but all it did was point to Hugh as the culprit. Clem's apparent motive of "being afraid of Hugh" wasn't even linked to Katherine's death. The only thing that would have meant hit-and-run charges could have been brought against Clem would have been the Van Borens telling the world about their bribe. It was ironic that Clem had been right about how killing Hugh was the only way for her to get off scot-free for what she did to Katherine – and yet here she was, being charged for a murder instead.

The verdict was read out: a minimum of eleven years in jail, which meant Clem could be out in the world again before she was thirty. I wanted to scream at the unfairness of it all – Clem had killed three people, had taken three lives, and only faced consequences for one death, which wasn't *enough*.

I left the courtroom without speaking to anyone, anger churning my stomach. Even now, Clem's money was helping her get off lighter than she deserved – having good lawyers had made a massive difference for her, and she came from such a *respected* family I bet it swayed the judge.

Instead of going out of the main entrance, where I knew journalists would be waiting to pounce, I slipped out of a side exit, bursting into the sunlight and squinting after the darkness of the courtrooms.

"Jess," said someone to my left. "Jesminder Choudhary."

An older Indian woman was standing next to me. She was wearing a smart black suit and was clutching a large handbag.

"Er…yes?" I asked.

We were in a busy street and it was broad daylight, but even so I took a few steps forward, considering whether the stranger-danger was sufficiently big enough to warrant me running away.

The woman smiled at me. "I'm Sunny Chopra," she said. "I have a background in investigative journalism—"

"Not another one," I groaned. "Look, I've told all the hundreds of other journalists that I'm not speaking to the press.

I don't *want* you to tell my story." I didn't want some crap puff piece about what had happened out there, something that trolls would tear apart and then point out all the holes they themselves had made.

Sunny smiled. "Journalists can be relentless, can't they?" she said. "But, actually, I'm now a commissioning editor at a publishing house – I wanted to speak to you about *you* writing your own story. I want you to take control of the narrative and blow the lid off the world of the elites who play with people's lives and think they can get away with murder."

I opened and closed my mouth, unsure what to say.

Sunny held out a card, which I took. "You can search for me online, check out my credentials," she said. "I don't need an answer now – whenever you're ready to discuss, if ever. But I've learned, over the years, that people with money can pay to control the story. Words are a powerful thing, Jess. Perhaps you should use yours."

EPILOGUE

So there we have it. That's what happened, as accurate as I can make it. I probably got a few bits wrong here and there, but I remembered all the most important stuff.

I'm in therapy now, which has been good, but you know what? Writing all this down actually did help. I guess Mum was right – thanks, Mum.

So, I've got a boyfriend who I love and – more importantly – I have a group of friends who lift me up and look out for me. I no longer walk around school feeling thankful to be there. I know I *deserve* to be there, as much as anyone else.

I still like writing – and my stories are getting more ridiculous every day and I absolutely love all of them – but I can't help thinking about Sunny Chopra's offer. Every so often I pick up her card, twirling it back and forth across my fingers. I did a stalk of her online like she suggested – she works at a place which has published some of the biggest-selling memoirs in history, and which have won all sorts of awards.

This notebook is almost filled up now: a tale about murder and betrayal and injustice… I'm one of the few people who knows what really happened to everyone, including Katherine Smith. Maybe the police failed her, and the legal system didn't give her the justice she deserved…but maybe, just maybe, I can.

I might not have money – but this book filled with the truth is worth something more. My story, my words, my voice – they are priceless.

I pick up the phone.

THE END

ACKNOWLEDGEMENTS

Thank you to my wonderful editors, Becky Walker and Sarah Stewart, for your guidance and enthusiasm. Thank you as well to the rest of the Usborne team for everything you've done for this book – Kath Millichope, Leo Nickolls, Hannah Featherstone, Deirdre Power, Gareth Collinson, Hannah Reardon Steward, Fritha Lindqvist, Jessica Feichtlbauer and Nina Douglas.

Thank you to my agent, Alice Sutherland-Hawes, for being so on board with this book from day one. And to the team at ILA, for working to find homes for Jess all over the world – thank you, Clementine Ahearne and Alice Natali.

I was lucky enough to be taught by many inspiring teachers. A special thank you to Erika Théron – I still have the "best original writing ever" award you gave me when I was thirteen.

To my critique partners – I don't know what I'd do without you. M K Painter, your advice is always spot on. And Tess James-Mackey – what a journey we've been on, from tentatively exchanging pages to debuting together. Thank you for telling me to always think bigger.

To my lovely friends – thank you for always celebrating with me. Thank you to Rachel, Ted and Annie, for all your insights into life at boarding school. And thank you to Matt and Alice, for reading everything I've ever written and being my biggest cheerleaders.

Lastly, thank you to my family. Mum, this book is dedicated to you, but you get an acknowledgement as well – for all those library trips when I was little, for all your encouragement and support, for everything.